Paris in Black

A Jeremy Winters Adventure

Lisa Mortara

Foil Books

Also by Lisa Mortara

Silver Blades

Snow Blind—Book Two in the Silver Blades Series

1989—A Jeremy Winters Adventure

In the Shadow of the Eiffel Tower

Chapter 1

Jeremy Winters swore he would never again accept an assignment involving a teenage girl. Give him blackmailers, counterfeiters, even would-be terrorists, and they could not come close to the deceptive charm and dumbfounding pluck of eighteen-year-old Solange Gautier. At first he had thought the Renseignements Généraux insane to assign him the job. The RG handled French police intelligence, not kids who turned eighteen while on summer vacation, then refused go back to school in September. Only the *kid* in question just happened to be the daughter of an assistant to President Mitterrand of France, and Jeremy Winters just happened to work for the RG in an unofficial capacity: a part-time "little-jobs" man—which, he eventually conceded, had proved a convenient match-up to the delicacy of the operation.

That was back in October of 1989. Now it was four months later—February, the start of a new year—and as he listened to a message from the same Solange on his answering machine, he marveled once more at his efforts to wrangle the wayward teen back to France from a commune in Amsterdam. "You remember me?" came the perky voice. "From Amsterdam and Brussels, last October?"

Remember? How in hell could he forget? *Solange,* who had hopped off the train in Brussels on their way back to Paris, leading him on a not-so-merry chase. Overall he would remember the job as a fiasco, if not for one penetrating ray of sunshine. He had met

Ghensie. The thought of the Albanian beauty still brought on a sensual sigh.

But *Solange*—what could she possibly need from him? The question sent his thoughts spinning back to that October morning in 1989.

It was the 12th, Columbus Day in America, Jeremy always remembered from his boyhood in the U.S. He had rolled into Amsterdam on the train on a quiet autumn morning. The sky shone a marbled blue and white, the leaves on the trees a shuddering gold in the cool breeze. As he walked to his hotel alongside the rippling waters of a canal he couldn't help seeing it all as a good omen. Didn't his RG boss, Benoît Rébert, assure him that Solange was already tilting towards returning to her parents and school? That the gentle pressure of a fingertip would turn the teen in the right direction? It might, Jeremy thought, be like gliding an iron over a wrinkle in one of his shirts, applying just enough pressure for the right number of seconds to smooth the crease without burning the garment. As a thirty-five-year-old lifelong bachelor, Jeremy had done plenty of ironing and the image made him crack a small smile.

When he managed to meet Solange in an Amsterdam café, his gentle but steadfast iron seemed to be doing the job. She'd talked to her parents beforehand and seemed receptive to Jeremy's benevolent presence.

"Yes, I'll be coming home," she affirmed to him.

"Good. I'll buy the train tickets."

"I just have to take care of one little issue."

And there his iron hit the first crease.

"I need to say a proper goodbye to Henk."

"*Henk...*" Jeremy echoed uneasily.

"The guy I've been living with." A matter-of-fact statement from a girl who reminded Jeremy of a 1970s hippie—long lank hair, grubby-looking jeans, finger-nails needing a good cleaning and filing. Still, she didn't look completely worse for wear from her communal living. Her blue eyes were clear and lucid, her face full with youthful freshness. Her parents shouldn't be too shocked when they saw her, and Jeremy was determined they would see her soon.

She assured him she would come back to Paris after tying up a few loose ends. "You don't need to wait for me."

If Jeremy's iron suddenly lost steam he tried not to show it. He cast Solange a wary smile. *Oh, he would wait all right.*

She might have read his mind. "Don't worry, Henk's okay with me going home."

Of that assertion Jeremy could hardly be certain, so he waited the three days it took Solange to finish her business and finally get to the train station. Thank goodness she looked clean and groomed, though he couldn't say the same about the young man who'd accompanied her, his blond hair long and stringy, his jeans frayed and mopping the platform.

She gave Jeremy an absent glance, then looked back at her companion. "Henk," she indicated to Jeremy, "came to see me off."

"Needed to see who she's leaving with," the young man said, drawing himself up. He spoke good English, like all the Dutch, and probably spoke it with Solange. In fact he looked like a West Coast beach boy, which inspired Jeremy to slip into another persona, one he'd abandoned almost twenty years ago—the youthful Californian.

"I'm from San Francisco, a friend of the family," he said. "Just volunteering to check on Solange."

"And to take her back to Paris..." The tall, lean Henk ran a hand through his hair, catching and working at a knot as he seemed to mull over Jeremy's words.

"If she wants," Jeremy said casually. "Her choice, since she's eighteen. But really, I was dying to get away from Paris. I miss California, but Amsterdam's a cool place too. I'd really dig staying on if I didn't have to get back to my bartending job in the Latin Quarter."

Henk stared. Solange looked astonished in turn. She knew Jeremy wasn't a family friend, knew he had been sent in some kind of vague official capacity, though she clearly hadn't let on about it to Henk. Alone with her, Jeremy had spoken in perfect French but was now conversing in the most colloquial American English.

"You're from *California*?" Solange said.

Jeremy nodded. "It's the coolest state in the U.S. I really miss surfing in Santa Cruz." Though he had never surfed in his life, he let out a nostalgic sigh, then shrugged and nodded towards the train parked next to the platform. "Anyway, I'm going to board now. I've got the tickets, Solange. I could load your duffel while you chat a little longer." He glanced at his watch. "Got about another three minutes before departure."

After a long couple of seconds Solange and Henk finally tore their gazes from Jeremy, shifting uneasily from one foot to the other as they looked at each other. Solange handed her duffel to Jeremy. "I'll be up in a minute."

Jeremy climbed aboard, the duffel in one hand and his own valise in the other. From the doorway he smiled at Henk. "You should check out California sometime." Then he headed into the corridor and found an empty compartment, where he swung the bags onto the luggage rack, then went to the window to peer out.

Solange and Henk were locked in a hug, after which

they disentangled themselves and held hands. At last their fingers unlaced and they moved a touch further apart. Jeremy checked his watch again, raising a knuckle to his teeth as the conductor blew his whistle. *Her bag's onboard; she won't leave it behind*, Jeremy assured himself. And in fact Solange hopped onto the train just in front of the conductor, who slammed the door behind her. The train lurched forwards, Jeremy met Solange in the corridor, and as the train picked up speed he could almost exhale a sigh of relief. *Almost.*

As the train raced through the countryside the two made stabs at conversation, Solange evasive about her sojourn in Amsterdam, Jeremy not much more forthright about his expatriate status.

"But your French is as good as your English," she insisted.

"My father was American but my mother's Belgian, and I've been living in Paris off and on my whole life."

She gave him a placid smile, then stretched her legs and rubbed her bare toes together. She had kicked off her shoes and was slouching on the plush seat across from him, feet up on the opposite seat. He was thankful no one else shared the space with them, could imagine the indignant glares, if not protests, in this first-class compartment.

Two hours into the voyage, her feet finally came off the seat next to him. She'd been dozing on and off, and now yawned and said, "You obviously prefer France to America..."

"It's where I've found opportunities." Jeremy hoped his answer sounded pleasant as well as succinct, for he didn't wish to elaborate.

"Anyway, it's great you can speak two languages so well." Solange was now putting her shoes back on. The train was pulling into its scheduled stop at Brussels

Central Station, and Jeremy appreciated her preparing for boarders who might join them. But no—as soon as the train jerked to a stop, she sprang up, snatched her duffel, and breezed towards the door.

"Sorry," she said over her shoulder, half apologetic, half flushed with urgency.

She dashed into the corridor, and after an instant of gaping in shock, Jeremy leaped to his feet and hurried after her.

In the corridor he found himself blocked by passengers filing in and out of the train. *Merde!* he swore, forcing his way through. He got to the door and scanned the platform, where a wisp of swaying red duffel disappeared into the crowd. "Solange, wait!" he shouted, and jumped off the train. He started in her direction, only to hear the conductor blow his whistle and the train door clang shut behind him. He whipped around. *His travel bag.* Wide eyed, he watched the train begin its electric march, gliding away on well-traveled rails. *Putain de merde!* he doubly swore. Then he turned back to the station and started to jog upstairs. "Solange, if I catch you I'll wring your silly little teenage neck!"

But he couldn't spot her either in the station's grand hall or outside. In fact he would never have found her if he hadn't gone to the telephones to call his RG boss Rébert and report his humiliating flop.

There stood Solange, making a call herself.

"Sorry," she repeated to Jeremy after hanging up. She gnawed her bottom lip as she met his glare. "I *did* say you could go on to Paris without me." She added a helpless shrug and smile. "Don't worry, I'll be going back, just not quite yet."

And there began the negotiations. Solange had business in Brussels, a friend to see. *No,* she interrupted Jeremy, *she wasn't going to meet Henk here. It was a woman friend.* And she would need a couple of days.

Jeremy's patience was evaporating like droplets of rain on hot concrete. "Listen," he said, forcing a personable tone. "Instead of talking here, let's take a walk outside. I know a café nearby."

She blinked a couple of times, then said, "You know Brussels?"

The question was unexpected. "Yes, my mother lives in Namur, not too far from here." Indeed his shoes had trodden the floors of this very station innumerable times.

"Oh." She shifted her weight, eyes giving him the once-over. Whether she was gauging his trust-worthiness, he couldn't tell. He couldn't figure this girl out at all—*he*, who had discovered a bombing plot during Paris's bicentennial last July.

"I guess we could stop for coffee..." she finally conceded.

He wanted to take her arm and relieve her of her duffel, but as he took a step towards her, she took one back, extending her hand for him to show the way. He consented with a nod and a silent sigh between clenched teeth.

He kept a sharp eye on Solange in the café Saint-Hubert. He didn't know what was behind her guarded expression, and he wished he could shift her duffel to his side of the table.

"You say your friend is a woman..." he said, after convincing Solange to stay for a bite to eat. A *small* bite for Solange, who ordered a meager Belgian waffle with powdered sugar, while Jeremy, to prolong their stay, ordered an omelet with salad, plus fries on the side. When his meal came, nervous second thoughts beset him—what would he do if she ran off now, leaving him with a tableful of food and the bill to pay?

But she picked up her fork and knife and seemed glad to cut into her waffle. "Yes," she said about her friend, "and she's expecting me before long."

Jeremy was relieved about the sex of her contact. He figured this improved his chances of getting Solange back to Paris by fifty percent.

"So, you need a day or two here in Brussels?" he asked, still hoping she might change her mind.

"*Two days*, she reiterated. "And you won't go back to Paris without me?"

Looking pleasantly apologetic, Jeremy shook his head. "Your parents—"

"*Right*, you're getting paid." Solange sighed but didn't argue. "I just want to make sure my friend Ghensie is doing okay before we leave."

Ghensie. That had been the first mention of the Albanian woman whose name and image would become branded in Jeremy's mind.

"Ghensie's a good friend," Solange said as they left the restaurant. "When I was on my own in Amsterdam, before I met Henk, she let me stay with her." Now, of course, Ghensie lived in Brussels—with a five-year-old son, Jeremy learned. "I'll be staying the two nights with them."

Jeremy grimaced to himself. *And he would have to check into a hotel and buy toiletries since the train with his valise was probably chugging into Paris by now*. Then there was that call to make to his RG boss Rébert, not only to report the job would take longer but to ask him to track down the valise. *Merde alors!*

"Don't worry," said Solange soothingly. "I won't ditch you again."

"*Promise...?*"

Solange returned a solemn nod. "It's just that my friend Ghensie is in an unstable situation. She moves from country to country—Italy, the Netherlands, Belgium— always in fear of being deported back to Albania. I just need to check on her."

After that, they parted ways, with Jeremy marveling at the newfound complexity of Solange and her peripatetic friend.

"*Ça alors*: our crackerjack Jeremy tricked by a schoolgirl!" Rébert joked, then agreed to retrieve Jeremy's bag from the Gare du Nord train station. "Just bring her back as soon as you can."

And so he did, but not before getting a chance to meet Ghensie the voyager, the woman on an odyssey from East to West. Black hair, blue eyes, high olive-tinged cheekbones, her Balkan beauty continued to stir his thoughts on the train back to Paris with Solange. He had longed to spend more time with Ghensie, to let his senses soak in her striking beauty, in the Albanian accent that echoed the exotic Balkan east.

That was in October. Now it was February and he would soon learn that the woman he had only fantasized about was in need of help.

Chapter 2

The leafless trees produced fanciful sketches against Paris's February skies. In the rue de Turbigo, Jeremy gazed out his living-room window following his phone chat with Solange. Hands in his pockets, he mused over the winter designs as if something elemental might be divined in branches that bared all. Perhaps something involving Ghensie...and him...

Jeremy replayed in his mind that small hour whiled away when Solange had invited him to meet Ghensie in Brussels—Solange to one side of him at the café table and Ghensie's little boy sitting next to his mother. Not having met an Albanian before, Jeremy imagined she looked Greek (the owner of his favorite Greek restaurant had blue eyes), then Slavic, though he did well not to share the latter opinion. Albanians were *not* Slavs according to Ghensie, but a people descended from the ancient Illyrians of the Balkan Peninsula. Still, there was no denying the mingling of ethnicities over thousands of years in that volatile caldron called the Balkans, and that such a mélange of coloring and features had created a very attractive result in Ghensie. Her five-year-old son appeared truly Slavic. Blond-haired, broad-cheeked, with an impish turned-up nose, the quiet five-year-old liked to draw, every so often peering up from his picture through kyrghyz eyes at the adults who spoke in French. Jeremy had wanted to ask about Ghensie's trek through Europe, but she seemed guarded when it came to personal matters, so he waited to ask Solange on the train back to Paris.

The compelling tale had been worth the wait.

Early in 1989, four years after the fall of Albania's communist dictatorship, Ghensie Berisha, twenty-seven, fled Tirana and her Muslim family—unwed, with her son Bekim in tow. That Bekim's father was a Bosnian Christian Serb had both helped and hindered the situation—yes, she had disgraced the family, but at least she hadn't *married* a Serb.

In fact, according to Solange, things might have turned out all right with her parents. They had gained a male grandchild and the Serbian father had beaten a retreat back to Bosnia. But then Ghensie's cousin Luan arrived to live with them. "He's evidently a shit," Solange had confided. "Always shaming her for dishonoring the family—the *only* way he can criticize her, since he's a failed engineering student, while Ghensie made the family proud by graduating from pharmacy school. So she finally left the country."

That was what Jeremy had learned in October, and today he and Solange would meet again when he would discover the extent of Ghensie's latest troubles. As the sun took its early, wistful departure, Jeremy couldn't help reflecting on his own recent misfortune. Béatrice, his ultra-Catholic Belgian mother, might have said, "The Lord giveth and the Lord taketh away." Though he had never been religious, Jeremy had to concede a certain cosmic truth in the saying. He had gone off to Amsterdam, delivered Solange back to Paris, received kudos and fat francs from Rébert of the RG, some of those francs even allowing him to have corrective surgery on his damaged, perpetually tearing right eye. He'd looked forward to Christmas...

Then fate had turned on him in the form of his American cousin's death. On 15 December 1989, Cousin Walter stepped off a curb in Norfolk, Virginia and was struck by a bus. Jeremy might as well have pushed Walter into the street himself, for the guilt he carried about the past.

He turned from the window, his chest constricting. It didn't bear thinking about. Better to look forward to hearing more from Solange. He checked his watch: finally time to go. He gathered his coat and keys and headed out to the Marais.

Sweeping the Café La Tourelle with his gaze, he almost didn't recognize Solange. Her hair was bobbed short and her face appeared leaner. For a few seconds he stood studying her reposing features. He sensed a nascent gravity grown over the last four months, though the look evaporated into cheery eagerness the moment she saw him. By the time he got to her table she was on her feet brushing cheeks with him. "Four months" since they'd seen each other, she reminded him.

As they sat, Jeremy expressed an approving smile. "You look older. Is it being back in Paris...or could it be school?" he wondered aloud.

"Maybe both," Solange allowed, granting him a subtle smile. *Defending her privacy*, Jeremy thought, and rightly so.

Yet he did repeat a bit of advice. "Whatever you do, don't leave school without passing your exams." They had discussed the matter back in October, Jeremy divulging his own experience of failing just one exam—German—which had scuttled his languages BAC. Without that diploma, an institutional wall blocked him like an invisible dog fence. His visions of going back to school and finally passing the miserable German exam had yet to play out, one more thing he had shared with Solange to illustrate the pitfalls of procrastination. He recalled her smiling in their compartment from Brussels to Paris, and nodding back with the politeness granted a well-meaning uncle. Today he would spare her any further harangues. He ordered a Leffe ale (since Affligem wasn't available) and they got down to the matter at hand.

Solange leaned in like an intent professional. "Ghensie's cousin Luan has been in Brussels for over a week now. As I said on the phone, he won't leave her alone, follows her everywhere, berates her on the street for disgracing the family, even in front of her son...And now two other Albanian men have shown up, or I guess they're Albanians from Kosovo."

"Lots of Eastern Europeans here now, with the fall of communism," Jeremy pointed out.

"But it seems they're following Ghensie too. What's it to them if she had a child out of wedlock?" Solange sat back, sober and pensive, and once again Jeremy sensed a newfound maturity in her. She brushed back her bangs, then leaned an elbow on the table, solemnly resting her chin on her fist. "Anyway, she's worried. She wants to move house for a while, somewhere she can't be traced till her cousin, and whoever these other guys are, quit harassing her."

In Belgium, Solange explained, Ghensie was considered an economic refugee from an unstable country. Tolerated for the time being, she worked in a pharmacy sorting and shelving products, and she generally kept a low profile.

"She's waiting for the government to give her official sanction to stay," Solange went on. "So she doesn't want to stir up trouble by filing a complaint."

Playing the waiting game for the government to decide her destiny. It took not only patience but discretion, which meant not going to the police to report fellow Albanians.

Jeremy understood that game. Still waiting to be

awarded a French passport, he himself felt at times merely *tolerated* in France. Plus he knew Italians in Paris with *official* refugee status under President Mitterrand's doctrine of protecting foreign Communists, and even they wanted no dealings with the police. This he had discovered the previous summer, in the midst of great personal drama working for the RG during the Bicentennial of the French Revolution.

Not only could he empathize with Ghensie, he found himself drawn to fellow expats like her. "Has she any idea where to go?" he asked Solange.

"No. She was thinking of coming to Paris but she'd lose the protected status she has for now in Belgium. Plus they might follow her here too."

"Then these guys must be full-blown fanatics," Jeremy said, secretly wishing she *would* come to Paris. He would like to see her again. "Are they trying to force her back to Albania?"

"I don't know, it's all confusing." Solange narrowed her eyes in speculation, then finished her café crème and released a little sigh. "This'll help me study this afternoon," she said, nodding at her cup and saucer, "though I'd rather have a beer with you."

The old mischievous look was back, and Jeremy took a light-hearted tone. "Nonsense—you'll be glad to do well in school." He glanced out the window at the little turret belonging to the Maison de Jean Hérouet on the rue des Francs Bourgeois. He scratched his chin. "Now where could Ghensie lie low for a while...?"

"I hoped you might have an idea since you know Brussels..."

He gazed at Solange, or rather looked through her, his thoughts percolating in tandem with the hissing of the café's espresso machine. Then he sat back and ran a hand over the waves of his close-cropped brown hair. "I'll go to Brussels and see what I can do," he told her.

"I've still got her address from last October."

Solange beamed a grateful smile, then added, "I wish I could come with you..."

"But you have school," Jeremy reminded her with two long sober nods. Then he flashed an affectionate smile.

Jeremy had good reason to go to Belgium. His mother, Béatrice, lived there. She had conveyed the news of his cousin's death in the U.S., she knew Jeremy felt responsible for the tragedy and had been nagging him ever since to come stay awhile. Well, the time had arrived. But before paying Béatrice a visit in Namur, he would stop in Brussels and renew his acquaintance with Ghensie. Maybe even try to get those goons off her back. He'd done a little job like this before—it shouldn't take long.

Chapter 3

The train from Paris charged to Brussels, a two-hour journey allowing for only one stop in Lille. In the calm of his compartment, Jeremy reflected on the time he was taking off work. It didn't bother him to ask for such favors. For four years he had been tending bar at Le Prince Blue Note, a jazz club on the boulevard Saint-Michel, and he'd been waiting since last September for a boost in his hours. So far nothing had changed. "No one wants to budge from his position," said Pierre, the manager. Jeremy couldn't blame Pierre or anyone else; jobs were scarce, one reason Jeremy had stuck it out at Le Prince. That, and his love of jazz. With extra cash flowing in from the RG, his life as an expat could be described as comfortable, if not all that he wanted.

And yet, did he even know what else he wanted? Just last summer he'd thought a position booking gigs at the club would be grand, a job that could open doors to delving deeper into the jazz world. Then came his pay raise from the RG, which solidified the oblique satisfaction he drew from carrying out their discreet little jobs. The offbeat creativity that came to him when solving delicate problems. The freedom. He didn't mind having to rough up the odd blackmailer or thief; as an amateur boxer he knew his way round a fistfight. He had lost control only one time, almost six years prior in a disastrous brawl with his cousin in Norfolk, Virginia. Jeremy had paid dearly with a jail sentence, plus the sickening reminder of having caused his cousin brain trauma. That Walter had wandered to his death in December drove the guilt home like a dagger to the heart. Jeremy would never lose control like that again. Once more he wondered if the RG had learned of Walter's recent demise. They certainly seemed to understand the mishap of six years ago, had practically hijacked him into their hire to dispatch certain off-the-record activities in return for perpetual renewal of his residency and work visa. If, in a sense, he felt hostage to the police intelligence services, the freedom of movement the RG offered was compensation.

Jeremy considered the barren brown winterscape beyond his window. At best, everything in life tended to be a draw, a wash, a compromise, though not always of the comfortable kind. He watched the fallow fields rush past him in reverse. In a few months they would be green. Winter-summer, give-take, constant change.

In Brussels, he booked himself into a little hole-in-the-wall hotel, his room dim and tiny, but cheap and located near Ghensie's building in the de Brouckère district. The former glamour of the quartier was renowned, its celebrated theater and music venues earning it the nickname The Little Broadway of Brussels. Then came the construction of two tall glass and metal structures in the 1970s, the cold, bare modernity of which famously ruined the sweep of the quartier's august nineteenth-century architecture. Many middle-class dwellers moved out and the newspapers warned of the neighborhood's impending *paupérisation*. Jeremy saw it differently: shops and the theater remained, joined by a diverse and lively population, another example of change and compromise.

He spent the afternoon scrutinizing the quartier, watching for guys hanging about bars and street corners, *mecs* who could be migrants from Eastern Europe, though he had no idea how he would determine if one happened to be Albanian. He caught sight of a bum sleeping in a doorway off the boulevard Adolphe Max, and mentally shivered for him; it couldn't be more than 5 degrees Celsius out. A knot of youths stood smoking on the sidewalk, forcing Jeremy to sidestep them. Nothing unusual struck him compared to the last time he'd wandered the neighborhood. He passed Ghensie's street a second time but saw no one lurking about her building. And now it was time to head back to the Îlot Sacré, where Ghensie and he would meet well away from her neighborhood. They had arranged their four-p.m. rendezvous on the phone, two days before Jeremy left Paris. He hoped nothing—or no one—would cause her to break it.

With that troubling thought, he changed his mind, crossing to the other side of the boulevard and posting himself next to a sidewalk newspaper *kiosque*. From there he could observe Ghensie's building, watching for her to exit in order to engage in a bit of counter-surveillance. He scanned the various magazine and newspaper headlines on the racks, then paid for a copy of *Paris Match*—easy to leaf through while keeping one eye on Ghensie's building. Then again, she could already be out and about. It didn't much matter; he would wait until fifteen minutes before their rendezvous, and if she didn't come out, he would make a loping dash to the café, arriving maybe five minutes late.

The point quickly became moot. The door of the building swung open and out stepped a black-haired young woman. Jeremy inhaled, pulling from his coat pocket a photo Solange had given him of Ghensie. He hardly needed it as he watched the woman turn left, then left again into the boulevard. He remembered her perfectly.

He kept to the opposite sidewalk, remaining a few

paces behind other pedestrians on his side. On the other side of the street, Ghensie clipped along like anyone striking out into the cold, bundled in coat, scarf, and gloves. Those in front of and behind her bustled along with equal purpose, breathing out steam, and no one appeared to be observing her on either side of the street. She turned left and Jeremy followed suit; so did one other person, a woman also swathed against the winter bite, a green cable-knit cap set at a jaunty angle on her head. Walking ahead of Jeremy, she followed the street up to the crossroads of rue Léopold, where she veered right. Ghensie slowed as she crossed the same intersection, looked behind her as if contemplating a last-minute turn into rue Léopold as well, but then continued on to the end of the street. Finally she turned right, having gone a block out of her way, glancing over her shoulder at intervals. She had her guard up, and Jeremy wondered whether she had spotted him; then again, her vigilance was probably preserved for her brother. Apart from Jeremy, no one tailed her the rest of the way down to the tiny, tucked-away Petite rue des Bouchers, where she entered their agreed café.

Jeremy waited for her to settle in, rolling up his *Paris Match* and slipping it into his coat pocket as he paced casually from one end of the ribbon-narrow street to the other. Satisfied he'd observed nothing suspicious, he finally ducked into the café. He had chosen the place himself for its small and narrow dimensions. From any seat inside you could spy who came in, and Jeremy immediately glimpsed Ghensie doing just that from her table. They exchanged tentative smiles, Jeremy broadening his own to reassure her as he crossed to her table and sat down. Her handshake was demure, a mirror of her smile, and again he was struck by her looks, the voluminous dark hair set against high, apple-round cheekbones, the dramatic contrast of azure eyes and olive skin. The lingering chill he felt from outdoors vanished.

Ghensie had already ordered a pot of tea and Jeremy did the same, confident in the long leisure their respective pots would afford them.

After thanking him once again for coming to Brussels, Ghensie asked after Solange. "From her phone calls she seems more settled. And yet, with our young friend you never know..."

"You're right about that," Jeremy replied, delighted they were on the same sunny wavelength. "She's back in school, *Dieu merci*, though she wanted to come with me today."

"And naturally you told her *no*."

Jeremy nodded. That Ghensie dubbed Solange their "young friend," he found fitting, since at age twenty-seven Ghensie had almost ten years on the still restless but good-natured teen. And the confidential smiles shared over the matter gave Jeremy the feeling of something quasi-conspiratorial passing between Ghensie and him—a playful familiarity he would happily nurse.

They spoke in French, the principal language of Brussels, though Ghensie had mastered some English and was fluent Italian. The latter was the third language they had in common, Jeremy having scored highly on his secondary-school Italian exam, and since then having kept the language dusted—if not thoroughly polished—by taking the occasional refresher course and reading Italian printed material. *If only he could claim the same about German*, though he said nothing about that bête noire to Ghensie, who finally initiated the topic at hand.

"It's my cousin Luan, along with two Albanian Kosovars he knows, who won't leave me alone. Luan is the only one who approaches me directly. The other two show up from time to time, though I've never seen all three together."

"I imagine your cousin wants you to return home," Jeremy suggested.

Ghensie blinked, almost deliberately it seemed to Jeremy, and his gaze paused on long dark lashes above sharp blue eyes.

"He was the one who drove me out," she countered. "He can hardly expect me to go back." She tilted her head, looking at Jeremy with an unsure eye. "My family is Muslim, and Luan has followed me across the continent to criticize me. But it's about more than religion—it's about control."

And Luan didn't like Ghensie's liberal western ways. She was a single mother, well educated. He ventured, "Might your cousin also feel inferior because you've got a pharmacy degree and he's got no degree at all? Solange told me."

Ghensie allowed herself a small smile. "I'm sure that's got something to do with it, although I'll have to get my immigration status settled before I can take the exams to be a pharmacist here."

"You work in a pharmacy, though..."

"Yes, and I'm thankful for it. But someday I hope to be the one standing *behind* the counter, addressing people's health problems."

Jeremy noted a wisp of sadness coloring her mostly determined expression. He nodded encouragingly. "I'm sure it will happen."

"In the meantime, I feel I need to live somewhere else for a while. With Luan or those other two hanging about, I'm afraid tenants in the building will complain, and then I could be in trouble with the authorities. If Bekim and I could temporarily move, they might get tired and give up. I know they've followed me everywhere, but I don't know what else to do." Her furrowed brow, far from rendering her unattractive, seemed burdened with the lonesome weight of her predicament, of her obligation to make a success of life for herself and for her son. It wasn't just success at stake, Jeremy said to himself, it was survival.

He felt it was time to talk about her little boy. "Your son," he said, "I remember him from last time I was here..."

Ghensie brightened at the memory. "Bekim is five now. Next year he'll need to be in school, though I've already taught him to read in Albanian and do simple arithmetic." Her eyes turned grave. "*School*—it will make everything different. Another reason I've got to be free of my cousin. He's already called me names in front of my building. What if he turns up at Bekim's elementary school?"

Jeremy shook his head. "Where's Bekim now?"

"With my neighbor, Sorina, a woman from Romania. She watches him while I'm at work. Her husband speaks some Albanian. They left Bucharest before the dictator Ceausescu was executed. We share a similar history in that. Enver Hoxha was bad enough for Albania, keeping us isolated like, how do you say, African bush people? But Ceausescu was a ruthless killer."

Jeremy's thoughts flashed back to last Christmas Day and the televised images of Nicolae Ceausescu and his wife slumped like sacks of potatoes after being gunned down by a firing squad. One photo captured the dictator's hat flying off as if desperate to escape association with its master's depraved rule. Political eruptions continued all over the Eastern Bloc, peoples flowing like lava into the West, liberated and unstoppable. The Soviet Union was teetering on collapse as they spoke.

As Ghensie's gaze became bleak, Jeremy's tenderness increased. "I'm going to try to help," he said. "First I'll make myself a presence in your neighborhood. Let your cousin and the other two think what they want. I'll walk you to work for a few days and walk you back home. In the meantime, I'll try to come up with a solution to your living situation." He had an idea, but first he needed to make a fairly tricky phone call.

Snuggled in their coats, Ghensie and Jeremy walked back to her building. When he noticed her shiver, he felt the urge to pull her closer. Nothing particularly intimate or chummy, just a desire to tuck her arm in his—companionship against the cold, arms linked against adversity.

When they turned into her street she stopped dead. Three buildings down, where she lived, a black-bearded man paced briskly back and forth on the sidewalk, hands in his pockets, a cigarette pinched between his lips.

"That's *Luan*," Ghensie murmured, arms crossed, mouth set in resentment.

At practically the same moment, Luan saw them and halted. His hands came out of his pockets to flick the cigarette into the gutter, then rest challengingly on his hips.

Ghensie glanced at Jeremy. "He won't react kindly to you."

"I imagine not," Jeremy agreed, his jaw tensing involuntarily as he surveyed the volatile-looking young man. "But we should proceed as if he's witnessing a perfectly normal street scene—a friend accompanying a friend home. I'll come to the door with you, make sure you're in, then leave. You've got my hotel phone number in case anything goes wrong. It'll take me less than five minutes to get back here if you need me."

Ghensie nodded, drew a resolute breath, then resumed walking at what seemed to Jeremy a deliberate stroll. Clearly she was used to dealing with her cousin.

In turn, Luan seemed accustomed to treating Ghensie with rudeness. He blurted out a question as soon as they drew nearer, a question aimed at Ghensie though his angry eyes were fixed on Jeremy. And though Jeremy couldn't understand his words, he physically registered their caustic, interrogatory tone.

"He's an acquaintance from Paris," Ghensie answered in French, as if *acquaintance* and *Paris* leant some business-like distance. "I'm going in now, Luan." Jeremy admired her cool, even tone, all the while tensing his abdominal muscles against the odd flying fist.

More Albanian spewed harshly from the high-strung Luan, his palms splayed, an incinerating gaze turned now on Ghensie. Once more she responded in French. "He's a friend of a friend. Other than that, it's none of your business. You do get *that* much in French, don't you?"

Luan puffed out his disgust, the short black beard that framed his jaw sustaining his air of menace even while his eyes betrayed confusion. Jeremy stepped forward, his height and build roughly matching that of Ghensie's frustrated cousin, and proffered his hand. Luan stared for an outraged instant, then took a rigid step back. Crisscrossing his thumbs, he made a thrusting gesture with the back of his locked hands. Giving Jeremy one last furious glare, he muttered something else in Albanian, then turned and stalked away. Jeremy was left frowning in wonder. He'd surely been insulted, though he had no idea how.

Chapter 4

I'll call you," Ghensie said, before thanking Jeremy and shutting herself in her building. He waited on the walk, watching the street for a good five minutes before at last heading back to his hotel.

True to her word, she did call, filling Jeremy in on what he had witnessed but not entirely understood: Luan's demand of an explanation concerning Jeremy, the suspicion he was some other *mec* Ghensie had picked up during her immoral wanderings. Ghensie had given Luan no further satisfaction, reiterating that he should mind his own business, which in turn led him to fling that bizarre gesture at Jeremy. Thumbs locked, back of the hands thrust outward, it represented the double-headed eagle on the Albanian flag—a mortal insult to Serbs, particularly those inhabiting Kosovo.

Jeremy, of course, was not a Serb, and if weren't for Luan's fierce hostility, would have laughed. Was there anything to truly fear in the situation—an actual menace versus a supreme nuisance? Whatever the case, Jeremy would stick by Ghensie. He had committed himself and he didn't regret it. Tomorrow was Sunday and he would take Ghensie and her little boy out sightseeing. Plus, he would definitely make that telephone call concerning her living situation.

At ten a.m. the next morning he arrived in front of Ghensie's building. Mercifully there was no sign of Luan.

"He's probably sleeping off a hangover," said Ghensie, once she and Bekim came down to meet him.

She glanced at her son; one of the boy's blue eyes was screwed up as he gazed back at her. "He only understands simple French, so we can talk with ease about *certain things*." She added a frustrated sigh. "I should be working more on the language with him or sending him to preschool, but I've been waiting to get settled, and now I'm dealing with this *mess*."

She shook her head as they struck out down the street, Jeremy giving her arm a small squeeze. "It'll get resolved," he said, though he was far from certain exactly how.

To Bekim, Ghensie reintroduced Jeremy as her Paris friend. "Remember, Jeremy was here last autumn," she prompted in French. Bekim gave Jeremy a hesitant smile, then a speculative tilt of his head. Not a trusting look by any means, thought Jeremy, but entirely understandable considering the kid's experience with Ghensie's bullying cousin.

They walked down to the Grand-Place. "Bekim loves this square," said Ghensie. "Loves how all the gilded buildings shine like gold." Bekim didn't reply, but gave a shy nod when his mother made the translation to Albanian. "He has a small bright coin collection, don't you Bekim?" Again she translated and the boy cocked his head, giving Jeremy a coy smile. He then yanked at his mother's hand, uttering something incomprehensible to Jeremy. "He wants to show you the swan," Ghensie said.

Jeremy knew exactly where they were headed but followed in dutiful silence. Le Cygne—the building of the old butchers' guild. Above the pediment of the tall wooden door stood a sculpted white swan, its wings splayed in glory, its beak, webbed feet, and the vegetation surrounding it, all painted gold. Jeremy smiled and nodded to the boy. Then more Albanian bubbled from Bekim as he pointed to the top of the building to the left.

"He's showing you the gilded equestrian statue," said Ghensie. "He says it's very shiny."

"So it is," Jeremy agreed, grinning and bending slightly to the boy. "But if you like statues I've got a funny one to show you." He turned to Ghensie. "Has Bekim seen the Manneken-Pis?"

He hadn't, which made Jeremy grin again and pat Bekim on the head. The boy shivered.

"He's just cold," Ghensie said. She looked up at the frigid grey sky then gave Jeremy an apologetic smile. "I am too, kind of."

"Right," Jeremy muttered. "We've been standing too long and we've walked a long way." He extended his arm to indicate the direction. "We'll take a quick look at the most famous statue in Brussels, then go have ourselves a warm drink."

Two short blocks later they stopped in front of a small, raised alcove. There, perched on a pedestal, stood the renowned statue of the legendary little boy who saved Brussels from burning by peeing on flames. Before Jeremy could tell the tale, and Ghensie translate, Bekim had burst into giggles at the sight of the bulging-bellied little boy, naked and streaming water into a fountain basin. One of his hands guided his little spout, while the other rested nonchalantly on his hip. Jeremy and Ghensie laughed along, and Jeremy was tempted to rough up Bekim's hair. The boy was becoming ever more likable. "Let's get you a hot chocolate," he told him, and left it to Ghensie to translate.

In a café off the Grand-Place, the threesome warmed themselves, Bekim with his promised beverage, Ghensie and Jeremy with coffee, Jeremy listening to mother and son exchange chatter in Albanian. Once more he studied the boy's features and wondered if Bekim resembled his Serbian father. His eyes, smoothed by the Mongolian fold, somehow made the lad look guarded as well as more vulnerable than his meager five years. A small stuffed bear sat in his lap, its beige fur looking worse for the kind of wear wrought by an active little boy. Jeremy had also owned a Teddy Bear at that age; he'd slept with it, though he couldn't remember ever bringing it to a restaurant. These idle thoughts meandered with the woody-caramel aroma of freshly ground espresso beans and the detached Albanian chatter that didn't require his concentration, all of which filled him with the relaxed, lazy sensation of leisurely weekend calm. That is, until he noticed Ghensie tense and straighten in her chair. She was staring over his shoulder. Bekim's eyes, aimed in the same direction, widened.

"It's one of the Albanian Kosovars," she said in a low voice, "outside on the sidewalk."

Jeremy turned round to see a coatless man, seemingly invulnerable to the bone-chilling cold in an open suit jacket, his shirt collar gaping and exposing a tuft of dark hair as he stared through the window at them. He was tall and husky, his head shaved and hatless, and his appearance seemed to frighten Bekim who now clutched his stuffed bear hard against his chest.

Jeremy turned to Ghensie. "One of your cousin Luan's associates?"

Ghensie nodded stiffly.

"Dressed to show how invincible he is?"

"Or how deficient in brain cells." Ghensie said, holding the intruder on the sidewalk in a nervous gaze.

"And you say he's never spoken to you?"

"Not so far."

Jeremy looked back again, just in time to receive a now familiar insult: the double-headed eagle, the same sort of thrusting of interlocked hands that represented the Albanian flag. The *mec* added a savage smirk, yet by the time Jeremy swiveled to Ghensie with a questioning look, then back to the window, he was gone. Taking Bekim onto her lap, Ghensie murmured something to him in Albanian and the boy laid his head on her chest.

Jeremy cast one last look out the window but saw nothing but the cold grey city. "Does this man also take me for a Serb?" he asked Ghensie.

Ghensie hesitated. Her face was wan. The cool condescension shown her cousin had evaporated. "The gesture was meant for me as well," she said. "Dominance, threats." She looked down at Bekim, who now faced the table cuddling his stuffed bear. She stroked his hair.

"Bekim's seen this guy too, I gather..."

Ghensie gave a grim nod.

"And they're both here to back up your cousin?"

Ghensie shifted her gaze slightly away and nodded.

Jeremy didn't argue with what he considered an alien religious logic. Luan, bringing along a couple bastards to unleash if Ghensie didn't somehow satisfy his honor? He watched her as she turned to Bekim and said something to the effect of, "Finish your hot chocolate," for the boy slid off her lap and returned to his seat.

Not knowing what to make of the strange situation, Jeremy scratched a couple of bristles on his chin which he'd missed while shaving in the sickly yellow light of his hotel bathroom. Too engrossed in the company of Ghensie and Bekim, he had also missed today's tail, failed to spot a big bald macho guy strolling about in the numbing cold with his chest hair exposed.

"You say this double-eagle gesture conveys force or dominance?" he asked Ghensie.

"Yes, and I'm sure it was meant to alarm us both.

29

He and Luan might have discussed it after the incident yesterday."

"*Discussed it*," echoed Jeremy, but Ghensie didn't comment further and again gazed away. Her blue eyes assumed an ocean-like infinity when she gazed off in this type of troubled contemplation, and Jeremy wanted to swim in their beautiful depths, discover everything about her.

He moved to stroke her arm then held back. "Has the other Kosovar shown this type of aggression?" he asked.

"No. He's shorter, has wispy blond hair, and almost looks mild-mannered, except for his cold eyes. Neither of them, before today, has threatened me with that gesture." She rubbed her forehead with both sets of fingers, as though massaging her thoughts might conjure a solution.

This time Jeremy did put a hand on her arm. "I might have an idea by tomorrow." He glanced at Bekim. The boy had been fussing with his bear, chatting with it in the singsong language universal to children, but now his curious, watchful eyes slid to Jeremy's hand on his mother's arm. Jeremy withdrew his hand to his lap. The boy might not understand adult speech but he surely understood body language. Jeremy would have to remember that about five-year-olds.

Neither Ghensie nor Jeremy observed anything unusual on the way back to Ghensie's building, this time taking the bus to spare Bekim from the cold. Jeremy hoped to be invited up to Ghensie's flat but took no offense when he wasn't. Her gratitude shone sharp and earnest in both gaze and tone of voice as she withdrew into her building, shunting Bekim in ahead of her, and Jeremy was left to walk back to his hotel, longing for their next meeting.

In his room he sat on the dodgy-looking bedspread of his single bed and dialed his mother's number in Namur. He would be coming...but with a friend. Surprised, Béatrice Winters waited to hear more, and learning of the saga of Ghensie's persecution she hesitantly agreed to the group visit.

"So they will be staying with me for a week?" she asked, the question elongated with a tinge of nervousness.

"Just about." *Maybe more*, Jeremy confided to himself, but he would deal with that when and if necessary. "I'll be there too," he reminded her. And if the plan worked, Luan Berisha might tire of his humiliating theater, realizing his pursuit to control Ghensie (to force her home? Jeremy was still not clear on this) merely showcased his own failures. Presumably, he would then call off his goons. But on that score, Jeremy couldn't be sure—especially if Luan were paying them, a thought that had struck Jeremy on his walk back to the hotel. Again he pictured the bald burly *mec* flashing that disconcerting double-eagle thing and wondered if the hostile gesture could be common to some kind of gangland activity. His stomach muscles steeled at the thought. He hoped the hell not.

Chapter 5

At five-thirty p.m. the next day, Jeremy and Ghensie sat in the same café where they'd met when he arrived in Brussels, Ghensie admitting that she feared a scene that would quake the block if her cousin caught Jeremy entering or exiting her building. She welcomed spending time away at Jeremy's mother's place. When he told her the train ride from Brussels to Namur amounted to a little over an hour, she said, "I could practically commute to my job at the pharmacy."

Jeremy wasn't sure if she was joking. "I think you'll need to take a short leave of absence," he countered gently, then feared sounding presumptuous. He had no idea whether Ghensie's pharmacy offered the kind of flexibility he enjoyed in his own bartending position, where all he needed was someone to cover his shifts. A temporary refugee, Ghensie probably had little in terms of legal protection. If she were dismissed, where would she go?

He was hesitant to say as much, for Ghensie was looking out the window, perhaps with those same bleak thoughts; a mood that seemed to seep into their intimate space with the liquid darkness gathering outside.

"I'm hoping they will give me the time off," she said, then turned back to Jeremy with a brighter expression. "I'm appreciated at the pharmacy. They don't just value the menial work I do, they allow me to discuss pharmaceuticals and medical conditions with them. They know that once I get my immigration status in order I can take the pharmacist exams and become one of them. They say they will even recommend me." For an eager heartbeat her eyes glowed with enthusiasm. Then her smile fell wan, and Jeremy could almost feel the gravity checking that brief outburst of optimism.

He wasn't sure how to respond. As much as he looked forward to spending a week away with Ghensie, he hoped she and Bekim would not have to stay long at his mother's in Namur. That Ghensie could return in time to keep a job that not only meant survival, but offered camaraderie and perhaps promise of a future career. He wanted to take her hand in a soothing grip, a passionate grip; he had ventured to touch her arm yesterday but now thought of Ghensie's cousin, their culture, that *honor* business, and the fact she couldn't even invite him to her flat.

So instead he leaned in with both arms on the table to express his empathy. "I understand about your job. I wish you didn't have to take time off, but I'm afraid all it would take is for your cousin or one of the Kosovars to follow you from the pharmacy to the train station, see which train you board, watch you leave, buy an identical ticket, then follow you to Namur the next day."

"I know," said Ghensie, "and I wouldn't want to put your mother at risk."

"Risk? My mother?" Jeremy frowned and shook his head. "As long as they don't know where we've gone, that won't be a worry. Plus I don't see why they'd hassle her. It's you who would get no peace." He smiled, drawing a breath to signal a change of direction. "Now, I'm counting on your cousin's laziness to keep him away from your building when we leave at the crack of dawn."

Three days later, Jeremy, Ghensie, and Bekim departed for Namur on the six-ten a.m. train. It was tar black when they left Ghensie's building in a cab, Jeremy wanting to avoid a tail, and if there were one, to at least confront it in the sparse pre-dawn crowd of the brightly lit Central Station. The pharmacy had given Ghensie only five days' leave, perhaps not long enough to bury Luan and the Kosovars in boredom, but sufficient to give her a triumphant air. While most of the passengers on the train remained taciturn, commuters absorbed in newspapers or dozing to the rock and hum of the train in the overly-heated compartment, Jeremy and Ghensie defied the sober mood and blackness beyond the windows with excited talk of how they would spend the five days away.

By the time they pulled into the station in Namur, pink was competing with grey in the wakening sky. Ghensie roused Bekim from a heavy slumber and shuffled him out of the station, where a taxi driver loaded their bags and ferried the trio to Jeremy's mother's address.

Béatrice had the front door open as the taxi disgorged the little group. Welcoming them into the house she gave Jeremy's arm a quick squeeze, her eyes telegraphing what he knew was solidarity over the death of his cousin. Words would have to wait. After issuing sleeping arrangements (Ghensie and Bekim in the guest room, with Jeremy bunking on a couch in Béatrice's sewing room) she offered the little boy hot chocolate and biscuits, while the three adults sipped coffee and made small talk. On the phone, Jeremy had requested his mother not bring up Ghensie's family situation, so they talked of her pharmacy schooling.

"Then you'll be looking to remain in Brussels," offered Béatrice.

"Yes, as soon as my immigration status is worked out," said Ghensie, in that optimistic voice that made Jeremy again admire her determined confidence under myriad pressures. Béatrice should be satisfied with the impression Ghensie was making.

He knew, however, that his mother had to be curious about the child, though she seemed to delight in his presence. "Are you hungry for something else?" she asked sweetly. "Does he understand?" she directed at Ghensie.

"Yes, he probably does, though his French is limited." She rephrased Béatrice's question in Albanian, which prompted a shaking of the boy's head and a squeaky *"Non, merci"* to Béatrice.

"Merci beaucoup, Madame Winters," Ghensie reiterated with warmth.

At intervals Jeremy caught Béatrice's inquisitive eyes lingering over Ghensie and him, and knew he'd be obliged to provide more details. For now, though, he was content to sit back and watch the reassuring scene—Béatrice Winters polite and hospitable, her discretion and charity something he knew he could count on. He observed her trim grey hair, elegantly swept-back and unchanged in style since she'd left the decade of her forties. He had never considered her frail, though next to Ghensie's sturdy frame and youthful posture she now seemed vulnerable, hesitant in her reactions. And she had also suffered grief over Jeremy's cousin's untimely passing, though it was a sorrow preserved principally for Jeremy.

"I thought I'd show Ghensie and Bekim the medieval citadel this afternoon," he said to the group, resisting thoughts that could land him back in a funk.

Béatrice nodded approvingly. "It's a sunny day and the views are wonderful from up there. Be sure to wear sturdy shoes—the cobblestones are steep and uneven."

Bekim beamed at Ghensie's translation of the proposal, and not for the first time Jeremy noted a mischievous glint in the boy's narrow blue eyes. Though he couldn't much communicate with Bekim, he felt the boy would never be boring. And that he liked.

Jeremy used his mother's car to drive Bekim and Ghensie into the historical center of Namur, from where they started their climb to the top of the 190-meter-high fortress. It overlooked the rivers Sambre and Meuse, with a cobbled path following the line of the old stone walls. A paved road ran near the footpath, reassuring Jeremy he could always go back for the car if Bekim were to flag. But the boy proved stalwart and eager, and it wasn't until they neared the summit that he began to grunt and sigh and slow. When Ghensie gave an apologetic look, Jeremy hoisted the boy onto his shoulders. Amid giggles from Bekim they continued to the top from where they viewed the city in miniature. Bekim, back on his feet, ran towards the old watchtower, a squat, circular stone structure with gothic-framed windows and arrowslits for archers. He shouted something in Albanian.

"He likes the flag on top with the rooster emblem," Ghensie explained. In fact a wind had kicked up, snapping the flag to rippling attention. Jeremy understood Bekim's joy, recalling his own boyhood delight in discovering every detail of the citadel, including its grassy slopes and how his mother would shout at him to stay clear of the low barrier separating the drop-off down to the river.

"Bekim!" called Ghensie, reminiscent of Béatrice thirty years ago. "Come back now, it's getting cold."

At least that much French the boy understood, his hatted, gloved, and scarfed form trotting back to them like a bouncing ball. Expressing as much joy on the descent down, he once more rode Jeremy's shoulders, squeezing his neck as if Jeremy were his trusty pony.

And the cheer continued when they arrived home, Bekim skipping through the door while hanging onto Jeremy's hand to the inquiring look of Béatrice. The look didn't escape Jeremy who freed his hand, turning the boy over to Ghensie, who in turn stripped him of his outerwear, whispering something that led him to take his crayons and bear to the kitchen table.

"I hope drawing will settle him down," said Ghensie. "You know, I couldn't ask for a better place to spend these coming days."

Béatrice invited her for a cup of tea in the kitchen and after Ghensie sat down next to Bekim, Béatrice slipped another meaningful glance at Jeremy, which he ignored.

Once tea was served, Ghensie whispered something else to the boy, who looked up and said in French, "Come see my picture, Jeremy!"

Jeremy bent close to observe Bekim's work, a yellow square with something spikey drawn in red at its center. Jeremy squinted. "Is that the flag you saw today?"

"And the rooster!" Bekim replied in Albanian, translated by Ghensie.

"Nice job," Jeremy told the boy, finally recognizing a skidding approximation of an outstretched red leg and orange claws.

"You know, Bekim, the rooster is the symbol of this region, of my homeland," added Béatrice. At Ghensie's translation, Bekim frowned studiously at his work, as though it now assumed a new importance and dimension.

"He's a *brave* rooster," Bekim declared in French, aiming a sideways smile at Jeremy in that sly way of his. When Béatrice turned her back, Jeremy roughed the boy's hair.

Chapter 6

S o, they'll only be here five days instead of a week?" Béatrice asked, once she and Jeremy were settled on the sofa in the sitting room.

Jeremy glanced at the ceiling, in the direction of the bedroom where Ghensie and Bekim had retired for the night, picturing mother and son tucked cozily into the double bed. "She only has a few days off from the pharmacy, but I wish she could stay longer," Jeremy stressed. "I doubt her cousin will give up stalking her after only five days. Still, she's worried about her job."

"You can't blame her." Béatrice aimed a curious smile at Jeremy. "And don't you think she might know her cousin better than you do?"

Though Béatrice's question made sense, she knew nothing about the two Kosovar goons and Jeremy decided to leave it that way. "I'm sure she does. It's just that this *Luan*, her cousin, takes offense at everything, thinks Ghensie has ruined the family honor because she's got a child. Up until now he's only been rude, but he's wound so tight...if he snaps..." Jeremy shook his head.

"So she had the child out of wedlock..."

Looking at his hands, Jeremy nodded. Things like this happened every day, and he hoped Béatrice would withhold any judgment.

"Is he yours?"

Jeremy stiffened in surprise, swiveling towards his mother. "No! What gave you that idea?"

"Ohhh," Béatrice drew out, "just the circumstances—the fact you wanted to bring the little boy and his mother here. The way you get on so well with him. Don't get me wrong, I like them both..."

"*Huh*," Jeremy half scoffed, rubbing his neck that now felt hot under his collar. "I met Ghensie and her son last fall through a mutual Parisian friend," he explained, sitting back against the sofa, hoping Béatrice would conclude the meeting had taken place in Paris itself. She was ignorant of his part-time work for the RG police intelligence services, and he didn't wish to lie about why he'd traveled to Brussels without taking a side trip to visit her.

Feeling composed now, he smiled affectionately. "I like them too, *Maman*. That's why I agreed to help get Ghensie's cousin off her back. And this"—he waved a hand at the room—"seemed the best option for now. Anyway, I'm glad you agreed."

"Ghensie seems like a good mother, and she certainly doesn't deserve harassment." Béatrice glanced down, smoothing her wool skirt where it met her pearl-tinted sweater. "You know, I wouldn't have minded if Bekim was yours. At least I'd have a grandchild." She didn't notice the downturned corners of Jeremy's mouth. It wasn't her first mention of grandchildren, and Jeremy never knew exactly how to handle her light-hearted semi-seriousness. As usual he said nothing, which by now she undoubtedly expected.

She reached over to take his hands in a warm grip. "So, tell me how you've been doing since Walter's death. I still feel bad about having left you at Christmas. Right after the accident..."

She had left on her trip the twenty-second of December, a week after Walter's death. *Walter Kelso*, who bore the same Christian name as Jeremy's father, the saxophonist Walt Winters. His demise almost twenty-one years ago had given Jeremy his first taste of tragedy. Winters, the musician, had enjoyed a spell of mini-stardom in Paris during the late fifties, persecuted and blacklisted for his communist affiliations in the U.S. but welcomed in France. When the family returned to the U.S. in 1964, the Winters' marriage collapsed and Winters took his own life five years later, prompting Béatrice to return to France with fifteen-year-old Jeremy. That Jeremy had found his father dead from a self-inflicted gunshot wound only intensified the trauma. The death of Walter, a cousin whom Jeremy had never liked, dealt a different kind of kick to his gut.

"You did well to take your trip," Jeremy said, repeating the same reassurance he had expressed on the phone in December. "It was already booked, and Haley and I had already planned to spend the holiday together." *Haley*—his estranged girlfriend at this point. In hindsight he wondered whether he could have handled that better, such as sharing more of his feelings at the time of Walter's death rather than alienating Haley with his gloomy moods.

"Haley, yes, such a nice girl." Béatrice nodded, her head atilt. "Does she know your Albanian friend?"

Jeremy didn't like where this conversation was heading. Things between Haley and him had cooled since Walter's death and then positively chilled with the return to Paris of Haley's former boyfriend. He had never discussed any of this with his mother and didn't plan to now.

"Ghensie and Haley don't know each other, *Maman*," he said matter-of-factly. "*I* barely know Ghensie. I might never see her again after I've finished helping her out." The latter thought troubled him, and perhaps Béatrice could tell.

"Mm," she murmured, a lilt of doubt in her voice. "Well, in about four days we'll know if staying here has helped." She put a hand on Jeremy's arm. "But I'm glad you're keeping busy. It's the best thing you can do when there's been a tragedy."

Jeremy nodded. He had been maintaining a delicate equilibrium since the catastrophe on the other side of the Atlantic. Walter had never been right in the head since his brawl with Jeremy almost six years prior. The whole calamity had centered on the possession of Jeremy's father's saxophone, once lent to Walter who'd assumed it was his to keep. Jeremy had traveled to Norfolk, Virginia to prove otherwise, and provoked by his cousin, had resorted to his boxer's fists. That would never happen again, he repeated to himself once more. If he said this aloud at this moment there would surely be a tremor in his voice.

As for the saxophone? Jeremy's prized possession now lay in shattered pieces under his bed, the victim of a different angry man.

That thought was sickening as well, although Jeremy managed a sympathetic smile for his mother. "Don't worry, *Maman*, I'm all right."

At times he needed to muster sympathy for his mother. Their relationship was an ambiguous tango, partly due to Jeremy's volatile youth, but mainly, thought Jeremy, because Béatrice had never forgiven her husband's adulterous affairs, making Jeremy an indirect target at times. Not that he had been free from blame. Could he not, for instance, have chosen a wiser place than La Coupole to take his father's young ex-girlfriend for a drink? Should he really have been surprised when they were spotted by a friend of Béatrice in such a stylish and popular place? Jeremy hadn't denied the dalliance, and though his father was already deceased, Béatrice had still lashed out: "Thank God I only had one child by an adulterer." That was thirteen years ago, and now Béatrice had expressed willingness to accept Bekim as a grandchild. Maybe it took a woman to understand another woman's logic.

"I only hope you're not putting yourself at risk in all this," his mother said, looping back to the subject of Ghensie's troubles.

"No," he said dismissively. "I think her cousin is a nuisance more than anything." At least he hoped that was the case, and left it at that.

The next day he drove Ghensie and Bekim to Dinant, a small town with another medieval fortress overlooking the River Meuse, the day after that they visited a bit of Liège, then that evening Ghensie reminded him it was almost time to return to Brussels.

"Your mother's been wonderful," she emphasized, "and I'll enjoy spending tomorrow with her, but the next day it'll be time to go home. I don't want to over-stay my welcome here and I can't take further advantage of the pharmacy's good will."

Jeremy disagreed with the part about overstaying her welcome, but kept his counsel. He gazed across the room into the kitchen, where Béatrice was straight-ening up and Bekim was drawing at the table, his bear propped next to his crayons. "I think Bekim enjoys being on vacation," he said with a wink.

"He likes it here, I know, and it would be nice to stay longer. But..." Ghensie shook her head, her brow furrowed in a frown of fatigue but also of determ-ination. Jeremy thought it a shame that a woman of only twenty-seven should have to shoulder multiple burdens and fight on multiple fronts, all on her own. To raise and support a child while navigating a slow, indifferent, even fickle immigration system should be challenge enough, without having to battle harassment from a wastrel cousin. Naturally the immediate needs of the child trumped all. In order to feed and clothe the boy she must work. Jeremy felt an urge to smooth that wrinkled brow with a kiss, slip his hand into the crook of her back and pull her into a deep embrace.

Instead he laid a hand on her shoulder. "I understand. We'll take the train back to Brussels together."

Ghensie shifted her weight, letting Jeremy's hand slide slowly off her shoulder. "You don't have to. Bekim and I can get back on our own if you'd like to spend more time with your mother."

"Of course you can," said Jeremy, his hand back in his lap. It wasn't that she'd flinched at his touch, he thought—he hoped—rather she seemed to draw herself up and move slightly away in a continuing posture of determined self-confidence. Her eyes, however, betrayed worry, and he found the combination intensely attractive.

"I know you're perfectly capable of getting around," he assured her. "You've traveled from Tirana to Brussels. But I don't mind riding back home with you. I'd like to hang around your neighborhood another couple of days and see whether our tactic is working."

He smiled and stood up. Ghensie returned a grateful nod, the smile in her own eyes a sliver less reserved than before. She rose and they went to the kitchen. Bekim was chattering to his bear which sat next to his drawing.

"It's a dragon," Ghensie translated, as they all looked on, including Béatrice. The body stretched out long and black, like a bloated snake digesting a prey. Because he'd been told it was a dragon Jeremy now recognized wings in the form of two splashes of green springing from the beast's sides. A blunted snout with spiking red eyes completed the ensemble.

"*Dragon*," the boy repeated in French, grinning up at Jeremy.

"Does it have a name?" Jeremy asked.

Bekim pursed his lips, his brow crinkling in consideration. "Not yet."

"How about your bear, *mon petit*?" asked Béatrice.

The boy understood, though he fired off his response in a lengthy barrage of Albanian. Ghensie took a step backwards, giving a nervous little laugh and said, "The bear's called Grizzly, and Bekim would like you to know that although he looks kind, and acts so most of the time, he can be terribly ferocious and bite your head off." She added an apologetic smile. "He gave it an Albanian name when we got it, but when we left Albania he changed it."

"*Greezly*," Bekim repeated with a rolled 'r,' his foreign pronunciation forcing his mouth into a grimace that bared his teeth.

Béatrice gave him three indulgent pats on the back. Jeremy wondered at the blaze in the boy's eyes before his features relaxed into a satisfied grin, a pinch of slyness at the corners of those smooth Mongolian folds. Not a boring boy, Jeremy reiterated to himself, and went to the phone to book himself back into his hotel in Brussels.

Their train pulled into Brussels Central at three-twelve p.m. and the three travelers, resembling more and more a cozy little nuclear family, disembarked and took a taxi back to Ghensie's building.

As the cabbie was setting the last of the bags on the sidewalk, Bekim asked a question in Albanian. The cabbie shot the boy a confused glance then looked at Jeremy, who paid him and sent him on his way while waiting for a translation.

It took a moment before Ghensie finally obliged. "He'd like to know if you're coming upstairs," she said, taking a half-step back from Jeremy.

His brows slightly raised, Jeremy gave a shrug.

They had encountered no welcoming committee. No Luan, no bald bastard, no eagle gestures to show how much their return was appreciated. Maybe the jerks had finally cleared off.

"I'm sure Jeremy is tired," Ghensie went on in French, which she quickly converted to Albanian for Bekim. "Lots to do after a stay out of town," she added for Jeremy's benefit.

"Right," Jeremy acknowledged without enthusiasm.

"Not that I've stopped being grateful for all you've done. Your mother and you treating us like family, not letting me pay for anything...which I wish you *had* done," she added with a little frown of rebuke.

Jeremy dismissed the idea with a shake of his head. "I only hope our tactic worked." He glanced up and down the street again. "So far so good."

Ghensie nodded, then smiled uncomfortably. "Well..."

"I'll call you tomorrow to see how things are going," Jeremy said, and received a firmer smile back.

As he walked to his hotel, he toyed with possible excuses to call Ghensie that evening. But when he entered the hotel lobby and crossed to the desk, a message was waved in his face. A phone call had already been made, and not from Jeremy to Ghensie but vice versa. The clerk handed him the paper which read: "Jeremy, please come back!"

He left his bag with the desk clerk and hurried out the door.

Five minutes later Ghensie buzzed him into her building. He took the stairs two at a time to the third floor and found her door open to the landing. Slowly he stepped over the threshold and into a setting of utter chaos. Ghensie looked at him in grim numbness.

Bekim was nowhere to be seen. Plenty, on the contrary, was on display in the living room. The room had spilled its guts. Credenza drawers overturned, items pulled off shelves and hurled in a heap on the floor. A circular umbrella holder lay on its side, its umbrella flung to the other side of the room. Books lay open as if gunned down from their shelves, some collapsing spine upwards, others landing spread-eagled, displaying their final words. Jeremy looked at Ghensie in astonishment.

"It's the same in the kitchen, and the bedroom and the bathroom," Ghensie stated, her voice wooden, though her eyes were glistening.

"And Bekim?" asked Jeremy.

"At my neighbor Sorina's—the flat across the landing—but she didn't see or hear anything. In fact the lock isn't even broken."

"Your cousin?" Jeremy asked after exhaling a harsh sigh.

"Not alone. He wouldn't know how to pick a lock..."

"But the other bastards might."

Ghensie nodded then shook her head bleakly.

"Have you had a good look around?" Jeremy asked, taking a step closer to her.

"Not completely, but nothing looks broken. Silverware is all over the kitchen floor, but no shattered glasses or plates. "Maybe Luan was here with them and kept them from wrecking the place."

She shot Jeremy a fleeting frown, which he caught and returned with a blunt question. "Why would those two want to wreck the place if Luan didn't? Aren't they here to back your cousin up? Isn't *he* calling the shots? Trying to get you to return home, or something?"

Ghensie didn't answer. Her eyes shifted to a pile of correspondence on the floor where they lingered before returning to Jeremy. She held his gaze in strange look of doubt. Finally she broke the connection and went to close the door and sit on the sofa.

Jeremy followed. She hadn't answered him so he asked if anything was missing.

"I don't know yet."

"Look Ghensie, I'd like to help—"

"I know, and you already have in a great way. But maybe I shouldn't have called you back here...it's just..."

"I don't blame you for being frightened."

"It's mainly Bekim I'm worried about."

Jeremy nodded.

"And if the authorities kick us out of Belgium, with all the trouble I'm attracting..."

"Let's not jump to conclusions. First, we need to be sure it was your cousin and his thugs who did this..."

Wearily Ghensie rose to fetch a piece paper left on the emptied credenza. She handed it to Jeremy and stood watching as he examined it.

It took a moment for the black image on white paper to take form. Then it registered loud and clear: a rough sketch of a double-headed eagle, wings sweeping out to both sides. *Putain de merde*, he swore to himself. *Fucking hell*. The belligerent message was obviously meant for Ghensie, but Jeremy couldn't help feeling targeted as well. Luan and the bald Kosovar had already flashed him the sign, but this was plainly worse. He started to hand the note back to Ghensie, then pulled it back. "What's this written below?"

Ghensie blushed, looking away. "It means...'For the whore and her new pimp'." Her voice was low and quivering with anger.

Jeremy grunted in disgust. He looked up at Ghensie who was gazing into the distance.

"I didn't want to show it to you," she said, "but now I don't know what to do." She allowed herself an uneasy pause, then sat down. "I'd better start by telling you the rest of what you don't know."

Chapter 7

Before I came to Amsterdam, then to Brussels,"
Ghensie went on to explain, "I was in Italy."

And there was this Italian...Ruggero Vairo, a
thirty-three-year-old collector of antique weapons who
the prior year had ventured to Albania in search of rare
finds. The country was still in flux after the dictator
Hoxha's death and border controls were loose, making
Tirana a rich market in which to buy most anything.
Ghensie, at the time, was working as an interpreter for
an auction.

"You speak Italian too?" Jeremy asked her.

"Practically everyone in Albania does. We've been
in Italy's sphere of interest since ancient Roman times.
Anyway, Ruggero took me out for meals in expensive
restaurants in Tirana and I showed him museums and
monuments. We got along well."

She paused to take another look around her
ransacked living room, shaking her head, then continuing in a wistful voice, "He offered to bring me to the
West. To Italy, where he has a villa and vineyards
outside Turin, and I agreed." When Jeremy's eyebrows
rose, she said, "I loved him..." For a moment she
glanced away. "I still do, to be honest. He doesn't have
children and he was kind to Bekim, and of course I
loved life in the West, away from the chaos of Albania
and from so much judgment about my being a single
mother."

Though Jeremy nodded respectfully at her pained
smile, he felt a prick of jealousy. He wasn't the first or

even the second man in Ghensie's life. And yet why should he think—no, *feel*—he should be? She was twenty-seven—naturally she'd been in love. He shook off this slight irritation and said, "Go on."

"Ruggero makes his living off the wines his vineyards produce, but his passion is antique weapons. His house has a whole room of them, practically a museum. He even has a sword from your American Civil War. He has daggers, dueling pistols, and this walking stick that holds a hidden sword..." Her voice had edged up with enthusiasm, but now came to a trailing stop. "Anyway," she resumed with an embarrassed smile, "he and his wife separated about a year before he met me."

"So he's divorced," said Jeremy, wondering where the story was leading.

"No, not yet...his wife lives in Lugano, Switzerland. Evidently she's a businesswoman herself. And Switzerland offers...how do you say..."

"Tax advantages," Jeremy answered dully, annoyance nipping at him again. Ruggero Vairo and his wife were well-off—so what? But that they were still married perversely pleased him.

"Right," said Ghensie. "Bekim and I lived with him for six months. I did translations in English and French for his wine business. But it became clear he wouldn't be getting divorced any time soon. It might take three years in Italy, depending on the circumstances. And it's not certain his wife will be staying in Lugano."

Jeremy was tempted to sigh out loud. Ghensie may still have feelings for this *mec*, but was she still *in love* with him, in that she could never get over him? "So that discouraged you...?" he asked.

"Not only that." Ghensie paused, lips pursed, staring ahead as if bracing herself. "Luan and the other two were already after me."

51

"Because you ran off with the Italian...?"

"Not exactly, although honor was part of it for Luan." She paused to take a stabilizing breath. Jeremy felt himself stiffen in suspense.

"Luan's associates are Albanian Kosovars, more reason to flash the double-eagle sign...but they're also traffickers in looted artifacts, mostly things robbed from ancient graves that should be handed over to the government as part of our country's national heritage. Kind of like Ruggero, the thieves came to Albania for opportunities, only Ruggero came to acquire things honestly." She hesitated, shifting uncomfortably.

"And there's more...?" Jeremy prompted.

Her eyes darted to him, as if testing him in some way. "Luan is involved in their activities," she said at last.

"Oh?"

Ghensie looked embarrassed, though she needn't have been. Given what Jeremy already knew about Luan it didn't take much to imagine him knee-deep in something illegal.

"Ever since his failure at university," Ghensie went on, "he's been on the lookout to make an easy profit wherever he can."

"In this case illegally..." Jeremy stated, impatient to hear the rest.

"Yes. It seems that while I was still in Albania he got involved with the Kosovar thieves, who somehow got their hands on some coins looted from an ancient grave. According to Luan, he was holding some of them at our house. He was living with us then, you see." Ghensie shook her head as if trying to order a torrent of thoughts too unruly and outlandish to explain. "I didn't know about any of it at the time, but then one of the coins went missing around the time I left for Italy. Luan first blamed Ruggero for stealing it." Once more she shook her head, the heel of her hand pressed hard against her forehead as she drew an intense breath.

"Why, because he collects ancient things?" Jeremy asked.

"Yes, but I'm sure he didn't steal it. I didn't know about the coins, so how could he have? But none of this matters to Luan—he hated Ruggero anyway, like he hates all men who have anything to do with me—and he must have passed his suspicions on to the other two."

Jeremy shifted his weight to look Ghensie straight in the eye, sensing what was to follow.

"The two Kosovars came to Italy, to Ruggero's country property, and ransacked his house. Bekim and I weren't there, but Ruggero was home to witness the invasion. He said they didn't steal or destroy anything, but they threatened to harm Bekim and me if he reported them."

"And so now they're threatening *you*..."

"They think I have the coin, or know where it is. That I'm keeping it to sell if I find the right circumstances."

Jeremy eased back on the sofa, tried not to let his innate skepticism show when he said, "But of course you don't have it..."

"*No*, I don't!"

"*Okay*," he said, giving her arm a reassuring squeeze. "But what kind of coins could be worth so much?"

Ghensie ran a nervous hand through her dark silky hair. "Again, this all comes from Luan, but he says they were 'found' in a burial mound in eastern Albania, near the borders of Greece and Yugoslavian Macedonia. The grave must belong to someone ancient and important, because the coins are silver and have King Philip of Macedon on them. Fourth century B.C. So..."

"They're worth plenty," Jeremy finished.

"But to insist that *I* have one of them…" Ghensie leaned forward and held her head in her hands, elbows balanced on her knees.

Jeremy watched her, sympathetic but also fascinated. "Philip of Macedon," he reflected aloud, "father of Alexander the Great…" He had a passion for ancient history, especially for the battles, encouraged and enriched by one of his favorite secondary-school teachers, whose instruction had included deep veins of culture and anecdote.

"Exactly," confirmed Ghensie, straightening again. "Luan says the name Philip is engraved on the coin in Greek, and an image shows a man's profile with a missing eye."

Jeremy felt a tingle of excitement spider up his spine. Philip's blinded eye: if this were the case, then the find was truly extraordinary. "And the rest of the coins?"

"Hidden somewhere else now, I assume, until they decide to sell them."

"I mean, are they all the same—identical image on them?"

"I don't know, I've never seen any of them."

Jeremy thought for a moment. "Could Luan have the coin in his possession? Keeping it to sell for himself?"

Ghensie shook her head. "I've wondered about that, but why go to all the trouble? He would get his cut when they sold the coins, anyway."

Jeremy nodded in acknowledgment. *Unless this particular coin was unique.* "Are there any other members of this trafficking gang?"

"Not that I know of. But what do I *really* know?" Ghensie sat up straighter, fixating Jeremy with the intense gaze of someone straining to find logic in the situation, of trying to protect Bekim and preserve their new life, and now, Jeremy figured, with the need to keep him as an ally.

"Luan won't talk about the other two," she said. "Tells me he just needs to get the coin back. But what can I do? Now that they've turned my place upside down maybe they'll believe I don't have it." She stood and started to pace in front of the sofa. "You should see our bedroom"—she tilted her chin towards the hall— "the contents of every single drawer strewn all over, everything yanked out of the closet and tossed in all directions. The same goes for the bathroom—cosmetics on the floor, Bekim's little toothbrush floating in the toilet..."

Ghensie's voice caught, she sucked in a breath. Panic seemed to deliver a punch, the storm of the chaos surrounding her crashing down in a deluge. She stood inhaling and exhaling until Jeremy reached for her wrist and gently pulled her back onto the sofa. He thought he felt her jumping pulse.

When she calmed, her expression seemed apologetic and weary. "Jeremy, I feel bad for not telling you the truth from the start. But I felt desperate to believe they would get tired of pursuing me. Please realize that I'm telling the truth. The fact that they insist I've got the coin makes going to the police even more impossible. Not only would my immigration status be questioned, but Luan and the Kosovars would claim I'm involved in the theft."

Jeremy felt semi-paralyzed by the dilemma as well. With a helpless hand he indicated the room. "Well, maybe after this they *will* give up. What else can they do?" Immediately he regretted the question, and suggested, "Maybe another move would be in order..."

Ghensie merely closed her eyes, and Jeremy sensed the exhaustion, the frustration, the *patience* conveyed in that simple quiet gesture. She had journeyed from Tirana, to the Italian countryside, to Amsterdam, to Brussels—always in haste and with hounds at her heels.

Which made him ask, "How do they always find you?"

She sighed and shook her head. "I keep in touch with my parents in Tirana. I didn't tell them about the move to Amsterdam. No one followed me there, still I decided it was time to get back in touch with them when I got to Brussels, that maybe Luan had finally given up. I told them not to tell him, but"—she shook her head again—"somehow he found out."

Ghensie seemed embarrassed, so Jeremy let the matter drop. Instead he asked, "Have you told your parents about their nephew and his activities?"

"Only that Luan harasses me. Not about the Kosovars. My parents are in Tirana, what can they do?"

They could inform the Albanian authorities of the theft of the coins, Jeremy replied to himself. Grave robbing, and particularly theft of antiquities, had to be a serious crime in any country.

"They would only panic for both me and Bekim," continued Ghensie before Jeremy could weigh in. "If they reported Luan, I would still get swept up in it, accused of possessing a stolen coin. I would like to move somewhere else near Brussels, where I can keep this job—I must keep this job—but it won't work, as you've pointed out, because they would no doubt find me."

"And if they step up their tactics?" Jeremy asked gently.

Ghensie held his sober gaze for moment, then rose, sidestepping the debris on the floor on her way to the window. She stood with her back to him. "Where would I go?" It was a hypothetical statement delivered to the anonymous, oblivious streets below.

Jeremy thought of his mother again, only this time he remembered Ghensie's words before they had left to stay with Béatrice Winters: *I don't want to put your mother at risk.* He had been none the wiser, and Ghensie had known exactly what she was talking about. Of course nothing had come to pass, their studied pre-dawn departure from Brussels all but guaranteeing they wouldn't be followed. No danger had presented itself. Ghensie could do the same this time if she left Brussels for somewhere else...

"You could come to Paris," he suggested. "Without telling your parents, naturally."

Ghensie slowly nodded, pacing each nod as if to respond *I thought you might suggest Paris*, entertaining rather than affirming the idea. That was Jeremy's interpretation, for he knew she was torturously divided between supporting her son and their future through her pharmacy job and protecting the child from harm. She didn't ask *where* she and Bekim might stay in Paris when she would once more start the punishing process of getting back on her feet. Frankly, Jeremy hadn't thought it through either. But Ghensie was now drawing out her silence as if unraveling an intricate ball of string, and he concluded she would eventually nix the idea.

Then she turned and faced him. "Would you take Bekim back to Paris with you?"

Chapter 8

Tomb robbers, antiquities theft and trafficking. Ruggero Vairo, unsuspecting Italian adventurer, smitten with Ghensie until threatened by Albanian Kosovar criminals. Ghensie racked by impossibly competing demands. Taken as a whole, the dizzying cocktail could cloud the mind of the steadiest thinker. But the request regarding Bekim had left Jeremy speechless. "Take time to think about it," Ghensie had said. "Whatever you decide I'll understand. We could try it for a week or so, until I see whether Luan and the Kosovars have decided to back off after searching my place. If they cause me more trouble I'll give notice at the pharmacy and come straight to Paris."

He had agreed to consider it. Problematic as the proposition appeared—he needed to get back to work, so who would watch Bekim at night?—he could not imagine getting in this far, only to back out and leave Ghensie to the wolves. Now, a day later, he was still mulling it over. What did he know about kids? He had no brothers or sisters, had suffered a difficult enough childhood himself when he and his family returned to the U.S. after his father's blacklisting—fighting boys who called him *red-butt* and *commie*, plus *frog-balls* due to his slight French accent. And yet, just picturing that turbulent time aligned him with Bekim. The boy was highly vulnerable in all this. Ghensie should give notice immediately and get him out of Brussels. Start her search for stability all over again...

Christ, he knew it wasn't easy, had seen it in her

eyes, or rather the poignant closing of them when he had proposed the move to Paris. He had wanted to take her in his arms right then, but held back, imagining the conflict and confusion already knocking about in her mind. And he had no idea whether an Albanian migrant would even be tolerated in France.

He shook his head as he reached the Mont des Arts, one of his favorite spots in the city, where the view of Brussels and its gothic spires unfurled postcard perfect. He stuffed his hands into his overcoat, having forgotten his gloves in Paris, while the humid cold sank its fangs into his ears. Still he felt invigorated by the height and sweeping space, his thoughts free to glide like a falcon over the dormant gardens below—maybe, he hoped, towards a possible solution to the dilemma of Ghensie and Bekim.

He pressed on towards the Parc de Bruxelles, next to the Royal Palace. He hardly encountered a soul—too grey and cold, and when he penetrated the park he found a space to himself amid lacy winter trees gowned in moss. With his handkerchief he wiped the damp off the corner end of a bench and sat down.

Next thing he knew he was no longer sitting, but on his hands and knees on the ground, his head slowly shaking from side to side, his nostrils filled with the scent of damp earth and decaying leaves. He raised a hand to his throbbing temple and received a kick to his ribs which knocked him onto his back. In a shaved second he identified the bald Kosovar and Luan, rolled away and lurched to his feet, taking a fighting stance. The big bald bastard charged, launching a blow at Jeremy's jaw, which Jeremy blocked, stamping on the man's foot and striking him in the solar plexus. The man gasped and Jeremy aimed for his throat, only to feel one of Luan's hands yank his coat collar and the other snake around his neck. The Kosovar, recovering his breath, barreled at Jeremy who gripped Luan's conveniently-firm arm and thrust his legs up to kick the bald bastard in the face. The blow clipped his chin, the man staggered back, and Jeremy hooked a foot behind Luan's, ready to throw him over his shoulder, when the Kosovar struck back with another kick to Jeremy's side. Both Luan and Jeremy toppled to the ground, Jeremy's fist struck Luan's jaw and a liquid crunch sounded, followed by an animal groan.

Then Jeremy's head was swimming from another blow. Once more he lay flat on his back, his opposite temple now pulsating, his eyes locked on the sight of a shoe's sole descending, then the crash of it onto his forehead. He forced his eyes open to see the Kosovar being shoved aside and Luan taking his place, his lips lopsided and leaking blood. With his knees he crashed onto Jeremy's chest, snatching a tuft of his hair, yanking up his head, then slamming it to the ground—up again then down into the dirt. Finally, over the amplified thudding in his ears, Jeremy heard the bald bastard shout out a command, followed by something that sounded like a gruff question. Luan halted, holding Jeremy's head by the hair in midair. Dumbly, Jeremy registered more Albanian as his head was released and Luan's knees slid off his chest. He squinted against the pain and static in his head, alien words still whirling about him in a cacophonous mist, until Luan stood and glanced around the park. Had he heard something? A faint whistling in the distance? Luan looked back down at Jeremy, put his fingers in his mouth, groping until he pulled out the tooth Jeremy had knocked loose with his scrappy blow. He stared at it, half disbelieving, half outraged, then threw it at Jeremy in revulsion. For good measure he spat a mouthful of blood and saliva that splattered Jeremy's chin. "*Fous le camp, loin de Ghensie!*" he further hurled in French, then stalked after the bald *mec*, who was already retreating out of the clearing.

For some long seconds Jeremy lay there immobile, his eyes closed. Finally he pulled out his handkerchief and wiped his chin. He tapped his head gingerly—his temples, the back of his head, his forehead, which hurt most. He fingered his ribs. They were sore but he could breathe all right, so he doubted anything was broken. *Still, what a fucking mess!* The bastards had blindsided him, and Luan had ordered him to *Get the hell out of here, away from Ghensie.* He closed his eyes again in disgust and dismay, then snapped them opened. A whistling again—close-sounding—then silence, apart from footsteps approaching, light ones, a delicate crunching of ground cover. With a groan he jerked to a sitting position. A little girl walked to within about three meters of him and halted, her stocking-capped head canted in query.

"Are you all right, monsieur?" she asked cautiously.

Jeremy sketched what he could of a smile, wiping his chin again to catch any stray blood that might appear menacing. "I'm just fine," he said. "Nothing to worry about." In fact, the soft damp dirt had probably saved his head from real trauma.

The child didn't seem convinced. She couldn't have been more than eight years old, yet her gaze penetrated him like a large-eyed alien studying its first human specimen. "My mother's on her way, I could go get her..."

"No, No, don't bother," Jeremy said airily. With a grunt he heaved himself to his feet.

She took a step backwards, still looking doubtful, even a little disappointed now.

"Thanks for stopping but I'll be on my way." With a few brisk strokes he brushed himself off and gave a cheery wave. "Bye, now!"

As he left the clearing his smile sank into a grimace. Expelling a deep sigh, he extracted his bloodied handkerchief from his coat pocket and tossed it into a trash receptacle.

In an ironic way, Jeremy's visit to the Mont des Arts did indeed relieve his indecision. When he told Ghensie about the fight with Luan and the Kosovar, she shuddered. She shook her head in worry at his bruised forehead and said, "You must leave. I'll never be able to thank you for all you've done, but now it's time to quit. That Luan has resorted to violence is a bad sign. He'll want revenge for the damage you've done him. Go back to Paris, Jeremy. Bekim and I will follow later if we must. It's even possible that Luan and the Kosovars have now come to the end of the line as far as the missing coin is concerned. The only thing left was to take it out on you."

Jeremy considered her as they sat in their usual secluded café in the Îlot Sacré, not believing that she really thought the attackers would stop there. *He* certainly didn't; in fact the assault on him had helped make his decision.

He shook his head. "No. I'm willing to take Bekim to Paris with me." He felt a slight twinge of unease, but still lifted his chin resolutely. He was not going to let those thugs win hands down, plus, if they did decide to make another move, at least the boy would be out of the way. He would find a solution for Bekim in Paris, options were already percolating in his mind.

Ghensie's expression tensed. Perhaps it had been easier to propose a separation from her son than to actually carry one out. Tentatively she nodded and suggested that if things calmed down in Brussels, she would come fetch Bekim and bring him back. Jeremy still thought it wiser that she come with them. "You really think those bastards won't physically harm you?"

She shook her head. "Luan wouldn't allow it. Plus he wouldn't want trouble with the police." And if needed she would resign from the pharmacy in a respectful and professional way, on the off chance they might rehire her in the future.

Jeremy didn't argue, though his muscles tightened inside. Luan and his pal didn't seem to care about the police when they jumped *him*. He knew how those fists felt and the thought of them landing on Ghensie made his stomach sink with nausea. "You should at least alert the pharmacy right away that there's a good chance you'll have to leave," he said.

She nodded, then thanked him again before they left the café to go their separate ways, Ghensie back home to relieve Sorina, the Romanian neighbor minding Bekim, and Jeremy to the Central Station to obtain two one-way tickets to Paris. Ghensie insisted on giving him the money, and after instinctively protesting, he conceded. As he accepted the Belgian francs he felt the silkiness of Ghensie's fingers and the urge to detain them in a heated grip. Their gazes met and he thought he glimpsed a fleeting spark in her eyes: eyes so young, yet wise. Balkan eyes—the rational West commingling with the sensual allure of the East.

They agreed Bekim and Jeremy would leave by taxi the following morning before dawn, a time Jeremy still judged propitious for stealthy exits. He hoped there would be no panic on Bekim's part—tears, fear, separation anxiety from his mother. The boy hardly knew Jeremy, and in a way it surprised him that Ghensie trusted him to this extent. And yet, from their first meeting, he had felt they shared a basic bond. Both had lived the migrant life. Jeremy uprooted at three-years-old and brought to live in Paris, then back to the U.S. when he was nine, and at fifteen, fatherless in

Paris. In this way he also understood Bekim's plight. And the boy liked him. Not that this overwhelmed Jeremy with confidence—in fact, now that the arrangement was a done deal he felt his nerves flare in protest. When he told Ghensie he would arrange for trustworthy care for Bekim during work evenings, her gaze seemed to turn inward. For a couple of silent seconds, their vaporous breath blending as they stood outside the café, Jeremy wondered if she felt as nervous as he did and would thus cancel the whole arrangement. He almost wished she would. Instead she said, "As soon as I get home, I'm calling Solange. She has promised to reciprocate my hospitality in Amsterdam. Well, now she can help watch Bekim."

Then just before they parted ways, Ghensie surprised him, firmly intoning, "No matter what happens here, I'll get to Paris as quickly as possible." She breathed in, nodded, then turned and left.

What did she mean? To reassure herself, Jeremy, or both of them? He thought about himself alone with the boy in Paris, the thugs still doing their thing in Brussels. Letting out a clenched sigh he headed for the station.

Chapter 9

I t was a good thing the boy could sleep like the dead, reflected Jeremy back home in his Paris flat. Bekim had been too sleep-dazed to realize what was going on at 5:00 a.m. that morning, when he, Jeremy, and Ghensie set off in a taxi to the station. By the time they arrived, Bekim had sunk back into slumber, Jeremy carrying him into the station to the platform, Ghensie following with the boy's backpack and bear. All three sat in the train as it stood idle next to the platform, Bekim still asleep. Ghensie got off right before the train began to roll out of the station. She waved shakily, though her smile remained steadfast, hope in her eyes as her mouth stretched firm. From Brussels to Paris Bekim roused off and on, only to wiggle into a different position then slip back into sleep. When he had noticed his mother's absence, Jeremy recited a phrase in Albanian taught to him by Ghensie. "Mommy will be here soon" seemed to satisfy the boy, since he clutched his bear and dozed off again.

Now the two sat on Jeremy's sofa in his flat in the rue de Turbigo—staring at each other—Jeremy having repeated the previous Albanian phrase, plus the Albanian for "It will be fine."

Until now Bekim had responded with an uneasy frown and a tightening of his grip on the bear, but this time when Jeremy trotted out the phrases he received a surprise.

"*Elle arrive?*" the boy replied in French.

Jeremy smiled in relief. *"Oui, tout va bien. Bientôt*

Maman va arriver!"

Another frown from the boy. He had obviously understood Jeremy's Albanian, demonstrating with French in return, so why the narrowed eyes and pursed lips? Maybe a sign of concentration? A step forward? What was the boy *thinking* about it all? He hadn't cried, though it was only ten o'clock in the morning and he might still be tired from the trip. The morning was cold, but it didn't matter, Jeremy would bundle the boy up again and take him down to the Square du Temple park. They'd had breakfast, Bekim had eaten without resistance (defiance being another behavior Jeremy feared), and now it was time for some exercise and distraction. Before they left for the park Jeremy checked his phone message machine, a recent and necessary purchase after a tense and fraught RG job the prior summer.

The voice that clicked on was that of RG agent Benoît Rébert himself: "Call me, Jeremy, I've got something for you."

While in Belgium, Jeremy had kept in touch with Rébert and also with his boss Pierre from Le Prince Blue Note jazz club. The latter had given him another three days off, starting this evening, but now Rébert had a job for him.

"Let's go," he said to Bekim, eyeing the phone one more time. He would call Rébert when they returned from the park when he would also call Solange who, according to Ghensie, expected to hear from him and do her part. One step at a time, he told himself—first and foremost, establishing friendship with the boy before handing him off to a minder. With Rébert's message lingering on the machine, however, Jeremy's steps might have to accelerate.

His nerves already felt the rush—*he had to get the boy*

used to things here—and as the two walked hand in hand down the rue du Temple towards the park, Jeremy impulsively picked the boy up and swung him onto his shoulders. Jeremy laughed in camaraderie, expecting the boy to join in, but the stuffed bear fell into the gutter and Bekim let out an ear-piercing screech. Jeremy squatted to retrieve the bear, keeping Bekim balanced on his shoulders, but the boy wanted down, wriggling off Jeremy, snatching up the bear and squeezing it indignantly against his chest. Jeremy could only wonder at what had gone wrong compared to the first time Bekim had ridden on his shoulders and giggled with glee. But then Ghensie had been at their side. He reached for the boy's hand, and after a silent moment Bekim dropped his frown and took it. And so the two continued down the sidewalk, Jeremy exhaling a large sigh of relief. At least the kid wasn't angry with him.

On the contrary, once they reached the park Bekim refused to leave Jeremy's side. They stood on the dirt path bordering the expansive patch of grass enclosed by its short chain-linked fence. Jeremy opened the little green gate and urged Bekim to go play. "*Va jouer*, Bekim," he said in French, gesticulating towards the lawn. But the boy stood his ground, clutching his bear and frowning imperiously ahead of him.

"Come on," Jeremy insisted, taking the boy's hand and pulling him onto the grass.

Halting, Bekim asked again, *"Maman arrive?"*

"Bien sûr qu'elle arrive!" Jeremy confirmed. He continued in French, "We're going to call her tonight when she gets home from work. In the meantime she wants us to have fun! *Fun*," he repeated, and dropped to execute five swift push-ups, followed by an attempt to stand on his head that failed in a flop to the ground, which he turned into a recovering somersault. Flat on

his back, he looked at Bekim. The boy finally gave in to a rush of laughter, trotting over to Jeremy to place a conquering foot on his chest. Jeremy gave a faux groan of defeat, then got to his knees and performed another somersault.

"Do you know how to do this?" he asked, brushing off his bomber jacket.

Bekim gave a tentative nod, so Jeremy put an arm around his shoulders, gently pushing him forward, but the boy proceeded on his own, dropping his bear and propelling himself forward. He sprang to his feet, snatched the bear back up and with a canted grin pointed to a slide across the dirt path from the lawn.

The slide was only about a meter and a half taller than Jeremy, yet the boy balked when he reached its ladder.

"Go ahead, I'll hold your bear," Jeremy said. "It's not very high and I'll be at the bottom to catch you."

Bekim continued to examine the slide, a wrinkle between his brows, and Jeremy could only sigh inwardly. *He doesn't understand.* With a series of pointing and swooping gestures he tried to pantomime what he'd said, but Bekim shook his head. He muttered something in Albanian, then finally managed in French, "*You,* you come with me?" He pointed to the top of the slide.

"Ah..." Jeremy's gaze slid up and down the silver slide, then over to where a couple of elderly men were chatting on one of the dark-green benches. Well, he decided with a wry smile, he couldn't look any more ridiculous than he had somersaulting on the lawn. "All right," he announced to Bekim. "Up we go!"

Thank God the boy was tired enough for a nap. After the park they had stopped for lunch at Jeremy's regular café La Gitane, which lay kitty-corner from his building, then he carried a fatigued Bekim up half of the six flights of stairs back to his flat, took off the boy's coat, and sat him on the sofa. He turned on the small tabletop TV and found a Tarzan movie, Johnny Weissmuller swinging in black and white from tree to tree. Within ten minutes Bekim was asleep, and Jeremy stepped quietly into the entryway to phone Rébert, Johnny Weissmuller's elephant yodel resounding from the living room.

"Glad you're back," the RG agent told Jeremy. "I've got a little job for you. Can you meet later this afternoon?"

Jeremy scratched his chin, glancing in the direction of the living room and the sleeping Bekim. "Could we try for tomorrow?"

"No problem, I'd like to get home early today anyway."

So the meeting was postponed until the next afternoon, Jeremy relieved not to have to trot out an excuse. Not that Rébert would have demanded one, or even allowed for an uncomfortable pause which Jeremy would have felt obliged to fill. Rébert didn't stoop to such pettiness, though he had been known to remind Jeremy of his duty to the RG in subtle, if complimentary, ways. *We're working on getting you French citizenship*. And, *France was glad to take your family in during the McCarthy period. We understand what you've been through and are grateful for the work you do with such finesse*. He never made Jeremy feel like a slave, though as an intelligence agent Rébert also knew how to *finesse his points*. Both men understood the game, a delicate dance at times, and throughout the five years Jeremy had been on the RG's payroll he'd rarely had reason to complain.

Late in the afternoon he rang Solange, who had returned home from classes.

"Ghensie called last night," she confirmed, expressing surprise and concern over the missing coin, Ghensie's ransacked apartment, and the attack on Jeremy. "So glad you're not terribly hurt, and so generous of you to bring Bekim to Paris."

"Well," Jeremy mumbled, part modestly, part uneasily, "I'll have him only till Ghensie gets here. And speaking of that, since Bekim knows you..."

"I'd be happy to watch him. I've got school, but I'll work it in whenever I can."

"Like tomorrow at 4:00, maybe? Until I finish with an appointment?"

"...Tomorrow," Solange considered. "Sure, I'll be free."

After thanking Solange and giving her directions to his place, Jeremy hung up and thought over the rest of what he planned to ask of her. If she could watch Bekim when he started back to work at Le Prince in three days, his mind would be lightened considerably. She could arrive after dinner, take care of Bekim until Jeremy returned, a little after midnight, then he would send her back to her parents' house in a taxi. She might not get enough sleep before school the next morning, her parents might object to the late nights, still she was eighteen, a legal adult. In any case he had another friend to call on for backup. A person who had helped him solve one of two explosive enigmas during the previous summer of the Bicentennial of the French Revolution. And if Louise Cholot were not available, he would have to approach Haley Morgan, his erstwhile girlfriend, with cap in hand.

That evening he called Ghensie in Brussels, with Bekim sitting on his lap at the entryway table. He let mother and son chat, giving Ghensie the opportunity to reassure the boy she would be joining him. The talk in Albanian seemed to go well, Bekim neither tearing up nor clinging to the receiver when Jeremy's turn came to talk. Without going into detail he mentioned Solange's willingness to watch Bekim the next day for a couple of hours. Ghensie approved, and what was more, she also told Jeremy she planned to give notice to her landlady and to the pharmacy. "The other Kosovar, the subtle one, followed me all the way home this evening," she said, "with that icy look. It's time to get out." It would still take at least ten days or so to close her affairs in Brussels, but Jeremy commended her wholeheartedly.

At least ten more days minding the boy and Jeremy had yet to face the first night. At nine o'clock, with this thought in mind, he turned his gaze from the end of the TV news to Bekim, who was kneeling at the coffee table with his drawings in front of him. Time for bed, according to Ghensie. He planned to put the boy to sleep in his own bed so he could stay up as long as he wanted before taking the sofa for himself. They could manage this way until Ghensie arrived.

Sidling up to the subject he pointed at Bekim's drawing. "*C'est joli ça,*" he complimented in French. "Is it a cat—*meow, meow*?"

"No." Bekim was adamant. He muttered something in Albanian, adding a shrill howling noise.

"A wolf?" guessed Jeremy, to which Bekim returned a broad grin.

"*Un loup,*" the boy repeated in French, and howled again.

Jeremy gave a dutiful though uneasy chuckle. The kid was cute, but *bedtime* had to be respected. He spoke the word, clasping his hands together and bringing them to his cheek in a sign for sleep that he hoped was universal.

And so it probably was, for Bekim returned a firm frown and shake of the head.

Jeremy repressed a sigh. "Okay." He was about to give Bekim a delay until nine-thirty, then changed his mind. "Ten o'clock," he said, "but no later." He picked up one of Bekim's crayons, marking a red 10 on a piece of drawing paper, then pointing to the number on his watch. Taking his time to weigh things, Bekim finally nodded. Did he operate this way with his mother? Either way, decided Jeremy, the leash might need tightening.

Bekim didn't last until ten. By nine-thirty he was nodding off on the sofa next to Jeremy and by ten he was stretched out, weighted in solid sleep and slack indifference to his environment. At eleven Jeremy chose to leave well enough alone. He removed the boy's shoes, brought a pillow and covered him up, and let him spend the night there.

That didn't last for long. Around midnight he heard whining and foreign mumbling through his open door. When he slipped out of bed and turned on the hall light he could see Bekim sitting up, rocking and hugging his bear as he continued to mutter and sniffle. The first night without his mother—what could one expect? Jeremy fetched some tissues and padded over to sit next to the boy.

"*Mami,*" was the only word he could make out, knowing from Ghensie it was Albanian for mommy. So he repeated the refrain "*Maman va arriver,*" draping an arm around the boy's shoulders and handing him the tissues to blow his nose. The sniffling lessened but the whining did not.

"*Okay,*" Jeremy assured, coming up with only one solution. "I'll stay here—nothing to worry about." He reclined against the sofa's armrest, trying to fit the length of his body behind the boy's, Bekim snuggling next to his chest and Grizzly the bear taking up his own slice of space. *How the hell could they get through the night like this?* But it wasn't long before Bekim slipped into steady heavy breathing and Jeremy considered wriggling out of the tangle of boy and bear and tiptoeing back to bed. Only he feared the same drama would repeat itself later in the night, so he wormed his way off the sofa, picked up Bekim and Grizzly, and carried them into his bedroom. He deposited them in bed, climbed in on the other side, and with a groan of relief, closed his eyes.

Chapter 10

Worry gripped Jeremy in the middle of the night, jarred awake as he was by a flying elbow from a sleeping Bekim. He had to shake himself to figure out what was going on. Then he scooted further onto his side of the bed and lay on his back, his thoughts projecting problems the boy could present, the kind of worries magnified into mountains in that state of sudden wakefulness. Why had he taken this leap? To lash back at Luan and his fellow thug, when neither might even care he had removed the boy from Brussels? No, it was more to help Ghensie and protect the boy from harm, he assured himself. And, taking charge of Bekim guaranteed he would see Ghensie again. That thought sent him drifting back into a comfortable sleep.

The morning presented its new light in which things looked more optimistic. Bekim had few possessions. A few winter garments, a new toothbrush, a comb, and probably what he truly valued: three toy cars, his crayons and his little coin collection, plus three slim picture books, one in Albanian, one in French, and one in Italian. *Italian.*

"*Parli italiano?*" Jeremy asked eagerly.

"*Sì.*"

So the boy spoke Italian, *and*, Jeremy found out, much better than French. He commenced naming and describing each of his toys, the language tumbling out of him in sketchy grammar but rich in the vocabulary of common conversation. Jeremy smiled with astonishment and a good-natured touch of envy: *the kid had lived only six months in Italy but had learned a lifetime of language; nothing more amazing than the nimble, sponge-like brain of a five-year-old!* It put Jeremy's own stilted command of Italian to shame, yet offered him built-in practice with the language and a more effective means to communicate with the boy. Ghensie wanted her son to learn French, and French would still be spoken but with Italian too.

Then there were Bekim's coins. The boy let him examine each one, but naturally none sported an image of Philip of Macedon, a fanciful but unlikely thought, which redirected Jeremy to the idea he'd had in Brussels. He needed to pay a visit to the library for a book on ancient coins. The one coin that had gone missing, presumably bore a rare profile of King Philip, a valuable coin that Luan and the bald Kosovar believed to be in Ghensie's possession. Jeremy's meeting with Rébert was slated for four p.m. in a café off the Place des Vosges this time, and Solange was due to arrive at three-thirty to watch Bekim. Jeremy checked his watch. Ten o'clock: plenty of time to go to the library at the Pompidou Center and get the boy out for some exercise as well.

As Jeremy held the landing door open, his eyes caught on the stuffed bear, snug in the crook of Bekim's arm. Yesterday it had fallen into the gutter, flecking fresh stains onto a beige coat already striped and spotted with the dirt of everyday, little-boy living.

"You could leave Grizzly here while we're out," he suggested to the boy in French, pointing to the sofa.

Bekim looked down at the bear, over to the sofa, and when his eyes returned to Jeremy they were stern blue pools.

"Just while we're at the library," Jeremy added in Italian.

A pause ensued, Bekim's frown deepening until fear flashed in his eyes. "Nooo!" he cried out, crushing the bear flat against his chest. *"Grizzly viene con me!"*

"D'accordo—d'accord," Jeremy pronounced in both Italian and French. "He can come with us."

The tensed muscles on Bekim's brow and around his eyes instantly relaxed. It wasn't two seconds before a smile sprouted on his still-flushed face.

"Right," Jeremy muttered in French, "let's go." Behind them he closed and locked the door, then led the way down the stairs, his own frown lingering.

Jeremy imagined he shouldn't really blame Bekim about the bear. At this moment of his short life, the boy probably saw Grizzly as the only constant he could literally hang onto. Life in Italy had to have been a seesaw ride as well, barely settling into a nice comfortable home and routine before having to flee Luan and the Kosovars.

And what about Ghensie's leaving behind her Italian lover? She claimed they still loved each other but did they bother keeping in touch? Phone calls, or a visit from this Ruggero Vairo to Brussels? Ghensie hadn't said, and Jeremy had refrained from asking. Having his house ransacked might have proved too much for the Italian, despite the adventurous spirit that sent him shuttling all over Europe in search of antique weapons. A lack of mettle to the man, perhaps, one that might play to Jeremy's advantage.

He smiled tentatively to himself, though chafing thoughts about Bekim returned as the two made their way along the sidewalk to the library in the company of the ragged, dirty bear. He had got the boy washed and dressed, his teeth brushed, his hair—short and straight—combed with its cowlick wetted down. *And this, after having received a humiliating beating by*

Luan and his partner in crime. But he hadn't taken the coward's way out by abandoning mother and child, and he still had the bruise on his forehead to prove it. Ghensie had yet to respond to any of his subtle gestures of affection. Not that he expected *payment* for the help he'd rendered. In fact he despised men who demanded that sort of thing. Merely a return squeeze of the arm, or, *God forbid*, a friendly peck on the cheek would be nice. *God*: that was the rub. *Religion*, modesty, restraint and the like. *Culture*. And yet all these things hadn't stopped Ghensie from falling into the arms of the *mec* Vairo, the idea of which prickled Jeremy all the more.

He looked down at Bekim and sighed. Not the kid's fault. His face was ruddy with cold and one red-tipped ear stuck out of his stocking cap. Jeremy slowed their pace to adjust it. When they arrived at the library, Jeremy steered them straight to the information desk.

Ancient coins: the librarian located several books on the subject, Jeremy settled with them into a vacant table, while Bekim sat next to him, his little backpack and Grizzly on the table before him.

"Coins!" the boy exclaimed in French, as Jeremy cracked one of the books open. "*Beaucoup*," he added, grinning.

"Bravo, you know the words in French." Jeremy pointed to the boy's backpack. "Now why don't you take out one of your own books to read." The boy obliged and Jeremy paged onwards, pausing to observe an ancient coin embossed with the image of Vercingetorix, the Gallic King's hair spiked with lime paste—brave and fiercely proud until the end, Jeremy mused to himself with a smile. He was leafing on when he heard Bekim muttering in Albanian and glanced over to see him tapping the large-print words in a picture book about a zoo. A golden lion dominated the page and near it a word that looked strikingly familiar. "What does this mean?" he asked Bekim in French, pointing at the word.

Bekim's finger jumped from the word to the image above. "It's a...a...*un leone*," he finally answered in Italian.

"*Lion?*" Jeremy said in French.

Bekim nodded firmly. The word in Albanian was *luan*.

"That's your uncle's name," Jeremy said, more to himself than to the boy. "So Luan means *lion*?"

The boy's confirmation was a nod and a hearty roar that sent Jeremy's gaze whipping round the room. "Shh," he said gently, his finger against his lips, "we're in a library."

"Grizzly is stronger than lion," Bekim said in a lower, almost belligerent tone, thrusting the bear at Jeremy.

"*Bien sûr*," Jeremy said, leaning away a touch from the filthy-looking thing. Stronger than a lion, he mused, stronger than *Luan* and his thugs.

Bekim continued to brandish the bear like a shield or a weapon, growling in a mercifully low volume. Jeremy almost regretted having brought the boy along. "Why don't you take out your crayons and paper and draw something?" he suggested, tracing his finger over the table in imitation of the act.

Without answering, Bekim sat Grizzly back on the table, shut his book, and started rummaging through his backpack. When the crayons and paper popped out, Jeremy pulled his own book back in front of him. From the corner of his eye he watched Bekim begin an outline in green. The kid flashed hot and cold like mercury gone mad. And God only knew what he understood about his uncle Luan.

Jeremy finally found photos of ancient Greek coins. Their images looked sedate and civilized compared to the riotous, offbeat, almost pop image of Vercingetorix. And there were many coins, flattened, uneven discs of silver or gold, including several commemorating King Philip of Macedon.

Only one, however, revealed a profile of a bearded man with a fleshy puckered eye socket. Philip, father of Alexander, had lost his eye in battle years before he was assassinated in 336 B.C., Jeremy read, and any one of these less-flattering coins should be considered a rarity, which answered Jeremy's question plus posed another. How much was a coin like that worth compared to the others? And were all the stolen coins of this variety? Ghensie claimed not to know. She had seen none of them, but either way, the missing coin clearly merited ransacking homes and threatening people. Jeremy could see no way clear for Ghensie, outside of reporting her brother and the Kosovars to the police...and that option circled round and round like a jackal waiting to bite back.

He felt a tap on his arm.

"*Regarde,*" Bekim said in French.

Jeremy gave an appreciative nod at what resembled a creature drawn with raised plates on its back. "A dinosaur?" he guessed.

"*Ouiii!*"

"Good job."

Bekim resumed his work and Jeremy gazed back into the middle distance. The sooner Ghensie left Brussels the better, without telling anyone where she was going. Certainly not her parents, but also not her neighbors or the pharmacy. Could she manage that kind of break? She would have to.

Once home, Jeremy continued to ponder the problem as he watched Bekim race his toy cars across the parquet floor of the living room. They were waiting for Solange to arrive, though Jeremy couldn't tell whether Bekim recalled the girl or not. He had expressed a non-committal shrug when Jeremy mentioned her name, and now Jeremy was starting to worry. He had to meet Rébert, and in the event Bekim pitched a fit at being left with another stranger, Jeremy would have to head out for his appointment regardless. He gazed at the TV, where an afternoon news report zeroed in on the deluge of migrants into Italy from former communist countries. In Asti, Albanians were being housed in the city's army barracks and the fire department had been summoned to resolve damage to the plumbing. Western Europe was on uneasy alert. Jeremy thought of the ever-changing faces of im-migrants sitting on the vast sidewalk of the République métro station. Not long ago an Easterner was sitting with his back against a building wall, a batch of tiny puppies next to him on a blanket. *We are all hungry*, read the man's sign.

At last the doorbell rang and Jeremy rose swiftly to buzz Solange into the building, standing with the door open to welcome her up the last flight of stairs and into the flat. The two exchanged brushed-cheek kisses, then turned to Bekim who had retreated to the sofa, Grizzly on his lap, part ally, part human shield.

"Bekim!" exclaimed Solange, bending low and flicking a strand of hair away from her eye. "I can't believe how you've grown."

The boy adjusted his grip on Grizzly, tilting his head a fraction and returning a guarded look. Jeremy shifted his weight nervously.

"You remember me," Solange continued to prod the boy. "*Solange*, who brought you *du pain au chocolat* from the French bakery in Amsterdam."

"*Du pain au chocolat*," Bekim repeated, a grin

finally breaking the mistrusting line of his lips.

"*Son petit pain au chocola-aï-aï-aï-aï-aï!*" Solange was singing Joe Dassin's little ditty about a pretty bakery lass and a fellow who buys his *pain au chocolat* in the bakery every day. Jeremy could hardly believe it. But it worked: Bekim shot off the sofa like a rocket and threw his arms around her.

Solange had passed the test. Relieved, Jeremy promised to take them both out for pizza when he got back, and then left them to their gleeful reunion.

Out on the sidewalk, on the way to the métro at Place de la République, Joe Dassin's silly little song kept replaying in his mind. Haley, Jeremy's on-and-off American girlfriend, liked Joe Dassin. A ten-year denizen of Paris, she had learned of the singer through her ex-boyfriend Luc, a Parisian born and raised. The same *Luc* who had now returned to Paris from a long professional stint in French Polynesia. Haley had insisted they were now "just friends," but Jeremy couldn't be sure. She'd had another boyfriend, Thierry, who worked for Air France and now lived in Argentina, but whose mother Haley kept in close touch with. Jeremy knew that neither situation should bother him and yet life seemed tenuous since his cousin Walter's death. It no longer resembled a spider's web, vulnerable, though tautly connected in its design and resilient to the most amazing of pressures. Life felt limp now, dangling from the weakest and ficklest of threads. Haley had received the brunt of his dark moods; they hadn't spoken for over a month. He needed to get beyond it all, beyond the angry dogs in the basement—shame, guilt, regret, with jealousy joining the pack—and their harsh harassing barks. He turned his thoughts towards Bekim and Solange, affection for the two coupling with relief at getting out of the house on his own for a while. To his further relief,

Solange had committed to looking after Bekim the first four nights after Jeremy returned to his bartending job. "Your parents won't mind your getting so little sleep?" he'd asked. "Don't worry, Jeremy, I can handle my sleep," she'd responded brightly. "I'd offer to take the fifth night too, but I've got a date." So that was that.

He took long leisurely strides, savoring the prick and tingle of chill air against his cheeks, curiosity over his meeting with Rébert teasing his thoughts. The RG hadn't given him a job since November. Although there was nothing unusual about a hiatus of two months, at one point in January he had wondered if Rébert might be granting him a kind of bereavement leave. Jeremy hadn't mentioned his cousin's death, neither had Rébert spoken of it, and yet the intelligence services had ways of learning such things. Now that a job was coming his way he would have his hands full, and it was probably time to call on another potential minder for daytime hours. But not on Haley—no, not yet.

Chapter 11

Benoît Rébert of the RG police intelligence greeted Jeremy with his usual brisk handshake. An habitual brief smile accompanied it, signaling that Rébert knew Jeremy fairly well, and even liked him, but also that their meetings remained of a business nature. Having arrived before Jeremy at the Café Victor in Place des Vosges Rébert was already seated, a glass of Kanterbräu lager in front of him. Late thirties, barrel-bodied, with a square head and ruddy complexion, he looked to Jeremy like a natural vessel for beer. That his origins were Alsatian merely boosted Jeremy's fancies of Rébert in a beer garden. A third of his Kanterbräu was already gone. Since the café didn't stock Affligem, Jeremy ordered a Kronenbourg and sat back to listen.

"You found your mother well in Namur, I hope," Rébert queried.

"Yes, thanks." Jeremy expected little more small talk. Rébert could flatter or put on a show of solidarity when needed, but otherwise his questions covering Jeremy's family and general state of being remained routine. He was a man who got down to business as efficiently as he swilled his beer. Jeremy liked that. He thought of Bekim back at his flat with Solange, a little matter unknown to Rébert, and yet his RG boss might have some useful advice regarding Ghensie's situation; maybe if Jeremy were to phrase her plight in hypothetical terms...he would keep that in mind.

"You've been following the news about Eastern

European immigration, I imagine." The intelligence man could have been tapping Jeremy's thoughts.

"I saw a report just before I left to meet you," Jeremy said. "Albanians swarming into Italy like locusts, wrecking the plumbing in the barracks where they're housed, and so forth."

"More like flooding than swarming. Literally paddling across the Adriatic using shovels for oars."

Jeremy gave a faint nod, feeling slightly uncomfortable with the way he had described Ghensie's compatriots. "I'm sure many have modern skills, though."

"But not always skills that benefit us." Rébert lit a cigarette, squinting against the smoke as he observed Jeremy.

"*Us?*" Jeremy asked.

"Haven't you noticed how many people from the East are here in Paris? Romanians, for example?" He took another swallow of beer.

Yes, Jeremy had noticed. Many were beggars, though from the universally tired and guarded looks of people holding pieces of torn cardboard announcing their hunger, it was hard to distinguish who was Romanian, Albanian, Bulgarian, or what have you.

"And crime has shot up since November," added Rébert with a look and shrug that suggested *It's only logical.*

He was probably right. Since the Berlin Wall had come down, mass migration overwhelmed the borders between Eastern and Western Europe, people cheering at collapsing a first set of barriers, only to be stymied and demoralized by those invisible gates guarding decent jobs. Crime inevitably followed, and that was Rébert's field, for the most part.

Over his glass, Jeremy eyed his boss. *So is he going to ask me to spy on beggars who might turn into thieves?*

"We've got our sights on a Romanian," came the answer, "a trafficker in stolen passports."

Passports again. Jeremy sighed to himself. The prior summer he had been assigned to investigate the possession of false passports by former communist Italian rebels given asylum in France by the Mitterrand government. The investigation had instead rerouted Jeremy to a rollercoaster trail of plots against the Bicentennial. "What do we have to go on?" he asked.

"The latest arrest was of a Romanian who had the bad luck to rear-end a police car. His passport was confiscated and determined a forgery. We've got the name of an intermediary supplier, but we need to get to the source, the forgers themselves. The supplier works out of a café off Place de la Bastille. We'd like you to make contact with him, ask to become a client. Tell him you learned of his services from your Italian political refugee friends. You're an exiled American, reviled at home, and you can't get a French passport. And you need one. Be sure to tell him you served time for a crime in the U.S. Your story," added Rébert with a sympathetic smile, "will ring authentic, I think."

So it would. Jeremy wouldn't have to lie much, if at all. He would have to recount the battle with his cousin Walter, five and a half years ago. After delivering a knockout blow, Jeremy had called an ambulance. Walter was rushed to the hospital while Jeremy was whisked off to jail. He did time, one month, convicted of misdemeanor assault since the fight had been mutually instigated.

But now Walter was dead and Jeremy was dogging Rébert to help expedite his request for citizenship, his own golden key to gilded gates guarding better job opportunities. Rébert had promised to follow up, yet nothing had materialized so far.

"I know what you're thinking," said Rébert, once more the mental eavesdropper. "And I want to emphasize that we're working on your case." His eyes took on a rare earnestness. "In the meantime your residency and work permits continue to be valid, plus you always have your U.S. passport if you need to travel."

More of the same. Jeremy exhaled audibly. "I *do* need that citizenship," he said with a firmness that lacked only the addition of, *or else.* But *or else what?* To quit working for the RG would be counterproductive to both his livelihood and to that very goal of obtaining French citizenship.

"I know you do," said Rébert. "And remember, the government is sympathetic to you, as they were sympathetic to your father back in the day. These things just take time. There are different types of time and the worst is *bureaucratic* time. It moves like a glacier." With that, Rébert stubbed out his cigarette and finished his beer. Jeremy could only offer a stiff nod. "Now," Rébert went on, "I'll brief you."

After Rébert left, Jeremy's thoughts wandered back to the issue of refugees, émigrés, expatriates, those who had the luxury of choosing to leave their native country versus those forced to flee. He guessed that Ghensie's situation incorporated a little of both and wondered if her Albanian passport was still good. He would have to find the right moment to ask that question, a question that could be as delicate as asking how much money she possessed.

Jeremy's RG assignment, on the other hand, would not require so much delicacy as it would the portrayal of raw desperation. In this, he could take his cue from Ghensie and from his Italian exile acquaintances, one of whom he'd had an affair with the previous summer. Stefania, her name was, and she'd once claimed she would rather rot in a French prison than be deported back to Italy to stand trial for rebellion against the state. In a way Jeremy felt the same about the America that had blacklisted his father in the fifties and whose sons Jeremy had brawled with as a boy to defend his pride and his family's reputation.

But none of that could be changed, and he now needed to consider how to cultivate his image as purchaser of a black-market passport. Rébert was clever in suggesting the Italian Reds as the word-on-the-street that black-market passports could be bought. Last summer's task to find out who among the Italians held false passports had come to naught, but now that the demand for forged documents was increasing with the waves of immigration coming from the East, Jeremy was headed back into the fray.

He left Café Victor with musings of Hugo's Jean Valjean and of all the other faceless victims of both fate, choice, or a combination of the two. During his métro ride home, the anonymous countenances gave way to the grinning faces of Bekim and Solange. He looked forward to seeing them both and hoped Bekim's buoyancy still held.

Indeed, it had not. Furthermore, he now barely noticed Jeremy, sticking to Solange as if the girl had replaced his mother. She was reading him a book, and when Jeremy sat down to join them, Bekim turned his back on him. Yes, the boy was complicated, but considering Solange would be taking care of him the next evening, Jeremy tried to view the boy's shifting loyalty as something useful— at least for now.

In the pizzeria, Bekim insisted he and Solange sit on the side of the booth opposite Jeremy. The boy held Solange's hand both leaving and returning to the flat, and now, as the three climbed the stairs, Jeremy was starting to worry how the boy would act when Solange had to leave.

His concern turned out to be warranted. Inside the flat, when Solange didn't remove her coat, Bekim refused to remove his. The minute her parting words began he belted out his now long, loud, familiar *noooo*! It was enough to bring the neighbors charging to Jeremy's flat to accuse him of child abuse—or even worse, child abduction.

Solange tried to calm him with her promise of returning the next evening, but tears drenched the boy's cheeks all the same. Finally, Jeremy suggested they call Ghensie again and Solange was able to slip out the door. Jeremy helped Bekim blow his nose and they headed to the phone.

"You're closer to leaving...?" Jeremy asked Ghensie in a tone just short of pleading. Yes, she was, and told Bekim the same, with Jeremy listening as he shared the receiver with the boy. Jeremy would have liked to press her for more details but decided against it with Bekim there, nor did he wish to let on that he was finding Bekim a *sacré* challenge.

Eventually the boy did settle down, asking Jeremy to read him his Italian book about a little boy in the Alps. *Robertino sulle Alpi*, it was called, Robertino reminding Jeremy of a little male Heidi.

"*Parli italiano in modo strano,*" was Bekim's only comment on Jeremy's reading. *So I speak Italian in a strange way*, Jeremy translated to himself. All things considered he would take it as a compliment. The mercurial boy was back on his side, and when nine o'clock came round Jeremy repeated the mechanics of the night before, letting the boy fall asleep on the sofa, but first convincing him to put on his pajamas. At eleven o'clock, he scooped up boy and bear and carried them off to bunk with him again. He would pass this nighttime routine on to Solange the next evening, and tomorrow he would get started on his new RG job which meant finding someone to mind Bekim for a few daytime hours. His first choice was Louise Cholot, and he prayed Bekim would not crumble into crisis at being handed off to yet a third party. *Providing,* however, that Louise was free and willing to help...

When he collapsed into bed he felt in a way more fatigued than he had last summer, dodging firecrackers during the Bicentennial as he rushed from the Champs-Élysées to the Louvre and beyond to forestall disaster.

Chapter 12

Louise Cholot was one of the sharpest, most intuitive people Jeremy knew. He had met her serendipitously during his investigation the previous summer, and she had helped him solve the mystery of who was stalking his ex-lover Stefania, all the while seeing through Jeremy's own cover of "Insurance Investigator." The fifty-something arm-chair-and-occasionally-street-active sleuth should be working for the RG herself, he'd told himself more than once. Jeremy kept his own part-time status with police intelligence services to himself, though he knew Louise had her suspicions; keen curiosity was in her admirable and attractive nature.

Attractive she was, and not just for her age. A fit outdoorswoman, she also exuded a confident, gracious style that charmed those in her company, Jeremy for one. As it was only February, he imagined Louise still settled in for the winter, and hinted as much when he called her from the phone in his apartment's entryway.

"I'm getting out to the Parc Montsouris for a jog when it's sunny," she replied. "But it's lovely of you to call, Jeremy. I'd wondered when I might hear from you again, apart from our exchange of Christmas cards."

"I should've been in touch before now," he confessed. "I've wanted to invite you out to lunch."

"No need to apologize. My phone works just as well as yours. So how have you been doing?"

Jeremy glanced in the direction of the living room where Bekim was drawing. "Well, some of the usual, and some of the not so usual...and yourself?"

"I could say the same. Christmas with my son, as I wrote, and then a week in January in the Dolomites watching some ski races. Now that there's more light in the day I'm getting restless to go hiking somewhere."

Louise Cholot was a widow, her husband having fallen to his death in a mountain-climbing accident fifteen years prior. Jeremy marveled that some handsome middle-aged fellow hadn't coaxed her into remarriage by now. He was sure men had tried, even younger ones.

"Glad to hear it," Jeremy said. "Always planning something exciting."

"And you, Jeremy, have *you* got anything exciting to report?"

Jeremy drew in a breath and answered with a speculative "*Mm.*" Louise had already picked up a scent. "As it turns out," he went on, "I've got another friend who's in trouble."

"Ah!" A friendly lilt to her voice hinted she wasn't surprised. "Another foreigner, by chance?"

Jeremy gave an apologetic little sigh. "I'm afraid so, only right now I'm taking care of her five-year-old son."

"*Ma foi*, Jeremy, your gallantry never ceases to amaze me!"

Jeremy enjoyed the bit of banter, but now he had to make his case. "Really, it's not a huge sacrifice, but it's true—I've got a five-year-old boy living with me for the time being."

"For the time being..."

"Well, until his mother comes from Brussels to get him. It's a long story."

"Things always are, so I won't ask for details, but how are you managing?"

"Not *too* badly...of course I've got my work and other things to attend to..."

"*Bien sûr*," Madame agreed. "And I imagine you could use a hand watching the boy..."

Jeremy's shoulders relaxed in relief. "I'm glad you understand."

"It's been a while since I've looked after a child, but I sense it's like riding a bike. When might you need me? This afternoon I have an engagement, but tomorrow I'll be free."

"Tomorrow would be perfect. You know I'm ever appreciative of your help. And your friendship," added Jeremy, moved by the fact that after three months of living their separate busy lives, Louise Cholot was as approachable as she had been that first day they crossed paths in a laundromat where he was making investigative inquiries.

They agreed that Jeremy would bring the boy to her house the next afternoon at two.

"Oh, before we hang up," she asked, "what is his name?"

"Bekim. Bekim Berisha. Berisha is his mother's last name. She's Albanian..."

"I understand."

"And the boy's French is limited, though he understands basic things."

"All right, I think I've got it. I'll keep him entertained."

Jeremy wanted to cross his fingers and add, *good luck*. If worse came to worst, and Bekim didn't like Madame, the kid would appreciate Jeremy all the more for coming back to retrieve him.

As Jeremy returned the receiver to its cradle, his right foot began to tap the parquet floor in a nervous beat. So he wouldn't be able to start his little job today. He sat thinking for a short moment before rising to join Bekim in the living room. Hands in his pockets, he stood observing the boy, who was on his knees at the coffee table coloring in the outline of what looked to be a raggedly-sketched mountain. The top remained white, while Bekim dragged a green crayon back and forth across the rest of it.

"Is this snow?" Jeremy asked, bending over and brushing the mountain's blank white peak with his fingertip.

Bekim nodded without looking up. "Snow."

The kid was clever—*why waste a white crayon to color what's already white?*

"And where is this mountain?"

"*In Italia*," Bekim answered, shifting from French to Italian.

"*Dove, in Italia?*" Jeremy pursued, squatting next to the boy.

Bekim paused to consider the question *where*. "*Dove abita Robertino.*"

"Ah, where the boy Robertino in your book lives. Do you remember where that is? *Ti ricordi dove abita?*"

Bekim finished coloring the verdant mountain shaft, slashes of green slipping across its lines like wild grass. Then he finally turned to Jeremy and said, "*In Piemonte.*"

For an instant Jeremy hesitated, then smiled back and nodded. The boy was wrong. The fictional Robertino didn't live in the Italian region of Piedmont but in an alpine village far above Lake Como, in Italy's Lombardy region. Piedmont, on the other hand, was home to Ruggero Vairo, the Italian viticulturist and antique arms collector. For six months Bekim and his mother had called Piedmont their home. The Alps stretched west over the region, and no doubt Bekim had visited them, and liked them, just as he'd evidently liked living in Vairo's home. Jeremy was tempted to ask the boy about Vairo, about what the three did together as a "family." Whether his mother still talked of Vairo, or if Vairo ever called. But he decided against it—didn't want to stir up the boy's feelings, thought it arguably dishonest to probe a five-year-old about his mother's former life with her lover.

Setting aside his own ambivalent sentiments, Jeremy patted the boy's shoulder. *"On se fait une promenade? Una passeggiata?"* he tacked on in Italian. But the glow in the boy's eyes told him that Bekim understood the French for *taking a walk*. "Hurry, let's get your coat on," he urged, using the edge of the table to lever himself back to his feet. He registered a slight twinge in the left knee, where he'd been kicked by a thug during last summer's RG job, and he couldn't help associating it with the pinch of guilt he felt about taking Bekim out on reconnaissance.

The Romanian was called Cornel Iliescu, a thirty-six-year-old refugee from the communist Ceausescu period. According to Rébert's information, the man had probably engaged in criminal activity back in Romania, though the intenseness of turmoil in the former Eastern Bloc made verification difficult. Either way, Rébert wanted to know who did the counterfeiting of the documents Iliescu sold. Jeremy would have to wait until the following day to engage his cover persona of desperate émigré in search of a passport. This afternoon, carrying a snapshot of Iliescu, and with Bekim in tow (if Ghensie knew, she would no doubt disapprove), Jeremy would limit himself to observing the *mec* who spent afternoons in a café called La Presque Bastille, near Place de la Bastille.

That Bekim was with him wasn't Jeremy's only concern. There was also the damn stuffed bear, more of an irritation, granted, than a concern, but eternally present and an ever-increasing eyesore. On their bus ride to the Bastille, Jeremy cast sideways glances at the grass-stains and gutter grime (all sorts of imaginable and unimaginable dirt) that streaked and glued the bear's beige fur. Could they not drop Grizzly off at the Laundromat for a thorough washing, or even lose him altogether? Of course the boy would stand for nothing of the kind, and Jeremy cringed at the thought of a siren of screeches and squeals and loud sobs resounding through the bus at the mere suggestion of even the first idea. The boy needed the bear viscerally, it seemed; Jeremy understood this, only wishing Bekim would trust him a bit more and brandish the bear a little less when he was upset. Then again, it must all be part of a small child's psychology, and Jeremy felt a pang of guilt for wanting to toss Grizzly in the trash.

They entered the spacious café, and from the photo he carried, Jeremy identified Cornel Iliescu at the far end. At least it seemed to be the Romanian, sitting at his table in profile. Jeremy would not get any closer today, and instead led Bekim to a corner table where Jeremy could observe Iliescu from afar. La Presque Bastille had ample seating, a space almost too big for clandestine meetings, thought Jeremy. He himself would have chosen a hole-in-the wall joint where he could monitor foot traffic more easily.

The Romanian sat alone drinking some kind of grog, it appeared, judging from the glass cup. His dark straight hair, longer on top than in back and on the sides, lapped over a prominent brow as he bent to write in a small notebook. He paused to take two quick sips of grog, then went back to his notations, a practice that repeated itself. The *mec* seemed methodical, and Jeremy wondered how many grogs he would have to order to complete his bookkeeping task, since only a quick scribble separated sips.

In the meantime Jeremy gave his order to a waitress, a *Croque Monsieur* for Bekim (the boy's own choice of sandwich, which might mean the kid was beginning to settle in) and an omelet for himself. He had suggested setting the bear on the floor while they ate, only to receive a fierce frown from Bekim.

His mouth half full, the boy pointed to a glass-covered sketch on the wall next to them. "What's that?" he asked in French.

Jeremy turned to look. "It's a drawing of the Bastille fortress being torn down." After a second's contemplation he rephrased his reply in Italian. "*Hai capito?*" he asked to check the boy's understanding.

Bekim tilted his head, then nodded. The boy's smile seemed wry, though maybe it was just those eastern eyes. He pointed to the drawing again and asked if it was a castle they were tearing down. "*Castello,*" he said in Italian.

"Yes, it's like a small *château,*" Jeremy emphasized in French.

More sketches of the Bastille in its various states of dismantlement checkered the wall and Bekim asked about the closest ones. Jeremy, all the while, kept an eye on Iliescu. A man was now arriving to sit at the Romanian's table. Iliescu snapped shut his notebook and smoothed back his hair. The two didn't shake hands, which told Jeremy the Romanian and his guest probably had frequent dealings. When Iliescu's gaze swiveled round the room Jeremy twisted back towards the wall, pointing at one of the sketches.

"How about drawing a castle when we get home?" he asked Bekim as he presented his back to the room.

"*D'accord.*"

"Good—then hurry and finish your *Croque* and we'll get going."

Jeremy stole glances at Iliescu as he waited for

Bekim to finally put down his fork. "You're not still hungry, are you?" he asked as he left money on the table. Without waiting for an answer he rose and ushered the boy out of the café. If the kid still had a rumbling stomach when they got home, he could eat an apple.

Back on the bus, Jeremy mulled over what he had seen. Iliescu sold fake passports and the man who had joined him might be an associate, or even a client. Both men looked respectable—jackets, collared shirts, the newcomer's jacket particularly well cut. Tomorrow, when time came to initiate his approach, Jeremy would dress accordingly. The new man had also entered the café in a stylish topcoat. Jeremy's three-year-old over-coat would do. In fact, better not to look too dapper as he played the desperate man in search of a passport. He could feel the role claiming him, soaking into him as he thought back to his meeting with Rébert and the ever-dangling promise of French nationality. His normal clothes would do just fine, his story would not need much finessing. No, not at all.

Chapter 13

Jeremy's shift that night at Le Prince Blue Note started off like many of his others. A five-year employee of the jazz club, he enjoyed some seniority, was appreciated for his knowledge of jazz and was held in esteem as the son of Walt Winters, former jazzman of the Paris scene. Many of the older jazz artists (the over-forty set) remembered the elder Winters, had played gigs or jammed with him, or had just enjoyed the opportunity to hear the man's music. Customers remembered him as well. Walt Winters' framed photo hung on the wall leading to the jazz cellar; the man's magnetism endured, some of it rubbing off on his son.

American Rita Mordenti, tonight's pianist, remembered Walt Winters and knew Jeremy to be his son. Before the show started she engaged Jeremy in a flurry of pleasantries, mostly her own reminiscences and compliments directed at the elder Winters. Jeremy nodded, smiling and thanking her, as was his custom in this type of situation. The son respected the father's legacy, even as he at times felt hamstrung by it. "I've heard *you* played the sax at one time, Jeremy..." she said.

Yes, he had, a long time ago, but his stint with the instrument had ended in the upheaval of his adolescence and his father's death. Five and a half years ago he had planned to begin once more by traveling to the U.S. to reclaim his father's instrument from his cousin. Despite the plan's tragic outcome, the saxophone had eventually returned to him. Tainted relic that it was, the stain of insane violence between Jeremy and his cousin still warm to the touch, it had nonetheless represented a link to his father and hope for the future. Naturally Rita Mordenti knew nothing of this history or how Walt Winters' saxophone now lay in its case under Jeremy's bed, a shattered remnant of itself, bludgeoned and dismembered by an intruder the prior summer. Since then, and especially since his cousin's death, the idea of playing the sax lay locked in the complex cellar of his guilt. And yet the itch to make musical magic never left him.

He felt it as Rita Mordenti's combo sizzled in the club's *sous-sol*, notes and beats and chords wafting up to him as he concocted non-magical drinks behind the bar. As was his habit he went downstairs during his break to listen. Rita's combo was performing their rendition of Claude Bolling's "Jazzy." Jeremy leaned against the back wall and let Rita's syncopated piano chords telegraph through him like stuttering bursts of electricity. The song was ending and he closed his eyes to breathe in the last hot currents of racing bass, crashing symbols, and fiery alto sax; then the release of Rita's final low, warm piano chords capped by the drummer's shimmering symbols. He opened his eyes and exhaled as if he'd never breathed before—a private climax, his blood hot and envious. That's how he always felt when the jazz was perfect—the melodies, the musicianship, the ecstasy of being lifted out of himself.

Always a touch reluctant when leaving the *sous-sol,* he returned to his terrestrial post behind the bar. His waiter friend Didier called out, "Mister Manhattan— *deux*!" As his nickname implied, he could make a decent Manhattan, and everything proceeded normally until ten-fifteen when he got a phone call, a rare occurrence at work.

It was Solange, and at the sound of her voice Jeremy tightened his grip on the receiver.

"Don't worry, Bekim's fine," she said. "I just wanted to tell you that Ghensie called and wants you to call her when you get home. She wants to talk to you while Bekim's asleep. I didn't want to forget to tell you..."

"Something urgent?" Jeremy asked, nodding at Didier who had arrived at the bar with another order.

"I'm not sure, I'm curious myself..."

"Okay, thanks, I'll take care of it when I get home."

Jeremy rang off, returning to his bottles and asking himself why Ghensie wanted him to call after midnight. A swell of applause rose from the basement. He dropped a slice of orange into the Américano he'd just finished mixing and placed the glass on Didier's tray. He checked his watch, his concern ticking back up. An hour and half to go.

It was after twelve-thirty when Jeremy stepped into his flat and saw Bekim curled up like a puppy on the sofa. Solange, sitting next to him with a magazine, stifled a yawn and said the evening had gone well.

All but the call from Ghensie, perhaps. Thanking her, Jeremy picked up Bekim and Grizzly and carried them off to bed, then returned to call a cab for Solange.

"Maybe you should call Ghensie first," she suggested.

"No," Jeremy decided, taking out his wallet to check his cash, "I don't want your parents to think I'm taking advantage of your time."

"They won't—they're still happy you brought me home from Amsterdam last October."

"Mm," Jeremy murmured. *She wants to see how the call goes.* "All right, I won't be long."

"Take your time."

He returned to the entryway to make the call. Ghensie picked up on the second ring, barely greeting Jeremy before launching into a declaration. "I'm coming to Paris soon. I've given notice at the pharmacy and my neighbor Sorina will let me store things with her. I should be there in three days, or so."

Jeremy took a step forwards. He didn't know quite what to say apart from expressing profound relief, which he didn't do for fear of sounding desperate to get Bekim off his hands. Why she wanted to report her news while Bekim was asleep, he didn't know. "And your furniture?" he asked.

"It's a furnished flat. I thought of having the pharmacy send my back-pay to your address but..."

"No, we wouldn't want anyone to track you." Jeremy sat down, rubbing his neck, knowing Ghensie would be hard-pressed to do without her last check. "How long will it take them to issue your pay?"

"I don't know. The end of the week, maybe. I'd like to wait..."

"Have you been accosted since we last spoke?"

"Yes," Ghensie drew out, frustrated. "Both Luan and the bald Kosovar."

Only to be expected, Jeremy thought. "The important thing is you're getting out of there," he emphasized.

"Luan asked to come up and visit, but I wouldn't let him. He said he wanted to spend time with Bekim. Of course that's nonsense since he's never cared much about Bekim. He'd just like to bully me more, so I told him no. But the Kosovar...he stopped me on the way home from the pharmacy..."

"And...?"

A hesitant sigh came down the wire. "He thinks you might have the coin—that I may have given it to you." The rest of her speech came in a torrent. "Naturally I told him it wasn't true, that I never had the coin to begin with and therefore neither do you. But I want to get to Paris, get Bekim, and find a place away from you in case the Kosovar bastard comes after me." Jeremy heard a sharp intake of air before Ghensie hurried to add, "I didn't mean that—I didn't mean I wanted to run away and leave you to those criminals. I'm sorry...I just don't know what to do anymore."

Stunned by Ghensie's first assertion, Jeremy hardly noticed the one needing an apology. "Never mind," he said. "Soon you'll be out of Brussels. The Kosovars don't know where I live, so when you get here you can stay with me, then we'll work on a place for you to live for the long term."

They ended the call in agreement. If the pharmacy could not issue her check within three days, she would ask them to hold it for her. Until when, who knew?

Jeremy replaced the receiver, his hand lingering heavy on it. He still felt shocked, though he told himself he really shouldn't. If Luan and the Kosovars thought Ghensie had stolen the coin, it wouldn't take much for them to suspect her of passing it on to him, either for safe keeping or to entice him to become her partner. He had, after all, spent a good amount of time with her in Brussels. *Luan*: more and more, Jeremy suspected the cowardly predator held the missing coin, conveniently blaming Ghensie and harassing her as a type of cover to keep his Kosovar partners distracted while he found a way to sell the thing.

Maybe.

And now that distraction would be channeled to Jeremy. *Definitely*.

"Did you get things squared away with Ghensie?"

Jeremy turned to Solange, who now stood behind him leaning casually against the doorjamb. "Well," he said, ambivalently leaving his musings, "she says she's coming to Paris in about three days."

"Oh." Solange took a step into the entryway. "And that's why she wanted you to call her so late?"

Jeremy didn't know what else to say. If Ghensie hadn't informed Solange of this latest development he didn't see why he should. Still, she kept staring at him with the look of an inquisitive, insistent schoolgirl who had caught her teacher out in a lie or some kind of dissimulation. Her arms were crossed, her head cocked skeptically. In truth she was doing him an immense favor by just being here at this hour, and he would need her to watch Bekim tomorrow night as well. He didn't want to alienate such an eager ally of both his and Ghensie's.

"Well," he began, "it looks like Luan and his Kosovar pals now suspect me of having the coin."

Solange stepped closer, her hands dropping to her hips. "*You?*" She looked at him more sharply. "Did they give you that bruise on your forehead?"

"Mm," Jeremy affirmed, offering a hapless shrug. "But there's no need to worry." He assured her that the thugs didn't know his address. Nor did they know his name, since Ghensie had introduced him to Luan as an acquaintance from Paris. No name, no address, so how could they find him in a city of nine million? By laying hands on Ghensie. All the more reason for her to get out of Brussels now.

Chapter 14

W e're taking the métro today," Jeremy announced, as he and Bekim left the building at two p.m. for Madame Cholot's. "She's a good friend," Jeremy had explained to the boy.

"What's the *métro*?" Bekim asked in Italian.

Jeremy answered in Italian, both for the sake of brevity and for the practice he was gaining in the language from this polyglot five-year-old. He described the trains that ran underground, pointing downwards and using his arm to weave the image of a snaking train.

Bekim's eyes stretched in wonder, then narrowed. "Is it dark down there?"

"No, no. There's lots of light, lots of people, kids too. My friend Madame Cholot is a very nice lady," he said after a pause, seeking to capitalize on the boy's interest.

"Nice like Solange?"

"Yes, but older. She's like a granny who likes to spoil her grandchildren," he added, counting on Louise Cholot to do just that.

Bekim seemed to consider this, then asked, "When will Solange come back?"

"Tonight. But you'll see, you're going to like Madame Cholot too."

As they descended the steps, hand in hand, to the Temple métro station, Jeremy felt Bekim's small grip tighten. Maybe he was still afraid of going underground. Maybe intuition told him he was going to be left with another stranger and recalcitrance was gearing up. Jeremy steeled himself.

Regarding the former, Bekim expressed nothing but sheer joy at the subterranean world—giggles as the train doors closed with their wind-breaking pneumatic sigh. "*Una scoreggia!*" he said with an exuberant grin.

Jeremy frowned in puzzlement, so Bekim blew a raspberry to illustrate.

"Ah, *un pet*," Jeremy said in French, smiling.

"*Pet!*" The boy puffed with pride at claiming this new vocabulary word, then repeated *scoreggia*, slapping Jeremy's thigh to encourage him to do the same, for indeed they'd each learned a new word for *fart*.

"*Scoregia*," Jeremy indulged him.

"No—score*gg*ia!" Bekim corrected, stressing the elongated sound of the double g.

Jeremy mimicked the pronunciation, glancing around at their fellow commuters. The two teens on the bench across from them didn't bat an eye, the girl engrossed in the French translation of Stephen King's *Misery*, the boy picking at a hangnail.

"*Bravo*," said Bekim, Italian style, grinning at Jeremy. The kid was both naïve and sophisticated in different measures. *His* pronunciation of *pet* had needed no correction. Oh, the advantage of a small child's brain!

In tune with her analogy to riding a bike, Louise Cholot seemed to relate to Bekim straightaway. Introductions were exchanged, Madame and Jeremy exchanged kisses on the cheeks, and Madame bent to shake the boy's hand. She was looking well and fit, Jeremy noted, in a pair of wool trousers and a snug sweater that flattered her slim strong form. She wore a pair of athletic shoes, which Jeremy soon learned meant a trip to the park was in store.

"But first a little snack," she said.

A crease of concern had returned to Bekim's brow, which didn't daunt Madame. "What a fine bear you have," she said, indicating Grizzly, who remained squished against Bekim's chest in a desperate love grip.

Bekim appeared to understand Madame's French, straightening slightly and loosening his grasp on the suffocated animal. He held it out slightly for Madame to further examine while Jeremy shifted his weight in embarrassment at the bear's filthy fur.

"He's called Grizzly," Bekim said in French, "and he's American."

"Oh?" said Madame, affectionately impressed. Jeremy raised his brows in surprise—Grizzly, *American*? The boy's imagination was like a dream-factory, inexhaustibly cranking out fantasies.

Jeremy stood by while Louise laid the dining room table with biscuits and tea. "Bekim might need a book on his chair to sit on," he told her.

"I've got plenty—dictionaries, atlases, a Petit Larousse..." Madame was a crossword fanatic, her apartment brimming with books.

At each of Madame's overtures to Bekim, Jeremy felt himself relax a bit more.

She gave the boy a frank gaze of curiosity as he sat propped up at the table. "Perhaps Bekim would prefer something other than tea to drink..."

"Hot chocolate maybe?" Jeremy conveyed in Italian.

Bekim nodded, while Madame gazed at Jeremy. "I didn't know you spoke Italian."

"I had lots of it in school. And, well, there *was* that business last summer."

Madame's lips and eyes sketched a knowing smile. "And Bekim speaks it..."

"So does his mother. They spent six months in Italy before coming further north."

Louise gave a reflective nod. Surely she was puzzling over this history though she asked nothing further in front of Bekim. Rather she said, "If all else fails, I can draw on the expressions I learned from all those mountaineering trips to the Italian Alps."

Clearly Madame knew how to handle the boy, and Jeremy was debating how to make his departure. Should he have a little tea first? Ease his way out?

In the meantime Louise went on, "When we're finished here we'll take the bus to the park for a little fresh air. There are lots of things for children there. Slides and swings"—she looped her hands through the air—"things to climb on..."

"Much bigger than the one in our neighborhood," Jeremy eagerly contributed in Italian.

Bekim seemed overwhelmed, his eyes darting between Jeremy and Louise as he tried to keep up.

"But first eat some biscuits," Madame said, nudging the plate towards the boy, "while I make hot chocolate." She shot Jeremy a knowing nod. "Have something hot to drink yourself."

More talk about the Parc Montsouris followed, Jeremy translating when necessary and affirming Madame. When he finished his tea he stood, thanked her, and looked at his watch. "*Oh zut*, I don't think Bekim and I have time to go to the park after all." He glanced at the boy with an apologetic smile and started to translate into Italian, but Bekim was looking worried before Jeremy had got his first word out. He braced himself for one of the kid's booming *nooo's!* but nothing of the sort followed. Only a dejected frown and welling eyes that made Jeremy look to Louise for help.

She said, "Bekim can still come to the park with me, Jeremy. You take care of your errands then come back to pick him up." Jeremy translated.

The boy squirmed, plucking his bear off the table and pressing it to him.

"The three of us can go—you, me, and Grizzly," said Louise, looking Bekim encouragingly in the eye.

It didn't take more persuasion or a translation. "I'll be back soon," Jeremy said, but Bekim was already clambering down from the table and didn't bother to reply. Exchanging a wink and nod with Madame, Jeremy took his leave.

On the métro to the Bastille, Jeremy went over his strategy for engaging the Romanian passport trafficker, Cornel Iliescu—an amazingly straightforward method, weaving Jeremy's own assault conviction and imprisonment in the U.S., with an added twist: the ensuing death of Walter. He felt strange using his cousin's demise for this job, but also thought he might face down more of his grief this way. According to this new version, not only had Walter died, but the state of Virginia was now looking to prosecute Jeremy for homicide, which would involve a request from the U.S. government for his extradition. Jeremy shuddered to think how real this scenario could be, and indeed felt his sense of guilt diminish a tad. He would call on this palpable chill when beseeching Iliescu for help.

Automatically he brushed off his overcoat as he exited the station. Underneath he wore a pair of black corduroys, laced black shoes, and a grey turtleneck sweater, a look not too dressy yet serious and respectful enough for the stylish Iliescu, who could conjure the means to freedom for a man living month to month on a part-time job—a man who might need to flee extradition at a moment's notice. Once more, it wouldn't take much acting.

His thoughts drifted back to Ghensie. Had *she* been

acting with her little deception in Brussels, hiding the truth about her cousin and the Kosovar thugs? *Acting versus dissimulating*: difficult at times to distinguish. What he knew was that he was now a target for Luan and the Kosovar thugs, and he could also channel the sensation of that danger in presenting his case to Iliescu.

He straightened his coat as he entered the café called La Presque Bastille. Now it was his turn to perform.

Cornel Iliescu was chatting with a woman who sat casually back in her chair while Iliescu leaned in to make his points. His dark hair flopped choppily forward while her blond hair streamed elegantly behind her, aided by an occasional flip of a casual hand. She appeared about Iliescu's and Jeremy's age. From a table where he could monitor the two, Jeremy ordered more tea, indifferent to whether he drank it or not, and focused on Iliescu: his staccato sips from a glass of beer, two at a time, his doing most of the talking and the woman most of the nodding. Iliescu jotted something in his notebook, the woman opened her purse, took out her own small notepad and did the same. The exchange lasted about twenty minutes, then she stowed the notepad, flipped her hair back again, and rose to put on her coat. Iliescu remained seated and held out his hand, which she shook by the fingertips before turning and leaving the table. As she crossed the café, Jeremy caught a full glimpse of her face. Their eyes met, hers blue with a flicker of curiosity, then she passed out of sight. She was pretty, and possibly in need of a passport.

Jeremy let another five minutes elapse, then rose, put his coat back on, and crossed casually to Iliescu's table. He stopped in front of the Romanian, who was scribbling in his notebook, his face so close to the paper that Jeremy wondered whether he needed glasses—which he did, pulling a pair from his jacket pocket and latching them on to give Jeremy a once-over. Without ceremony Jeremy pulled out a chair and sat down, his hand shooting over the table in greeting.

"Jeremy Winters," he introduced himself, his voice firm and eager. "I've been looking forward to meeting you."

No hand rose to meet Jeremy's, only cool silence and a neutral gaze from the Romanian.

"You *are* Cornel Iliescu, I hope?" asked Jeremy with a faux note of doubt.

Amused arrogance lit the Romanian's dark eyes. "And who did you say is asking?"

"Jeremy Winters. I've heard Monsieur Iliescu can work wonders, and frankly I'm in need of a miracle."

Allowing himself a half-smile, Iliescu closed his notebook and removed his spectacles, laying them on the table. His expression returned cool blandness. "A miracle, eh...?"

"I can only hope," said Jeremy, wondering if he'd finally passed inspection. He extended his hand again and this time Iliescu deigned to give it a tepid shake, before brushing the hank of hair off his forehead, his head jerking in a gesture not unlike that of his previous visitor, the blonde. Jeremy smirked to himself. Iliescu was a vain *mec*.

"I imagine," he said, "you're looking for something you can't get through...ordinary channels?"

Jeremy gave a slow nod. "I need to obtain permanent residency in France—a document that'll also enable me to move to another country, if worse comes to worst." Humbly, Jeremy cleared his throat. "I'm looking for the means to disappear with a different name." He drew a breath and sat back, folding his hands on the table and frowning at his thumbs as he worked them against each other—the sign of a nervous, concerned man.

Iliescu summed up the situation. "You need a French passport but you're not French—Monsieur *Winters*, is it?"

Jeremy returned a sober nod.

"Funny, you speak French like a Frenchman."

"I've lived here off and on a good part of my life."

"So what *are* you, then?"

Jeremy shifted in his chair and leaned in. Presenting his most fervid, hopeful expression, he commenced to tell his tale: from the blacklisting of his father in 1958 to assaulting his cousin in the name of both his and his father's honor, and finally the untimely death of Walter.

Then came the climax: "And now, you see, the U.S. is threating to force me back to prison." His fingers still laced, Jeremy massaged his knuckles, an authentic case of nerves coming on. Eyes sweeping Jeremy from hands to face and back, Iliescu seemed to be speculating—on whether Jeremy was telling the truth? On whether the business would warrant the time and risk?

"Anything you could do," Jeremy started to add, "I—"

"Who told you about me?"

Iliescu's interruption wasn't brusque, rather firmly inquisitive. Jeremy relaxed his hands. He was still in the game. "I have Italian friends, political refugees who've needed this type of service to avoid getting deported back to Italy. I don't know exactly how they managed, but your name's been mentioned as a person who understands these matters." Jeremy added a respectful nod.

"Italian Communists..." Iliescu's crooked smile

crept back. "If the political Right comes to power here in the next presidential election, they'll all be in your situation." He let out an offhand *humph*. "In that case I might be glad your friends know my name."

Still under Iliescu's diagnostic eye, Jeremy drew a deep and silent breath. This was the closest the Romanian had come to a concession.

"Well," he said, "your story is interesting. I'll take a look into it. Have your friends told you how much the kind of document you need costs?"

"Does it matter, the cost of staying out of prison?"

Iliescu's dark eyes scrutinized him anew, hawkish, disconcerting. Was he gauging what could be siphoned from a desperate American? If so it didn't concern Jeremy, for if the RG wanted the counterfeiters they would have to pay the price.

Iliescu finally nodded. "Meet me back here in four days, at three o'clock."

Rising, Jeremy shook Iliescu's hand again. "*Merci*—until Saturday." As he crossed the café towards the door, he took a last look over his shoulder. Iliescu's nose was buried in his notebook again, his hair back dangling over his brow, his pen busy as a worker ant. No doubt his scribbles included the name *Jeremy Winters* and *Italian Red Refugees*. Iliescu hadn't asked for an Italian name, though Jeremy had one at his disposal. He would keep it pocketed for future use. As he pulled up his collar and made his way towards the métro station, a subtle smile of satisfaction broke the sober line of his mouth.

Chapter 15

By the time he reached Louise Cholot's building, Jeremy's smile was replaced by a nervous working of his jaw as he readied himself for Louise's account of Bekim's behavior. He punched in the access code to the building and rode the elevator to the fourth floor, where Madame's door opened almost instantly after his ring. Two cheerful-looking figures faced him on the threshold.

Jeremy's smile crept back. Both Madame and Bekim looked content, Madame flashing a smile of welcome, Bekim granting Jeremy his shyish, slant-eyed version.

"Bekim and I have had a productive afternoon," Louise said. "Plenty of fun at the park, snacks, some books to look at. Oh, and Bekim has drawn a magnificent dragon," she added, beaming down at the boy.

At Madame's instruction Bekim padded off to fetch his drawing while Jeremy nodded gratefully at Louise. "He wasn't any trouble, then...?"

"Not a bit. We got along like two old friends."

The boy seemed to prefer the company of women. If so, it made a certain sense considering his history, and on the whole Jeremy couldn't blame him.

Returning to the entryway, Bekim stopped next to Madame with his drawing.

Jeremy took his time scrutinizing it, cocking his head and stroking his chin, one eye noting the boy's intense frown of anticipation.

"Bravo!" he finally pronounced, and the boy

returned a triumphant smile.

"Will you stay a little longer, Jeremy?" asked Louise. "I'm sure Bekim wouldn't mind drawing us something new..."

Her tone carried a hint, her gaze a knowing look. Polite as she was, she no doubt expected him to explain this new undertaking of his. So he settled in the living room with her, while Bekim drew at the kitchen table. He told her everything, most everything at any rate, considering the original assignment concerning Solange was RG business. He summed up Ghensie's plight, Luan and the Kosovars and their threat to implicate her in their crime if she went to the police. Jeremy shook his head as if hearing it all for the first time and added, "Her immigration status is tenuous as it is."

Louise's nod was more grave than sympathetic. "That's all understandable, but now they're after you. If they *do* find out where you live...?"

"I know." He sighed inwardly. *I know.*

"And you believe everything in her account? I don't doubt you," she went on, "but you say Ghensie is a friend of a friend, that you've only known her a short time..." With her pause, Louise's gaze grew more sympathetic, and Jeremy wondered if she suspected a possible romantic complication.

"You're right," he conceded. "I don't know her all that well, but she and the boy are definitely in danger. I've seen her cousin and one of the Kosovars in action."

"In action?"

Jeremy hadn't mentioned the beating he took. No need to frighten Madame. So he related the bald Kosovar's threatening behavior at the café in Brussels, mimicking the hand gesture of the double-headed eagle. "Ghensie says it's especially nationalistic and hostile on the part of Kosovars."

"I imagine so," murmured Louise. "Kosovo is part of Serbia, though the ethnicity of the inhabitants is mostly Albanian. I've read of the restiveness there and violence between the Albanian and Serbian Kosovars."

"Bekim's father is Serbian."

"Oh," said Louise, a catch of surprise in her voice.

"An affair she had five years ago." Jeremy hadn't meant to put it that way, as if Ghensie were alone to blame. "They were both students," he hastened to add.

"Life can unfold that way," Madame said with a sigh of understanding.

"He's not in the picture anymore."

"I don't imagine it was easy for her family."

Louise was aware of Ghensie's Muslim background, but another item Jeremy hadn't mentioned was her initial lack of forthrightness concerning the coin. *Too long and complicated*, he'd rationalized. *Too damning of Ghensie*, he knew all too well.

"In any case," said Louise, "I'm sure you're right about the coin's value. I can't conceive of any leader, even today, who would countenance his image being carved like that. Your president Franklin Roosevelt, I've heard, refused to let himself be photographed in his wheelchair. Then again, losing an eye in combat and continuing to lead armies could be considered a badge of honor."

Jeremy nodded in speculation. They were sipping port, cocooned amidst shelves of leather-bound books and marquetry-inlaid tables as dusk gathered outside. Below, in the Place de l'Abbé-Georges-Hénocque, trees were beginning to shiver in growing gusts of wind. Jeremy figured it was time to head home.

He thanked Louise once more as he rose.

"Don't hesitate to call on me again." A wink followed, and Jeremy knew it conveyed not only Madame's willingness to watch Bekim but also her eagerness to help solve the greater problem.

They strolled into the kitchen to check on Bekim. "What are you drawing this time?" Louise asked him.

His blond head popped up to reveal his creation— an entity with a mass of outstretched tentacles colored black.

Jeremy asked if it was a jellyfish, translating for Louise, but Bekim shook his head.

"What are those two nobs at the top?" asked Louise, pointing at the creature.

Bekim tapped the two spots with his crayon. "Two heads."

"Two?" Jeremy asked absently. He glanced at his watch; they needed to get going.

"Our eagle has two heads," Bekim explained. "Like you made with your hands."

"Eagle?" Louise echoed, guessing at the Italian.

"With two heads," Jeremy stated, his lip curling. "You know," he told Bekim in Italian, "that's not a polite thing I did with my hands. I was only showing Louise that it's not the kind of thing you do in front of people."

"I know." Bekim bowed his head. Then it shot back up. "*Mami* says if I draw something it can't hurt me."

Jeremy pinched the bridge of his nose in bemusement. When he translated for Louise, she said, "A bit of psychology, I imagine. The magic of taking power over a fear by reproducing it. Or something like that."

Jeremy looked back at Bekim's paper, wondering how such a clumsy, amorphous drawing (feathers that looked more like pasta stuck to a fat body) could allay fear, but he guessed it was no different from the power the boy seemed to ascribe to his scruffy toy bear.

Dutifully, Jeremy and Louise praised the drawing and then stepped back into the living room while Bekim packed up his things. Louise whispered, "Not only do the walls have little ears, they have little eyes as well."

Jeremy understood all too well. In the future he would need to watch what he said and did, no matter which language he happened to be speaking.

Back in the flat Jeremy threw together a meal of packaged ravioli and sauce from a jar, and when Solange arrived he barely had time to brush cheeks with her. Bekim's arms were clamped tight around her waist again, and as Jeremy flew out the door the boy cast him a sly smile. A little lady's man.

Solange would watch Bekim nights through Thursday. Friday she had a date, in which case Louise had said she could substitute if Ghensie hadn't arrived yet. Saturday he would again meet with Cornel Iliescu, and by then Ghensie should definitely have arrived—and thank goodness. He wanted to call her to see how things were going but decided to wait. She said she was coming—he need not pester her like a child.

As things stood anyway, Bekim seemed to be warming to him. The boy adored the métro. They raced underground from one end of the city to the other, Bekim delighting in the farting doors and perhaps even more in sliding his ticket into the turnstile slot and plucking it out when it popped up on top. He pointed out the varying colors of plastic waiting-seats on the platforms of different stations, declaring, "I like the red ones best!"

Yes, things were going much better, however by the time Thursday afternoon came, Jeremy still hadn't heard from Ghensie. Louise Cholot would watch Bekim Friday night, but he would still have to ask either her or Solange to look after him on Saturday when Jeremy would meet with the Romanian—unless Ghensie called from the Gare du Nord that very day, announcing, "I'm here!" He could only hope.

While they waited for Solange, Bekim asked Jeremy to read him his Italian book, the one about the boy Robertino in the Alps. "Solange doesn't know Italian." The statement was matter-of-fact, though Jeremy felt a flush of warmth all the same.

"Well," he encouraged, "she can read you your French book, right?"

"But I like Robertino best."

As they sat side by side on the sofa, Jeremy opening the book, another surprise utterance came from the boy in Italian. "*Tu sei mio papà adesso?*"

Jeremy's eyes shot up from the book. "*Cosa?*" he said in shock and perplexity.

Bekim repeated the question, this time stressing the *tu*. "Are *you* my dad now?"

The inner warmth Jeremy had just felt now turned to a heat that burned his cheeks. What to say? "Well...who was your dad before?"

"Ruggero. He was my daddy. But he's gone now."

The Italian *mec*, Vairo, Jeremy muttered to himself. *On the contrary, your mother had to leave him. And for now your mother is not in the picture either.* The thought stung Jeremy, a dart from his conscience that even he could cause the boy further distress by disappearing from his life. Then the only thing left to cling to would be the ever-faithful filthy, grimy Grizzly. He glanced at the bear propped on Bekim's knees. It didn't stay there long, for another wonder took place: Bekim lifted the bear and sat it in Jeremy's lap. "Grizzly likes to hear you read too."

Jeremy felt his mouth fall open and couldn't manage to close it.

After a moment, Bekim asked, "Aren't you going to start?"

"Sure," Jeremy said with a nervous chuckle. "Just

hang on one minute." He checked his watch: almost seven o'clock—Ghensie should be home at this hour. "I just need to make a quick call."

He sat Grizzly on the sofa and went to the phone in the entryway, dialed Ghensie's number, and waited. And waited some more. Evidently she didn't own an answering machine. He hung up, his nerves rattled. She could still be at the pharmacy, or walking home, or attending to last-minute business before leaving for Paris. Or, *the Kosovars*...

He inhaled deeply. No need to panic, he would try her later. He returned to the living room and sat back down. Bekim handed him the book and returned the bear to his own lap. "Can we start now?" he asked, his blue eyes blinking in eagerness.

"Of course we can." As Jeremy smiled at the boy in sober reflection, Bekim edged closer to him.

Jeremy opened the book to the story's beginning, the little Robertino dressed in something like lederhosen as he climbed a grassy Alpine slope. His black dog followed, a red bandana and a bell tied about its neck. "Robertino hates to stay indoors," Jeremy began. He took a surreptitious look at Bekim and found the boy's brow furrowed in concentration. After a moment's hesitation he gave the kid a pat on the head, then went on reading.

Chapter 16

That night, on a break from work, Jeremy left the club for a pay phone and redialed Ghensie. This time he waited eleven rings before reluctantly hanging up. Ten o'clock and she still wasn't home. She should be calling *him* by now, letting him know she would arrive by Saturday, the day after tomorrow. *If* she was able to call, he reminded himself anxiously. He headed back to the club, telling himself not to worry until he had a solid reason.

Back in his flat after midnight, with Solange on her way home in a cab, he debated trying Ghensie again. He stood by the phone, then changed his mind, not wanting to come across as an alarmist. She could be out with a friend or simply in bed asleep by now. He would wait until tomorrow morning.

The next day still produced no satisfaction. "*Merde*," he swore aloud, all but slamming the receiver down. *If he just had a clue as to Ghensie's plan.*

Maybe Bekim heard him, for he bounded into the entryway, but only to ask if they could take the métro somewhere again. "We might have to stay home today," he told the boy. He didn't want to miss a call.

Bekim hung his head in his disappointment, but at least he hadn't mentioned the topic of fatherhood so far today—*Sei tu mio papà?*—nor was he voicing objections to staying home.

"We'll leave for Louise's a little early," Jeremy conceded. The boy seemed pacified, giving two exaggerated nods then scampering back into the living room. Jeremy reckoned they could take a few detours around town on the métro before arriving at Louise's, where Madame would be waiting to watch the boy that evening. In the meantime Jeremy pondered tomorrow's meeting with Cornel Iliescu. Who knew how the Romanian had sized him up? He must have come off somewhat credible or Iliescu wouldn't have offered another meeting. At this point, the appearance of desperation meant everything, Jeremy decided. Iliescu must respond to his plea. But should he offer to pay any price for the passport? Should he risk presenting the image of an American with negligible financial worries?

He picked up the receiver again and dialed Rébert, who welcomed the update. "Sounds like Iliescu might believe you. As far as being taken for an American with deep pockets...well, of course we'll have to agree on his price, but don't act like it's easily affordable. You're a desperate man whose pockets are shrinking by the day. Tell Iliescu you're lying low, expecting to be summoned at any moment by the French Ministry for Internal or Foreign Affairs."

Jeremy nodded towards an invisible Rébert, having conveyed what he had told Iliescu about fearing imminent deportation. He didn't mention the inspiration of his cousin's demise. That was a private affair, more comfortably shared with a stranger like Iliescu, in a contrived, detached context.

They rang off, and three hours later Ghensie had yet to call. It was Friday, a workday, though by now Ghensie's employment with the pharmacy should have been concluded. Jeremy dialed her again, listened to another interminable string of rings, and replaced the receiver with a loud *clunk*. Then he felt like snatching it back up and giving himself a knock on the head. Ghensie would have canceled her phone service by now, probably had evacuated the flat altogether and was staying with her Romanian neighbor. And yet why wouldn't she call from some other phone? *If* she could. The same old *what-ifs* revolved round and round in his head like relentless windmill blades as he paced the entryway before heading back into the living room.

One of Bekim's toy cars, a Lancia Fulvia, came careening at his foot. The boy cackled at the collision and Jeremy smiled distractedly. "Can we go yet?" he implored Jeremy.

With a sour look Jeremy checked his watch. "Yeah, we can go."

Madame Cholot agreed to watch Bekim the next day and even offered to keep the boy into the evening while Jeremy worked. He thanked her heartily but told her he would be off Saturday and Sunday. As for Saturday afternoon, he would let her know the next morning, apologizing for "leaving you hanging like that."

By the time Bekim and he returned home after midnight, Jeremy's nerves felt like they might fire through his skin. As soon as he got the door open his gaze leaped to the answering machine next to the phone. The light was blinking and he made to lunge towards it, then thought better of it, deciding to put Bekim to bed first. When Jeremy finally set the machine's tape rolling he heard Ghensie's voice rise from the speaker. Her "I'll be in Paris tomorrow morning" sounded like the angels announcing the birth of Jesus. She would arrive at the Gare du Nord on the ten-o-five train from Lille.

He would be there to meet her.

He said nothing to Bekim about his mother's impending arrival. Instead, the next morning, after straightening up the apartment and changing the sheets on the bed, he got the boy bundled up and told him they would strike out on "a new métro adventure," hedging against the possibility that something might go wrong. If for some reason Ghensie didn't show, God forbid, the boy wouldn't be distressed. And if things went as planned—*they had to*—Ghensie's appearance would be like a Christmas surprise.

When they got to the station Jeremy found the arrival platform, and there they waited.

"Are we taking a train now?" Bekim asked, his eyes ablaze with curiosity and enthusiasm.

Jeremy responded with a nonchalant smile. "No, we're waiting for a friend of mine."

The boy stared back at the empty tracks, then looked up again. "Is it a boy or a girl?"

That was a question Jeremy hadn't anticipated. "Well…"

Around them people paced and milled and strode to and fro, voices mixing with clacking heels on concrete, their echoes crescendoing under the station's high vaulted roof and giving Jeremy an excuse to cup his ear and ask, "What did you say?"

Then the train appeared. Jeremy pointed to it and smiled broadly.

He saw no one resembling Ghensie. Passengers descended from an interminable number of train doors, dodging one another, some hurrying to make a connection on a different platform, others methodically dragging their luggage towards the exit. And Jeremy continued to scan the crowd, he and Bekim stationed next to the nose of the train where Ghensie would have to pass if she were to leave the platform. *As long as she had made the train*. The thought set Jeremy's foot tapping.

Suddenly Bekim gave a yelp. Jumping up and down, he yelled, *"Mami, Mami!"*

Jeremy looked hard at the woman with short blond hair and knit cap while Bekim launched himself into her arms. The woman looked Bekim up and down and seemed satisfied. Yes, it was Ghensie, cosmetically transformed.

Incognito, she later told Jeremy in French once they were back in his flat. "I purposely stayed in Lille for two days, and I didn't see Luan or the Kosovars."

"Good," said Jeremy. He wanted to ask why she hadn't called him earlier, but just having her next to him on the sofa made him soften with relief—maybe she had been short on money. "Since your cousin and his gang have no idea where I live," he went on, "we should be fine for now." He glanced at Bekim, who was drawing at the coffee table, always wondering how much French the boy understood. "You and Bekim will take the bedroom," he told Ghensie, "and I'll sleep here on the sofa."

Yes, she had arrived safe and sound, thank God, and she was looking good. The haircut smacked of Nordic sophistication and, coupled with dark eyeliner, made her all the more enticing. Thanking Jeremy again for his generous support she granted him a hug. It was their first, and feeling the soft, sensual curve in her narrow waist, he vowed it would not be their last.

At that very instant Bekim set down his crayon and hopped up onto his mother's lap, once more parking Grizzly with Jeremy.

"Oh!" said Ghensie in surprise. Her glance traveled from the bear to Jeremy to Bekim. "I can see you two have gotten on well!"

Jeremy gave a modest shrug.

"And Grizzly looks ever the worse for wear," she said with an embarrassed little laugh.

Jeremy smiled along with her. At this moment the bear and its appearance couldn't have mattered less to him.

Ghensie had arrived with only two suitcases, the rest of her goods (which weren't many, since she'd been renting a furnished apartment) stowed with her neighbor Sorina in Brussels.

"And no one else knows you've left?" he asked.

"Only Sorina and the people at the pharmacy, but I told none of them where I was going."

"Not even your parents...?"

"No—*not this time*."

He allowed himself a small sigh of regret. "I'm sorry about your career at the pharmacy."

For a brief moment she dropped her eyes. Then she looked up past Jeremy's shoulder, her gaze now level and stoic. Her lips parted but words seemed to fail her. She simply nodded.

They all went out for lunch that day, and when they returned Jeremy left Ghensie and Bekim to settle into the warm flat while he struck out for his rendezvous with Cornel Iliescu. "Errands to run" would become his refrain, his cover for his work. The trees at Place de la République, having surrendered their leaves to winter, now resembled a skeletal escort flanking Marianne, the statue symbolizing the Republic. A frigid breeze snapped sporadically as he reached the métro station, and when he emerged at Place de la Bastille a white-grey sky released a riot of snowflakes, furiously assailing Jeremy's face.

For Iliescu's consumption he was wearing the rougher, down-scale attire of jeans and knit cap and had relinquished his tailored overcoat for his more louche-looking bomber jacket. He hurried through the blizzard with long lunging strides and entered La Presque Bastille appearing all the more urgent and harried. He waited until he spotted Iliescu before removing his cap, and only did so once he reached the Romanian's table, sighing and shaking off the snow as if he were indeed the most distressed and desperate of men on the run from a super-power. He stuffed the cap in his pocket and held out his hand. This time Iliescu responded promptly, though his tepid grip could hardly be taken for a sincere welcome.

Jeremy was invited to sit, and when the waiter arrived Jeremy glanced at Iliescu's cup and saucer, film from a finished espresso glossing the cup's interior, and ordered the same. Iliescu leaned in, flicking back strands of dark hair that again hung over his forehead like grass over a sand dune.

"Monsieur Winters," he began with a genial smile, rolling his r's in an accent that became more pronounced the longer he spoke, "I'll begin by saying that I am disposed to helping you...but naturally I have a question or two." He broke off to light a cigarette. He hadn't smoked during their first encounter, but that Iliescu now smoked Dunhills, a luxury British brand, didn't surprise Jeremy. Iliescu sat back, taking two short drags— quick, methodical puffs. He smoked, thought Jeremy, like he drank, in obsessive little increments.

Jeremy waited out the pause without changing expression.

Then Iliescu spoke. "First, let me say that I'm curious about a previous visit you made here. No doubt you wished to *sound the terrain*—the correct French expression, I believe?" He gave a vague, abstract smile and took two more quick drags of his Dunhill. "You see, Monsieur Winters," he said through a stuttering of smoke, "you were spotted here, you and a small blond boy. He had a stuffed bear." Iliescu stifled a mock laugh with his fist. "Excuse me, but the unfortunate-looking creature sat right on your table."

The waiter arrived with Jeremy's coffee but Jeremy stared straight through him in silence, the turbines in his mind cranking at high gear.

Chapter 17

The congenial noise of the café—clips of chatter, sporadic laughter, the chink of cups on saucers— faded in a heartbeat, extinguished by Jeremy's accelerating thoughts. *Why hadn't he waited until Louise was free to watch Bekim before coming here that first time? What would an extra idle day with the boy have mattered?* The two questions occupied about a second each in Jeremy's mind and then hindsight became a luxury he could no longer afford. Cornel Iliescu, trafficker in counterfeit passports and who knew what else, was studying him, brows arched, head slightly atilt, in what was either suspicion or mere curiosity. With no time to deliberate, Jeremy went with the truth. It had served him well so far and he hoped it wouldn't backfire.

"He's a friend's boy," he told Iliescu blandly. "I agreed to watch him that day and thought I'd just check to make sure this café was your spot."

"Ah." The Romanian smiled and nodded as though this were the most reasonable of banalities. "Only..."

Jeremy waited for the caveat. Iliescu took two more drags of his cigarette then stubbed it out with meticulous precision, a hank of hair falling back to dangle over thick dark eyebrows. The man could muster a sinister air, though to Jeremy he looked more shrewd than menacing, more cocky than dangerous.

"*Only,*" Iliescu repeated, "my sources say the boy comes and goes with you every day." He spread his hands, his smile amused. "You do understand that I have to learn about my clients before doing business with them."

Jeremy didn't comment. He had been followed, Iliescu knew where he lived and no doubt where he worked. He wasn't surprised. He had given his true name and it wouldn't take a genius to discover his haunts. What gave him cold pause was Iliescu's specific interest in Bekim. And now, of course, Jeremy could not fabricate being on the run, sheltered by some Italian communist or another.

Continue with the truth, or at least a half-truth, he told himself. "My girlfriend's son," he said of Bekim. *And say as little as possible.*

Iliescu went on in the same humoring tone. "Ah, a girl with no family here...?"

"That's right."

"Do you consider *her* family?"

A girlfriend, family? What was Iliescu probing for? Jeremy shrugged, kept his tone neutral. "Not at this point." He said nothing of Ghensie's sharing his flat yet imagined Iliescu and his crew would surely find out. In fact Jeremy would have to tell his concierge who, without offering objection, had also remarked on Bekim's presence in the building.

Iliescu took his time digesting Jeremy's answer. Suavely he smoothed back his hair. Apart from his overcoat, folded neatly in half over the back of his chair, he also wore a smart leather jacket, black and soft looking as a baby's skin—expensive, probably Italian. He folded his arms and gave Jeremy a matter-of-fact stare. "So you're willing to drop her and the kid if you have to get the hell out of France..."

Jeremy matched Iliescu's tone and stare. "I may have no choice if the U.S. government gets its way."

"Hmm." Iliescu nodded his understanding, though Jeremy detected a fleck of amused condescension in his gaze. "One more question—the Italian Reds you mentioned, the ones who've heard of me. What are their names?"

At last. Jeremy wondered why Iliescu hadn't asked this in the first place. "A guy called Mirko Mazzini mentioned you last year before he skipped the country."

"*Mirko Mazzini...*" Iliescu, his eyes narrowed and tentative, seemed to be tasting the name in his mind, rolling it around like wine on his palate. "Never heard of him," he finally pronounced.

"Well, he's gone now—fled to Marseille where he got hold of a passport, then flew to Cuba, Italian agents on his ass right up till his plane took off. You have to admire that," Jeremy added with a smirk.

"*Do you?*" It was more a challenge than a question, and Jeremy found himself shifting in his seat as Iliescu leaned in and glared at him. "*Really?* You think Cuba is a better place than France?"

Jeremy marveled at the touchiness of the Romanian trafficker. The former East Bloc denizen had known communism and its strangulation of *all* kinds of entrepreneurial endeavor. "No," Jeremy conceded, suppressing a smile. "Mazzini just needed a country that would never deport him. I personally wouldn't choose a communist country, and I certainly understand people wanting to leave one."

Iliescu's glare receded. He sat back and gave a dismissive grunt, as if recalling that politics ranked decidedly below a lucrative sale. "You have to go where you can survive," he allowed. "I don't really give a shit which country *you* have in mind." He pushed his empty cup away. "Five thousand francs for a French passport under a new name." He paused as Jeremy's brows came together. "Or you can pay in dollars—eight hundred."

Jeremy inhaled and rubbed the back of his neck as if trying to get his head around the massive figure. "No discount for being referred to you?" he half joked with a feeble smile.

Iliescu shook his head, not deigning to comment. "I'll give you four days to return here with a decision."

After evincing what he hoped looked like a modestly pained expression, Jeremy nodded. "I'll work on getting the money together and be back in two, if you don't mind."

"Come back in three—I still have some research to do, and bring a photo-booth picture of yourself."

Jeremy drew himself up with a determined sigh. "Whatever it takes for a ticket to freedom."

The métro train rocked on its rails shuttling Jeremy home, his thoughts oscillating along with it. Iliescu was on to Bekim and it wouldn't take long before he discovered Ghensie, for why else had the trafficker put him off another three days? Clearly to gather more personal information, perhaps also to ascertain if Jeremy could afford the passport. Would he nose around Le Prince Blue Note where Jeremy bartended, if he hadn't already? Would he look into the story of Mirko? No problem with the former, and the latter, the account of Mirko's escape, was one hundred percent true. Of course Mirko had never cited Iliescu, but how was the Romanian to verify that with Mirko living in celebrated exile in Havana? The train jerked around a corner and Jeremy's thoughts swung back to Bekim. Naturally he shouldn't have brought the boy to the café, but little did it matter since Iliescu would have discovered him anyway.

Tailings and *stakeouts*: criminals indulged in the practice as much as cops did, which brought him back to Ghensie. Luan and the Kosovars knew she had been employed at the pharmacy, and they might also be aware of her Romanian neighbor Sorina. That Sorina or the pharmacy could receive a visit from a couple of enquiring thugs with Albanian accents made Jeremy's grip tighten on the support bar.

He had given Ghensie a spare key, and when he got home he found she'd been to the market and started dinner. "I'm making Belgian stew for us," she announced as he peered into the kitchen. "I hope you don't mind?"

No, he didn't. His cooking talents were embarrassing. "If you can't find something, ask me!"

Outside, snow was still falling, damp and dissolving now, and the warmth of the flat enveloped Jeremy like eiderdown. Bekim was watching television, while the fragrance of beef gravy infused with ale drew Jeremy back to the kitchen, almost allaying the concerns that had chilled him on the métro. Ghensie stood stirring a simmering pot. Had the story he'd invented for Iliescu been true he would have slipped his arms around her and caressed the curves of her narrow waist.

Instead, he pulled out a chair and asked her to sit for a moment. "I'm very glad you're here, things are going to be perfectly fine with the three of us in the flat." Then, with focused calm: "But I need to ask about the friends and colleagues you left back in Brussels. You said you told no one where you were going, but could you have mentioned my name?"

Ghensie frowned in concern. "No, you were only in Brussels a short time."

"Nothing to the people in the pharmacy..." To which Ghensie shook her head. "Or your neighbor Sorina..."

And here Ghensie paused. "I've thought about

these very same things. Believe me, they worry me too. I did mention to Sorina that I had a friend from Paris. That was back before you were attacked in the park. But I never said your name."

As Jeremy continued to observe her, Ghensie caught the drift. "You're thinking Luan and the Kosovars might try to force information Sorina doesn't have. But they would have to contend with her husband too. I don't think they would risk harming them, considering Sorina and her husband are legal residents and would surely go to the police."

Still Ghensie looked distraught. She blinked and bit her lip, seeming to fight her fear—right when she had just arrived in Paris and was trying to settle in and make a nice meal for Jeremy.

"We should be all right," he said, patting her hand. "They don't know my name and Paris is an enormous city." He stood up. "So let's open a bottle of wine and get it breathing before dinner...you don't mind alcohol, do you? I mean there's beer in the stew..."

"As Muslims we're not that strict in Albania, at least not in my family." Entertaining a second thought, Ghensie gave way to the balm of laugher. "I couldn't begin to count Luan's binges!"

As Ghensie returned to the stove Jeremy retrieved a special bottle of Châteauneuf-du-Pape to christen Ghensie's arrival. It might not make the best marriage with Belgian stew, but Jeremy wanted to celebrate. When he sidled past Ghensie she gripped his arm and laid her head on his shoulder. Only for an instant, but this time she didn't thank him again, and he appreciated her not linking the gesture to gratitude— that perhaps she sought physical contact with him in and of itself.

Outside, it had stopped snowing. The white of sky and snowflakes was giving way to the bleed of dusk. For a moment Jeremy basked in the warm glow of the transition, then pulled the curtains shut.

Over the next couple of days the little threesome developed a routine. During morning hours Ghensie went looking for work while Jeremy watched Bekim. She told Jeremy she would accept any kind of employment, menial as it may be, and although Jeremy knew labor laws were strict he said nothing to dent her spirits. He, after all, had been responsible for encouraging her to come to Paris. It was the right thing to do, the only solution at the time, and, he admitted, the desirable one. He recalled her soft hand on his arm, her cheek on his shoulder, and it still seemed right.

Both Monday and Tuesday morning Ghensie went out with a list of shops and restaurants Jeremy had helped her compile, and each afternoon she returned still unemployed. Her hope held undiminished, she had only been at it for two days, yet Jeremy couldn't help judging the quest all but futile since she had no work permit. He tried asking at Le Prince, but Pierre, the club's manager, just shook his head sympathetically. "I can't consider her for any kind of job without proper papers." And French work permits, he went on to explain, were granted first and foremost to foreigners who were nationals of the European Economic Union. When Jeremy cited her job in Brussels, Pierre just shrugged as if to say *who can figure out the Belgians?* When Jeremy brought up her East Bloc refugee status, Pierre could only advise presenting her case to the Préfecture de Police. "They're the ones who sort out work permits and can advise on refugee status."

Jeremy conveyed this to Ghensie who took a half step back, and before she replied he understood her fear. "I can't get involved with the police." Jeremy wondered if she would ever feel comfortable interacting with any of the authorities. Her position vis-à-vis the stolen coin and her immigration status left her about as free as a prison inmate. And so Jeremy considered appealing to one of his Italian communist acquaintances. Although the Red refugees were prohibited from working he knew some obtained under-the-table jobs. He could always inquire.

The thought came to him during his Tuesday afternoon meeting with Cornel Iliescu, for Iliescu had indeed verified Jeremy's story about Mirko Mazzini, the Red who had escaped to Cuba.

"*Mirko le miraculeux*," Iliescu said cynically, as he and Jeremy sat face to face once more. "What a coup—I hope he enjoys living in a police state!"

Jeremy didn't comment, other than to ask if Iliescu had finished checking him out.

"For the moment." Iliescu sat back and sniffed twice. "Seems your girlfriend is back. Quite the happy little family when the three of you go out."

Jeremy was hardly shocked. Though he hadn't spotted Iliescu per se shadowing him, he had noted the repeated appearance of a redhaired man who wore a loden coat, even indoors.

"Things are fine for now," Jeremy answered, in reference to his little household, "but my girlfriend knows I'm a dead-end prospect and she's looking for a job so she and her son can move out."

Iliescu seemed to genuinely chuckle at that. "And so you are! One of your Red pals agrees, though he didn't know you were now a wanted man."

"I'm not talking to anyone these days," Jeremy said, wondering whom exactly Iliescu had unearthed among the Red companions. "The fewer who know the better."

"Mm," Iliescu appeared to agree, giving the air another couple of speculative sniffs. "So I'll sell you the passport, and here's a good reason: "Your girlfriend has been heard speaking an Eastern European language to her son, so I reckon they're immigrants just like you. What are they, Bosnian?"

"Albanian."

"Albanian, of course," said Iliescu, as if recalling something. "Anyway, once you slink off to Spain, or wherever you plan on going, they'll go their separate way and keep their profiles low. *No police*. I'm sure you've heard that tune before." Iliescu's smile was smug.

Jeremy left a passport-fit photo of himself with Iliescu, and they made another appointment to meet the following Tuesday in order to exchange money for goods, this time in a different café. As Jeremy left he noted Iliescu's face buried again in his notebook, his hair flopping back over his brow. Now that the strands were in his eyes he didn't bother to sweep them away. The *mec* was decidedly bizarre, full of tics and slick vanity—and, to be sure, animal street-smarts. Jeremy would keep these qualities slotted, for part two of his plan had yet to begin. And to get it started, he crossed to a café across the street and, making sure no one had followed him, took a window table and waited. Waited for Iliescu to leave La Presque Bastille, and then tailed him home.

Chapter 18

A happy little family," was how Cornel Iliescu had referred to Jeremy, Ghensie, and Bekim. In truth he wasn't terribly far off. Though the specter of Luan and his thugs still hung over them like a not-so-distant disease, and Ghensie hadn't found work, they enjoyed their afternoons together. Ghensie seemed always to have money for food shopping and Bekim's behavior had ceased its frenetic yo-yoing. No more defiant *nooo*'s since his mother's arrival, in fact he even let Ghensie take some soap and water to Grizzly. So far the boy had yet to repeat his question about Jeremy being *papà*, and Jeremy enjoyed the company and all round warm tranquility of the household.

But naturally Ghensie needed to work, so one afternoon, while Jeremy was out on his own, he stopped at a phone booth and called the Italian political refugee Pietro Grimaldi, who enjoyed protection by the French state but who was also not allowed to work. Jeremy knew several Italian Reds in this position, sheltered under the socialist Mitterrand Doctrine, though enjoying little else in terms of support from the French state. Pietro, for example, had a pittance to live on and was instructed to keep his nose clean. In short: *step out of line and you'll be on a plane back to Italy where there's a prison cell reserved for you*; and *not* toeing the line included trying to get a job. Yet those with a will found a way, Jeremy knew. He didn't ask Pietro who did or didn't hold jobs, nor, of course, did he ask if Iliescu's network might have contacted Pietro. Instead he appealed to a sense of refugee solidarity— daring perhaps, since the two had clashed over that very issue the previous summer. And though they would never become friends, a basic understanding had formed between them. From Pietro, in fact, Jeremy had learned of Mirko Mazzini's escape to Cuba. Mirko and Pietro had been not only *Compagni* in arms but companions in love as well, and Jeremy had acquired empathy in this respect too. He trusted Mirko was well in Cuba, expressing as much on the phone.

"He's okay. I only hear from him in code, so not very often."

Jeremy acknowledged the risky logistics of covert communication, then started to state his own case. "I know that none of the *Compagni* are officially working," he said, "but..."

Pietro grunted. "Well, *you're* not like us, so what's up?"

Jeremy tolerated the bluntness as patiently as he did Pietro's perpetual cynicism, a product of their history from the previous summer. "I've got this friend," he began, "a refugee with no work permit...she's willing to do any kind of work she can find, and I thought—"

"Ah," Pietro interjected, and Jeremy knew his revelation of a female friend had piqued Pietro's curiosity. Last summer Jeremy had also defended a young woman, who along with Pietro's companion Mirko had been at the center of the explosive debacle that sent Mirko fleeing to Cuba.

But if that memory disturbed him, Pietro didn't let on. Instead he said flatly, "She must be foreign and not from the European Community."

"Right on both accounts."

"And she's in some kind of trouble."

"True again." Jeremy was loathe to explain more.

On the surface the situation might resemble last summer's entanglement with Stefania, Pietro's fellow Red refugee. But there the similarity ended.

"And you want to *rescue* her," Pietro went on.

Once more Jeremy ignored the sarcasm. "She's Albanian and she's got a five-year-old son to support. She needs work."

A weary sigh followed. "All right," said Pietro, "I'll look into it and get back to you. Same number?"

"Yes...but she might answer the phone if I'm not there, so in that case I'll call you back."

"Right..."

Jeremy expected Pietro's *au revoir* at this point, but instead a pause persisted.

"Jeremy?" Pietro finally said, this time without sarcasm. "Be careful."

Though Ghensie was nothing like Stefania, Jeremy couldn't help appreciating Pietro's concern. The women looked nothing alike, Stefania a petite redhead, confidently seductive, and in the end, maddeningly manipulative. Instinct told him the latter was not in Ghensie's nature, even though bouts of doubt sometimes harried him like a pebble in his shoe. And if she possessed the missing coin after all? He didn't think so and hoped the unease he felt might eventually mutate from the proverbial pebble into something like a grain of sand in an oyster's shell. His analogy surprised him: since oysters produced pearls, what kind of precious commodity did he expect to blossom from this entanglement?

The thought stuck with him when he entered his flat and was bulldozed by Bekim, the boy's new way of greeting him that led to an interlude of sporty roughhousing. Jeremy enjoyed the games, continued to enjoy the home cooking, enjoyed observing mother and son together, though mostly he was engaged in watching Ghensie—still feeling that pebble in his shoe, wondering what else might lie in the shadow of her history. And waiting—waiting for a further sign that she would like this little household to function at its physical fullest.

As they sat on the sofa, a film on TV, he was tempted to report his contact with Pietro but thought it better to wait in case the endeavor to find Ghensie work fell through. Bekim, on his knees drawing at the coffee table, suddenly turned and launched himself onto the sofa, bouncing into Jeremy's lap with a whoop. Ghensie gave a startled laugh, then ordered him to calm down. "You're going to hurt Jeremy," she said. Jeremy dismissed the warning with a wave and Ghensie, with a helpless smile, said, "I'm afraid he just likes you too much."

As Bekim bounded off the sofa and back to his crayons, Jeremy wished Ghensie would say the same regarding herself—*I just like you too much!* Yet might she then expect to live with him on a permanent basis? He had asked himself the inconvenient question before and like then he now shrugged it off. For the time being this cozy little ménage suited him. Luan and the Kosovars were on the loose, danger remained to be dodged, and what better way to protect them all than by keeping them under one roof? It was the only conclusion that made any sense.

That, plus phase two of his plan targeting Cornel Iliescu. With that in mind he checked his watch and slipped into the entryway to make a quiet call to Rébert, who at four o'clock should still be in his office.

"Five thousand francs is doable," said the RG boss. "Seems not too high or too low. And Iliescu hasn't acted overly suspicious?"

"I've been tailed, but that's understandable."

Rébert acknowledged as much. "So we'll need a secure spot to get you the five thousand." As Jeremy was pondering this, Rébert provided the solution. "I'll send a man to Le Prince while you're on shift. He'll leave the money in the club's restroom." After they worked out the details Rébert added, "Next we'll have to get you closer to Iliescu's organization."

"I've already come up with something."

Rébert weighed what he heard and agreed. "It's worth a try. Just don't get caught." This parting cliché meant nothing and everything. Naturally it was Jeremy's responsibility not to get caught. But if he did, he would be left teetering like a tightrope walker with no net.

Thursday evening a man in an overcoat and gloves entered Le Prince. Non-descript, apart from a bushy head of muddy-brown hair, he ordered a Negroni without ice, then asked for the restrooms. Upon his exit he swept out of the club, leaving the cocktail Jeremy had prepared untouched on the bar. Jeremy looked at his young co-barman Laurent, spreading his hands in quizzical disgust.

"*Connard*," Laurent swore after the man. "Should I go after him?"

Jeremy shrugged. "I'll have a look outside." He crossed to the entrance, opened the door, and glanced up and down the sidewalk of boulevard Saint-Michel. Turning back to Laurent, he shook his head sourly. *What people will do to get away with a free piss.* Before returning behind the bar he took a detour to the men's room and unearthed a fat envelope from the bottom of the trash. Tucking it inside his shirt beneath his apron he rejoined Laurent. "At least he didn't vomit in there," he said, and Laurent gave a nod of relief.

Tuesday of the next week Jeremy prepared for his meeting with Iliescu. Leaving Ghensie home this afternoon felt particularly uncomfortable, for her spirits were low and he sensed she would have liked to accompany him on his afternoon "errand." She still hadn't found a job, despite the well-known existence of employers who turned a blind eye to the pesky protocol of work permits. The Italian refugee, Pietro Grimaldi, had yet to call back, and Jeremy wondered if he would. Today, though, he had to concentrate on his meeting. Success in part one of his plan *must* lead to an opening to part two.

Before leaving the house he pinpointed the location of Iliescu's new café in his *Paris par Arrondissement* guide. The new café lay in the Romanian's home *quartier*. Jeremy had followed him to his neighborhood in the southern corner of the Thirteenth arrondissement, only to be surprised at how close Iliescu lived to Louise Cholot. The café was even closer to Madame's building, he soon discovered, and as he walked past that building he lowered his head and lengthened his stride.

The café was a cave compared to La Presque Bastille, four tables to the right of the bar, filing two in a row towards the back wall. At a table in the last row sat Iliescu, his hawkish gaze nailing the entrance. He nodded to Jeremy then nodded to the barman, who stepped out of the room into a service area in the back, leaving merchant and client alone under a low, domed brick ceiling that rendered the room shadowy in the rustic style of a wine cellar. With no one else occupying the café, Jeremy was alone in his observations, wondering who would serve customers who might stroll in. As it was, not even he was served, and as he sat, Iliescu wasted no time in pulling an envelope from his jacket and holding it suspended in front of him.

Flashing a smile, he flapped the air with it twice, its

contents rattling with promise. "Your ticket to freedom."

The smile seemed almost guileless, probably the most honest Jeremy could expect from Iliescu, and that was encouraging. He slid his own envelope out, the inside layered with cash like a *mille feuille*. The two white envelopes crossed the table and both Jeremy and Iliescu verified their contents. Leafing through the passport, Jeremy found the page with his sober photo and unremarkable new name: Martin Jacques Duroc. He was no expert in judging the quality of the facsimile but that hardly mattered. His role was to act satisfied, and he expressed as much to Iliescu once the Romanian finished counting his francs.

"Drinks," Iliescu shouted, once envelopes had been stowed, and the barman, brawny and impassive, reappeared with casual indifference. "Something for my friend," Iliescu told him, indicating Jeremy. "The drink is on me, though I'm sorry I can't stay to join you."

He moved to leave, his chair scraping the floor, but Jeremy stayed him with an outstretched palm. "I've got something else to put to you."

Iliescu shot him a sharp look. Jeremy nodded for him to sit. It took a couple of seconds bolstered by Jeremy's persistent stare for Iliescu to comply. And when reluctantly he did, Jeremy leveled his gaze and said, "I'd like a job in your organization."

Slowly Iliescu sat back, and for the first time Jeremy observed a sort of baffled wonder on the Romanian's face.

"I'm almost broke," Jeremy confessed, once Iliescu agreed to order a drink for himself. "As much as I'm grateful, the five thousand has set me back. If the order comes down from the French government to pick me up, I'll have to cut and run—might not even get to the bank."

"And your accounts would be frozen before you got there." Iliescu had recovered his nonchalance and was observing Jeremy in sidelong curiosity. "So you think it's imminent, them picking you up..."

"I've no choice but to plan on it. And when it happens I'll have to leave my job, my flat...everyone." He paused, staring at Iliescu with stark determination.

"But then you would leave *my* employment as well," Iliescu pointed out. "*If* I decided there's a spot for you."

"I would let you know, but yes, that's the way it would have to be. I'm not looking for a career," Jeremy added, frowning earnestly, "but if I can lend a hand, maybe in your tailing operations..."

Jeremy received a crooked grin, so he leaned in with a wry smile of his own. "I could do the job better than one of the last guys you had following me. A *mec* with lots of red hair and a loden coat he never takes off." Iliescu demurred and Jeremy pushed on. "I tailed *you* home after one of our meetings...rue du Docteur Tuffier, I believe?"

A flush, rosé in tint, lit Iliescu's face while a red menace filled his eyes, and in the tense pause that followed, Jeremy almost wished he'd checked his boldness. But Iliescu surprised him. His expression righted itself and he broke into a mighty laugh, hank of slick hair flapping on his forehead. He smoothed it back and called for a second round of drinks. "I like you, Winters, you've got balls. And I can always use extra muscle, temporary as it may be."

Extra muscle?

Iliescu soon clarified. "Tailing work would be wasted on a man like you. What I need is someone to apply a little pressure now and then on wayward individuals. The Italians say you're tough. And you did have that experience in prison thanks to your boxing skills." Iliescu threw a couple of mock punches, and Jeremy lowered his eyes. "Now, now," Iliescu joked, shaking his finger. "No need for modesty. I appreciate all kinds of talent! Come to La Presque Bastille Friday, same time. I've already got something in mind, something right up your alley."

Chapter 19

Jeremy walked the four blocks to the Tolbiac métro station, buffeted by a cold, stubborn February wind, while his thoughts rocked from his initial success with Iliescu to the Romanian's knack for turning the tables on him. Would he have to act as enforcer for the Romanian? It shouldn't surprise him, not after having spilled his pugilistic history during their first meeting. Playing up his rage and playing down his regret regarding the fight with his cousin had unwittingly led to the accomplishment of that second goal: counterfeit passport in his pocket, Jeremy now had a foot in the door to Iliescu's underworld, albeit one that caused him some worry.

On the métro train he examined the passport. "Martin Jacques Duroc," entrepreneur, was born in Lyon and now lived in Switzerland. Border stamps attested to his having crisscrossed Europe and Britain. Before sliding the booklet back into his pocket he gave the photo a longer look: *So, Martin, are we up to acting the thug?* This would be a new role, potentially messier than any of his RG assignments. He had never been asked to commit violence. The majority of his intelligence work entailed shadowing individuals, with an occasional assignment to infiltrate petty criminal activity. Last summer he oiled his way into the company of a couple of vandals bent on disrupting the Bicentennial; right before that he was tasked with unearthing fake passports among the Italian *Compagni*, counterfeit documents a perennial vexation to the authorities. No one had asked him to hurt anyone, and the closest he'd come to exercising his fists on the job had been to convince a haughty antique-shop owner to stop blackmailing the wife of an assistant in the government. Even then Jeremy hadn't started the fight, but merely defended himself with a blow to the belly of the smug Monsieur Blanc, following up with a couple of casual threats and a menacing squint from his red-rimmed left eye.

He had to admit that his red eye—damaged by his cousin in their fight five years ago—came in handy at times. Until his surgery last November the eye also watered uncontrollably, which occasionally added a surprise advantage of its own, but mostly amounted to a *sacré* pain in the ass. The perpetual tearing had now ceased, yet enough red remained to make him look menacing if he desired. He'd caught Iliescu examining it on the sly and now wondered if the Romanian had seen potential there as well: a withering squint backed by a set of jack-hammer fists.

And yet he could speculate all day about Iliescu's intentions only to learn on Friday that his assignment was to discover if a certain person of interest owned a Pit Bull. As for Jeremy's eye, everyone took a second look when they met him—Ghensie and Bekim included. The attention could be uncomfortable, though he never took offense and usually offered "an accident" as explanation. Normally that ended the interest, except in Bekim's case who had asked, "Did it get poked?" Which led Jeremy to fib about a pencil and a rubber band.

Seriously, he needed to rope in his thoughts. It wasn't as if Iliescu would ask him to murder someone, at least not until taking careful time to probe Jeremy's character at length—and by then, Jeremy emphasized to himself, this business would be wrapped up.

He was nearing home, the métro pulling into the République station, and soon he would be met by a flying tackle from Bekim while inhaling the aroma of some herby dish conjured up by Ghensie. The image mellowed him, smoothed rough edges of resentfulness, of defensiveness, impulses he had carried from his youth and that in turn served him well in dealing with men who deserved a comeuppance.

As he walked to his building in the direction of the sinking sun, thoughts of an already warm flat, a warm dinner and even warmer company repulsed the wind's icy gusts, and when he opened the door to his flat he braced himself good-naturedly for a blitz from Bekim. Instead he found the boy curled on the sofa watching television. He cast Jeremy a brief glance, then turned back to his cartoons. Ghensie came from the kitchen, spicy scents wafting in her wake, plus a look of doubt. It was warm in the flat, just as he'd eagerly anticipated, but the warmth felt spiked with friction. Something was wrong, and as Ghensie lowered her eyes before explaining, he steeled himself for the worst, the thing that hung precariously at bay, like the threat of fire in the tinder-dry forests he remembered as a boy during California's hot summers: *Luan and*—

"Bekim has something to tell you," she said, breaking Jeremy's grim reverie. She shot the boy a reproving frown. "Go on," she prompted him, "sit up straight."

The boy obeyed and Jeremy shifted an uncomfortable gaze from him back to his mother. Bekim gave a sheepish frown. "I'm sorry I opened your case," he said.

Jeremy stared back dumbly, then gave Ghensie the same clueless look.

"He means the music case under your bed," she explained. "He shouldn't have been poking around in your private things—"

Jeremy barely heard the rest of the extended apology, so relieved was he that nothing traumatic had befallen the household. "It's all right," he said to Bekim, who had now stiffened in suspense. "I'm not upset." He said the words in French and then in Italian to reassure the boy, his thoughts then moving to the mutilated corpse of the saxophone under his bed.

"It was a saxophone," he clarified, the instrument in question now scarcely recognizable. "And somebody broke it." He searched for terms the boy could relate to. "A person who wasn't very nice. But that was a long time ago and everything's fine now."

All the while Ghensie listened, head atilt. With a small intake of breath she parted her lips to ask something, then closed them, leaving Jeremy a quizzical stare. Jeremy glanced at Bekim then back, as if to hint *I'll tell you more later*.

That evening, Jeremy wrestled with just how and what to tell her. As they sat on the sofa, well after Bekim had gone to bed, he fiddled with the television remote, zapping back and forth between channels, hoping to find a program that would absorb their attention so he could delay, or perhaps avoid completely, the subject of the saxophone—the desecration, the mutilation, the murder of an object that had once leapt magically to life under the fingers of his father, an object that Jeremy had held in nostalgic reverence regarding the past while assigning it promise for the future, despite its role in the disaster involving his cousin. But someone with a grudge had destroyed it last summer.

Jeremy would not be going into those details and was still hoping he could ignore the whole messy matter. He didn't trust himself to master his feelings. He didn't want Ghensie to pity him. And it looked as though he might just succeed in dodging or at least delaying the situation, for he had found something on TV that made Ghensie still his hand on the remote.

"A Maigret movie with Jean Richard," she said with enthusiasm. "I used to watch these films dubbed in Italian when I was in Albania. Now I can watch it in the original French."

"I'm glad," said Jeremy, settling back against the sofa cushions, letting his legs sprawl in contentment.

"I love the psychology in the Maigret stories. He's a police detective who doesn't just want to catch a murderer, he wants to *understand* the criminal's mind."

Jeremy agreed. He too liked Maigret.

"Which makes me wonder," Ghensie went on, "who would be insane enough to wreck a musical instrument so thoroughly...'a bad person,' you told Bekim."

Jeremy sighed to himself in resignation. "Shall we wait until after the movie?" he asked hopefully.

"I don't mind hearing now." She nodded at the television. "I already know the movie's plot."

All right then, he would skip the lengthy and difficult parts and tell her more or less what Bekim already knew. A vandal had invaded his flat, sparing nothing, and the police had never caught him.

"They couldn't find *anything* out?" she wondered aloud.

Jeremy shook his head—certainly a lie of omission—and trusted that would be the end of it.

Ghensie didn't pry into his feelings, though she asked, "Did you play it much, the saxophone? I mean, could you have bought another one to replace it...?"

"No..." Jeremy's tone was open-ended, since he was responding to two different questions. He still kept an eye on Maigret, hoping Ghensie would think that *he* didn't want to miss the plot.

"You never played it?" she insisted.

"No."

"But you've kept the broken pieces..." Ghensie looked so confused, a look Jeremy had become fond of, how her lips pursed in a partial pout that he always felt like kissing.

He finally faced her and yielded a slight confession. "The pieces are still there out of sentimentality—it was my father's."

"Oh..."

"He died when I was fourteen," he continued, since she clearly expected more.

She shifted sideways on the sofa to better engage him. "So you've sort of kept the remains..."

The *remains*—how perceptive. "I guess so," he said casually, turning back to Maigret.

"You must have felt horrible to see it that way..."

The question made sense, what with the saxophone's bell caved in, each of its mother-of-pearl keys shattered, and its mouthpiece crushed. At the time he had passionately wanted to make the vandal pay. Instead he told Ghensie, "It was hard at first, but I've gotten over it—just haven't brought myself to throw the thing away."

Ghensie squeezed his arm. "I understand."

He went still as a deer in the woods. Ghensie's touch felt hot, even through his shirtsleeve.

"You've suffered a double loss..." she said, her hand still resting on his arm, her eyes radiating sympathy and compassion, plus a hint of the same spark he felt in her touch.

He couldn't keep sitting in a slouch. Risking the loss of her hand on his arm, he straightened himself and assured her the trauma was well behind him. "Always better to look towards the future and new possibilities."

"To new friends, for example," said Ghensie, her

hand sliding to his.

"*To new friends*," he echoed slowly, gripping her hand. Only a sliver of space separated them on the sofa and their gazes melded as much in wonder as in anticipation. Ghensie drew a deep breath, closing her eyes then opening them as if inhaling something heady in the air between them. Jeremy pulled her against him. He felt her breath catch, then her hands found his waist and encircled it. His mouth found her lips and pressed. Her lips parted and he accepted the invitation.

When he slid his hand under her sweater, she gave another shudder, this one stiff. "Are you all right?" he asked.

She inhaled heavily, exhaling a whispered "Yes." Then she glanced at the hall towards a sleeping Bekim.

"If you're afraid he might wake up..." said Jeremy, still stroking her smooth warm back.

With a soft laugh she said, "He sleeps like a bear in winter, it's just that I'm always checking."

Jeremy murmured his understanding, then moved his lips to the silkiness of her neck. His embrace took them down on the sofa, where their hands began to wander, testing, feeling out flesh as well as boundaries. There seemed to be none of the latter and soon even the barrier of their clothing began to drop away, piece by piece in tune with the urgency of their bodies. Jeremy reached up and turned off the lamp, and if a neglected concern remained, the darkness swallowed it.

The next morning he rose well before Ghensie and Bekim, already used to getting up earlier so as not to have Ghensie tiptoeing around the kitchen in fear of waking him. Sleeping on the sofa left him with the odd ache and tightness in his back, but this morning he stretched like a pampered cat, savoring thoughts of the night before. He slipped on his robe and trod lightly to peer through the crack in the bedroom door. Up until last night Ghensie had kept it closed while she and Bekim slept in his bed; now the open door signaled to Jeremy that a barrier really had been broken. He nudged the door a fraction more and caught Ghensie's blinking eyes. She smiled lazily at him. Things were just fine.

Over coffee, before Bekim got up, they acknowledged the delicacy of the situation, Jeremy giving a nod to the awkwardness regarding the boy. Then Ghensie surprised him with a practical viewpoint. "We are adults, Bekim is a child. I would prefer him not to discover us romantically entwined, so we should be careful."

Jeremy agreed, though he continued to ask himself how she and the Italian Vairo had lived their six months together. Did they occupy separate bedrooms, all the while Bekim calling Vairo *papà*? Jeremy doubted it. Ghensie had once professed love for Vairo, though whether she still loved the Italian, Jeremy now judged conveniently irrelevant. And then there was the lovemaking. He had found Ghensie experienced. And why not—he had to be her third lover, at least, which again made him wonder about her Muslim background. (He had once exchanged kisses and heavy petting with a Muslim girl, Paris born, but who nevertheless expressed shame and quit seeing him.) Yet Ghensie was an Albanian Muslim—of a different ilk, in her own words. It had taken a while, but she'd finally come round. Maybe she hadn't been ready yet, maybe Ruggero Vairo was truly starting to fade from the fresco of her life. Jeremy should be grateful— grateful for no regrets or indecision on her part, few complications in other words. And on the whole he was. Yes, mystery continued to swirl around Ghensie, but for now Jeremy was content to let it waft in and out of his sphere like an ocean breeze, one that swelled sails but didn't much rock boats.

Chapter 20

As it went, things notched up for the better. The next day Pietro, the Italian Red refugee, called with a tip about under-the-table employment.

"You said she's Albanian, so I found a guy who hires Eastern Europeans, no questions asked. She'd be working at home...at your place I guess, attaching the backs of pocket watches—old fashioned retro things, I guess."

"Well, whatever it amounts to I appreciate the favor. Would she have to pick the watches up and then drop them back off?"

"Not sure how it works but I've got the location, so she'll be able to find out for herself." He stated the address of a *quincaillerie,* a hardware store, and when Jeremy finished writing it he thanked Pietro again. The work seemed odd—it probably didn't pay much—and he wondered who this curious employer was.

When he told Ghensie, she looked surprised as well. "I've never done anything like that," she said, shaking her head in wonder. "But it sounds pretty easy..."

The next morning they agreed that Jeremy would watch Bekim while Ghensie took the métro to the rue Pernety in the Fourteenth arrondissement. There she would enter the designated store, stating an Italian *Compagno* had recommended her for a job. According to Pietro they would understand the reference.

The setup sounded nebulous, on the shady side at the least, and when Ghensie said, "I'll be back as soon as I can," her eyes darting to Bekim, Jeremy could detect a tinge of apprehension in her voice.

"I can come with you," he offered, "make sure everything's on the up and up, that they won't take advantage of you...I'll just have to check if my friend Louise can watch Bekim."

Ghensie returned a grateful smile and took his arm warmly. "As much as I'd appreciate that, I think it might alarm whoever it is who might hire me—you know, if a Frenchman accompanies me. I know," she preempted Jeremy, "you're not French but you sound like a native and it might spook them. I think I'm going to have to navigate this on my own."

If he hadn't been entrusted with Bekim, Jeremy would have followed her to this strange place of employment—or whatever it was, considering its employees took watches home with them—and positioned himself outside to keep watch. As it was he would have to leave her on her own. Not that she wasn't used to managing by herself; still, people took the protective presence of the authorities for granted, a knowledge that lay dozing somewhere below the conscious state of most good citizens. Not so for the precarious migrant. He hoped Ghensie would indeed return soon. Not only for his peace of mind, but in order to get to his rendezvous with Iliescu on time. It would not do to arrive late.

"When is *Maman* coming back?" Bekim's question, asked only about fifteen minutes after Ghensie had gone out, took Jeremy by surprise. Lately the boy paid little attention to his mother's comings and goings. He must have scented something amiss in the air, in spite of Ghensie and Jeremy's speaking in hushed tones out of earshot.

"*Maman* will be out for a bit like she always is in the morning," Jeremy told him.

Bekim shot him a nervous frown. "Is *Mami* scared?"

Mami, Maman, Mamma, the boy juggled Albanian, French, and Italian with curious facility, though Jeremy had figured out a thing or two: Bekim always addressed his mother directly as *Mami* (the Albanian), while when talking to Jeremy he referred to her as *Maman* and *Mamma,* depending on which language they were speaking. And yet when fear or doubt dug into him, he shrank back to his elemental Albanian.

"*Mami's* not scared," Jeremy stressed in Italian, maintaining the intimate Albanian term.

Bekim's mouth tensed as he padded over to sit on the sofa, pulling Grizzly onto his lap. He squeezed and pulled at the bear until Jeremy thought its fur would come out in clumps.

"Listen," he stressed softly but firmly, "*Mami* will be back soon and she'll probably bring us some goodies from the market. Doesn't that sound nice?" Who knew if Ghensie even planned to stop at the market, though its mention was worth an attempt to distract the boy.

And after a lengthy pause, in which Bekim gazed at the window in what seemed almost adult speculation, the boy gave a tentative nod.

Strange child, thought Jeremy. What the boy needed was some solid fun. "How about going down to the rides at Saint-Paul?" he suggested.

A shorter pause and a firmer nod.

"Well, let's go then." Jeremy watched Bekim slide off the sofa and head for his coat.

"Don't forget Grizzly," he added.

"No, he'll stay here this time."

Jeremy's eyebrows rose. "You're sure about that?"

Bekim repeated two firm nods. "Grizzly can wait for *Maman.*"

Back to using *Maman*—a sign that confidence and security had been restored. And so they left the flat, Grizzly sitting on the sofa, holding down the fort, and Jeremy shaking his head in wonder.

The rides, located on the vast sidewalk next to the entrance of the Saint-Paul métro station, consisted of a little carousel with a rotating car, plane, boat, and spaceship (at least it looked like one to Jeremy); it had bestowed joy on the children of the Fourth arrondissement for as long as Jeremy could remember, the kind of carefree joy that adults rarely experienced. As he watched Bekim go round and round, his yellow airplane atilt and set higher than the other little vehicles, a sad note played in his mind. The boy, at only five years old, probably hadn't enjoyed many truly carefree moments in his short life. As Bekim circled to the tune of "Ciribiribin," looking like a little aviator in his stocking cap, Jeremy waved at him and hoped that this half an hour or so could be one of them.

They returned to an empty flat, where immediately Bekim snatched up Grizzly and marched from room to room, looking for his mother.

"*Maman* will be home soon," Jeremy emphasized. The phrase and its various iterations were making Jeremy feel like a trained parrot, and he wondered whether Bekim was becoming inured to *Maman va arriver*, if a five-year-old's psyche even functioned that way. At least, so far, the promise had not been broken.

Ghensie really should arrive within the next half hour, or so, Jeremy told himself. He wanted to leave for La Presque Bastille by two-thirty, which gave him another hour and a half. Bekim had picked up his Albanian zoo book, his brow creased in concentration as he sounded out words, his index finger underlining each one.

Jeremy found the alien sounds irritating without an interlocutor, so he asked, "Would you like me to read Robertino to you?"

Bekim halted for an instant, then shook his head without looking up. "Grizzly wants to hear *this* book." And on he read, at times stuttering and stumbling his way over some part (Jeremy could at least make that much out), but mostly seeming to enunciate quite clearly. Jeremy wondered whether he could have memorized the book, which was as smudged and tattered as his bear. At any rate, he figured the boy wanted to be left alone with the language that evoked his mother.

Fortunately, within the half hour, *Maman* did return. The doorbell on the landing rang, which made Jeremy start, for no one usually entered the building without either having a key or being buzzed in, and Ghensie had keys. So when he opened the door he gave another start at seeing her there, until he focused on her baggage, the two boxes she was carrying. "I followed someone in downstairs—I didn't want to drop these."

Bekim barely let her set the boxes down before hurling himself at her.

"Did you thank Jeremy?" Ghensie asked him, after hearing about the rides at Saint-Paul.

Once the boy had done so, red-faced and with a tremor in his voice, Jeremy stressed, "Don't worry, we'll do it again."

The boy didn't know where he stood half the time, floundering in the shifting sands of forced pere-grination that had become his and Ghensie's life for at least a year. On the bright side, Jeremy concluded as he rode his métro train to the Bastille, Ghensie seemed content with the little job given her by the French couple running the hardware store. Whatever the legitimacy of this pocket-watch assembling sideline, she had assured Jeremy of the couples' good intentions. "They were particularly approving when I mentioned the exiled Italian *Compagni*."

Now, he told himself as he climbed the stairs out of the Bastille station, *may my own little job go as smoothly*.

Iliescu sat by the window today (Jeremy had never seen him twice at the same table), nose in his notebook, stubborn stalks of hair flopping over his forehead. As he approached, Jeremy noted the Romanian was wearing a rich-brown sharkskin suit. Presenting the allure of a slick benefactor? A lord with many resources with which to reward his loyal retainers? If so, Jeremy wondered what else the Lord Iliescu might be dabbling in, apart from illicit passports. His head rose slowly as Jeremy stood before him, making Jeremy also suspect that one such retainer had already alerted Iliescu to Jeremy's presence in the café.

Iliescu slicked back his hair before giving a condescending nod at the chair across the table. "So you weren't skittish about coming back...no second thoughts?" he asked, looking imperiously askance. Then to Jeremy's quizzical frown: "Not everyone accepts my offers, and I can't really blame them..."

Dominance, Jeremy confirmed to himself while sliding into his chair. *You, Winters, will soon be subject to* my *orders*. All along Jeremy had considered the hierarchy of this little criminal pyramid, Iliescu somewhere towards the top. He was probably in his mid-thirties, around the same age as Jeremy, and yet he felt the need to immediately communicate his power, which in a way only betrayed the very lack of self-assurance he tried to project. Over-confidence scuttled by lack of confidence; tics, vanity, and now a hint of insecurity: Jeremy logged them all for the future.

He ordered a coffee, watching Iliescu light a Dunhill and take two of his fidgety drags.

"Well," Jeremy said, slipping into studied earnestness, "I need to get started if I'm going to earn some money."

Iliescu returned a satisfied grin. "True enough. And as I told you before, I've got a job that will let you show off your skills."

Jeremy waited. *Which skills?*

Perhaps Iliescu sensed something in the pause—and didn't intuition play its part in this business?—for he pulled abruptly at his shirt cuffs, one, then the other, two short tugs. He crossed his legs, then sat inspecting Jeremy—a long look, sweeping from his head down to his belt buckle then back up to his expectant eyes.

Had he still not passed muster? If not, why would Iliescu have asked him back? No, he was merely making Jeremy wait, another petty pressure. Purposely, Jeremy shifted in his seat and intensified his regard, open and candid as a teen's at his first job interview.

Iliescu finally broke his stare and yawned. "*Patience*," he said, recovering from the yawn. "You need it in this business. That and commitment. In your case, with the job I'm assigning you, you'll need to prove that you won't back down."

Jeremy remained silent, his gaze impassive. *To hell with playing the eager puppy.*

"So you can tail someone as well as spot a tail," Iliescu resumed with a sage nod. "That, you've proved. Now I want you to teach a lesson to the idiot whose tail you made." He took two more quick puffs of his Dunhill and stubbed it out. "Our redhaired friend, the one you nailed when you were out with your Albanian girl and her kid. He's fucked up before. Now he needs to pay. And you'll carry out that punishment. I want you to tell him I've fired him, then give him a working-over. Nothing that will put him in the hospital—we don't want inquiries—just a little reminder that his work's become shit and this is the end of the line."

To Iliescu's face, Jeremy reacted with bland acceptance. He concurred that Carrot-top was a fuck-up, shrugged with an *oh-well* smile—the slacker had brought it on himself—then frowned studiously as Iliescu informed him of the meeting he had set up between Jeremy and said slacker, a Moldovan called Florin Rusu.

But when Iliescu dismissed him, Jeremy left the café chanting *putain de merde* to himself. *Shit, shit, shit!*

Chapter 21

Unable to keep this "job within a job" off his mind, Jeremy nonetheless tried to keep Iliescu's orders from contaminating his mood when he got home. Ghensie was already at the coffee table bent over her watches, attaching their backs then repacking them carefully. Boxes sat next to the sofa, Bekim's cars came skidding at his feet, and Jeremy had the sudden impression the flat had shrunk in the last couple of hours.

He surveyed the clutter, wondering if there might not be a more convenient work area, when Ghensie tuned in on that very thought. "Sorry about the mess," she said, after reaching up to lace her fingers in his. "I might take this into the kitchen, work there, then clean it up and store it before dinner."

"Whatever you think," Jeremy said, giving her hand a warm, approving squeeze, then sitting down next to her. "Is it complicated, this stuff?"

"No, they taught me on the spot; it just takes attention to detail." She put down the watch she was working on and gave Jeremy an optimistic smile. "And you've concluded your business successfully?"

"Mm," he affirmed with an evasive shift of his gaze. He could tell from the quizzical lilt in her voice that she would like to know more about his afternoon comings and goings, which he stubbornly stuck to calling "errands," never describing what kind. And in this, he would have to maintain his own mantle of mystery. Only his former girlfriend, Haley, knew he worked for the RG, and he had never revealed the specifics of any job.

Haley—for an awkward moment as he crossed to the kitchen for a beer, he felt her pull, pictured her soft chestnut hair bouncing in a wavy frame around her face. Her green eyes peering mischievously at him behind glasses, which when discarded before sex left those eyes looking larger and more scintillating in their desire. He suddenly wished to meet her for coffee. After all they did have much in common, including a healthy respect for each other's privacy. She understood Jeremy's reticence when it came to his RG work, even though as recently as last October she had hinted that he might be hiding more than necessary behind the RG aegis. Then there was that period of dour silence he'd inflicted on her when his cousin died, which happened to coincide with the return to Paris of Haley's ex-boyfriend—all in all, not the makings of a merry couple's cocktail. Yes, he would like to see her, to catch up, but the idea of the Frenchman Luc lurking in the background was as chafing as sandpaper.

He returned to the living room and looked at Ghensie, bent again to her watch, and wondered if to her mind their having had sex now meant a right to know more about him. But she was intent on her work and seemed to have lost curiosity about his comings and goings. Standing next to her, he caressed her back and kissed the top of her head, eliciting a smile though her eyes remained locked on her watch. He sat down and nuzzled her neck with light kisses to which she reacted with a soft little laugh, just in time for Bekim to come charging at them with his cars. He made a loud revving growl, yanking at Jeremy's hand for him to come play. "Bekim," Ghensie scolded, "I'm trying to work." Jeremy felt the message could also apply to him and let his fingers trail to the small of her back under its sweater, just to give the silky skin a tickle before he retreated to the floor with Bekim. *They would both be good boys, for now.*

The next day, with one free day left before his assignment to "sort out" Iliescu's ex-employee, Jeremy suggested the three of them visit the Natural History Museum. Getting out and about, stretching his legs and his senses, made him feel alert to a day's possibilities however vague and distant they may be—joining the city's pounding pulse, with its car exhaust smelling of energy and forward movement. At home, his newfound intimacy with Ghensie added a sense of satisfaction, but he was beginning to feel the crunch of confinement in the small flat—almost always some kind of noise, space inexorably disappearing from counters, dressers and tables, the disarray of the bathroom (a tiny space he wasn't used to sharing and which now included hair bleaching paraphernalia, since Ghensie felt it safe to remain a blonde). And if he could only switch sleeping places with Bekim.

Yet when he was out on business and time came to come home in the afternoon, he did feel contentment. Dusk sliding in like low piano chords, softening with each reprise, in sync with the sky blushing purple; that purple cloak's warm embrace, bestowing permission to shut down milling thoughts of his past and his future, the cocoon set to deepen with a full rich kiss from Ghensie when he entered his flat.

That night when he returned late from work at Le Prince, he and Ghensie made love and after that moment of completion, the release of himself into her, he felt his sense of purpose intensify: to protect Ghensie and Bekim—and himself—from Luan and the other predators, to see the situation through to the end. Though a bit clichéd, at this stage that purpose felt immediate and as valid as anything. And if Luan and company were to surface in Paris, he could always go to Rébert as a last resort. Migrants who fell victim to a crime could apply for legal protection. Too bad the crime must precede the protection, Jeremy thought, feeling a heaviness in his chest.

The following day he couldn't help reflecting that the very man to whom he was supposed to teach a lesson might be an illegal migrant himself, who could also seek legal protection as victim of a crime—namely the roughing up Jeremy was ordered to give him. Unlike Ghensie, however, the Moldovan himself was part of a criminal association, which should discourage any temptation to talk to the police. In effect, Jeremy's two jobs, his RG assignment and his orders from Iliescu, were entwined like mating snakes, and for Rébert, tidily removed as he was, Florin Rusu's "lesson" would pose no problem.

Still, Jeremy resisted the idea of using his fists unprovoked. He wasn't even boxing these days. He had planned to return last autumn when the weather cooled; then came the job in Amsterdam and afterwards Walter's death, and well...things hadn't entirely righted themselves. He could only think of one approach to the task set by Iliescu, and he hoped it would work.

Iliescu had set up the meeting with Florin Rusu in the same café in which the exchange of money and passport had taken place.

Once more Jeremy whisked through that neighborhood—Louise Cholot's neighborhood—his stocking-capped head bent low, until he reached the café. Upon entering he was mildly surprised to see a table of lively individuals, before his gaze swooped over them to light on Rusu in the back. He looked left to the bar—the same guy as last time, drying glasses. When he glanced at Jeremy it was only to give a nod and a tilt of his head towards Rusu. Jeremy passed the table of three animated men who were tossing back their drinks and chattering in an Eastern European language. He felt like a foreigner in this Balkan-like atmosphere located only a block from Madame Cholot's building.

Rusu, at the table behind the group, looked down at his newspaper as Jeremy approached. He sat with his green loden coat on and his great bush of red hair— lots of hair, Jeremy noted, for a middle-aged *mec* who had to be over forty. As Jeremy stood before him, his cap stuffed in his jacket pocket, he firmly cleared his throat, forcing Rusu to look up with a face pinched with irritation.

"I was told you would be here," Jeremy said, skipping greetings and introductions, his thumbs hooked matter-of-factly in his jeans pockets.

A nervous rustle came from the newspaper as Rusu set it down. "I don't know who you are but I'm meeting someone soon, so if you'd move along..." He shooed Jeremy, a futile response since that *someone* was standing before him.

Jeremy pulled up a chair and plunked down opposite him. Rusu looked truly offended now, first rearing up and then settling slightly back, like a posturing dog sensing he was physically outmatched. He was in fact shorter than Jeremy, at least in the torso, and his build was dumpy at best. Jeremy doubted Rusu had ever done enforcement work for Iliescu, and this made him fear his job might become both simpler and more difficult: though the *mec* would be easy prey, Jeremy didn't like uneven matches, especially now that he was tasked to be the aggressor. Under the table he flexed a fist—his tactic *had* to work.

"You're meeting *me*," he told Rusu. "Didn't you

know?"

Now the Moldovan seemed genuinely thrown. He edged back a bit more and shook his head. "No—"

"Cornel Iliescu sent me, I thought you knew that."

"*No*," Rusu insisted, after a pause which left him further shifting in his seat, his frown more confused, and his Moldovan accent thickening. "*Iliescu* was supposed to come."

If it hadn't yet dawned on Rusu, it definitely had on Jeremy. Iliescu had played Rusu, telling the Moldovan he would join him and then leaving Jeremy to deal with the joke plus carry out his job. "He's not coming," said Jeremy more glumly than he would have liked.

Rusu sputtered, offense puckering his face again, his chest puffing out. "But...but..."

He was both barking and backpedaling, and Jeremy gave him a silencing smirk and shake of his head. "Iliescu sent me to tell you to clean up your act. Actually, you'll have to get another gig because he's fired you."

Rusu's eyes grew larger, though he said nothing.

"You *do* remember me?" Jeremy went on pleasantly. "I definitely remember you. I've never seen a dumber tail. Iliescu decided you need another line of work and I can't help agreeing."

Rusu squirmed and blinked twice, a fish surprised at being tossed into a boat. He pushed away from the table, his chair shrieking against the tile floor. "You're lying! You've got no right—"

"*To come here?*" Jeremy finished for him. "How do you think I knew where you'd be?" His eyes swept the café, his hand following. "How did I find you in this charming little place that reminds me of a wine cellar?" He noticed that the three men at the table behind him had paused to watch and listen.

The barman was watching as well. In a few quick

strides he was out from behind the bar and standing over Jeremy and Rusu. "Take it back there," he said in his own seemingly Eastern European accent. With a jerk of his chin he indicated a corridor down which the restrooms were probably located. The same direction in which he had disappeared the day Jeremy met to exchange money and goods with Iliescu. "Go," he now ordered, when neither man stood. "There's a storeroom on the right."

Jeremy slid out of his chair and stood facing Rusu, thumbs once more hooked resolutely in his pockets. Rusu rose hesitantly, his eyes darting to the door leading out to the sidewalk. Jeremy shook his head, mouth set in a line of warning. "First, we settle this," he said. When Rusu finally stepped into the aisle— nowhere else to go— his face had turned defiantly red. Jeremy took a step towards him, the barman extended a meaty hand in the desired direction, and the two filed down the hall.

The storeroom was small and cold, no radiators, just metal shelves with boxes, plus a table with a chair and a cup and saucer on its corner. Items to keep a vague eye on, Jeremy noted, while pursuing his plan. The carrot-top Rusu had allowed himself to be baited, emitting sarcastic grunts and sighs of outrage while they had marched down the hall. *Who the hell did Jeremy think he was?*

Now, though, in the sterile chill of the storeroom, its door closed behind them, the Moldovan's expression had turned blank, almost studiously blank. Time to resume provoking him.

So Jeremy said, "Iliescu wants you to learn a lesson before you move on, though you'll probably fuck-up again."

"If he's kicking me out, he can tell me himself,"

countered Rusu with a shrug. "I'll wait to hear from him personally. In the meantime, what else do you want?" With these words his chin pitched up, a spark of challenge back in his eyes.

Jeremy met it with a condescending smile. "You know how you gave yourself away tailing me? For one thing, your red mop stands out like a revolving police light, and you were ridiculously obvious when you eavesdropped on my conversations last week, sitting practically at the next table in that loden you always wear. Jeremy eyed the coat derisively. "Do you sleep in it too? *Imbécile*."

Rusu still wouldn't bite. Not a flinch, not a twitch of the eye, let alone a balling of fists preceding the first punch. He merely shifted his weight and slipped his hands in his coat pockets. "Well, maybe I did show my hand in the Gitane. Isn't that what it's called, the café across from your building?" He canted his head in mock search of his memory. "Yes," he said with a smile, "La Gitane. You and your little family—your bull-necked woman, her little brat of a boy." Rusu's sneer made Jeremy's jaw tense. "I heard the two of them speaking Albanian—Muslim scum. Can't you do better than a couple of West Balkan mongrels?"

Heat rose through Jeremy. "You'd better respect your betters, Rusu, you're not worth a single piece of lint on her coat. You're a shit, a fucking flunky—can't find better work and can't even hang on to this piss-poor job." The fingernails of his right hand were scratching his palm.

But Rusu merely laughed. "Turkish mutts, the both of them. She's a phony blonde, I can tell. And what's her kid, part Serbian pup?"

Rusu had scored a couple of lucky guesses, though Jeremy was hardly going to satisfy the piece of shit with a confirmation. Now both of his palms were itching. He took two stalking steps towards Rusu, backing him up against a shelf of boxes. Then he saw Rusu's hand fly out of his coat pocket gripping a knife. He heard a click, barely glimpsed the gleam of a blade before blocking Rusu's arm and throwing a punch to his solar plexus. Rusu bent in half though not without swinging wide with the switchblade, slashing Jeremy's forearm, which luckily lay swathed in the stout leather of his bomber jacket. He kneed Rusu in the throat then leaped back, amazed that the turd, who was now on his knees, still clung to the blade. Rusu lunged desperately, slashing so closely that Jeremy barely had time to kick the knife out of his hand. He snatched it up, then with one thick-soled Oxford brogue, delivered a final kick to Rusu's torso, plus one to the side of his face (in case Iliescu looked for proof of the job). Rusu withered like a punctured balloon, after which Jeremy collapsed the switchblade, pocketed it, and paced out of the room, leaving Rusu in a panting, wheezing heap on the floor.

Passing the bar Jeremy received an "*Hé*" from the barman, who added a questioning stare. A winded Jeremy waved towards the storeroom. "He's resting," which netted a knowing nod from the barman. Jeremy left the café, checking the sleeve of his bomber jacket and shaking his head. The jacket was ruined. It had been a gift from his mother a year ago last Christmas and he hated the idea of parting with it. It had served him well today, saving his arm from a probable set of stitches, plus he just plain liked it. Heading to the Tolbiac métro station, he fingered the switchblade in his pocket. The confrontation hadn't gone exactly as planned but had turned out satisfactory in the end. Plus he now owned a switchblade, an item he hadn't possessed since his teen years in San Francisco. Emitting an adrenaline-filled laugh he gave the weapon a triumphant squeeze.

Chapter 22

Jeremy's adrenaline leaked away. As the métro train swung and clattered on its tracks he began to analyze his handling of the Rusu affair. What had he expected from the man? Certainly not a knife in a public place. He had dealt with that surprise deftly enough and could almost be lulled into thinking he had played an expert hand. He had baited the man, all the while reasoning that Rusu would throw a punch, which would in turn justify a rough response. Yet it was Rusu, with his unexpected taunts about Ghensie and Bekim, who made Jeremy almost lose his cool and throw the first punch. And that bothered him. *Not smart, Jeremy—must do better in the future.* Especially if he were to continue infiltrating Iliescu's network.

He reached into his pocket, once more fingering his new acquisition. Spoils of war, he supposed, a trophy for having at once bested Rusu, carried out Iliescu's orders, and advanced in his own RG assignment. But what to do with the switchblade now? Hide it away for now, he reckoned.

So when he got home he made an immediate detour to the bedroom, pulled the saxophone case out from under the bed and ditched the knife in it. It was Bekim who worried him, and considering the boy had already discovered the saxophone, there should be no reason for him to reexplore the instrument. He closed the case and pushed it back into its metaphorical tomb. Then he took off his slashed jacket and hung it at the far end of his armoire, bunched with clothes he rarely wore and then went to enjoy a civilized dinner *en famille*.

Now though, when he considered Ghensie at the stove and later while she was correcting Bekim's table manners, he couldn't help thinking about Rusu's insults targeting Albanians. The Balkans were a cauldron of roiling rivalries and ancient grudges, Jeremy knew that, but the vehemence in Rusu's words—*Muslim scum, Turkish mongrels*. The Muslims Jeremy knew in Paris were certainly not scum, and Ghensie fit a fairly modern image of a Muslim woman. Maybe it was time to ask...

The following afternoon he did just that. The little threesome had made a jaunt to the Square du Temple. The day was clear, with the kind of dry distant cold that didn't chill the bones, the sun sparkling as it arced ever more westerly in the month of February. Jeremy and Ghensie were sitting on a bench while Bekim played on the slide—it was a good time for an intimate chat.

"Yesterday," he began tentatively, "I heard a Moldovan guy in a café making unkind remarks about Muslims in the Balkans." He gave her hand a squeeze. "It made me angry but I didn't say anything, mainly because I don't know enough about the religion or the culture of the area where you're from."

Ghensie's sigh suggested comments such as those he'd heard were nothing new to her. "*Moldovan*, was he?"

"I gathered that much."

Ghensie eyed him curiously but didn't question Jeremy's ability to distinguish Moldovan from other Eastern European ethnicities. He was glad he didn't have to explain.

"Well," she said, "I'm used to prejudice, especially from non-Muslims from the Balkans, and now Moldovans, it seems. These people probably consider themselves Christians, though they don't always act that way." With a mild smile she breathed in and looked out over the park and its pale-blue sky, clearly enjoying the afternoon's crisp clear air. "Here," she said, addressing the tranquil scene, "in the West at least, most people wouldn't think of insulting me and my own." She waved at Bekim, perched at the top of the slide, and received a grin in return before the boy went plummeting down with a shriek of ecstasy.

When the boy reached the bottom Jeremy clapped loudly. Bekim waved, hopped off, and raced back around to the ladder.

"That guy," said Jeremy, still observing the boy, "insinuated that Albanian Muslims are...half Turkish, so to speak."

Ghensie swiveled to face him and answered adamantly. "We are *not* Turks. And whoever this guy is should be reminded that Moldova also had the Turks in their house. Albania fought to liberate itself from the Ottoman Empire, just like the Greeks and others did. Yes, most of our population is Muslim, but many of us are Sufis, very different from Orthodox Muslims." She paused, then added more gently, "In that we have much in common with the Christian faith."

This surprised Jeremy. Sufis? He had heard of them, but mainly in connection to the famous Whirling Dervishes. And speaking of whirling energy, Bekim came jogging up to join them, his cheeks and ears glowing red. Ghensie tugged his cap down and asked him if he wanted to go home. The answer was a resounding "No," after which he pivoted and ran back to the slide.

"He likes to take a break now and then," said Jeremy. "Maybe just to check on things in your sphere."

"Yes, back and forth like a puppy. I guess it's his

age. Plus," she added in a less light-hearted voice, "he's had his share of upheaval." She stared ahead at the children's recreation area, and though she wasn't looking at him, Jeremy gave a nod of understanding. Still, her use of "puppy" in reference to Bekim, reminded Jeremy of the Moldovan Rusu and his slur "part Serbian pup."

"Is Bekim Muslim, then?" he asked, looping back to their discussion.

"Normally," Ghensie answered after a thoughtful pause, "a child is considered Muslim if his parents are Muslim. Bekim's father, on the other hand, is a Serb, a Christian by definition. That has always been one of Luan's objections—not only was Bekim born out of wedlock, but to a non-Muslim father." She paused again, this time lowering her eyes. Perhaps she felt a brush of shame, Jeremy thought, and he gave her hand another squeeze.

"I adopted Sufi Islam while I was at university in Tirana," she went on, looking directly at Jeremy now. "Many conservative Muslims hate Sufis. Luan is a good example. Don't ask me why, but he is much more extreme than my parents. Granted, he's a hypocrite, but that's beside the point.

Jeremy nodded wryly.

"I said Sufism has much in common with Christian principles," Ghensie continued, her gaze bright and earnest. "We believe in peace, tolerance and most of all, from what I've learned, *forgiveness*. Like the Christians, we want to love God, not fear him, and in loving and serving others we get closer to God." She touched her chest. "God is in the heart, our ancient teacher Rumi said, and love is there too. And where there is love, there is forgiveness. Though they aren't Sufis, my parents forgave my transgression. So, you see, there is hope for Orthodox Muslims as well. And my parents love Bekim. But to answer your question about my little boy being Muslim? Yes, in that I'm raising him to be strong in Sufi love, tolerance, and compassion."

Jeremy was staring at Ghensie in what must have seemed edification. His lips parted, though he didn't know quite what to say.

"You didn't expect a speech," Ghensie joked, squeezing his hand in return.

"Maybe not, but I'm glad to learn." He put his arm around her and pulled her close. She let her head rest on his shoulder.

"Sufi poets write of love," she said in a murmur. "Sufism doesn't see women as 'fallen.' The poets speak of human desire as a symbol for the soul's longing for God. I'm not sure I always believe in God, but when I feel my heart beating in unison with another's, I agree He must be near."

Jeremy imagined their hearts beating in unison this very moment. "I like your poets," he said. He was struggling with what else to add, still in semi-wonder, still not sure of the extent of his feelings, when Bekim came bounding up again to sit with them. Once more Jeremy thought of the Dervishes.

"I never knew much about Sufism before," he said, "but I've heard of the Whirling Dervishes."

Ghensie sat up straight. "Have you? That's wonderful. *They*, I think, are our greatest representatives. Would you like to see one of their performances? There's one on right now in Paris."

"Really?"

"I saw it in this week's *Pariscope*," she said, referring to the city's weekly publication that "scoped out" exhibitions, films, and artistic performances of all kinds.

"Well, I think you at least should go. I can watch

Bekim..."

"No, it would be even better for you to see it. I'll ask Solange to stay with Bekim."

"All right, in that case..."

"Good, I know how to get tickets!"

The rest of the week spooled out with work. Ghensie continued her job with the pocket watches, hauling the watches to and from the apartment in two large messenger bags. Jeremy worked his shifts at Le Prince. He also met with Rébert to turn over the money Iliescu had paid him. The RG boss lauded Jeremy's ever-increasing penetration of the Romanian's operation, told him to hang on to the passport (which Jeremy had hidden in an inside pocket of his ruined bomber jacket) for the duration of the job, and when learning of Jeremy's skirmish with the Moldovan Rusu, said: *watch your step, we don't want any deaths, including your own.* As for Iliescu, Jeremy had heard nothing from the Romanian since their last meeting. He must have heard something about the *lesson* taught to Rusu, either in direct complaint from Rusu himself or from the barman, an obvious Iliescu retainer. In any case, Jeremy enjoyed the respite, and when his night off work came, he and Ghensie prepared to go see the Whirling Dervishes.

Jeremy commented, "If Paris weren't a mecca where you can find most any kind of performance, I'd say this coincidence was ordered just for you." He was happy to see Ghensie absorbing the city's life, and for the first time they were going out in the evening as a couple, Jeremy in a grey wool suit and dark blue-and-burgundy striped tie, Ghensie wearing a dark-blue satin dress. Solange was successfully enlisted to watch Bekim, though Jeremy could see she would have liked to accompany them. Ghensie must have sensed it too, for she invited Solange to come to dinner the next evening.

"You really do look lovely," Jeremy repeated to Ghensie, as he helped her shed her coat and they took their seats in the Eleventh arrondissement theater.

Pre-performance music wafted from the stage over the audience—sounds of the Silk Road, of the Grand Bazar of Istanbul, Jeremy imagined as he watched the musicians weave magic with drums, flutes, and fat-bodied stringed instruments.

Ghensie grasped his hand. "This is very exciting for me, so have patience with my enthusiasm."

"I'd never have thought of it on my own," Jeremy assured her. "So I'm here to enjoy myself and learn."

"Okay," she said, releasing his hand and pressing her fingertips together in prelude to another speech. "You're going to see four stages to the Dervishes' dance. Really, it's more a prayer than a dance—to focus the mind on the God within us as well as on the whirling world and universe on the outside. That's why they turn round and round. It's about being at one with everything." She paused, taking in Jeremy's slightly confused expression. "You'll see," she whispered, as the audience's chatter morphed gradually into a collective murmur. A bearded man in a long black cape and tall cylindrical hat stepped on stage. Simultaneously, the lights dimmed and a soft, intimate glow enveloped him. Facing the audience, he began to speak; his words, heightened by a microphone, filled the theater in a kind, conversational fashion.

He spoke of the "oneness" Ghensie had mentioned, the striving for unity with all things through love and mystic prayer. How the Sufi movement started when Muslims joined mystic Christians in ancient Syria and how it spread throughout the Ottoman Empire with the Whirling Dervishes, the emphasis on love and tolerance versus rites and rituals. Plurality over absolutism.

Jeremy felt he was entering a different dimension. He looked at Ghensie. "You'll see!" she whispered.

And so he did. At the end of the dance, he could only marvel at what he'd witnessed. The Dervishes, in their long twirling white skirts and cylindrical hats, spun into the first stage of the dance—described as "Moving towards God," by the instructor, who was actually in charge of the performance, strolling among the dancers as they whirled towards stage two—"With God," and stage three—the "Ecstasy" of the union. Now and then the leader touched a dancer's sleeve. "To make sure they keep their balance," Ghensie explained, "because they've left themselves behind in this phase— ego, family, everything around them." And then on to stage four, the final phase, the "Coming Back," the return to the self.

Throughout, the dancers appeared to be in a trance: eyes half closed, heads tilted to one side, their movements as soft and graceful as a butterfly's, only much swifter; their sense of direction as honed as the radar of a bat. Jeremy couldn't get over the skill of it— but it really seemed much more than a skill...

"More like moving meditation," said Ghensie at the end of the performance. "Whirling in harmony with all things in nature, from the body and its circulating blood to the revolving stars and planets. The Buddhists speak of this universal unity too," she added pensively. "Shows we're all really 'one' as humanity."

The philosophy was comprehensible in an abstract way, though this type of mystic ecstasy wasn't some- thing Jeremy felt keen to experience any time soon. Better to watch the exquisite practitioners and share the spirit of good will and community. But yes, he was glad he'd come, and now he knew more about Ghensie. He squeezed her hand again.

"Sufism isn't an easy philosophy to practice," she mused. "It takes constant work, and I'm still behind." She gave a helpless shrug. "Life gets in the way."

So it did. That night, while he and Ghensie made love, Jeremy thanked the Sufi poets. The next day he received a call from Iliescu, congratulating him on a job well executed and instructing Jeremy to meet him the next day. How to reconcile the heights he had just come from the night before, that whirling crystalline air to the fetid underground of Iliescu's trafficking world? If there was any unity involved, it was a *sacré mystère*. And with that thought, he moved forward with the Iliescu assignment.

Chapter 23

Iliescu observed Jeremy askance, his notebook and cigarettes on the table next to his drumming fingers. They were meeting in a different café this afternoon—not in the Bastille quarter, not in the cave-café in the Thirteenth arrondissement—but in one that bordered the Ninth and Tenth arrondissements at the end of the short rue de l'Abbeville. Smaller by far than La Presque Bastille, it seemed more suitable to Iliescu's need to keep watch over foot traffic, thought Jeremy. He wondered if here, as at the cave-café, there was a complicit barman. He couldn't tell, for this man, like the barman of La Presque Bastille, never stopped moving—pulling draft beers, working the espresso machine, filling glasses and plates for the fairly packed tables, occupied mainly by an older, male clientele. Some sat alone with their newspapers, others chatted in pairs, none of them looked particularly shady.

This café, like La Presque Bastille, seemed to serve the purpose of "arranging things," as opposed to executing hard business of a potentially compromising nature. Before sitting Jeremy glanced around again.

"Expecting someone?" Iliescu asked him, his gaze a cross between skeptical and irritated. His fingertips drummed in quick spurts of two: *thump, thump—thump, thump.*

"No, no one." Jeremy shrugged. "Just wondering whether you've got a point-man like at La Presque Bastille."

"Why? Would you prefer a job like that? The Rusu

job too much for you?" Jeremy didn't reply, and finally Iliescu barked a cynical laugh. "Don't worry, Winters, you did well enough. *But*" he said, adding a pause for effect, "from what I hear, our friend Rusu got up your ass. Says you're on the touchy side when it comes to your woman."

Iliescu looked amused. Jeremy swore to himself, was tempted to ask whether Rusu had also mentioned pulling a knife and still getting bested. But he stayed silent and Iliescu waved a dismissive hand.

"No matter. I'm going to pay you for the work. My barman friend says he found Rusu panting and sweating like a pig. Had to pull him to his feet to get him out of the place." Iliescu nodded in satisfaction. "So, here's your reward." He pulled an envelope from his jacket and slid it across the table. Jeremy picked it up and counted the banknotes inside—six hundred francs.

"Not bad for an hour's work, eh?"

Jeremy nodded, tucking the envelope into the inside pocket of the old black peacoat he had now substituted for his bomber jacket. "Do you ever pay in dollars?" he asked.

"I accept dollars, but I don't pay out in them."

Jeremy gave a little shrug. "It's just that on the run, dollars—"

"Are more useful—*I know*. So just go to the bank and exchange what I gave you for a hundred bucks if you want. Iliescu sounded annoyed. Then his tone changed. "Have you heard anything about when the cops might nab you?"

"Nothing specific, but I'm trying to get as much cash together as possible beforehand."

"Well, I wouldn't pay six hundred an hour for tailing someone, if you're still thinking of that kind of work."

Jeremy shrugged again. "I can do other things. You might even need a courier—messages, and so forth." *Passports to deliver*. "Frankly, I'd rather not risk getting arrested."

Iliescu appeared to consider this. Or maybe he was pondering something else, because he asked, "Are you still planning to take off on your own...no woman, no kid?"

Jeremy hesitated a long moment under Iliescu's probing gaze. From the start, the Romanian had rooted around after Jeremy's personal ties—strictly business, of course, collecting leverage, naturally—only in this case, Jeremy couldn't imagine what the bastard was after.

"She's hardly rich, your Albanian girl," he continued. "Coming and going from your place with those bags, I'm guessing she's found some kind of sketchy work." He paused, head canted, and Jeremy stiffened inside. *Putain de merde*: so Ghensie was being tailed now. But what could he do?

"You're not saying much, Winters." Iliescu smoothed back his hair and leaned in over the table, his polished leather jacket creaking softly. "You want to protect her, I know—I *understand*. And you'd like to take her and the kid with you when you run." He sat back again. "Correct me if I'm wrong."

Jeremy waited for the burning in his chest to ease. Iliescu was casting bait. His conclusion about Jeremy and Ghensie could only seem logical, and Jeremy could think of no advantage in contradicting it. To the objective observer, the sight of Jeremy, Ghensie, and Bekim leaving the house together—Jeremy's arm at times around Ghensie, his hand occasionally clasping Bekim's—could only smack of a family unit.

"Sure, I'd like to take her with me," he finally said with a casual shrug. *He'd swallowed the fly floating on the stream, now where would he be pulled?*

Iliescu lit a cigarette, took a couple of quick pulls and exhaled with apparent satisfaction. "Depending on how much work you're willing to do, I might also be able to get your Albanian girl a French passport."

Well, well, Jeremy thought, gazing from Iliescu to the table and back. So here hung the real hook: offering to help Ghensie in order to further indebt Jeremy. "You'd do that when I'd have to cut loose at any time?"

Iliescu displayed his palms. "You want to work, right? I'm just offering a choice in how you'd like to receive part of your pay."

Jeremy shook his head in doubt—for Iliescu's consumption, but also in real doubt about involving Ghensie. For now he pushed that concern aside and asked, "How long would it take me to work off another five thousand francs?"

"Ah, you see, now that you're my employee you're entitled to a discount."

Avoiding Iliescu's smug smile, Jeremy made a show of twisting his coffee cup in deliberation. "How much, then?" he finally asked.

"Three thousand. You could make the amount doing five 'strenuous' jobs, about an hour's worth a day, or in a couple of weeks doing the work I'll need done now that I've fired Rusu." A smirk accompanied this last bit.

Jeremy drew a contemplative breath, his eyes meeting Iliescu's, then nodded sagely. "I'll think about it. But let me get started with what you need taken care of next."

After observing Jeremy for a moment longer, Iliescu sniffed a couple of times and said, "Fair enough. In the meantime, I need you to check out a certain individual." When Jeremy cocked his head in interest, Iliescu asked him if he had a camera.

"A camera? Sure."

"One with a telephoto lens?"

"No...but I can borrow one."

"I need pictures of a guy as he comes out of his mistress's flat. Preferably with her on his arm."

"Mm," Jeremy murmured with a twitch of a smile. "So you also deal in blackmail."

"Not exactly, in this case. Let's call it insurance on someone I'm dealing with. Anyway, I've brought photos and an address for you."

"In which category would this job fall? As high as the Rusu job?"

"Not quite, but higher than a simple tailing task. Get started right away. I need goods on this guy."

Insurance, Jeremy repeated to himself as he left the café for the Bonne Nouvelle métro stop. Another *mec* like himself that Iliescu sought leverage on. Only on Jeremy the goods were Ghensie and Bekim, two irregular migrants who could be compromised if Jeremy crossed Iliescu. Could giving the go-ahead to procure a passport for Ghensie make Bekim and her more vulnerable? He wasn't sure. On the other hand, agreeing to Iliescu's proposal might get him closer to the source of his investigation. And when eventually Iliescu asked for a passport photo of Ghensie—and for three thousand francs, for which Jeremy would *not* apply to Rébert...but he was getting ahead of himself. Now he simply needed to get started with his new task. He had time to make his decision about the passport.

Grimacing, he started down the métro stairs.

When he got home, Ghensie reminded him that Solange was coming to dinner. It was his second night off work.

"Solange, Solange!" chanted Bekim, circling around Jeremy as if Jeremy were a maypole. When the boy finally came to a halt, Jeremy tousled his hair and went to hang up his peacoat in the bedroom armoire, buttoning it so as to shield the inside pocket with the six hundred francs from view. Then he headed to the kitchen, a steaming new aroma drawing him along. "Something smells deliciously different!" he said, and kissed Ghensie on the neck.

"Do you like lamb?" He did. "Onions?" *Bien sûr.* "Yogurt?"

"*Hm?*" He did, but usually not for dinner.

"You'll like it in my recipe."

"What about Solange?"

"I've made this dish for her before. Oh, and of course there'll be rice."

Jeremy kissed her again, then drifted back to the living room. Bekim was squatting on the floor making droning noises with his cars. Jeremy sat down and picked up the copy of *Paris Match* from the coffee table. He tried to read an article but his thoughts kept turning over Iliescu's offer: agreeing to a passport for Ghensie might indeed help him zero in on the forger, but it could also risk Iliescu getting too close to Ghensie. He might want to meet her, and that thought made Jeremy's chest burn again—*no*, that would never happen. Did Iliescu even know Ghensie's name? He hadn't asked, so it seemed doubtful at this point...

Bekim must have noticed his pensiveness. "Will you play with me?"

Jeremy gazed back absently.

"No one'll play with me."

The kid looked forlorn, and welcoming a respite from his deliberations, Jeremy folded himself down onto the floor to join him.

"*I'm* using the Alfa Romeo" (a new car Jeremy had bought him—racing-car red). "You get the Porsche."

Jeremy smiled as Bekim gave him the little black

car, pieces of its paint chipped off.

After a few sporty collisions they heard the interphone buzzer. Bekim leaped to his feet, shouting, "Solange!" Game instantly abandoned.

It was the first time all four had spent time together since last October, in the café in Brussels. Plenty of small talk ensued: news of Solange's studies and Ghensie's curious job, of a jazz accordionist's appearance at Le Prince Blue Note, and of Bekim's improved French. Then, after dinner in the living room, once Bekim had gone grudgingly to bed, Solange asked about Luan and the Kosovars.

"We haven't heard a thing," said Ghensie. She touched the wooden coffee table in superstitious French fashion.

"And they don't have my name or address," Jeremy emphasized.

"We're all doing fine here," said Ghensie.

Solange's gaze roamed the room more intently than it had when she'd first arrived, thought Jeremy. Certainly, the tone of the household had changed and he suspected she could tell.

"You know we appreciate all your help, Solange." Ghensie said. "I couldn't have made it this far without you."

Solange, whom four months earlier Jeremy had found flippant and self-absorbed, now seemed modest about taking due credit. "But," she said, a complicit grin aimed at Ghensie, "Jeremy's the man of the hour. He helped get me out of that stupid situation in Amsterdam, and now he's here for you."

Ghensie gazed sharply at Solange. "If I remember right, it was your parents who contacted Jeremy about coming to take you home."

"Someone my parents knew. When you're the

daughter of a minister, you know...it was all a bit hush-hush."

Ghensie looked at Jeremy with a curious gleam in her eye. But she said nothing more, and neither did Jeremy, nor did Solange who was now observing the two of them with a placid smile inferring further speculation on their domestic evolution.

With a perky lift of his brows, Jeremy proposed, "A little nightcap?"

Solange left late in a taxi and Ghensie began the clearing up.

"We could put it off until tomorrow morning," Jeremy suggested as Ghensie collected glasses. He followed her into the kitchen, took the glasses from her, and set them on the counter.

When he nuzzled her neck, Ghensie edged away. "I hate dirty dishes in the morning."

"A one-time occasion," countered Jeremy, cupping her hips in his hands.

"I just want to finish this and go to bed," she said politely, as she started running water in the sink.

Something uneasy in her voice, he thought. What was bothering her? He recalled the sharp curiosity in her eyes when Solange alluded to her parents' connections; it reminded him of the expectant tone in her voice whenever she asked how his solitary outings went. She wanted to know more.

"*Oh*," she added, in that same inscrutable tone, her back to him at the sink. "I forgot to tell you that someone phoned for you a couple of days ago while you were out. He wouldn't leave a message and just said he would call back."

Well, then he probably will, thought Jeremy with a touch of annoyance. Kindly, he said as much, then lifted his hands to massage Ghensie's shoulders.

a.m. It was late and they could both use a good night's sleep. They did the dishes together, then kissed and went their separate ways to bed.

Jeremy rehashed their conversation as he lay on the sofa. Yes, to some extent he was deceiving Ghensie about Iliescu, but with no ill intention—on the contrary, he only wanted to shield her as effectively as possible. He had no more wanted Iliescu to learn about her than Ghensie had intended Luan and the Kosovars to turn their suspicions on Jeremy over the missing coin. Neither had been completely honest with the other, and now Ghensie felt her own unease about him, just as he had felt his about her, because once deception has made an appearance, it's not easy to dismiss—despite talk of caring and manifestations of affection.

But this latter was the only thing that felt real to him, solid and dependable: Ghensie's soft fingers, her sensual murmurs, her caring embraces. They all gave him a sense of completion while helping to silence those barking dogs in his internal basement of guilt. Her warm touch—Ghensie's hands always felt warm— her lips brushing his ear. Those images were now with him as he began his descent into sleep, into that silky liquid stage where he was just conscious enough to choose the images he wished to take with him. At least at first. As he sank further he fell into a dream-state, the two of them pulled into hard lovemaking, he in the dominant role, after which the image flipped and she was looking down on him—a hot, electric thrill that then turned into an odd unease as he stared into suddenly strange, unfamiliar eyes.

He woke to a pale light penetrating the patch of sheer curtains he always left exposed to distinguish whether it was night or day. A remnant of some dream was still with him, though he couldn't remember details, something unsettling that strummed through him, heavy and discordant.

He got up and pulled the curtain and sheers open. A greyish-white sky presaged a damp dreary day.

In the kitchen he guzzled two glasses of water, his throat and mouth parched from last night's spicy lamb and multiple glasses of an economical Saint-Émilion. For a while he sat on the sofa, drinking coffee and watching *Télématin*, the volume low—the sun, according to the *méteo*, would not even give a wink today.

At eight o'clock he left host William Leymergie and crossed softly to the bedroom door, opening it a crack. Bekim was on the floor, rolling the little Alfa Romeo to the sound of "*tsh-tsh*."

"I see you!" he launched at Jeremy, who put a finger to his lips.

Too late, Ghensie opened her eyes, and smiling she motioned Jeremy over to the bed. "Come lie down."

Jeremy glanced at Bekim, who eyed him for an instant before going back to his car. In his bathrobe and socks Jeremy strolled over and stretched out on the bed. It felt marvelous. He could have spent a good half hour savoring the caress of the plush mattress he used to take for granted. Ghensie reached for his hand.

So nice. Until Bekim sent his car careering towards the wall then jumped onto the bed between them, separating Ghensie's and Jeremy's hands. He lay flat, his own hands behind his head in clichéd relaxation, forcing Ghensie onto her side to make room. Jeremy sighed to himself. It was a scene common to a thousand families on any given morning: mother and father, and little one in the middle, the epitome of family intimacy. Although he appreciated being invited into the circle, he felt strange. There was the residue of that heavy discord he'd felt earlier. And he wasn't used to this type of intimacy, had never spent the morning in his parents' bed. He felt he was being squeezed, not just by Bekim in the middle but by something vice-like inside himself.

"I'm getting hungry," he announced to his bedmates. "Who wants breakfast?"

"I do!" Naturally that was Bekim. Ghensie just winked and cast him a contented smile.

Back in the living room he felt his chest expand with air. He walked over to a chair and picked up Grizzly. So, Bekim had left him there all night. Was it the first time? If not, Jeremy hadn't noticed before. He sat down, the bear dangling from his hand, his thoughts drifting like the lazy grey clouds outside the window, everywhere and nowhere.

The job assigned by Iliescu was reminiscent of past RG tasks. Jeremy had borrowed a telescopic lens for his camera from Rébert and now, at eight in the morning near Place de la Nation, had the subject and his mistress in its sights as they exited the woman's building. Who this guy was (both his photo and the man himself looked like a youngish, mustached Roger Vadim) and what he represented to Iliescu, the latter hadn't said; and in the end why should it matter to Jeremy, whose only concern should be winning Iliescu's confidence? Still, his interest was piqued. *Click, click*, first shots completed.

And while on the subject of "confidence," he thought of Ghensie. She was right, he should take her deeper into his trust by introducing her to a friend or two of his. He still felt vigilant about her situation, didn't want many people involved, yet one friend stood glaringly out: Louise Cholot knew Bekim and, more to the point, Jeremy owed her a lunch, now more than ever.

"Your friend Louise is a lovely person," Ghensie said, as they returned home from the brasserie in the Fifth. "I'm glad she was able to take care of Bekim. And he seems *very* fond of her." As for Bekim, he had regaled Madame with everything he had done since last seeing her, including riding the elevator to the top of the Tour Montparnasse, and he had insisted they visit the Parc Montsouris again.

"*Can we, can we?*" he'd chanted to Jeremy.

With an encouraging smile from Louise, Jeremy gave an absent nod, his thoughts already tugging him back to the Iliescu case.

There were more photos to take of the Roger Vadim lookalike, though not all work would involve daylight hours. Iliescu wanted a good and *compromising* shot of "Vadim" and his girlfriend entering the latter's building at night, preferably arm-in-arm. For that Jeremy would have to wait until his next night off from Le Prince. In the meantime, he spent an entire morning shadowing his target: the suited Vadim leaving his girlfriend's building to a rendezvous at the coiffeur's (though Jeremy couldn't see much difference other than a trimmer mustache), then on to a café for a café noisette; afterwards, taking the métro south to a location inside a courtyard near the porte de Vanves. Jeremy waited outside, alternating sitting on a low concrete wall and pacing the sidewalk, but after half an hour Vadim still hadn't come out. Jeremy finally left, although not without casting a backwards glance at a guy wearing glasses, two pedestrians behind. Jeremy had seen him in Vadim's café...he thought. Before dipping down into the métro, he looked back again, but the *mec* had melted away.

Being tailed while tailing? Iliescu making sure

Jeremy was doing the job as assigned? He was supposed to record Vadim's exits from his girlfriend's building in the Twelfth—snap photos suggesting infidelity, at most follow the couple to catch them in a kiss, or checking into a hotel, which hardly seemed likely since they had the girlfriend's place. In other words, he hadn't been authorized to launch his own quest regarding Vadim. A half sour, half-amused smile twisted Jeremy's lips. Iliescu might not be pleased with his overstepping of orders.

Chapter 25

On the métro home Jeremy wondered if the same *mec* he had spotted while following the adulterer Vadim was also tasked to tail Ghensie. If not, how many Iliescu minions were scurrying about Paris like so many sewer rats? Once more he considered doing counter-surveillance when Ghensie went out alone, only he would need to find someone to watch Bekim at the spur of the moment and, *merde*, that seemed impossible. He could only hope that since Iliescu now knew Ghensie's routine and surmised she was working under-the-table, the tails would end. Bad enough that *he* couldn't work in peace, but this shadowing of Ghensie amounted to an invasion of his domestic life and a possible menace to those he held dear. Amidst the juddering and clangor of the métro, he rubbed his face in frustration and made a decision to confront Rébert, suggest they wrap up the job, arrange for Iliescu's arrest and have done with it.

"No," the RG agent replied when the two next met in the café near the Bourse. "Why back out when Iliescu's giving you more work?" Rébert shook his head in baffled disappointment. "Just because he's having you shadowed? It's the nature of his work."

But Ghensie...

He was tempted to confess to Rébert, words rallying in his head and heaving towards his lips—but he managed to resist. Without proof of a crime against her, Ghensie could be deported from France. Iliescu's tailing of her wouldn't count as harm, and mentioning it would only raise questions about her immigration status. He almost wished Luan and the Kosovars would show up, even if they might implicate Ghensie in their crime. For all he knew they could be stalking about Paris as he and Rébert spoke. Swiftly he banished the thought.

"You weren't followed *here*, were you?" Rébert asked.

Jeremy shook his head. "I took an especially roundabout route."

"And these photos you're taking of the Vadim lookalike—why don't you take a shot of him for us too."

Jeremy thought about it and agreed. "With a different camera and film, and provided I'm not being followed."

Rébert seemed satisfied, though he then considered Jeremy with a slight frown. "Anything you need? Making ends meet with your latest raise? There will be a big chunk more when we bring down Iliescu and his forger."

Jeremy obliged Rébert with a neutral nod. Since last summer his RG income had almost doubled. *Ouais, plus de fric.*

More money. But helpful as it was, it would never replace French citizenship, and a *real* French passport. A furtive thought drifted to the Martin Duroc document tucked away in his damaged bomber jacket; the idea that he could look into the quality of the forgery. Ask someone out there with knowledge of these things, before he would have to give it up to the RG. *If* he became forced to hand it over...

"And yes," said Rébert, surfing dangerously close to Jeremy's wave length, "we're still working on your citizenship matter." He took a breath, but Jeremy cut him off:

"I know: *it takes time*."

Rébert's gaze persisted, the kind of tilting regard that angles to make sense of something. Jeremy glanced out the window at the stock market building and its hallowed white columns, an exquisite beacon of the *France of the French*.

"You're restless today," said Rébert, breaking his gaze to light a cigarette, smoke streaming haltingly with his next observation. "Everything okay at home?"

Jeremy looked back at him with raised eyebrows.

"I know you live alone, but things can still get complicated. Personal relationships, and so forth...or maybe you've got a problem with this assignment..."

"I'm fine."

"You can always ask if you need help..."

"Right, thanks." Second thoughts must have escaped Jeremy's tone, for Rébert leaned in on his forearms, concern mirrored in his corrugated brow and narrowed eyes. The gravity of his barrel-like bulk, the four years in age he had on Jeremy, his thinning hair, inversely suggesting wisdom accrued, and now his sincere concern, made Jeremy almost yield to trusting this man whom he had known for six years. *Almost*—if not for the pricking reminder of just what he represented to the RG, the purpose that trumped everything else: he was the agency's convenient instrument on the streets, no more, no less. What did Ghensie matter to them?

With that in mind, Jeremy met his handler's eyes straight on. "I appreciate your asking, but everything's all right."

Rébert let his look linger a couple of seconds longer, then sat back. The two men exchanged per-functory nods, then tossed back the rest of their beers.

With the arrival of his next night off, Jeremy prepared

to set out to take photos of Vadim entering his girlfriend's building.

When Ghensie noticed him packing up his camera equipment in the bedroom, she stopped and stared. It was just after dinner.

"I need to get some night photos of this guy," he explained, glancing back at her as she stood in the doorway.

"*Night photos?*"

"Mm," he affirmed, zipping up his bag. "I'm getting close to the end of the job."

"And you have to take pictures of this person at night..." Doubt clouded her voice and face.

"Just trying to photograph him with his girlfriend," Jeremy confessed, reckoning the truth might end the discussion more quickly than anything else.

But it wasn't that simple. "Blackmail?" Ghensie uttered, the cloud in her eyes turning dark.

"*No.*" Jeremy scratched his head in annoyance. "I *told* you, I'm not working for the underworld or any type of criminal organization. It's confidential business, though."

Ghensie's sigh betrayed an impatient edge. Still she made no comment and moved aside as Jeremy left the bedroom.

Would they go back and forth like this forever? he wondered.

Apparently not. By the time he got to the door Ghensie looked diminished, her sturdy shoulders deflated, her fallen features meek as she watched him sling on his overcoat. She was at his mercy. She lived here at his pleasure. Hunched, submissive, her look did not please him at all. It wasn't Ghensie and it didn't suit her, and he felt like a shit for practically scolding her. "I won't be late," he said softly, taking her by the hands.

She didn't pull away, and he was grateful. He put

his arms around her and whispered, "Thank you for being here."

When they released each other, she gave a small smile and nod, a bit of the old spunk back in her eyes.

They exchanged a quick kiss, he waved at Bekim, and then he left the flat.

At a little after ten-thirty he returned home, with nothing to show for his evening out. Vadim's mistress, whom Jeremy now nicknamed "Bardot," had come home at just after ten, alone, with only her purse on her arm. Jeremy found her every bit as attractive as her namesake "Brigitte," and with his second camera he snapped a couple of photos of her entering her building—night shots, highlighting the curve of her hair and hips in silhouette. That night, when he and Ghensie made love on the sofa, he deemed this make-up sex its own reward.

The following morning, when Vadim still didn't appear at Bardot's place, Jeremy took the woman's photo once more for Rébert as she exited. He didn't blame Vadim one iota for fancying her and wondered what nationality she was, with her high forehead and cheekbones, dark eyes contrasted by voluminous blond hair. In Paris, it rained races and ethnicities, even more so since the Wall had come down, and no one really looked out of place. Iliescu worked with Romanians (he and the barman at the cave-café had exchanged words in their native language), Moldovans, and who knew what other flavor of immigrant. Though Jeremy hadn't gotten close enough to hear him speak clearly, he figured Vadim could come from most anywhere in Europe—probably the East again, given the *mec's* Stalin-like mustache and Iliescu's predilection for hiring those who were most "manageable." And the girlfriend....Jeremy did wonder about her...

With another sweeping glance behind him, checking for a possible tail, he filed into the crowd after her as she struck out down the sidewalk. He hoped to finally get a photo of her and Vadim in at least an embrace. He also needed a snapshot of Vadim for Rébert, and since he had no other commitment for the day, why not follow the sway and bounce of Bardot wherever it might lead?

The pursuit took him towards Place de la Nation. She was probably heading for the métro station, Jeremy figured, until she rounded the Place and turned into boulevard de Charonne. There, she stopped in front of a drab seventies-looking building, its wrought iron sparse and blandly straight, and pushed its buzzer. It didn't take long for the door to click open. She threw a glance behind her and ducked inside.

Vadim's address? Jeremy asked himself. A morning versus an evening tryst? For half an hour he waited across the street at a newspaper kiosk, examining every title of magazine, newspaper and comic book on the racks. Finally, he puffed out a sigh and decided to leave. If this were the married Vadim's residence, why would his mistress be visiting him here? Why, Jeremy complained to himself, glancing at his watch, was he wasting his time?

Because of that glance over her shoulder...

Vadim's girl suspected someone of following her. Jeremy took another long look around him—shops, a café, a florist, multiple recesses where a different sort of tailer might lurk, one who had his sights set on Bardot, while easily picking out Jeremy in counter-surveillance. Instinctively, he transferred his bag to his opposite shoulder and removed his cap. It was time to go. He gave one last look at the dull building across the street. Could Vadim be renting a flat there for his affair? Not likely since he and Bardot were already nesting in her place. If it *was* her place...Iliescu had said so, at any rate.

Christ, this inane adultery assignment was pushing him farther and farther from his principal RG business. Getting him nowhere. He thrust his knit cap into the pocket of his peacoat and headed out of the neighborhood at a brisk stride.

He was sick of it: tired of tailing and being tailed. Fed up with pursuing Iliescu's minions—*sick of Iliescu, period*. Tired of this prolonged RG job in which he had to play the minion himself. How long did Rébert count on this lasting? He had never given Jeremy an assignment that stretched out with no end in sight. Even the job last summer hadn't trailed out indefinitely. Rather than mindlessly shadowing people, he had been tasked to procure information from the political refugee, Stefania. Cozying up to Stefania versus to Iliescu made for quite the pleasant challenge, and, God knew, it was never boring. In fact, when Rébert had pulled him off the job, Jeremy had silently refused to let go—and, unbeknownst to Rébert, his recalcitrance had paid off.

What a contrast to this crap. Did Rébert even care how long this could last? Probably not, for as the RG boss continued to reiterate in one form or another, "You're perfect for the job." Who else could have passed all of Iliescu's background checks but Jeremy, the disgraced and allegedly hunted American in pursuit of a route to freedom? Hot embarrassment filled him as he again registered how close to the truth the statement was. Yes, he had been disgraced, gone to prison, and now toiled at jobs he had once found stimulating but now considered confining—everything was confining when you lived in a country but were deprived of its citizenship. He wanted that French passport and he wanted it now, a passport whose middle page displayed the name and optimistic face of *Jeremy Paul Winters*, rather than the dull phony stare of Martin Jacques Duroc.

He got off the métro at Place de la République, starting the ten-minute walk home in a drizzling rain. He had loaded his bag but forgotten his umbrella. He forced his mind to entertain thoughts of a good meal, a fast-moving evening at Le Prince, and a return home to a romantically-inclined Ghensie. *Oh,* how he felt a need for that kind of evening. He pictured his return home: he would embrace Ghensie with both passion and affection, give Bekim a couple of twirls around the living room; Ghensie would be working on her watches, Bekim's attention would gradually scamper away, and Jeremy would open an Affligem and sink onto the sofa with the novel he was reading in Italian. Then dinner, and...

A horn honked, causing him to jerk back. He had just begun to cross the little ribbon of street that separated rue du Temple from his own rue de Turbigo, neglecting to check the miniscule stoplight in the middle of the crossing. Jeremy watched the Renault station wagon advance through its own green light, then looked left again before crossing. And in that one-second interval he caught sight of something else.

Putain de merde! The *mec* on the other side of rue du Temple was watching Jeremy while wiping rain off his spectacles with his scarf. Now he snapped them back on, turned on his heel, and started back towards Place de la République.

No, you don't—not today! Jeremy wiped rain off his face and struck after him, crossing against a red light, with more angry horns trumpeting at him from both sides. At a jog, his bag banging against his side, he chased the spectacled stalker who maintained a striding retreat towards the Place. At the end of rue du Temple he turned right towards the métro station, and before Jeremy could catch up, the bastard was halfway down the stairs. Jeremy plunged down after him, tried to take the stairs two at a time, but was stymied by his bag and the slick steps. The *mec's* coattails flapped around the corner into the station.

A station that teemed with commuters. By the time Jeremy spotted his prey it was to see him inserting his ticket into a turnstile slot. Against the strap of his bag, Jeremy struggled to unbutton his coat and extract his transport pass, while the *mec's* ticket sprang up and the turnstile revolved. When Jeremy's turn came to insert his Carte Orange ticket, the ticket failed, the word *annulé* blinking on the little screen. Jeremy swore and tried his ticket again, and this time the bar turned to let him through, only to have his vision blocked by more swarms of commuters. Which way did he go? Jeremy couldn't tell, started to merge with the crowd heading towards Line 3, then stopped and let his arms flop to his sides. There were nine lines running through this station; how would he find the bastard, and if he did catch him, what would he do in the confines of a cramped, public métro platform? He envisioned the same scenario if he followed him onto a train. Was he willing to chase the piece of shit all over Paris? Either way, it didn't matter. He had lost him.

He fumed all the way up the station stairs, only to arrive at the top with rain now cascading on him. All he wanted to do was get home, flop down on his sofa and guzzle a beer.

Still, Iliescu would hear about this!

Chapter 26

No, Iliescu *would not* hear about the tail. At least not from Jeremy. Yes, he wanted to confront the fucker, fling in his face that he had spotted yet another of his inept employees, and demand that the shadowing stop. But then, if Iliescu just laughed, telling Jeremy he would now have to teach another slacker a lesson...?

No, he repeated to himself as he climbed his building's stairs, he would keep this to himself but remain watchful. He understood that a character like Iliescu trusted no one, including, and perhaps especially, his new hires. He had ordered a tail on Ghensie that could still be ongoing, so why dwell on the inevitable? Iliescu might even mean for Jeremy to know he was being shadowed. ("Don't get too *comfy* or think you can take liberties!") He would never wriggle out of Iliescu's claws until Rébert decided it was time to close in on the trafficker and shut down the source of the forgeries. And until Jeremy got cozy enough with Iliescu to identify the source, he would have to tolerate being tailed and endure what for now seemed a vicious cycle. Gritting his teeth in distaste, he stopped, drew a calming breath, and resumed his climb.

By the time he entered his apartment, he was feeling more weary than angry, He hung his wet bag, coat and cap on hooks next to the door before moving on to the living room, where Bekim was playing a game with Grizzly and his cars. He looked up to say "*salut,*" and "Do you want to play?"

"Maybe later," Jeremy told him, crossing directly to the kitchen to get a well-deserved beer. He found Ghensie packing up her watches for the day.

"All finished?" he asked, after giving her a peck on the cheek.

"For now. I might work a little more after you leave for work."

Jeremy nodded absently as he retrieved a bottle of Affligem from the fridge and popped off its top with an opener, both of which he left on the counter.

Ghensie came up behind him, scooped up the cap and put it in the trash bin under the sink, then returned the bottle opener to its drawer.

"Right," said Jeremy with a brief smile. He was tired. He fetched a glass and poured out his ale. "I think I'll read for a while."

"And I'll start dinner in a while. Don't worry," she said, a slight edge to her tone, "it'll be ready well before you have to leave."

"Who says I'm worried?" Jeremy set down his glass. When Ghensie shrugged and turned away, he caught her arm, pulled her back, and took her into the embrace he'd imagined before setting off after the bastard with the glasses. But she felt like a sack of cement in his arms. "What's wrong," he asked, releasing her.

A second shrug suggested "nothing" and "everything." She surveyed him with a skeptical eye. "You look exhausted. You're getting up too early to go out, and you don't come home until late."

True, but his RG hours had always been irregular, and now especially with Iliescu intent on getting photos of Vadim and his girl at all hours.

Ghensie was right, though. He wasn't getting enough sleep and he could feel it in the dull ache behind his eyes, even in his facial muscles as he smiled at Ghensie and said decisively, "I won't be going out early tomorrow." He took her hand and kissed it. "Come and sit in the living room with me. We can look at your new *Pariscope* together."

Glancing at her watches, almost all of which were packed up, she nodded.

Before settling on the sofa, Jeremy removed his monthly transport pass from his peacoat (the *Carte Orange* that had momentarily malfunctioned at the métro turnstile) and set it on the entryway table next to his keys. He would be switching to his overcoat tonight. On the table he found a note he had overlooked when he came in.

"Haley called," was written in neat cursive.

Jeremy glanced towards the kitchen, then picked it up. As he gazed at the name, a fresh breeze seemed to waft over him and he felt a feathery lift in his mood. Haley had been thinking about him, just as he had been thinking about her, not long ago. They had shared a love of jazz, of the cinema, of each other's bodies...Then his thoughts returned to Ghensie. He pocketed the note and walked slowly to the living room.

Ghensie was standing at the window, gazing at a rain that now danced in spurts against the window. His glass of beer sat on a coaster on the coffee table, next to the little Pariscope magazine. He thanked her for bringing his beer, and when she didn't respond he watched her for a moment longer. Finally he lowered himself onto the sofa, took a long sip of the Affligem, and picked up the Pariscope.

"Any good movies this week?" he asked casually.

Slowly Ghensie turned and came to sit next to him, her expression distant, speculative. "I haven't checked," she said, just as distantly.

"Well, there's always something to see in this city."

Instead of picking up the magazine she continued

gazing ahead, with the same odd look that he wished she would explain.

He thought of Haley again, how up until a couple of months ago they had seemed to understand each other pretty well. Then again, Haley was a thirty-three-year-old American expat, not a twenty-seven-year-old migrant on the run with a child. At twenty-seven, Haley had already been ensconced in Paris with her trust-fund money.

He didn't want to compare the two. And he was too tired to address Ghensie's mood and how it could relate to her having exchanged a few halting words with Haley on the phone. He took another swallow of beer, then set it down and let his head rest back against the sofa cushions. He had just closed his eyes for a second when he heard the flutter of pages being turned; when he opened them Ghensie was laying the Pariscope back on the table.

"You probably need rest and space," she said.

He lifted his head. She spoke in a matter-of-fact tone, but he still caught the discontent in her eyes.

"You're too burdened with all this," she went on, a hand indicating the living room, including Bekim who was crashing his cars into Grizzly, the bear kicking them back, naturally by way of human hand.

Jeremy looked back at Ghensie. In the kitchen he had found her edgy. Now she suggested he needed space and rest. "Maybe just rest," he said.

"Of course," she said, looking away.

He sat up and wrapped an arm around her. "But as for *space*, please don't worry. No matter what happens, no matter *who* calls (and here he hoped she understood he meant Iliescu as well as Haley), you need to know I won't abandon you. Remember, we're in this together here."

She gave his hand a slight squeeze and nodded.

Jeremy glanced back at Bekim, who was now rolling his cars more slowly. He peered up, caught Jeremy's eye, then bent back to his game.

The boy's French was improving at a galloping rate. Did he know what *abandon* meant? Could he have gleaned his own little idea of "commitment" from Jeremy's words?

Jeremy gave Ghensie a smile, then relaxed against the cushions again, deciding there and then he would sleep in tomorrow. After staring ahead for a moment longer, Ghensie sat back too. For a long while neither of them spoke.

From the floor resumed the explosive sound of crashing cars and then a little-boy roar from Grizzly: "You can't hurt me!"

While Jeremy's thoughts trickled back to Haley.

The next morning Jeremy roused only when hearing Ghensie's delicate steps and light clinks and chinks in the kitchen. He had the day ahead of him, it was only nine o'clock, and just maybe he could capture a shot of Vadim and his girl. It was Saturday, and if they'd spent the night together, the couple might go out for a late café breakfast.

He left just after ten o'clock, both cameras in the bag on his shoulder and no tails behind him—at least none he could perceive. *But should he care, anyway?*

No, he felt good. On his way to the métro he stopped at a phone booth, slipped inside and dialed Haley's number. As the rings added up, he wondered what he would say if a male voice—Luc's voice—answered. Would he grudgingly identify himself before asking for Haley? Better to hang up? He almost did so now, when suddenly the ringing ceased, replaced by "Allô?"

"Haley..." Jeremy pronounced in English, with

relief.

"Ah, you called back..."

"Of course. It's good to hear your voice."

"Yours too." She gave a nervous little laugh. "In fact, I was surprised it wasn't you who answered when I called yesterday..."

"...Well, I've got a roommate." And when he was met with silence, "Just someone and her son I'm helping."

"Someone and her son." The tone was just shy of skeptical. "She sounds foreign."

"Albanian—a long story, but it has to do with a job I did for the RG. This woman is trying to gain residency here, but she's been harassed by men from her country." He stopped—didn't want to say too much or too little. "A complicated story...But I can't believe so much time's passed since we last spoke."

"I hope you don't think that's my fault." The response was neutral but immediate, and Jeremy knew she was right.

"No," he said. "I've been wanting to talk to you...thinking about you..."

"It's been over a month..."

In the glass phone booth Jeremy's nod was reflected back to him. "I know, I've had some jobs lately."

"RG jobs?"

"Yeah." It was good to speak English again, to talk more openly than he did with almost anyone else. "And you...things status quo?"

"More or less. No big changes. I just wanted to check on you."

Check on him: code for *to see if we're still friends*? "I've missed you," he said. "Was hoping we might get together for coffee, or something."

"I'd like that. When it's convenient for both of us."

The line went quiet again. Then Haley said, "Should I leave it to you to call back?"

"Yeah. Great. I'll do that."

When they hung up, Jeremy felt strangely light-headed. They would finally meet again. Maybe Haley had distanced herself from Luc. But what did it matter, as long as she didn't expect the full rundown on Ghensie. *Ghensie*. Where was he going in all this? Were Haley and he both capable of falling for two different people? He didn't understand the mystery of it and wasn't exactly comfortable with his double longing. But *longing* he did have, the need to at least see Haley in the flesh and get the measure of her now.

He left the phone booth, checking his watch. It was almost ten-thirty and who knew if he would find Vadim at Bardot's? The métro sped him to Place de la Nation, where he got off and made his way to the café across from Bardot's place. He ordered a pot of tea, a beverage he could prolong during a stakeout and which he didn't mind abandoning if he had to leave in a hurry. Naturally, he paid up front, then sat back and let his thoughts glide from Haley to Ghensie and back, keeping an eye on the building across from him and a hand near his camera bag.

He didn't expect anything, but chance dropped a gift in his lap half an hour later when the door of the building opened and out stepped Vadim and Bardot, both bundled against the cold. Instantly Jeremy was on his feet, towing his bag to the door and readying his cameras. Vadim and Bardot were chatting on the sidewalk.

First, Jeremy took out the camera whose film was destined for Iliescu, and which the Romanian wanted delivered undeveloped. He stepped out into the recessed entrance of the café and took two shots. Then he did the same with the second camera—the photos for Rébert. The two lovers lingered, and Jeremy switched back to the first camera, positioning it against his eye. And lo and behold, Vadim and Bardot kissed. *Snap, snap, snap.* Jeremy couldn't get enough. Then the two broke apart, and after beaming at each other, turned and walked separate ways, Jeremy's eyes darting triumphantly between them.

Chapter 27

The job for Iliescu was finished, proof of Vadim's infidelity coiled in Jeremy's camera like a sleeping snake. He could finally go back to the Romanian, hand him the film in the Nikon, and if only he could say *Now please confide in me*! With that cynical thought, he struck out for the Nation métro station. Bardot was strolling a block ahead of him, so he kept his distance, admiring the seductive spring and sway in her step. She was probably on her way to catch her own train, he thought, before watching her head around the square. Shifting his bag crossways over his chest, Jeremy fell into step after her—just a touch of curiosity to satisfy, one final itch to scratch. And he smiled at his good instincts when Bardot arrived at the very same address as before, rang the bell, and was buzzed in. Not, however, before tossing a glance behind her.

He waited ten minutes. Vadim had gone his separate way, so someone else in there waited for Bardot, and she clearly wanted to meet that person in absolute privacy. Another affair? The cheater Vadim cuckolded in his turn? Hardly a novel idea, but still one that might interest Iliescu.

Jeremy was about to leave, when the door to the building swung open and out stepped Bardot, setting off again. Ten minutes: hardly time for a tryst or much of anything else, so what was she up to that excluded Vadim? Jeremy had no idea, but as she made her way back towards Place de la Nation he felt a magnet pulling him after her.

Once more he embarked on an extended métro trek, riding in the carriage behind Bardot's. He stationed himself next to the door where he could lean out discreetly to check whether she got off. After fourteen stations, she finally did—at Montparnasse, only to engage Line 13 going south. By then Jeremy was sure she would end her journey at Porte de Vanves, the last stop before leaving Paris proper, where he had followed Vadim.

And indeed, there she surfaced, Jeremy on her heels, crossing the street and clipping down two blocks, where she entered the same courtyard as Vadim had. And where Jeremy in turn had been followed by the bespectacled *mec*. He looked around—no sign of Iliescu's hire—and after twenty minutes of pacing up and down the street, asking himself what could be going on besides an extramarital affair, Jeremy muttered a couple of minor curses and walked back to the Porte de Vanves station. On the métro wall map he verified the most efficient route home. It would take close to an hour, back up Line 13...

He paused, was reminded of the Pernety station on the line, located in the neighborhood where Ghensie obtained her watches. He had meant to check the place out, get his own measure of the French couple who not only sold tools but transacted under the table to have pocket watches finished. Now seemed a convenient opportunity.

The rue Pernety comprised three short blocks, with only one hardware shop, and in no time Jeremy was entering the world of tools, chains, wire, everything he expected to see in a neighborhood *quancaillerie*. The quarters were typically cramped, shelves stuffed to overflowing, but he found no middle-aged couple manning the counter. Instead, Jeremy exchanged *bonjours* with a lanky youth sporting dark stubble and a wool scarf wound round his neck in a fashionable knot. He couldn't have been older than twenty-five...perhaps the couple's son.

Jeremy gave another glance around the store and asked about padlocks.

"*Bien sûr*," answered the clerk in a dry monotone. Behind his counter he was leafing through a car magazine and indicated the location with a casual wave of the hand. Whether Jeremy actually found what he was looking for didn't seem to concern him. But Jeremy did find the padlocks, and edging sideways down the narrow aisle, he chose the cheapest model and returned to the counter.

"Wasn't there a couple running this store?" he asked casually.

The young clerk snatched up the lock and without looking at Jeremy said, "They're not here." *Sullen kid, resents holding down the fort*, thought Jeremy in his most charitable judgment.

He paid for the lock, said *merci* and *bonjour*, and received a mumbled *au revoir* in return. Back on the métro, he wasn't sure how to size up the situation. He wouldn't mention it to Ghensie. He had sensed nothing untoward, just a skinny, grumpy kid who clearly didn't like his job—anything but a phenomenon. If Ghensie dealt with him from time to time, she never mentioned it, and therefore neither would he...for now.

As the train approached the Saint-Lazare station he joined the crowd at the door. A transfer to Line 3 and he'd be home in twenty minutes. Not, however, before he stopped at a phone booth to call Iliescu. He looked forward to handing over the film, and since he was still no closer to gleaning the source of the passport scheme, Jeremy decided it was time to go out on a limb.

Two afternoons later he met the trafficker in his new café of business off the rue Poissonnière. In the Café Bonne Nouvelle Jeremy placed the roll of film on the table and slid it towards Iliescu. "This should give you all you need."

"The two of them kissing, eh?" Iliescu's smirk lasted all of a second, then his expression turned serious.

"In front of her place," Jeremy confirmed.

Iliescu nodded.

He should be congratulating me, thought Jeremy, *instead of peering at me like I'm not being straight with him.* Jeremy thought of his chase after the spectacled man, having caught him in flagrant spying. Surely the *mec* wouldn't have reported his failure to Iliescu, if he was indeed Iliescu's man...

At last Iliescu broke his stare. "As far as payment..."

Jeremy's thoughts snapped back to the decision he'd made before coming here. "Put it towards a passport."

"For your Albanian girl."

"That's right."

Iliescu seemed satisfied with Jeremy's choice. He picked up the roll of film and gave it couple of shakes. "If this is as good as you say—fifteen hundred francs. Which means you've paid for half of the passport."

Unable to suppress his surprise Jeremy responded with two hesitant nods.

"What?" said Iliescu, amused. "I pay well for good work. You probably spent quite a few hours on this assignment. And even if you only put in three, a *kiss* is worth...well, a lot."

"And to earn the rest?" Jeremy asked.

"Depends." Iliescu pocketed the film and sat back. "Still want tame assignments?"

"Any more photos I could take?"

Iliescu shook his head. "Not for now. He sniffed couple of times. "But I've got some tailing you could do...still, I hate to see your talent go to waste on small stuff." He let the words hang there, this time free of sarcasm. "Or," he resumed, "you could take care of a little matter concerning a guy who owes me money."

Jeremy groaned to himself. He thought about Bardot and her sketchy movements about town, suspicious enough to perhaps warrant a reward of confidence from Iliescu—or maybe not...

"Having a hard time deciding?" Iliescu leaned in, the same quizzical glint in his eye that suggested more than simple curiosity.

Jeremy gazed back. *Yes, he was*. And he had other concerns. "If we have the passport made," he stated firmly, "I don't want my girlfriend involved."

Iliescu made a mock choking sound. "But she *will* be involved. Who's the passport *for*, the pope?" Finally a dose of sarcasm.

"I *mean*," Jeremy countered, "that she's not to know where it comes from. And don't even ask to interview her."

"Calm down, Winters. I'll only need her photo when the time comes."

Jeremy nodded. Of course Iliescu would ask for a passport photo of Ghensie, but Jeremy would not let the game get that far. More money remained to be earned to pay for the passport. *Jobs*: which to choose, shadowing one person or roughing up another?

He sighed to himself and chose the latter—the better to gain Iliescu's admiration.

"So who needs leaning on?" he asked.

Rébert asked the same question when he and Jeremy next met and Jeremy handed him the second roll of film.

"Some guy who owes Iliescu money," Jeremy told him.

Rébert looked down at his espresso, taking his time to stir in the sugar. They were sitting in the basement café of the FNAC mega book and record store in the rue de Rennes. Jeremy had arrived early, spending an hour browsing the store before finally taking the escalator down to the *sous-sol*. No tails, he'd assured Rébert. In fact, apart from a young couple comparing music cassettes at their table, Jeremy and Rébert were alone in the little café.

Rébert finally let his spoon clink against his saucer and looked back up at Jeremy. "I know you don't like pushing people around for the hell of it, and I don't want risky violence like last time..."

"But I need to do whatever will win Iliescu's trust."

Rébert hesitated before giving a sober nod. "Just don't get in the way of a knife again, and let's hope we can wrap this up soon." Rébert blinked, seemed on the verge of saying something else, then gave a final nod. He looked worried. And Jeremy was glad.

The target this time was a sorry specimen, Jeremy concluded, shaking his head at the photograph. A married man, a family man with a decent job, but who had a thirst that could never be quenched and who would probably end up drowning himself in the process: he was an inveterate gambler, with a penchant for the horses.

So, it appeared Iliescu was also a loan-shark. The image, thought Jeremy, fit him even better than trafficker of passports. Slick hair, shiny suits, sharkish grins following sardonic comments. The obsessive, oily leverage he accumulated on everyone who had any-thing do to with him. Iliescu was a greasy roach that needed to be flattened.

Jeremy studied the photo of the man who owed Iliescu money. Marcel Coste: a turkey neck, weak eyebrows that arched like a woman's, dark droopy eyes that registered sleepy surprise at being caught in the gleam of a camera's flash. *Pauvre con*, pathetic schmuck, he would likely never escape Iliescu's jaws. Jeremy would need to stoke the distaste he felt in order to do the job.

He turned the photo over, where on the back Iliescu had jotted down both Coste's work and home addresses. Jeremy would not be going to the latter. The embattled *mec* managed a bistro near the Normandie cinema on the Champs-Élysées, and according to Iliescu's trackers he sometimes stopped for a movie on the Avenue before going on shift. Probably an interlude of respite, of pure illusory escape.

So having received information on Coste's work hours, he commenced surveillance of the strip of the Champs-Élysées nearest the restaurant. And, Jeremy had to admit (for in general he avoided the teeming avenue), there was plenty to watch: meandering tourists of every color and shape, age and ethnicity, the clatter of heels and swell of chatter, not quite eclipsed by the whoosh and roar of traffic next to the wide sidewalks. Litter here, trash bin trawlers there, a busker offering low-key relief from glitzy storefronts, and all overseen by the imposing presence of the Arc de Triomphe.

Jeremy stationed himself near the George V métro station, only a couple of blocks down from the looming monument. Arriving a little over two hours before the start of Marcel Coste's shift, he killed time window-gazing (sunglasses on the Avenue about the same price as a night in the Ritz), checking out the newspaper kiosks (mayor Jacques Chirac and his big plans for the

Avenue's overhaul), pausing awhile to listen to the New Orleans style clarinet player (his music case speckled with coins, including Jeremy's own copper-colored ten-franc piece). Finally he stopped for tea at a café within view of the métro station (idly confirming that the opposite side of the Champs-Élysées sported sparse foot traffic, matched by fewer stores and cafés due, Jeremy had always heard, to its shaded exposure).

For four days straight he repeated the afternoon routine, only to observe Marcel Coste come gliding up the métro escalator around four o'clock and make his way zigzagging through the throng to his bistro. Jeremy had taken to reading his paperback Italian novel while sipping his Assam tea, when on the fifth day, just after one-thirty, he almost missed Coste walking right past his restaurant. Jeremy jumped up, jostling his table, and strode after him, right up to the wide, open entrance to the Normandie cinema. There he stuffed his novel into the inside pocket of his peacoat, then gave a determined squeeze of the switchblade in the outside one. The knife he had snatched off the Moldovan Rusu would prove useful today.

Chapter 28

The cinema Normandie had a long entrance hall, and by the time Jeremy arrived at the ticket counter behind Coste, his hand was tense in his peacoat pocket as it fingered the switchblade. After sneaking it out of the saxophone case at home, he'd practiced snapping it open and squeezing it shut—in the bathroom, of all places, the only area of privacy he could count on in his flat. The release button was small, the role the blade would play in his strategy, risky but essential.

Coste bought a ticket. Jeremy did the same, barely registering the name of the movie he had paid to see. Coste stopped at the snack bar to buy a box of Dupont d'Isigny, Jeremy standing to the side, pretending to check something in his small address book. When Coste crossed into the auditorium, Jeremy followed, waiting at the back while Coste chose a seat—thankfully not towards the front. Jeremy waited another five minutes until the lights lowered and the ads rose on the screen; after that, another five minutes until the previews started. Then he walked down to Coste's row, excused himself as he made Coste rise so he could pass, only to sit down next to him.

Coste gave Jeremy an irritated grunt, no doubt thinking, *You make me get up just to sit right by me?* But in the dark, relieved only by slashes of glint from the screen, Jeremy was in silhouette, unrecognizable from his presence in the lobby. Coste turned back to the previews, settled himself more comfortably, and popped a candy into his mouth. As Jeremy had eased past, he could sense the slightness of Coste's build, how he could push him back in his seat with the heel of his hand.

Jeremy glanced at the two seats between Coste and the aisle, crossing his fingers that they would remain vacant. No one sat behind them.

Coste flipped another candy into his mouth. The sound from the previews blared deafeningly. Jeremy considered the time almost right, if not for the stragglers who continued to arrive. He waited for the movie to start, the movie whose name meant nothing to him. A movie that now crept onto the screen with little noise. Remaining stragglers found their seats. The perimeter around Jeremy and Coste stayed clear.

Then percussion filled the air, followed by heavy electric guitar—good cover noise, Jeremy judged. He gave the switchblade in his pocket a little squeeze. On the screen a gang was now stalking the streets at night, leaving Jeremy and Coste well covered in the murky shadows of the auditorium. The introduction credits drifted away, the gang now breaking into an establishment, neon light coloring their brutish faces blue. A man in the upstairs apartment hears noise below, loads a gun to protect his store.

Jeremy looked at Coste: not the kind of film he would expect the beleaguered *mec* to choose, hardly a relaxing escape from Iliescu's tightening noose.

The police arrive and guns explode into the dark neon blue.

Jeremy's adrenaline spiked. It was now or never. He pulled out the switchblade, hit the button, and pressed the blade against Coste's ribs. "Don't move. Don't make a sound or I'll slice you and no one will hear you squeal or notice you slump dead." With his left hand Jeremy reached around and gripped Coste's shoulder, and felt it wither under his touch. "We need to talk. So I want you to stand up slowly and make your way back out of the hall and into the men's room."

"But...?" Coste's quivering objection barely reached Jeremy's ears, swamped as they were by police sirens on the screen, gunfire, glass erupting, gangsters grunting and screaming.

Jeremy nudged the knife another millimeter. "It's not good to owe Cornel Iliescu money. Now, if you want to live to see the end of this film, get up and do as you're told. *Slowly*," Jeremy repeated, clamping down on Coste's shoulder.

As Coste began to rise, Jeremy felt him shrink under his grip. "Don't try to run," he warned, "because I'll catch you. Someone will always catch you. Now keep your mouth shut and move."

They made their way down the aisle, pressed together, Jeremy careful not to trip on Coste's heels. They reached the door, Jeremy opened it, and they passed into the cinema corridor. The door eased closed and they were bathed in silence.

One hand on Coste's shoulder, the other holding the blade to his ribs, Jeremy walked him to the men's room, hardly needing to worry as Coste had gone white and weak-kneed. Inside, Jeremy quickly verified they were alone, then forced Coste into a stall and locked the two of them in.

Keeping the blade trained on Coste's belly, Jeremy gave a cynical look and stated the obvious: "I hope you've got the rest of Iliescu's money."

Coste drew a long shaky breath and exhaled in the same manner. "I still need more time." He winced, and the fear in his face couldn't have been more extreme if he had been facing the guillotine.

Merde, Jeremy swore to himself. Now he would have to turn up the toughness. He squared his shoulders and gave Coste his most incinerating frown, relying on his bloodshot left eye to heighten the menace. He pushed Coste so that he almost fell onto the toilet. "You lousy shit. Don't you care about your family, your wife and kids?"

Coste evidently did, for his lower lip went slack and as he closed his eyes a shudder rippled his shoulders. When his eyes opened again, they were wide in supplication. In a strong, determined whisper, he said, "I'd kill myself for my family, if I knew you all would stop."

Jeremy slapped his left hand on his hip, his lip curling in disgust. "How heroic. You'd go that far but you won't stop gambling. How the fuck do you explain that?"

Jeremy was about to give Coste another shove when the door to the restroom opened and someone walked in. Jeremy clamped a hand over Coste's mouth and lifted the blade's tip to his neck. Both men held their breath, Coste rising onto tiptoes, while they waited for the explosive rush of a flushing toilet. Then the splattering of water in the sink and the clanging of the rolling towel dispenser. And finally, the thud of the closing door.

Jeremy let out a breath and lowered the knife back to Coste's quivering belly. "*Answer me!* How the hell do you account for what a miserable fuck-up you are?" Jeremy's question was sincere, as he had drawn on a visceral repulsion at such weakness and stupidity, plus anger that the *mec's* mess had become his own.

Coste lowered his eyes and gave a doleful shake of his head. Looking back up he inhaled haltingly, then took a half step forward to meet Jeremy's knife. Its point dented his shirt. His eyes swelled wider, a half-crazed stare filling the stall. "If you kill me," he said, his voice surprisingly firm, "will Iliescu stop? Will he spare my family?"

Jeremy felt an urge to recoil, but he was already backed against the stall door. He withdrew the blade a fraction as he gaped in awe at the insane bastard. But Coste wrapped his hands around Jeremy's and pulled the knife closer, the tip of the blade slipping into the gap in his shirt against his skin.

"Step aside," Jeremy yelled, nausea clawing at him. Coste's face was tense as a drum, his eyes still frozen wide in his plea. Jeremy yelled again. "I said move away from me!"

Coste finally shook himself from his nightmarish trance and stepped back against the stall's side wall.

"I want you to disappear," Jeremy continued, shock and revulsion magnifying his hard and hostile tone. "And so does Iliescu." He waved the blade at Coste. "We never want to see you again."

Coste's face slackened, then contorted into a grimace. "The money..."

Jeremy drew a stabilizing breath and released his words in menacing staccato. "We're cutting you loose. You're a sick fuck and we want nothing more to do with you. So leave and never, I mean *never*, come near us again. Or I *promise*, I'll slice you open from your throat to your dick." Jeremy unlocked the door and threw it open, stepping out of the stall with his blade still aimed at Coste. "Now get out!"

Coste left the stall, head bowed, and started towards the door. Then he stopped and turned writhingly around. "I can't...can't hold it any longer."

Jeremy's eyes raked him from chin to crotch. *Lucky he hasn't pissed himself already.*
He jerked his head towards the urinals and Coste quickly crossed over to them. As soon as Coste's back was turned, Jeremy folded the switchblade, tucked it into his pocket, and strode out of the room—out of the

cinema and down into the métro, where he hopped onto a train that couldn't take him far enough away from the Normandie. He still tasted the stain of nausea, smelled Coste's terror-stricken sweat. Couldn't get those wide gulping eyes out of his head. Hoped his own distasteful, brutish behavior had shaken some kind of sense into the man. As for Iliescu, Jeremy wasn't worried. Inside his closet, in the breast pocket of his damaged bomber jacket, along with the Martin Duroc passport, lay an envelope containing the entire sum owed by Coste as quoted by Iliescu. Courtesy of RG Agent Rébert. Jeremy couldn't wait to slap it on the table under the bastard's nose.

Shelling out the money hadn't pleased Rébert, though he recognized his own part in directing Jeremy to dive deeper into Iliescu's organization. "Let's hope for a breakthrough soon," he'd said, with a nod that left no mistake that the "let's" meant Jeremy.

As for Iliescu, the cash came as a mild surprise. That was how it struck Jeremy as he sat across from him in the Café Bonne Nouvelle the next day.

"It didn't take you long..." Iliescu commented, arching a curious eyebrow.

"A week," Jeremy confirmed, "with some not-so-subtle pressure."

"Well, good." Briskly Iliescu scooped up the envelope and filed it in his jacket pocket. "You think he'll be back for more?"

"He'd be a fool." Jeremy conjured the memory of a quaking Coste. "When I mentioned his family he almost pissed himself. Talked about suicide. Wanted me to do him in right then and there. I think you're well rid of him."

"And *should* I be thankful to be rid of him?" Iliescu wore his crooked, contentious smile; he seemed back to normal compared to their last meeting.

"In my opinion, yes. He's too unstable, could have a nervous breakdown and end up babbling the whole story in some psych unit."

"Mm." Iliescu smoothed back his hair, seemed to mull this over as if considering choices on a menu. "You could be right," he finally said, giving a dismissive shrug.

Jeremy let out a long, silent breath. When his glass of ale arrived he wanted to guzzle it down in relief. "And the passport? How close am I?"

"The passport, *bien sûr*." Iliescu sniffed a couple of times, his eyes darting to the bar and back. "You've earned quite a few points with this job," he said, patting his jacket pocket. "Sixty thousand francs I've recovered, thanks to you. Thing is, I'm going to be changing forgers. Having trouble with my usual person."

Jeremy leaned in. "Something I can help with?"

Iliescu grunted back. "In a way you already have." When Jeremy's brows rose with interest, Iliescu just shook his head wryly and waved an end to the discussion. "For now we'll take a break. I'll let you know when there's anything more I need."

"But I *will* get the passport...?"

"Yes, you've nearly earned it."

"I want it done right," Jeremy stressed. "It's got to be as good as my own."

Iliescu gave him an icy look. "I don't contract bad work."

"I just want to make sure I get a good product, since you're having problems." Jeremy eased back and took a sip of beer. "I can lean on someone if necessary."

Iliescu looked amused. "Developing a taste for hands-on work, eh?" He nodded. "Just hang on. I'll let you know what I decide soon enough."

Jeremy left the café, his thoughts a blizzard of excitement and confusion. *What was going on with the forger? How could he get more information out of Iliescu? And how in hell had he, Jeremy, already helped in the matter?*

Despite the riddle—even because of it—he felt good, sensed progress in the making. He inhaled a big draught of cold air, and just before ducking down into the métro he glanced back towards the café. His smile lasted all of a second. And then his face fell. The stalking *mec* with the glasses stood watching him from across the street. As Jeremy met his eyes, the man tapped a finger to his forehead in what looked like a salute.

Chapter 29

Jeremy couldn't believe it. Was the spectacled *mec* inviting a repeat of last time's chase? He had appeared at Jeremy's meeting place with Iliescu—what a waste of time and money. Rooted to his spot on the sidewalk, Jeremy watched his stalker turn and walk away, away from Jeremy and away from Iliescu's café. Jeremy lingered another few seconds, frowning in indecision, until finally his feet started moving down the métro stairs. Something wasn't right, but he couldn't spend time trying to decipher it now.

Iliescu's riddle took precedence. Supposedly Jeremy had helped with the forger problem. How? And what was the problem in the first place? As Jeremy made his way home, his thoughts sifted through the jobs Iliescu had assigned him—a total of only three, with two of the three seemingly straightforward. The Coste assignment couldn't have been more clear-cut. Jeremy tasted nausea just thinking about it. In the case of the Moldovan Rusu, Jeremy had punished failure as well as proved his suitability for Iliescu's organization. That wasn't to say, however, that Rusu was everything he seemed. Who knew the extent of his service to Iliescu? *Past* service, at any rate, with Iliescu having dismissed him over two weeks ago—*presumably*. So, ticking off a third finger left Vadim, and what did Jeremy know about that character other than his romantic and blackmailable entanglement? Vadim... perhaps he warranted further investigation.

Jeremy's métro train pulled into the République

station, and as he made his way towards the exit he was reminded of his humiliating counter-pursuit of the spectacled stalker. How everything had worked for the bastard while conspiring against Jeremy, from Jeremy's clumsy camera bag to the malfunctioning of his *Carte Orange*.

On his way out of the station he grimaced at the turnstiles on the entrance side. Not that glitches didn't occur with regular tickets, but the bastard had been lucky while Jeremy got screwed. He wondered how long this mocking stalker had been in Paris, since he was still using regular métro tickets versus the much more economical *Carte Orange*. Not only residents benefitted from the monthly pass but also people on extended stays in the city, since a two-week pass could be acquired as well. The guy might be one of Iliescu's new recruits from Romania or Moldova. *New to the city?*

Maybe. As he climbed the stairs to his flat, the pesky thought wouldn't subside. Even Ghensie had a *Carte Orange* and she hadn't been here a month. When he entered the flat and kissed her in greeting, a shadow of foreboding passed through him that continued to follow him about the house. Finally he sat down at the kitchen table and asked Ghensie pointblank if she had sensed the presence of someone following her recently.

"*Sensed* someone following me?" she asked, looking up from the watch she was working on.

"Well," Jeremy said, with a nervous clearing of his throat, "I mean if you'd noticed someone following you, I assume you'd tell me..."

Ghensie laid her watch on the table, alarm creeping into her eyes. "Jeremy, what's going on?"

Nothing, he hoped. Things had been nice so far, Ghensie a good sport despite his reticence concerning his private work, and in the face of calls from Iliescu and Haley. The hint of hackles raised after Haley's call, the little flare of jealousy, he had even found endearing. He wanted none of this changed, let alone threatened from outside.

He leaned in, and gathering his calmest voice, said, "Lately someone's been following me."

Ghensie flinched and stiffened. "*Who?*"

"That's just it, I don't know...could have something to do with those photos I was paid to take."

"Your *detective* work..." Ghensie sat back, her frown revealing not only skepticism but apprehension.

Jeremy nodded. "The work's nothing dangerous, but I just wanted to check with you, in case..." He halted, conflicted over what to say next.

"*In case?*" Ghensie repeated cautiously. Her worried gaze darted from Jeremy to the watches spread out on the table and back again. "I'm not aware of being followed but that doesn't mean anything. What does this person look like?"

"He wears a grey parka jacket with the hood up and rimless glasses, has light eyebrows, could have fair hair..."

"*Fair hair.*" Ghensie's echo seemed a leaden pronouncement. "The second Kosovar, the one you've never seen, has blond hair, but I've never seen him with glasses, and he wasn't wearing a parka in Brussels."

For a moment Jeremy stayed silent.
Glasses in and of themselves didn't mean much. His waiter friend Didier at Le Prince wore them when his eyes felt tired. Even Iliescu donned his spectacles from time to time. And only Rusu was stupid enough to keep wearing the same coat.

He reached across the table to take Ghensie's hand. "Nothing is certain right now. This guy's probably been sent by the man I worked for. I finished the photo job, so now I'll no doubt be left alone." Which wasn't strictly true, given Jeremy's ongoing status as RG operative in Iliescu's operation.

Ghensie shook her head, and Jeremy expected to be questioned about his work again. But he wasn't. Rather she said, "Unless *I* lay eyes on him, we'll never know whether Luan's second partner has come to Paris."

"He wasn't your main stalker in Brussels..."

"He followed me twice, the first time with Luan. No threatening gestures like the bald one that time in the café. Not even any words—just a cold, drilling stare, letting me know that none of them would forget that miserable coin they think I stole."

Jeremy recalled the bald bastard's vicious face, all but plastered against the café window, and that double-headed eagle gesture meant just for him. His jaw clenched as he pictured Luan and the goon jumping him in the park. But neither time had the other Kosovar made an appearance. Perhaps he gave the orders, or maybe he preferred a different style of harassment. A less aggressive *mec,* the cool kind who saved the worst for last...

When their eyes met again, Jeremy sensed Ghensie might be thinking the same thing. "Well," he reasserted firmly, "most likely it's something left over from my photo job—no reason to think it's not."

"The job connected to the Romanian." Ghensie's lips parted, Jeremy feared the voicing of further suspicions, but she only said, "I hope you know what you're doing."

Jeremy sat back and gave a stiff nod. He would have liked to point out the scale of Ghensie's own fine mess, that she was a risk-taker as well—

A sudden bellow came from the bathroom. "*Maman!* Bekim yelled. "There's no toilet paper!"

Ghensie smiled and rolled her eyes. "He's been in

there for half an hour."

With that she got up to attend to the situation, and Jeremy figured it was just as well to keep his peace. As of now the spectacled stalker remained an unknown quantity. Better to concentrate on bringing the Iliescu job to a close, and after that, as he had told Ghensie, the stalker might very well disappear too.

The next day he received a call from Rébert. With the roll of film developed, there was interesting news.

Rébert laid a photograph on the table in the same café where they had last met, in the basement of the FNAC megastore.

"Right," Jeremy said, scanning Vadim and Bardot. "I took the picture across the street from the woman's building. I also took one of them kissing, for Iliescu."

"Good for Iliescu. But this one is better for me, because it shows her straight on."

"*Her?*"

"Manon Lemaire."

"And him?" Jeremy pointed to Vadim.

"As far as his photo goes, he's not in our records."

"But *she's* in your records?"

"That's right. Been arrested for cigarette smuggling."

"*Her?*" Jeremy repeated. *Tiens*, what do you know? Bardot—Manon Lemaire, that is— working in a criminal ring. Manon: the name of the famous protagonist in Abbé Prévost's *Manon Lescaut*. Jeremy had read the eighteenth-century novel in secondary school, and from then on associated the name with women who charm men into submission, render them hopelessly obsessed and driven to ruin.

"But *he's* Iliescu's man," said Jeremy, his finger tapping Vadim's image. "He's the one Iliescu wanted compromising photos of." Jeremy shook his head, perplexed. "Still, I've followed this woman twice now on her own. And both places she went, she looked behind to see if anyone was tailing her."

"Where?"

"An apartment building near Place de la Nation. Then to a courtyard near the Porte de Vanves—Vadim went there a different time. I could follow her again, but if she's got nothing to do with Iliescu..."

"As far as we know, the cigarette smuggling didn't involve him. It was close to ten years ago, and Manon Lemaire, because it was her first offense, didn't do time."

Just like the heroine Manon Lescaut, mused Jeremy. And just like Manon Lescaut, this woman had got started young. "She must be about thirty," he said.

"Thirty-one. And yes, I'd like you to tail her again."

"Another thing," said Jeremy. "Last time I met with Iliescu he said he was having problems with his forger. When I asked if I could help, he said I already had."

"And...?"

"Nothing else for now, but it seems we might be on the right track."

Rébert's smile expressed cautious optimism. "I'm beginning to have hope we'll get that sixty thousand back soon."

Naturally, Rébert meant the sixty thousand francs the RG had given Jeremy to pay off Marcel Coste's gambling debt. Jeremy added his own conspiratorial smile of hope.

So, this modern Manon was a crook (or had been one) and Jeremy had somehow helped Iliescu with his forger problem. By photographing Vadim and Manon/Bardot in a kiss? It seemed the only lead, and Jeremy resigned himself to another stakeout of the woman's place.

This time he would only take his pocket-size camera.

"You're going out early again," Ghensie said, as he was getting ready to leave in the morning. "You *have* finished the photo job…"

"Well," Jeremy answered uneasily. "The photo part, yes."

"But there's more?"

Jeremy gazed about the living room (an automatic if not evasive gesture). Bekim was drawing in the kitchen. "It's complicated," he said. "I haven't been working directly for the Romanian. It's an agency that put me on to him, and they want to know if there's anything else going on with this guy."

"An *agency* now. I know it shouldn't concern me but it makes me wonder what you actually *do*, Jeremy, apart from tending bar. *Tending bar*—that *is* real, isn't it?"

The corners of Jeremy's mouth turned down in exasperation. "Yes, of course it is. Le Prince Blue Note jazz club, Fifth arrondissement, boulevard Saint-Michel, corner of rue Monsieur Le Prince. Would you like to visit me there some time?"

Only a trickle of sarcasm leaked from Jeremy's speech, but it didn't escape Ghensie whose brow was still creased with concern and whose face now flushed red. "If that's an actual invitation," she said, in a tone that quavered to maintain dignity, "I'd love to. But yes, I believe you."

Jeremy could only offer a conciliatory smile. First she had doubted him, now it seemed she believed him, at least about Le Prince. About the other, he wasn't sure. She had cause for skepticism, considering his sketchy movements these past two weeks—almost all of February, really, since the month was now coming to a close. A solid three weeks on the Iliescu job, with no definitive end in sight. He couldn't tell Ghensie about it and neither did he wish to extend his semi-lie about his "detective work." But he knew she was worried, worried about what trouble could befall Bekim and her through association with him, on top of her own entanglements with the underworld devils she knew.

"Listen," he said, giving her hand a squeeze, "on one of my nights off—soon—we'll go out, just the two of us and listen to some jazz at Le Prince. You've introduced me to your Sufi music and I'll do the same with the stuff I enjoy." Noting her features soften, he went on, "As for the other, my detective work, well I report to the police when I need to. So there's no need to worry." Or was there? Her face had tensed again, lips retracting into a line. "Don't worry," he repeated, pulling her into an embrace, one that felt uncomfortably one-sided.

When he released her, she asked him if he would be home in time for her to go fetch more watches. "If not I could always take Bekim with me…"

"No, no need, I'll be back early." She had never before suggested dragging Bekim back and forth across the city on her dodgy watch runs. Yet Jeremy understood her motive today. She worried about Luan and the Kosovars, she felt uncomfortable about what *he* did, and now he had mentioned the police, a two-edged sword at best for immigrants like her. She was testing him. "You just stay put," he stated adamantly. "I'll be back in time."

The last thing he saw when he left was her fragile smile; then the door clicked shut.

Chapter 30

Ghensie's fearful look was still with Jeremy as he descended the stairs and left the building. Since they had been together he couldn't think of a time they'd been truly free of worry or suspicion. Perhaps the night of the Whirling Dervish performance, when Ghensie filled the air around them with not just her spiritual views but an unabashed *joie de vivre*. And he? Jeremy had never been one to let his thoughts and beliefs gush from him, partly due to natural reticence, partly because of the caution that had become second nature for his RG work. He had confided in Ghensie about the destruction of his father's saxophone, though even then he hadn't told the whole story—about Walter's part, and Walter's end. Yet she had done the same back in Brussels—fudging the story of Luan and the Kosovars, waiting to reveal the true magnitude of the problem until he was solidly in her corner...

Merde, it wasn't worth rehashing. Only the present mattered. For all the tangle and knots of worry and suspicion, a line of contentment had been cast to him, and he wanted it to last.

After three hours of stakeout across from Manon/Bardot's building, plus a trip down to the Fourteenth arrondissement to check on the courtyard property at Porte de Vanves, Jeremy headed back home—no sighting of Manon or Vadim. They could be using a car, however inconvenient in central Paris, though they would still have to exit the building to access it.

And when would Iliescu call again? Jeremy wanted to press the bastard to reveal the forgery problem. Hadn't Jeremy provided leverage-quality proof of Vadim's adultery, thereby deserving some trust in return? Or was the cheating even the real issue...

The RG knew nothing about Vadim but plenty about his girl, Manon. With his network of informants, Iliescu too had to know about her cigarette-smuggling past.

Yet it all came back to the photos—photos proving Vadim and Manon's intimacy. So far only Manon had acted suspiciously, with her secret drop-ins to the building in her neighborhood. But something strange was going on between the two, with both Vadim and Manon separately visiting the Porte de Vanves location. How much did Iliescu know about their movements around the city?

Jeremy's train pulled into the Temple station, the end of the line for him and his ruminations, which for now had hit a bang-your-head-against-the-wall impasse. Instead of walking straight home, though, he crossed over to the Monoprix in rue du Temple to buy another toy car for Bekim. Gifts for a child meant as much to the mother, he couldn't help reminding himself, and he wanted back firmly into Ghensie's confidence.

As it was, they barely had time for pecks on the cheek before Ghensie headed out to exchange her watches, her two shoulder bags crisscrossed against her chest. Bekim was on his knees drawing at the living room table when Jeremy slapped the miniature fluorescent-green 1965 Ford Mustang next to his crayons. Whoops of joy and thanks erupted and, as Jeremy had anticipated, he was pulled onto the floor and into a bout of racing and crashing.

It was after four o'clock when Jeremy wondered why Ghensie hadn't returned yet. She must have stopped for some last-minute thing for dinner, he figured, and in that case she would be laden with bags.

He looked at Bekim. "Why don't we go down to the corner and see if *Maman's* on her way, and give her a hand with her bags?"

At the rue du Temple they stationed themselves by the newspaper kiosk next to the métro entrance. Whether Ghensie got off at Temple or République, they would see her coming, even if she were backtracking from the Monoprix. Jeremy's eyes kept flashing from the street to his watch. Bekim started kicking the handrail post at the top of the métro stairs, asking if they could go back home and get his new car. To distract him, Jeremy bought him a Lucky Luke comic book at the kiosk.

"Can't we go home and read it?" the boy asked. "I'm cold."

"Yes we can," Jeremy announced, for at that moment he spied Ghensie marching down rue du Temple, her bags banging at her sides. "Come on," he said, grabbing Bekim's hand. "There's *Maman*."

Maman looked pale and exhausted, and not, Jeremy was to find out, because of her burdensome bags of watches.

"I've seen him," she told Jeremy in the kitchen, once Bekim was ensconced on the sofa with his comic book and car.

Her expression was grave, her voice low, and Jeremy didn't have to guess to whom she referred.

"The guy with the glasses," he stated.

Ghensie returned two grim nods. "The second Kosovar." She gave a shudder. "It took me twice as long to get home trying to lose him."

Jeremy stood rigid. Was she *sure* this was the second Kosovar? He asked whether the man was wearing a hood.

"The hood was pulled back, showing his thin blond hair. I recognized him even through his glasses."

"And you managed to lose him?"

"I think so...I'm not sure..."

"And he didn't try to approach you?"

Ghensie shook her head. "No acknowledgement of me whatsoever. He just followed my same path as if the whole thing was pure coincidence."

No fleeing, no flashing a mock salute as he'd done with Jeremy, but certainly no coincidence. "And Luan and the bald guy...?"

"No sign of them." Ghensie paused, while Jeremy waited for the inevitable: "But they might not be not far off."

No doubt, Jeremy thought. "The guy with the glasses has followed me to this neighborhood," he said. "I should've suspected something of the kind earlier."

Jeremy started to pace while Ghensie stood hugging her arms.

"How could he have found us?" he questioned aloud, to no one in particular and with no expectation of an answer.

Instead, Ghensie reacted as if he had lobbed a dart. "Not from anything *I* did," she answered in desperation, her hands splayed.

"I didn't mean that." Jeremy stopped pacing to put a reassuring hand on her shoulder. "I'm just trying to figure out what could have happened."

He could feel Ghensie relax a bit. "I know," she said. "But as I've said before, my neighbor Sorina is only aware that you're from Paris, and at the pharmacy they don't know anything. I've never mentioned your name to anyone." Ghensie shook her head and looked down at the floor, while Jeremy gazed sightlessly into the distance past her shoulder.

He inhaled deeply, his jaw clenched—it had finally hit him. "The hotel in Brussels."

"What?"

"My hotel near your flat. They had my address." He looked at Ghensie with a frown of resignation. "Not your fault; not anyone's, except the poor bastard desk clerk they probably bullied the information from. It was a shoddy place to begin with," he added with a regretful shake of his head.

"You could call them to find out for sure..."

"Yes, well there's no point now. But," and he hated to have to say this, "now that we've been compromised..."

"We're not safe here," Ghensie finished. "None of us are, including you."

"Listen," he said, "on my own I can handle this guy. Later, if the others show up, we'll see. In the meantime I think you and Bekim should go into hiding again." When Ghensie's stare deepened he added, "I've already been thinking about a back-up plan for this type of event. I'll ask Louise Cholot if you can stay with her for a while."

Ghensie looked doubtful. "It would be a great imposition."

"I don't think she would see it that way. And it's been a long time since Bekim's been there, and back then no one was following me."

Ghensie fell silent, non-committal but ever pensive. "I know this should be a police matter," she finally said, "but..." She gave a helpless lift of her shoulders.

"But what can they do if we don't mention the theft of the coins?" Jeremy completed.

"Without that they wouldn't take me seriously, and with it they would question my honesty."

And detain you for immigration irregularity, Jeremy added to himself, because he hardly needed to remind Ghensie of the stingingly obvious. "And they can't offer protection if a crime hasn't been committed," he said instead. "That's why going to Louise's is the best option for now."

"Are we going to see Louise?" Bekim stood in the doorway, eyes wide and expectant, bright-green Mustang in his hand.

Ghensie's response was a flaccid smile, so Jeremy picked up the slack. *"Mais bien sûr!"* he told the hopeful boy. He glanced at Ghensie with an encouraging nod.

Jeremy didn't rush to phone Louise Cholot. Having convinced Ghensie of the logic of the move, he could now mull over one other option. But first he decided to call the hotel in Brussels, after all. Discover just who had entered the establishment and strong-armed a clerk for information that should have been kept confidential—if that was indeed what had happened.

Introducing himself went smoothly; explaining the anything-but-banal situation was awkward, and when Jeremy finally made his point, a portentous silence followed, then the gradual filling of dead air with hemming and hawing from the clerk.

"Has *anyone* asked for my name and address?" Jeremy repeated, this time in a steely tone. "They would have inquired about a man from Paris who stayed in your hotel during the week of the fifth of February."

The clerk sounded young, his voice barely grown into a baritone, and after another spell of dead air he let out a third nervous sigh. "Well, yes, I suppose something like that did take place...I was told so, anyway."

"Was it one man who came in...two, or three?"

"One...at least that's what I heard."

Or what you witnessed firsthand, Jeremy scoffed to himself, though he couldn't blame the youth for not wanting to admit to breaking hotel regulations; nor could he blame him for collapsing under threats from someone like the bald Kosovar bastard.

"*One*, okay," Jeremy repeated in a milder tone. "Did he have an accent—Eastern European-ish, maybe?"

The clearing of an adolescent-sounding throat: "I suppose so—I mean I'm not sure what kind of accent...but I think he was eastern European, yes..."

"Was he tall, short, wearing glasses, maybe?"

"Not very tall, but he definitely had glasses..." The kid was trying in earnest now. "He didn't look very tough, but the way he talked..."

"You're doing fine," Jeremy said, as if he were a psychology-trained police interrogator. "So he managed to come away with my name and address..."

More dead air on the line. "It's all right," Jeremy reassured, "I'm not going to get you in trouble."

A nervous breath made its way down the line. "I guess he did. I'm sorry."

"Mm," Jeremy reflected. "And I suppose no one reported it to the police."

"I...you see, the boss here..."

"Never mind." Jeremy had his answer: if the incident had been reported in Brussels, the Paris police would likely have been contacted. "Just one more question: do you remember what color hair the guy had?"

"...Blond."

Bien sûr.

Jeremy hung up and went back to the kitchen. Ghensie now had her watch operation set up, though instead of working she was staring off into the distance.

"I called the hotel in Brussels. You were right to suggest it."

"And it was the hotel people who told?"

"Mm-hm. A scared kid behind the desk gave the blond Kosovar my information."

Ghensie's face fell, as if sinking from inescapable guilt for everything that had befallen the household. "I'm sorry...sorry—"

Jeremy cut her off with a shake of his head. "We've got to go on from here and keep our minds looking forward."

"Right," she acknowledged. "And I've been thinking of an alternative. Bekim and I should stay in a hotel."

Ghensie hadn't been alone in coming up with this option. Jeremy had considered it and found the idea clinical and impersonal. A hotel, where Ghensie and Bekim knew no one, where no allies would call if things turned sinister.

No, he didn't like it, but he understood why Ghensie would prefer it. "That's a possibility," he allowed in a cautious tone. "Maybe for just a few days. I still think Louise would be happy to lodge you."

Ghensie looked back into the distance, perhaps reconsidering the two options. "The blond Kosovar," she stated instead, "the one who's never approached me—shows up alone at your hotel in Brussels and now here in Paris..."

"Right," Jeremy said with a knowing nod. "So where *are* Luan and the bald thug?"

Chapter 31

The absence of Luan and the husky bald Kosovar did indeed loom large in Jeremy's mind, larger than the physical presence of their cohort with the glasses. But he couldn't dwell on the unknown. Time to get on with what they had to do.

In that regard he gave in (at least for now) to Ghensie's preference for staying in a hotel. She and Bekim could ride out at least a few days there while Jeremy braced for a confrontation with the spectacled stalker. He would warn the bastard off—*we don't have the coin!* And if that didn't work, then a good roughing-up might send this silent *mec* back to the cave out of which he had slithered.

On the recommendation of a friend, Jeremy made arrangements in a discreet two-star hotel off the boulevard de Port-Royal, near the border of the Fifth and Thirteenth arrondissements. His waiter friend, Gaétan from Brussels, had stayed there, and during that stay Jeremy had frequented the lobby and found the atmosphere intimate and friendly. He only worried about Ghensie and Bekim having to go out for meals. Too much exposure no matter where they stayed in the city could be risky, for which reason he planned to pursue a variation of his original option. If that worked out, Ghensie and Bekim would only have to stay in the Hôtel Petit Mouffetard for two or three days.

Ghensie packed for a brief sojourn away, leaving most of her things in the flat. *It will only be temporary,* they told each other through reassuring smiles and caresses, gestures only to be followed by furtive frowns and looks of regret.

Jeremy continued to count on Louise Cholot, though for now he kept this to himself. Bekim hadn't forgotten her either as he now struggled to understand why they were going to a hotel.

"It's like a vacation, Bekim," was how Ghensie put it. "We're having a little holiday in a hotel."

A puzzled frown from the boy: "For how long?"

"A few days or so."

A longer puzzled pause: "But can we still go see Louise?"

Jeremy cut in whole-heartedly. "*Definitely*. I'm going to call her very soon, once I help you and *Maman* settle into your hotel room." Here, Ghensie shot him a quizzical frown of her own. "Yes," he reaffirmed, "we *will* visit Louise." *And if plans go accordingly,* he told himself, *you'll soon be staying with her in phase two of your temporary relocation.* It was the only tactic that made sense. Ghensie, considering her odyssey from Tirana to Paris, via Italy, the Netherlands, and Belgium, had to know that better than anyone, even though pride and privacy were strong inhibitors. Someday this yearlong journey would end, despite the competing variables in the "stars."

They made the move on Jeremy's next night off, a taxi rolling up in front of his building in inky darkness. The driver loaded two bags into the trunk while Ghensie, Bekim, and Jeremy squeezed into the backseat. In the sparse, pre-dawn traffic, the cab streaked south across the Seine and almost the entire Fifth arrondissement, slowing through the village-like Mouffetard *quartier*, from where it coasted down to the boulevard de Port-Royal before snaking back to the tiny rue de Valence.

Once Ghensie and Bekim were settled in their

room, Jeremy métroed back home, already missing the warmth of their pressing bodies in the cab, feeling the weight of a heavy hollowness when he got home—an empty space that for the first time in a month was silent as a tomb.

Such a crushing contrast to the pre-departure commotion which even included an argument over Ghensie's pocket watches. She was bringing both bags with her. "I'm almost finished with this batch and I have to return them or else it will look like I've stolen them."

Despite her distress Jeremy pointed out, "You can't risk the exposure of going back to that shop."

"I have to. The older couple are semi-retired and their son is not the cooperative type."

To himself Jeremy couldn't help agreeing. He had no difficulty picturing the sullen young son (undoubtedly the same kid he had dealt with when buying the padlock) demanding punctuality from those he deemed of a lower station, while sitting on his ass ignoring potential customers.

"I'll take the watches back when you've finished them," he'd told Ghensie.

She had hesitated—no one in the shop knew Jeremy—but inevitably agreed. He would also pass on the message that it would be a while before Ghensie returned for more watches, something which also caused her to stiffen, but to which she bleakly agreed— no one would wait for her to come back to the shop; they would find some other desperate soul to do the work. *The end of another job, the kind not easy to find.*

The next morning, after rising to a palpably empty flat, Jeremy called Louise. Madame asked after Ghensie and Bekim, which allowed a segue:

"You're kind to mention them. In fact, in a way that's why I'm calling."

Madame was nothing if not intuitive. "It sounds as if you need help."

And so Jeremy related the most recent development in the almost month-long saga of the missing coin and its bloodhounds, combined with Ghensie's precarious immigration status.

"So Ghensie seems to be caught between the hammer and the anvil."

"Exactly. She and Bekim are in a hotel for now, but it might be wiser if they stayed in separate places." *The third option of which Ghensie was so far unaware.*

"Hmm," Madame murmured after a pause that made Jeremy start pacing the entryway with the phone in his hands. "And a possibility would be for me take one of them in...?" When Jeremy didn't answer outright, Madame spared him further awkwardness. "Come over and we'll discuss it."

Split them up, he explained to Madame, as they drank coffee in her living room. *Separate the possible targets*. That had been Jeremy's modified plan and Louise agreed to its logic, particularly as it applied to Bekim. "It might keep the boy safer, plus he already knows me."

Jeremy nodded appreciatively. "Luan and the Kosovars are hunting Ghensie and me, but I can't rule out them targeting Bekim to put pressure on his mother."

Madame shook her head. "Jeremy, you *do* attract exotic situations." If a tiny smile hadn't followed, and a conspiratorial twinkle hadn't lit her eye, Jeremy might have been tempted to reconsider Louise's involvement in his plan. Sheepishly he glanced down at the cup and saucer in his hand.

"You know," Madame went on, "I'm mostly concerned for *you* in all of this. I understand your not wanting to involve the police at this stage, but eventually..."

Jeremy looked back in earnest. "I can take care of myself as far as this guy in town goes. If the others show, then you're right, I might have to call on help." Second thoughts hit him again about Louise's part in the plan. "But maybe I've been too presumptuous in asking you to get involved."

"Jeremy, I'm old enough to make my own decisions. And as you know from last summer, I'm not the faint-hearted type."

Indeed she wasn't. Her husband, Jean-Baptiste Cholot, had died in a mountain climbing accident. Her own fit, fluid lifestyle allowed her to switch effortlessly between cosmopolitan Parisian and energetic alpine hiker. And last July, on behalf of Jeremy, she had indulged in a discreet bit of spying herself. Hardly a middle-aged homebody, she was a risk taker in her own right. She was part of the club.

"So of course I'll take Bekim," she said. The un-crossing of her toned nylon-clad legs and the clacking of her cup and saucer on the coffee table seemed to punctuate that decision.

If only Jeremy's concerns could end there. He had yet to present his plan for Bekim to Ghensie, and that was only part one.

That afternoon he delivered bread and cheese, water and Orangina for Ghensie and Bekim's lunch, but he could already sense a feeling of confinement in the room. Ghensie had little space on the small desk to work on her watches. She had to scold Bekim for jumping on the beds. The boy asked if there was a park nearby—"*big*, like Louise's," he added. Jeremy took the hint. "Be patient a little longer," he told him. He preferred to broach the subject of Louise to Ghensie while they were alone.

That evening, his second night off work, when he returned to the hotel in one of his circuitous fashions, Ghensie suggested they go out for dinner. "We can't go on having you bring things in to us," she told Jeremy, "as much as we appreciate it. The hotel personnel will get suspicious."

She was right. The hotel provided breakfast, but if Ghensie and Bekim never set foot outside for other meals, that would indeed arouse suspicion. Risks would have to be taken; movement around the *quartier* couldn't be avoided altogether.

"You choose the restaurant," she said to Jeremy. "I'm paying."

Across the boulevard de Port-Royal, they settled into Le Canon des Gobelins, a close, informal brasserie whose memory Jeremy cherished from his childhood. Its attraction for a small boy? The model of a nineteenth-century cannon showcased on a table inside the restaurant. Jeremy asked if they could sit near it so he could relive the experience, this time through the eyes of Bekim. He was rewarded by the boy's enthusiasm and at one point, when Bekim left his chair to further observe the little cannon, Jeremy snatched the opportunity to present his plan to Ghensie.

"What do you think?" he asked, after quickly delivering the proposal. He glanced at Bekim who was explaining to Grizzly what Jeremy had said about the cannon.

Ghensie's answer surprised him. "I'm glad you brought it up again," she said. "I didn't want to ask after turning you down the first time, but I think staying with Louise would be good for him. I'd remain at the hotel, of course."

Jeremy didn't go into any of the clinical calculations behind the idea, which Ghensie might well have considered herself.

They made the transition early the next evening, again by taxi but with Jeremy taking Bekim alone. The boy didn't seem to mind, looking at the move as another phase in their "vacation," one that involved the sprawling Parc Montsouris and Madame's rambling apartment. With all the confusion and disorientation the boy deserved a pampered break, thought Jeremy. Besides, with this second move, who could trace him? It wasn't lost on Jeremy that Louise lived relatively close to Iliescu and his cave-café. Still, the park lay in the opposite direction, a good bus ride from Madame's building, and in general he had strong hopes for a timely shutdown of Iliescu's network. With that in mind he would have to get back to surveillance of Manon. But first he called his former girlfriend Haley to arrange the meeting they had both looked forward to.

It would be a welcome reunion—and play a part in the second phase of Jeremy's plan.

"Is it still your favorite building?" Jeremy asked Haley, looking out the café window at the Conciergerie in the middle of the Seine. They were on the Quai de la Mégisserie on the Right Bank, and nostalgia was in the air. The ancient fortress called the Conciergerie rang as evocative to Haley as the little cannon at Gobelins did to Jeremy.

"It was the first magnificent thing I witnessed here," she said. "You can never forget a sensation like that." She gave a little shrug of her lean shoulders. "But I guess I take it a bit more for granted now." Her green eyes smiled at him, an inquisitive smile, though a patient one. What had they each been up to during these almost two months of separation? Luc had returned to Haley's life, and jealousy wasn't the only sensation Jeremy had suffered—and felt ashamed of. He had envied Haley herself, whose trust fund allowed her to live in the city of her dreams without the anxiety of having to support herself. Today, though, he felt different. As they sat in the café Flora et Fauna, looking out at the ancient Île de la Cité, he felt fairly competent with what he had accomplished over the month of February—namely getting Ghensie out of the clutches of Luan and company in Brussels, and sharing his flat with her and Bekim like many a normal adult.

Yet Ghensie and Bekim weren't his family. As he gazed across the table at Haley, at the same smile that hinted at mischief and spontaneity in life, he realized how rooted their bond remained—their shared English language, the jazz that buzzed in their blood, their spontaneous treks all over town to purchase an album with a single song they fell in love with and desired to make love to. How could he explain longing for both Haley and for the warm little ménage he shared with Ghensie? *He couldn't.*

He wanted to ask Haley about Luc, felt he couldn't get a current understanding of her without knowing whether she and Luc were lovers again. But he balked, and in the meantime Haley asked an equally appropriate question of him.

"Are you still lodging your Albanian friend?"

Jeremy looked her in the eye, searching for that same wonderful wavelength they had shared from last May to December—until Walter died and Luc returned.

"No," he answered carefully. "The mother's in a hotel and her son's with another friend." He watched Haley give a neutral nod, the absent kind that says, *That's nice, so now you've moved on to something else.* But of course he hadn't, and that was a further reason he'd come to her. "I've ended up helping them quite a bit actually."

"The woman and her son?"

Jeremy frowned as he nodded. "It's developed into kind of an intrigue, to tell the truth..."

"*Intrigue?*" Her eyes were pert behind her glasses, that spark of curiosity always lying in wait and now ready to spring with questions. She knew about some of his little intelligence jobs, had helped him puzzle out the targets of last summer's attack on major Paris monuments. "Something to do with the RG?" she asked.

"No. But it turns out that the Albanian woman, her name's Ghensie, is being stalked by her cousin and two thugs from Kosovar, all because they think she's taken one of their antique coins." Naturally he couldn't stop there and ended up explaining the whole business, strategically leaving out his romantic entanglement. "But in a way the RG work *is* connected," he told her, explaining how he had met Solange.

"That was the assignment you didn't want to tell me about last fall," Haley pointed out with an ironic smile. "I remember you said it was *confidential*."

"And it was. But that was back in October and now it's over and this mess has taken its place."

"So these Kosovars are dangerous, but you can't go to the police..." She shook her head. "What kind of personal stake do you have in this, Jeremy?"

Jeremy sighed. *Time to confess.* "I guess I got a little too involved with Ghensie while trying to help."

Haley sat back, letting out a softly amused "Ah." Perhaps not too amused, for her eyes assumed a distant look.

"And *Luc?*" asked Jeremy. "Are you two still *just friends?*"

Haley's far-off gaze turned rueful, and Jeremy gave up seeking an answer. After two months who could assign blame on either side?

Haley seemed to agree. "So what's your next move with Ghensie and her son?"

"Well, with one of the Kosovars back on her trail I've got mother and son separated. But I don't know how long Ghensie should stay in a hotel. She can't go out much and it looks suspicious if she doesn't."

"I see." She tipped him a knowing smile. "So it might be convenient if someone took her in..."

Jeremy shrugged and showed his palms.

"Someone like me..." she said.

Jeremy couldn't help gaping in surprise, though he had come there with the very same idea.

"Don't look so shocked," she said, a corner of her mouth turned wryly up. "I might just do it."

Chapter 32

Jeremy and Haley parted, with Haley willing to consider taking Ghensie in. "Give me a day," she had said, which suited Jeremy fine, for he would still have to convince Ghensie of the move. She was proud. Allowing Louise Cholot to look after Bekim was one thing. Accepting shelter from a stranger she had never met, let alone Jeremy's ex-girlfriend, made for quite a different proposition. Jeremy didn't want her to feel humiliated or even humbled, but how else would she be able to go on hiding and not attract attention?

Haley was reasonable, well-meaning, and having gone through her own travails in Paris she didn't shy from a dicey situation. It was one of the reasons he liked her and why they had gotten on so well together. In a way, she was like a young Louise Cholot. Gutsy girls attracted him on many levels. When they kissed goodbye, though with only a peck on the lips, he stood watching her walk away along the *quai*.

The next morning, per Rébert's instructions, Jeremy posted himself across the street from Manon/Bardot's place but after two hours, without a glimpse of either her or Vadim, he gave up the surveillance. He could not—*would not*—stay here all day; neither would he continue to shuttle back and forth between the Eleventh and Fourteenth arrondissements just to look at suspicious addresses. He had to talk to Iliescu. Why had the man still not called? He stopped at a phone booth, dialed Iliescu's number but got no answer and had to leave a message. Then he headed back to Ghensie's hotel.

"I just talked to Louise and Bekim," she said. "He's enjoying the attention. It would be nice to see him, though, and thank Louise in person."

Jeremy shook his head. "I know, but you mustn't leave the neighborhood. I'll go by Louise's and thank her myself."

Ghensie's eyes shifted to the desk in the room. "All my watches are finished and ready to go back."

"I'll take them," Jeremy said. Ghensie was perched on one of the twin beds while Jeremy sat on the bed across from her. The room barely allowed space to cross paths. It felt stuffy though Ghensie had opened the window for a bit before closing it against the cold.

"I don't know if they'll give you more," she said of the watches. "They might not trust you."

This surprised Jeremy. He thought they both understood that her pocket-watch stint had likely come to an end. All the same, there was a gleam of hope in her eyes that he didn't want to disappoint. "I can ask," he said tentatively.

"It's a great imposition, I know, but the money helps buy food."

Jeremy marveled at the spunk that still buoyed her. Pitched forward on the edge of the bed, she projected firm enthusiasm, readiness to dive into more work. He wanted to sit beside her and assure her she needn't worry about money at this moment. An urge in him mounted to hold her, to...

Then he thought of Haley, equally plucky and willing to help. He felt an aching desire to keep both of them close. "It's no problem," he said of the watches. He almost added, *I can pick up Line 6 at—*. But he stopped himself in time. She didn't know he had already inspected her hardware store. "Tell me the address again," he said, leaning forward and giving her hand a squeeze. "I'll take them back right now and ask."

"If we're lucky the older couple will be there."

Jeremy hoped so as well. Things were hard enough.

And so they would continue to be. When Jeremy arrived at the shop in rue Pernety the kid with the permanent glower was the only person behind the counter. Verifying he was the sole customer on the premises, Jeremy released a determined sigh and crossed the store to meet him.

The kid, who had at first only slightly raised his gaze from his magazine, now stared in confusion at Jeremy's shoulder bags. *Look familiar, do they?* Jeremy telegraphed mentally to him. If he didn't recognize Jeremy from the previous visit, the kid was now interested.

"*Bonjour.* I'm here to deliver these watches on behalf of a friend," Jeremy stated, setting the bags carefully on the counter. "Are your parents in?"

For an awkward second the young man continued to stare at the bags. Then he looked back at Jeremy and uttered an annoyed, "*No they're not,*" as if Jeremy had no business making such an impertinent enquiry. "And your *friend* shouldn't expect them to be. I've told her they're retired." He sharpened his gaze at Jeremy. "And why didn't *she* bring the watches in?"

Patiently Jeremy watched the kid puff himself up, then he replied as if dealing with a twelve-year-old. "She happens to be busy. You *would* like the finished product, wouldn't you?"

The kid gave Jeremy a sour look and pulled the bags towards him. He looked inside one, checked the contents of one of the boxes, then slung both bags behind the counter.

"Okay," he said grudgingly, "but if she wants her

pay she'll have to come for it in person."

Jeremy breathed out a silent sigh. He had half anticipated this. "I told you she was busy," he said, in the kind of reasoned tone aimed at a child, "and *I've* been instructed by her to receive payment."

The kid shook his head. "*Désolé—pas possible.*"

Sorry—not possible? Jeremy leaned in, his bloodshot eye narrowing in a menacing squint. "You'll turn over the pay," he said in a leaden voice, "and you'll do it *now*." So much for the opportunity to ask for more watches. It had been futile from the start.

The kid backed up a step. He cleared his throat and raised his chin. Though lean of build, he was taller than Jeremy and seemed to take nervous heart in the fact. "*No*," he countered.

Suit yourself, but don't think you didn't ask for it. Jeremy leaned in further, grabbed the wool scarf the kid was wearing, and gave it a hard jerk. Before the kid could react, Jeremy grasped his hair with his free right hand and shoved his face onto the glass surface. "If you don't want this nice counter shattered, you'll remove the one hundred-eighty francs you owe from the till and hand it over."

The kid placed his hands on the counter's edge, but before he could push off, Jeremy hammered both sets of knuckles with his free fist. The kid groaned, flailed for about two more seconds, then went still. "*Okay*," he yielded in a muffled voice. Jeremy let him up slowly, one fist poised to strike if the kid changed his mind. Instead he observed an outraged young man rub his fingers and slink over to the cash register. Face scarlet and scowling, he pulled out what he owed and handed it over with trembling hands.

"Thanks, but I'd still like the bags back."

If it were possible for a face to grow any redder, thought Jeremy, it would explode.

"They're *ours!*" the kid shouted, tears sprouting on his lashes.

"Oh...?" Jeremy said, in good-natured surprise. "In that case, *excuse me.*" He pocketed the cash, said a half-amused *au revoir*, then pivoted and walked out. In truth he hoped never to see the little prick again.

When he brought Ghensie's pay back she thanked him with relief, then looked at him with doubt. He had returned with no bags. "The young guy was there..."

Jeremy nodded; he really was sorry.

"And he wouldn't give you more watches..."

Jeremy shook his head. "*Hardly*—he's a spoiled, stubborn, shit of a kid. He didn't even want to hand over your pay."

This said, Jeremy could sense an almost combustible fury radiate from Ghensie. "How *dare* he! Who does he think he is?" She started to pace but was stymied by the desk and the corner of the bed. She turned back to Jeremy. "He's in love with his power now that his parents are retiring. I'll have to deal with him myself."

"Ghensie," Jeremy stated firmly, "*do not* take the risk of going there."

"But he—"

"He's a crook, what do you expect? Let it go for now." *And for good*, Jeremy added to himself, picturing the kid's sizzling face. "He's an angry young man—stay away from him."

Ghensie inhaled, closed her eyes and breathed out the kind of sigh that seeks to calm and contain things. Jeremy hoped Haley would call this afternoon with a positive response so that Ghensie could at least have space in which to pace if she wished. Maybe Haley had already left him a message. He was fairly sure she would take Ghensie in, otherwise why say she would consider it? In fact he wondered if the gesture might even be an olive branch of sorts, or proof that she still fancied adventure. That she hadn't turned into a domestic little mouse these last two months with Luc.

With these thoughts he left Ghensie, who had calmed enough to turn on the television in the room. He was glad he'd purchased an answering machine last September. Iliescu might even leave a message, if the bastard felt like returning his call. And what if he didn't? Jeremy checked his watch. The hour was perfect for dropping in on Iliescu in his café.

Jeremy almost missed his opportunity. As he walked into the Bonne Nouvelle, Iliescu was packing up his things—notebook, cigarettes, glasses. Before he had a chance to stand and swing on his coat Jeremy plunked down in front of him.

"Glad I caught you," he said with a tight smile.

Iliescu registered a look of surprise before his face became a pinched frown. "You haven't, I'm on my way out. I told you I'd call when I decided on a job for you."

"That's not why I'm here. I need that passport and I'm willing to pay the balance." Jeremy sat forward, trapping Iliescu with his most anxious and determined look. "I need it *now*."

An uncomfortable moment passed before Jeremy received a response. Iliescu's circumspect eye was back, the clinician observing his wriggling specimen.

"What's up, Winters? Is your American FBI, or whatever, closing in?"

"*Yes*," Jeremy lied. "I'm ready to run but my girl needs her documents."

"Right." Iliescu's tone rang falsely sympathetic. So far he hadn't uttered Ghensie's name, but Jeremy couldn't rule out the trafficker having knowledge of it. He was glad Ghensie was tucked away in her hotel, away from Iliescu's tentacles.

"*But*," said Iliescu, "you'll have to wait a little longer.

"Your forger issue…"

"Mm. Looks like I'll definitely have to change providers."

Providers. An interesting choice of term. Why not *men*? Jeremy couldn't remember Iliescu using the term *man* at any time regarding the subject.

"I don't have the luxury to wait," Jeremy said, this time more calmly. "Let me run a photo of my girl to your man and get it done fast."

Iliescu gave an abrupt laugh. "I thought you were concerned about a *quality* document."

"No time now. Is his work really that bad?"

"Let's put it this way: only choose a man to do a man's job."

When Jeremy cocked his head, Iliescu waved a dismissive hand. "Never mind. If I can arrange something I'll let you know in a couple of days. Otherwise you'd better just look out for number one." He pointed a pale finger at Jeremy's chest.

Don't worry, Jeremy replied to himself. *I will.*

Chapter 33

Jeremy left the Bonne Nouvelle and headed straight to another café where he ordered himself a Kir royal. Not having long to linger, he downed the drink quickly, its champagne making for a symbolic celebration.

For he did have something to toast, and after turning over Iliescu's words in his mind to be sure, he left for the nearest phone booth and called Rébert.

"Well, well, so it's our dear little Manon," said Rébert.

"Must be. Iliescu inferred a *woman* was his problem and Manon is the only person my photos could've helped him with."

"The photos might not have been about adultery at all," said Rébert, "which means the Vadim look-a-like's probably involved in the forgery business as well."

"Could be that Manon was double-crossing Iliescu so he wanted photos of them both."

"Possibly. At any rate, I'll get cars out to watch all three properties." With a sigh of cautious satisfaction, he added, "We'll make arrests soon."

Jeremy returned the receiver to its hook with a gratifying clack, yet when he stepped out of the phone booth a strange sense of anticlimax filled him. One monumental weight had been lifted from his shoulders, true, but until all the arrests were made—including and *especially* Iliescu's—he would continue to crack his knuckles in nervous suspense. He might still receive a call from Iliescu about the passport he did not actually want. Better not to answer his phone. Let the machine pick up so he could screen his calls like lots of people did these days.

He inhaled a draft of cool, damp air; not the frigid, brittle air of just last week, but a softer, smoother current, a whisper of spring to come, though he wouldn't count on it soon. Nor would he truly breathe easier until Ghensie was out of the hotel.

He re-entered the phone booth and called her, proposing an early dinner, when he would broach the idea of her staying somewhere else—that is, as long as Haley called beforehand...

And she did, just as promised. The call came while he was home ironing a shirt for work.

"Glad I caught you," she said. "I wasn't sure what time you'd leave for Le Prince."

He appreciated her dependability, especially now. "Perfect timing. And everything's okay with you?" he asked, not wanting to hurry her response.

"Yeah, and it's also okay for your friend Ghensie to stay with me for a while. You didn't say for how long but—"

"Not long," Jeremy was quick to interject, desperate to see the situation resolved.

He never knew how Haley would have finished her sentence, though he imagined she might have said something to the effect of: *but it can only be for about a week.* Or: *but Luc and I aren't completely split up.* What he preferred to imagine was: *but she can stay until you get things sorted out.* After he hung up, though, picturing Ghensie and Haley in the same flat made him rub his face in mounting nervousness. How would he act around them, and what would they say to each other in his absence?

He met Ghensie at the hotel and they walked to a

restaurant two streets down, where over her pizza margherita she once more floated the idea of visiting Bekim.

Jeremy peered at her but kept his patience tethered. They had agreed *he* would check on the boy and thank Louise. What was her hurry in seeing him when she had gone a week without him while still in Brussels? Then again, what did Jeremy know about the throes of being a parent?

"For safety's sake let's stick to our plan," he gently reminded her. "I'll go to Louise's tomorrow."

"Thank you," she said, though her tone still betrayed concern. "I hate to nag you because you have enough keeping you busy..."

"Not really. I'm completely finished with the photo job," he told her in order to end the awkwardness.

"You don't have to explain anything more about that. You've done plenty for us already."

Jeremy appreciated the words but wondered at Ghensie's hesitant smile, gracious in a way, distancing in another. He really didn't know what to expect, didn't know how *he* might show gratitude in her position—in her *prison-like* position. He couldn't imagine it.

In the meantime she went on about Bekim. "I bought him a coloring book, if you could take it to him."

Of course Jeremy would, though he questioned how far from the hotel Ghensie had ventured to buy the gift. He didn't ask. Nor, at this moment, did he feel comfortable raising the subject of Haley and her offer of hospitality. Once more he thought of the two together. Yes, he confirmed to himself, he wanted Ghensie to move, but he would wait until checking on Bekim and reporting the boy's high spirits: *how much cheerier to stay in a home than in a hotel.*

He left the hotel for work, hoping to soon again cross paths with the spectacled Kosovar, who hadn't made an appearance since Ghensie's sighting of him. If only he would show up in Jeremy's neighborhood, or even at Le Prince (at night, outside the club, would be ideal). Anywhere away from Ghensie and where Jeremy could deal with him however he must, *with whatever it took*. For now Jeremy preferred not to think that completely through.

The next morning he called Louise and was invited to lunch. He did laundry beforehand. The apartment was clean, Ghensie having insisted on undertaking domestic tasks. He left the little things as they were— the left-behind toy cars on the coffee table, the clutter in the bathroom, for soon Ghensie could surely return.

The laundry completed, he hung around the neighborhood, buying razors at the Monoprix, stopping for coffee at La Gitane, the café diagonally across the street from his building. He loitered as long as possible, moving on to scan the periodicals at the kiosk next to the Temple métro entrance, nattering with the fellow who sold him his newspapers, then finally pacing the length of Place de la République, all the while keeping a sharp eye out for the Kosovar. But the man refused to oblige. Where the hell was he? Who was he following now? *For he had to be tracking someone.*

Finally Jeremy left for Madame Cholot's, as usual posting himself next to the door on the métro train, alert to who got on in the neighboring carriages. Follow me, *please*, he invoked the Kosovar—I'll run you out of our lives!

Lunch with Louise and Bekim seemed to have a sense of normality. The boy asked when he would see his mother and seemed satisfied with Jeremy's assurance of *soon*, then went on to enlighten Jeremy about his trip to the Zoo de Vincennes. Later, while Louise and Jeremy finished their wine and drank coffee, Bekim having scampered off to the living room to color in his new book, Jeremy lowered his voice to speak frankly. "I hope he's not too much of a handful."

Madame, pouring the last of the Sancerre *rouge* into Jeremy's glass, said, "He's not." She set the bottle down, her eyes focusing on the table where she pinched a breadcrumb from the tablecloth and dropped it in her plate.

"Because," Jeremy went on, "Ghensie and I can't thank you enough for this. Taking him to the zoo went above and beyond." He added a good-natured chuckle. "I hope you enjoyed it too."

"Mm," Madame confirmed with a distracted smile. "Just watching his enthusiasm was enjoyment enough." Again she paused to pick up a crumb, half studying it before letting it roll off her fingertips into her plate. Jeremy wondered if he should thank her once more, knowing perfectly well she wouldn't expect it and indeed would not like him to do so.

He finished his wine then asked, "Is there something else I could bring to make Bekim's stay here easier?"

Madame eyed the doorway. The door to the living room was open so Jeremy got up, and after glancing at Bekim who was coloring on the coffee table, eased it closed to a crack.

Madame rubbed her fingertips together, ridding them of further stray crumbs. "No," she replied, "we've got all we need, but thank you for asking. Everything's fine, the boy's completely cooperative, talkative as can be. His French is making great strides, though at times I wonder at some of his comments."

Jeremy's frown prompted her to continue. "Bekim has an amazing imagination. I know," she added, "all children do, more or less, but his is particularly intense; you must have noticed the way he engages with his bear, as if it were real..."

Jeremy nodded, started to say something, but was preempted by Louise. "Not that that's abnormal for his age, but sometimes he refers to it almost ferociously, saying the bear protects him and will rip to shreds anyone who crosses it—that it has magical powers. A bit extreme, don't you think?"

Jeremy nodded again. "Oh I've noticed, and all I can think is it probably has to do with his chaotic background. The bear's the only constant in his life," he said, expressing what he had theorized from the beginning. Still, he knew all too well how irritating the behavior could be; it had tapered off with Ghensie's arrival, yet now that mother and son were once more separated, Jeremy could imagine it springing back with a vengeance.

"Yes, that makes sense," Louise agreed, "and I don't hold anything against the child—he's never been anything but lovely with me, but he said something rather strange when I asked him how *Grizzly's* magical powers worked. He said he didn't know, only that his cousin told him so."

"His cousin?"

"Exactly. *Luan,* he said. Isn't that his mother's cousin, the one who's been hounding her for the ancient coin?"

Jeremy opened his mouth to speak but found it paralyzed by the pistoning of his thoughts.

"According to Bekim," continued Louise, "he was told by Luan to keep the bear close to his skin, because only in that way would the bear protect him. Protect him from exactly *what*, I'm not sure unless it's from those Kosovars. Then he got panicky because Luan told him to keep it all a secret..." Louise trailed off, observing Jeremy's deepening frown. "But you don't think..."

He did. Why hadn't it occurred to him before? *Grizzly.* He and Madame locked eyes and nodded. *We need to examine that bear.*

"The coin could be sewn in wherever there's a seam," said Louise.

"You'd think Ghensie might have noticed."

"Depends on where it's sewn."

"*If* it's there somewhere." Jeremy rubbed his chin vigorously and stood up. "I've got to find out."

"Be careful, Jeremy. If the boy knows nothing about this entire business, taking the bear from him could cause trauma. He says he hasn't told anyone else, not even his mother, that Grizzly's magical because Luan swore him to secrecy. So let *me* look. I'll wait until he's asleep tonight and examine the bear thoroughly."

Jeremy nodded. "In the meantime I'll tell Ghensie." He checked his watch. He could head over there before going to work.

Louise rose to accompany him back to the living room, where there was no sign of Bekim. They exchanged curious glances. "*Bekim,*" Madame called out, walking towards the hall to the bathroom. "Are you in there?" she asked through the closed door.

No answer.

Jeremy glanced at the abandoned crayons and coloring book. Grizzly was not with them. "*Bekim,*" he echoed about the room.

Madame returned from the hall. "He's not in the bathroom or in his room, or my room—"

A roar exploded from behind the sofa and out jumped Bekim, brandishing Grizzly like the severed head of Medusa. Jeremy closed his eyes and braced for the worst.

But the boy merely burst into laughter. "You couldn't *find* me!" he cried in delight, more giggles spilling from him.

Jeremy and Louise exchanged looks of reassure-ance.

"It seems he didn't hear anything, thank goodness," Louise murmured in the entryway, as she gathered Jeremy's coat for him. "All the same, he has an astonishing imagination." When Jeremy returned another quizzical look, she said with a wry smile, "Oh, he's got more tales! I'll tell you another time."

Chapter 34

Jeremy would have liked to hear the rest from Madame but he needed to tell Ghensie. Yes, Bekim was precocious and imaginative, yet if Jeremy was on the right track about the coin, nothing else Madame had to report could prove more astonishing.

Luan hiding the coin in Bekim's bear. Jeremy couldn't wait to hear Louise's news after searching Grizzly tonight. As the métro charged towards Gobelins and Ghensie's hotel, his thoughts raced with it, and when he got off, his heart thumped as he covered the long block to the rue de Valence and Ghensie's hotel. At the hotel's reception he asked the clerk to ring Ghensie's room, drumming his fingers on the counter.

"No need, monsieur," said the young woman. "Madame Berisha has gone out."

"Gone out?"

The woman nodded.

Where, he wanted to ask, knowing quite well that asking would not only be impertinent but also futile. Desk clerks didn't inquire about their guests' comings and goings. Still it was well past lunchtime, so where could Ghensie be? Out buying another present for Bekim? *Merde*, he hated not knowing.

He left the hotel to search stores and cafés in the neighborhood, and there were plenty, with Jeremy entering and exiting practically all of them. *Nom de Dieu—if she wasn't around here, where the hell could she be?* After a long stretch of aimless wandering well beyond the neighborhood's confines, he returned to the hotel, where he received a shake of the clerk's head and a polite *désolée, monsieur*—Madame still hadn't returned.

"She did say she was going out for a late lunch," said the clerk, after observing Jeremy's slumped shoulders and worried expression.

He thanked her for the courtesy, all the while fuming: *a late lunch—where, up at Montmartre?* Extremely imprudent to be out this long—down right irresponsible! He wrote a message instructing Ghensie to call him at Le Prince as soon as she got in, and after handing it to the clerk he left, heaving a huge sigh of exasperation.

He could barely get through his shift at Le Prince, watching the phone as if someone might steal it out from under him, responding cagily to comments about his agitation by both his waiter friend Didier and his co-barman Laurent. Once more Didier asked when he'd like to come to dinner, having extended invitations on the part of his wife since Jeremy's break-up with Haley.

"It's not like we're estranged," Jeremy responded, when his friend made reference to it again.

"*Tant mieux.*" Didier gave a triumphant smile. "I've told you before, Haley's not a girl you want to let get away."

"*I* think he's got someone else at home," said Laurent, throwing a playful elbow at Jeremy. "Always in a rush to get out of here."

His colleagues' comments wafted past like a mildly distracting wind. Only one thing registered: Didier's mention of Haley. He still had to convince Ghensie to move. His excitement about the coin had practically pushed it from his mind. And as his shift continued at an insufferably slow pace, Jeremy could only long to get Ghensie safely ensconced in Haley's flat. When he hung up his apron for the night Ghensie had yet to call. He went into the back office and phoned the hotel.

"Madame Berisha's key is in front of the cubby with a message left for her earlier," the night clerk reported.

Jeremy's heart sank with nausea. He swung on his coat, telling Didier and Laurent he had to leave right away, and headed out the door. He might have imagined Laurent launching the parting comment: "See what I mean!" but his mind felt encased in ice. And yet Laurent would have been wrong, for instead of going home Jeremy took one of the last métros of the night straight to Ghensie's hotel.

The night clerk frowned as Jeremy entered. It was twelve-thirty.

"*Bonsoir*. I'm the one who called about Madame Berisha," Jeremy explained, "and I left that message in her box this afternoon." He pointed to the cubby marked room 35, its key hanging in front of it like a sinister omen. "So she hasn't been back to the hotel..."

"If you're the one who left the message, you must know." The man eyed Jeremy with barely concealed impatience. *Why not just come back tomorrow?*

Jeremy hardly noticed for the sledgehammer-like blow he felt. Ghensie had been gone all afternoon and evening. He didn't want to leave the lobby. Maybe she would come breezing in any minute with a story of meeting a band of tourists and painting the town with them. How unlikely, but at this point how welcome the news would be.

"If you'd like, you could leave another message," the clerk suggested.

Jeremy thanked him but declined. He wanted to wait awhile, but knew he wouldn't be tolerated hanging about the lobby into the wee hours. He headed reluctantly out the door. What else could he ask of the clerk when it was entirely natural for a hotel guest to be gone all day and evening, exploring everything the City of Light had to offer?

She went out for a late lunch, the day clerk had said. And that, Jeremy surmised, feeling a ruthless clenching in his chest, was when trouble must have struck. *But trouble with whom?* Luan and his bald buddy had yet to make an appearance, so that left the spectacled *mec*.

Once he reached home, questions and unpleasant scenarios kept battering Jeremy's brain so that sleep offered no relief until dawn. Then he went down like a felled tree until eight o'clock, when he staggered out of bed and called the hotel again—only to learn nothing new, except now the day clerk was concerned.

"Could she have stayed out all night with friends?" the woman asked.

"I don't think so, but I'm going to look into it," he said, assuring her that Ghensie would never skip out without paying, and that at any rate *he* had secured the room with his own credit card. He hung up and called Louise.

"Jeremy," she said, "you sound anxious, so I'll give you the news right away. It seems the coin has been sewn under the bear's tongue. Thoroughly but awkwardly, considering the spot."

For a couple of seconds Jeremy stood immobile, his thoughts like a forked river, coursing in separate directions. "The coin, *yes*! Were you able to remove it?"

"Not yet. I'll need enough time to sew the bear back up again. But it's there—I can feel it." When Jeremy didn't reply she said, "I could remove it tonight... Jeremy?"

"...Maybe you should wait..."

"If you say so, though it would be nice to verify that

it truly is the ancient coin." When another pause ensued, Madame asked Jeremy what was wrong.

"*Oh, mon Dieu,*" she exhaled when he told her. "And whoever has Ghensie will think Bekim has the coin."

"I'm not so sure." He had given this thought as well. "It seems only Luan knows where it is, and for all we know he's still back in Brussels. Whoever took Ghensie must think *she's* got the coin."

"But they'll put pressure on her since she doesn't know where it is. Jeremy?" she prompted when he gave no answer."

He was thinking Madame was right in that *they*— this nebulous *they*—might also insist on knowing where the boy was.

"You're right," he said. "As a precaution I've got to move Bekim again." And he didn't need to add, *both for his and for your own safety.*

Madame agreed. "But Jeremy, I'm still more worried about Ghensie. She won't reveal Bekim's location, do you understand? A mother never would."

True enough. Ghensie had to be found before...before God knew what happened.

Jeremy told Louise his plan and they arranged to move Bekim that night after dark. Jeremy was off work and could fetch the boy. "And Louise," he said, "I'm going to contact the police." He gave her Rébert's number in case an emergency arose before he got there. *There, he had done it*—taken the first step in involving the RG.

In the meantime he returned to Ghensie's hotel, paid the bill, and convinced the personnel that Ghensie had decided to move. He collected her things and brought them back to his place. Then he sat down and did some cold contemplating. Had Ghensie truly been kidnapped? There was no evidence of such and the only culprit, as of now, could be the spectacled Kosovar. But how had he pinpointed Ghensie's whereabouts? Jeremy was sure he hadn't been tailed either going to or coming from the hotel—not by either the spectacled *mec* or his known cronies. His thoughts swung back to Luan. Ghensie's cousin could never reveal the coin's location to the Kosovars. If he were caught double-crossing them, they might well kill him. But if another partner existed, one neither Ghensie nor Jeremy had seen? Jeremy shook his head—he had been meticulous in his movements around town, alert to the repeat appearance of a face, of a color, of an article of cloth-ing—from block to block, from métro stop to métro stop.

Ghensie herself was hyper-vigilant, constantly looking over her shoulder when she and Jeremy left the hotel for a meal.

So where had she gone? He couldn't imagine her leaving without telling him, without taking Bekim. *She went out for a late lunch*—nonchalant and in no hurry, by the day clerk's tone. *Calm*, in other words; unlike the day before. Jeremy pondered that last encounter in the hotel when he had returned with no watches. Ghensie had flown into a rage over the kid in the hardware store: angry, indignant, desperate. *Desperate* enough to do what? In a sudden flash of intuition, Jeremy rose, grabbed his coat and keys, and stalked out of the flat, slamming the door behind him.

The métro ride to the rue Pernety in the south would take at least half an hour. *Too long*. So Jeremy jogged up to Place de la République and hailed a cab. In four p.m. traffic the métro could conceivably be faster, though he felt better tracking his progress in a taxi, urging the cabbie on versus traveling trapped and blind underground. Seven years ago he had been a taxi driver himself and often alluded to the fact when he found himself in the passenger seat.

So he did now, adding to the young driver, "And if you make it fast there'll be a fat tip for you."

They arrived in rue Pernety with Jeremy pulling out cash before the cab came to a halt. As soon as he felt the final jerk of the brakes, Jeremy verified the meter and shoved a wad of francs at the driver. He threw open the door and bolted out, leaving the cabbie to count the money and stare in wonder at Jeremy's generosity.

Then the pace decelerated. Slowly, Jeremy opened the door to the hardware store and drifted in. The kid behind the counter looked up and locked gazes with him in semi-shock. He said nothing until Jeremy reached the counter, when he backed away, uttering, "Stay away from me or I'll call the police!"

Casually, Jeremy swept the store with his gaze. "*Really?*" he said. The two of them were alone. "And what will you tell them?" He leaned in, forcing the kid to back up against his shelves. "That the foreign woman came in yesterday asking for more under-the-table work?"

The kid's wide eyes shrunk to a nervous squint. "I don't know what you're talking about."

At that, momentum kicked back in. Jeremy vaulted over the counter and snatched him by the shirt collar. "I think calling the cops is a *fine* idea. Get it all out in the open, including everything you're doing behind the scenes here." Jeremy released him, walked down to the phone on the back counter and lifted the receiver from its cradle.

"She was here," the kid blurted out, red-faced and jittery.

"*And?*"

"She *did* ask for more work. I couldn't believe she came back after what happened when you were here..."

Jeremy slammed the receiver down and strode back to the kid, keeping his temper carefully calibrated. The kid wasn't wrong to marvel at Ghensie's reappearance after Jeremy had manhandled and humiliated him. Of course Ghensie knew nothing of that twist of events.

"And you turned her down, I suppose," he stated.

The kid nodded. "She argued but I..." He inhaled a stuttering breath. Jeremy raised his brows and dipped his chin in a not-so-subtle prompt.

"...I told her that I couldn't take a chance on her anymore."

"*Did* you? In a reasonable and gentlemanly tone, I imagine...?"

The kid looked away, muttering, "I just told her: *no more work.*"

"And then what?"

"She left."

The tall, gangly youth, flattened against the shelves, his head bent to the side, was probably telling the truth, Jeremy decided. The kid might be a crooked little prick, but Jeremy couldn't really picture him taking off after Ghensie just for the hell of it. Besides, Ghensie was sturdy enough to kick the lazy weed's ass.

He took a step back and cast his gaze at the door. "Was anyone else in the store when she was here?"

"No."

Jeremy glanced around the place with a smirk. "You don't do much legitimate business, do you?"

The kid's face turned a brighter hue of red. Jeremy watched him open his mouth then close it after glancing at Jeremy's hands, whose fingernails were scraping their palms. In reality the gesture was purely contemplative, but Jeremy took satisfaction in the effect it produced.

"Was anyone hanging around outside while she was here?" he asked.

The kid gave a defensive shrug. "How was I supposed to deal with her and watch who was out on the sidewalk at the same time?"

"So there *was* someone outside..."

The kid shook his head in frustration. A high grunt accompanied the gesture as he tried to sidle away from Jeremy and instead found himself bounced off the shelves behind him. The tins rattled and the kid covered his head. Jeremy gave him a couple of more shakes for good measure, then said, "As soon as I take you down along with your *merchandise* I'm calling the police. I've got nothing to lose."

"All right, all right!" The kid's hands flew up in surrender. "When she left, there were two guys outside. One took her by the arm and they all walked away together."

Chapter 35

Outside the hardware store, Jeremy stared blindly ahead of him. Ghensie had walked away with two men? *Nom de Dieu*, what did that mean!? He had tried to coax a description of the two, but the kid insisted he couldn't remember. "I was just glad to be rid of her!" Given the kid's trembling state, Jeremy saw no reason not to believe him.

Without wasting time to call ahead, Jeremy headed straight back to Louise's. In a hushed tone he shared the news about Ghensie, then called Haley while Madame packed Bekim's things. With Ghensie perhaps in the clutches of the Kosovar, the boy was again at risk.

"Is this still our vacation?" the boy asked, completely befuddled. Madame held his backpack while he clutched Grizzly, squeezing the bear in nervous spurts.

"Absolutely," Jeremy confirmed. "We're going to stay with a new friend."

"But I like staying *here*. And *Maman* is supposed to come soon."

Jeremy and Louise exchanged quick glances.

"Why isn't *Maman* here yet?" Bekim's question was more protest than inquiry, his mouth a tense line, his gaze exuding both fear and frustration. "I don't *want* to move again."

"Soon we'll go home, and *Maman* will join us." Jeremy tried to pour conviction into his tone but Bekim wasn't having it.

"But where *is Maman*?"

Jeremy turned to Louise, who at first looked loath

to lie but then came to his support. "*Maman* is tied up right now, just some business. You go on with Jeremy to his friend's, and you and I will see each other soon."

The boy's eyes darted between the two adults, finally resting plaintively on Jeremy, who urged, "You and I and Grizzly are going to have a fine time!" And while Bekim went back to his room to retrieve one of his toy cars, Jeremy murmured to Louise, "Tonight I'll remove the coin."

Bekim needed to remain safe, but he must also stay in as familiar an atmosphere as possible, Jeremy had concluded. Wherever she was, Ghensie would agree. He had to get the boy sorted out, and then he would try to figure out where Ghensie could be, although he already knew he had no clue. *No clue*—his intuition had come to a halt with the hardware store.

At least Bekim would be safe in the relative anonymity of Haley's domicile, which would in turn contain Jeremy's reassuring presence. Fortunately Haley hadn't objected to the change of plan.

Granted there would be work to do, and Jeremy started by trying to humor the boy on the taxi ride over. "My friend Haley is American," he touted, "just like your bear Grizzly."

Bekim said nothing, frowning at first at Jeremy and then down at the bear.

"You *did* tell me he was American," Jeremy reminded the boy. "Is your bear as mighty and brave as the great American grizzly bear?"

At first Bekim hesitated, shifting on the bench seat and gripping the stuffed animal more tightly. Then he nodded firmly.

"Good," said Jeremy, the "magical bear" motif concocted by Luan playing in his thoughts. "But Grizzly's not the only powerful friend you have. You have me and Louise, Solange, and now a strong American woman from grizzly bear country."

Bekim squirmed again, repositioning the bear against his chest. "Is *she* magic?" he asked, his frown uncertain.

"Well, Bekim, 'powerful' and 'magical' aren't the same thing. Grownups have the ability to protect you—much more than your bear has. Can you tell me how Grizzly is magical?"

Bekim stayed quiet for a long moment. "I don't know," he finally said. "But Luan does."

Jeremy left it at that, his thoughts turning back to Ghensie and the men who had escorted her away. Either of the two could have staked out the hardware store—the spectacled Kosovar who had previously followed her home from there, or maybe someone Ghensie hadn't recognized at all. For that matter, even Iliescu knew about her connection to the shop. *Iliescu*: Jeremy still hadn't heard from the piece of shit, and he was now glad for it.

His hand on Bekim's shoulder, Jeremy stood before Haley in her doorway.

"Welcome," she said in French, inclining her greeting towards Bekim. Her short, fluffed brown hair and wide green eyes gave her a pert, inquiring look, though as she scanned both Bekim and Jeremy a slight awkwardness trailed in her smile. Jeremy understood. She had expected Ghensie versus Bekim, and Jeremy's hurried explanation over the phone must have left her wondering how to proceed.

"I guess you and Bekim can sleep in the spare room," she told Jeremy, after ushering the two into the house.

Bekim took a step closer to Jeremy, leaning against the tall man's legs. Jeremy reached for his hand. "That sounds fine." He thanked Haley again and led Bekim to the bedroom to drop off the boy's things—everything but Grizzly, of course, who remained crushed in the boy's embrace.

As they drank tea in the living room, Bekim sipping a small glass of Orangina, Jeremy picked up his previous narrative about America. "I told Bekim you come from the great Far West," he said to Haley," his faint nod signaling the importance of the narrative in terms of gaining the boy's confidence. It was true in any case, for Haley hailed from Reno, Nevada.

She adroitly took up the thread, smiling confidently at Bekim. "I come from a place surrounded by lakes and mountains."

"And you like going into the forest," Jeremy prompted.

"Oh, yes."

Bekim sat stone still on the sofa next to Jeremy, pondering Haley's words and perhaps her entire presence. She was taller than most French women, and in heels she easily reached Jeremy's height, something Jeremy hoped might lend an extra aura of wonder and strength in the little boy's eyes.

"Have you ever seen any bears?" Bekim finally asked, looking equally fearful and hopeful.

"I have, as a matter of fact, when I was camping at Lake Tahoe. They'll steal your food if you don't lock it up."

Bekim drew an audible breath, his small torso tensing. "Were you scared?"

Haley's eyes held firm in what Jeremy figured could be a quasi-lie. "No."

"Are those bears *magic*?"

"No," she repeated gently. She glanced at Jeremy who returned an approving nod.

"Bekim's bear is called Grizzly," he informed her

matter-of-factly, "and he's also American." Noting the wrinkle between Bekim's brows he resisted slipping Haley a subtle smile.

"My bear is little," the boy said, his grip shifting on Grizzly.

"But he's strong and brave." Jeremy caught Haley's eye. "Since you're used to living around bears, would you like to hold him?"

Not just Haley's, but Bekim's brows rose at this unexpected question. "Could Haley hold Grizzly," he pressed, "since she's a strong woman and understands bears?"

Jeremy was sure Haley had to stifle a laugh, though she quickly recovered and said, "If you'd like me to, Bekim."

After an awkward moment of deliberation, Bekim shimmied off the sofa and took three tentative steps over to Haley in her armchair. He held out the bear, ambivalence still in his gaze.

"It's a nice bear," said Haley, before accepting the ragged, stained creature, which had recently again fallen into the gutter.

Jeremy nodded, continuing to smile. Haley was playing her part well. She didn't hold the bear long, though, and gingerly gave it back to Bekim. She and the boy watched each other for a moment, Haley's smile close to wilting under Bekim's extended examination of her. Finally she rose, announcing she had to see what was in the fridge for dinner. Single with no children, Haley, like Jeremy, had little experience with kids. Jeremy was only two years older than Haley, had sheltered Bekim for only a few weeks, but still felt he had amassed a belly-full of experience due to this never-ending saga.

After dinner, once Bekim had drifted off to sleep on the sofa, Jeremy and Haley reverted to English. He updated her on the details of the latest events, to which she half asked, half stated: "Then you *will* call Rébert..."

"If I knew it would help, I'd call him right now. But I need more to go on."

"The hardware store isn't enough of a start?"

"Like I said, I don't think the kid knows anything more, and he'll just repeat that Ghensie walked away with two men. Plus..." Jeremy paused awkwardly, "bringing the kid into it would only point out Ghensie's illegal work."

Haley looked away. They were sitting at the kitchen table, and after a moment's meditation she reached to refill her glass with mineral water.

"You don't approve of her working under the table," Jeremy stated flatly.

"It's not that. I understand people wanting to work at anything they can find to stay in a country."

And so she should, Jeremy reflected, since he knew Haley had done so herself ten years ago.

"I just don't understand your priorities," she went on. "If the police find her they'll know she's here illegally anyway."

Haley was right. Still, Jeremy wanted to offer Rébert a better lead. Who could Ghensie have walked off with, and what could Rébert do with such a vague reference? He might investigate any shady person connected with Ghensie, and probably with Jeremy as well. The police fished far and wide, which meant they could cast their nets even to Brussels. But with Luan and the bald Kosovar missing in action and their spectacled partner's whereabouts unknown, how much progress could they make?

Jeremy sharpened his focus on Haley, who now rose to clear the dinner table. *Priorities*, she had mentioned. Might she be wondering whether *she* was still a priority for Jeremy? He wanted to tell her that she was. He wished he could explain his divided longings for both her and Ghensie, but since he hadn't grasped the situation himself, he didn't want to risk tromping on Haley's feelings.

Priorities: he got up from the table to have a look at Bekim. In sleep the boy's mouth hung slack, his arm relaxed next to Grizzly.

He turned the television down low and walked back to the kitchen to announce: "I think we can start the operation."

Haley looked back at him over her shoulder.

"Operation *Grizzly*," he clarified.

Carefully Jeremy lifted Bekim off the sofa and carried him to bed, a maneuver reminiscent of the first nights the boy slept in his flat. Only this time Grizzly stayed behind. Haley had already retrieved some sewing tools.

"Mm-hm," said Jeremy, fingering the inside of the bear's mouth. "It's right under the tongue." He handed Grizzly to Haley, who sat poised with a seam-ripper.

And before long, *voilà*, she extracted a small metal disc. For a couple of seconds she stared at it, eyes gleaming as if she had assisted in the birth of a god. Then she handed it to Jeremy, who felt his heart leap. The coin was worn dark and uneven around edges, but it had been cleaned sufficiently to reveal a bearded man in distinct profile. "Could it be him?" Jeremy asked, expecting no particular answer. The image portrayed thick wavy hair and a strong straight nose. And, Jeremy added in a hopeful voice: "his eye looks puckered."

"It does," agreed Haley, huddled next to Jeremy as they both examined the face on the coin. "Let's turn it over."

The reverse side featured the bearded man now naked and on horseback, and most important of all, both Jeremy and Haley could decipher a name: *Philip*, with hand-carved letters phi, lambda, and pi. Their eyes met in joyful amazement.

"It's fantastic!" Haley said.

Jeremy nodded reverentially. "Now I wonder about the rest of the coins. If this is the only one showing Philip of Macedon's blind eye, I can see why Luan stole it."

"The *value* of it," Haley echoed, shaking her head in awe. "Minted over two thousand years ago."

They took turns holding and admiring the coin. Then sighing in satisfaction, Jeremy stood and pocketed it. "I'm keeping this as close as possible. Don't want to put anyone else at risk."

Haley nodded in acknowledgment.

"If you don't mind," he said, "I'll run over to my place and get some clothes and things. Bekim shouldn't wake up—he sleeps like a dormouse."

"Like a *log*, you mean," said Haley, substituting the correct English simile for the French one. "Go ahead— I'll sew up the bear while you're gone."

Jeremy thanked her, then struck off on the fifteen-minute walk to his place, hands in his pockets, his left hand fingering the fantastic coin while his mind grappled with the drama and intrigue it engendered. The *danger* of it—for this was why Ghensie had disappeared, there was little doubt of it. He could almost feel menace in the friction of the coin between his fingers.

He approached his building from the shadows, looking for loiterers on the sidewalks. Up in his flat, he remembered to call Louise.

"I would love to see it," she said of the coin. "But more importantly, are you going to call the police?"

He told her he would. With the reality of the coin now unchallenged, maybe Rébert could pull out all stops.

"And Bekim's all right?" Madame asked. "Because there's that little matter of the other thing he told me..." At Jeremy's prompting she cleared her throat and said, "He says his mother was supposed to be a man."

"What?" was all Jeremy could say. *Ghensie was supposed to be a man?*

"I tried probing for an explanation, but the boy offered nothing more." When no comment came, Madame said, "You're speechless. I understand. I felt the same way when he told me."

"He's dreaming," Jeremy finally replied. "*Inventing.*"

Louise agreed. "Or he's projecting that his mother is more powerful than she should be as a woman. Similar to the bear magic, perhaps. Anyway, I thought I'd pass it along."

Jeremy thanked Madame once more for all her help, then hung up. What would the boy come up with next? How did such a claim chime with the workings of his little psyche? More importantly, *where was Ghensie?*

Chapter 36

Jeremy clamped his hand back on the receiver, ready to lift it and call Rébert at home, when the phone came to life on its own, trilling under his fingers.

He stiffened, picked up the receiver and was greeted with a familiar, accented voice. "*Winters*, my friend!"

"Iliescu..." Slowly he pulled out a chair and sat down.

"You're a hard man to get hold of. I've been calling all evening."

"I *do* have the answering machine..."

"Don't like to mention business on them. Anyway, I called to say I can get that passport for your girl."

A lengthy pause silenced the line. *Where was Rébert? Why hadn't Iliescu been arrested by now?* Jeremy didn't have time for this. "Look," he finally said—

"I'll only need her photograph. You *did* get that for me?"

"I..."

"Come on, Winters, don't tell me you haven't taken care of that, after pressuring me to come through for you." Iliescu sounded exasperated.

"Well, she's..."

"Listen, do you want the passport or not? I don't have time to waste."

Neither do I, thought Jeremy. And he began thinking fast. "I *do* want the passport, and I have the

290

photo. We had a little spat, but things are okay now."

Iliescu grunted. "Bad timing when you need to cut loose and run."

"Right..." Jeremy stood, lifting the phone's base with him. "I can bring you the photo soon."

"How about now?"

Another pause on the line. It was ten o'clock at night. What was the hurry? "You're available *now*?" Jeremy asked tentatively.

"Why not? You know I don't punch a time clock."

Jeremy let the sarcasm pass, though he still questioned the hour of the meeting. "Where?" he asked.

"Let's make it La Cave Hénocque. It'll stay open for us."

The *cave* café with the wine-cellar motif, where Iliescu carried out his tougher sort of business—where Jeremy had been tasked to rough up the ex-employee Rusu and been almost knifed in return.

He told Iliescu he'd be there in half an hour. Before hanging up, he pressed the button to end the call, then dialed Rébert.

"*Finally*," said the RG agent. They had picked up Bardot and Vadim but hadn't been able to locate Iliescu.

"Then I'll meet you at La Cave," Jeremy said. Rébert told him to enter the establishment first in case Iliescu hadn't arrived yet. Rébert and his men, in unmarked cars, would wait outside for a signal.

Jeremy rang off and called Haley.

"Is Bekim still asleep?" he asked.

"Yes..." Haley drew out with curiosity.

"Good. Do you think you can handle him if he wakes up?"

"What...?"

"Because I've just talked to Rébert and we've got to

meet."

"About Ghensie?"

"I don't have time to explain, but I'll tell you when I get back."

"Then go—and be careful."

Before going out he thought about hiding the coin in the house. Inside his demolished saxophone sounded reasonable. But when he recalled the break-in last year, the vandal finding and destroying said saxophone, he decided against it. The coin was nowhere safer than on his body.

From Place de la République Jeremy launched into another cab ride south across town. While his eyes tracked the road, his thoughts branched off to Ghensie. He had to enlist Rébert's help and maybe tonight would prove the ideal time. Thanks to Jeremy, Iliescu would be delivered on a silver platter, and after the bastard was arrested and carted off, Jeremy would present his case. He hadn't thought seriously about where to begin, though the coin seemed the obvious starting point. He patted his pants pocket.

The buildings around the Place Hénocque lay dark and still, shuttered and tucked in for the night. Jeremy saw no sign of Rébert and his men but knew he wouldn't be able to identify their civilian vehicles. They would remain owls in the shadows until Jeremy gave the signal at the right moment from inside the café. He would simply rise and go look out the window as if fearing imminent arrest by the authorities. Iliescu would write it off as understandable neurosis.

The café presented its own dark façade, its closed sign discouraging lingerers. Instructed by Iliescu, Jeremy was to knock twice, pause for two seconds, rap twice more, then, after two more seconds, execute four knocks.

And it worked. The door creaked open, barely enough for Jeremy to slide inside, then closed, the operation carried out by Iliescu's favorite barman.

In penumbra Jeremy entered the tiny establishment, the only light a dim glow emanating from ceiling bulbs above the two back tables. There sat Iliescu, cloaked in black—black turtleneck, black jacket, black gloves on his table—melding sinisterly with the milieu. A strange welcome, Jeremy thought. He would have liked to walk straight to the window nearest the light and show himself, but that would have been premature. Iliescu must not suspect his involvement in the trap.

With a jerk of his chin Iliescu motioned Jeremy over to his table. The barman followed, then disappeared down the hall while Jeremy settled across from Iliescu.

He greeted the Romanian with regret in his voice, then said, "Seems I won't be needing that passport after all."

"...Ah no?" Relaxed back in his chair, Iliescu took a couple of short puffs from his cigarette, before observing, "Yet you came all the way down here."

"You owe me money—the pay for the photo job and for collecting that gambling debt. I won't have time to wait for a passport."

"And your girl?" Iliescu studied Jeremy with a sharp eye, breaking only to stub out his cigarette with equally sharp deliberation.

"She's not coming."

"Oh...?" Iliescu shook his head in mock sympathy. "And you didn't want to tell me over the phone."

"I held out hope until the last. But it doesn't matter—I just need the money and I can't wait any longer." Jeremy shifted uneasily in his chair, exhaling and preparing to get up and have a look out the window for pursuers.

"Before I pay you, I want something in return."

Jeremy demurred. "In return?" He started to rise again but was interrupted by a loud bang. Iliescu had picked up the heavy glass ashtray he was using and slammed it twice on the table. At that moment the barman re-entered the room, followed by none other than the spectacled Kosovar. The two men formed a barrier to the aisle. Iliescu stood as well, leaving Jeremy blocked at the table.

"We want the coin," said the Kosovar, his grey eyes impassive as a surgeon's behind his spectacles.

Slowly Jeremy stood up, his incredulous gaze taking in the two men. "Where is Ghensie?" he demanded.

"Quite safe. And as long as we get the coin, nothing will happen to her." Tonight was the first time Jeremy had heard the Kosovar speak. His French was as good as Ghensie's—educated, it seemed—and his voice flowed mild, his tone reasonable. Just the opposite of the testy, tick-ridden Iliescu. The Kosovar's wispy blond hair seemed to match the mildness of his voice, and Jeremy mistrusted him all the more.

"The coin," Jeremy stated, keeping his left hand well away from his pants pocket. "You've obviously decided Ghensie doesn't have it, so why not let her go?" It was a futile plea, though he had to try. As his gaze continued to sweep the three men surrounding him, criminals all of them, he shuddered inside at the thought of Ghensie at their mercy.

"Don't insult us!" Iliescu chimed in, red-faced and agitated. "Either you or the boy has it, and you'll turn it over to us!"

Jeremy drilled him with a cold stare. "And *you*— how did you get involved?"

Iliescu lifted his chin in a triumphant smile. Clearly

he enjoyed having lured Jeremy into a trap. "Our new friend," he said, nodding at the Kosovar, "is a smart fellow. After following you to me, he made an offer, and seeing an interest in the matter I couldn't refuse."

"So you're getting some kind of cut..."

"I can arrange for the sale of *all* the coins." Iliescu sniffed, his hands resting confidently on his hips, his smug grin seeming to project pride in all of his black talents.

"Never mind about that," the Kosovar cut in. "Is the coin with you or the boy?"

"The boy knows nothing about it."

"Then where did you put it?"

Where did *I* put it? Jeremy asked himself. Why had Luan not been mentioned? Did no one yet realize his part in this? "*Luan*," Jeremy said aloud. "Why don't you ask *him*?"

A corner of the Kosovar's mouth twitched almost imperceptibly. "Forget about Luan, he's out of commission."

Out of commission. His pulse ticking up, Jeremy repeated his scan of the three: the volatile Iliescu, the silent but muscular barman, the smooth and stolid Kosovar. Jeremy again resisted touching the pocket where the coin practically burned through to his thigh. Where were they keeping Ghensie? How could he get to the window and signal Rébert?

His gaze shifted between the Kosovar and Iliescu. "I won't say another word until I see Ghensie."

"You want to see her?" The Kosovar's eyes displayed an almost touching curiosity, which made the blow that followed feel all the more potent. When the Kosovar withdrew his fist, an unprepared Jeremy was left doubled up.

The barman moved in and grasped one of Jeremy's arms, the Kosovar took the other, and Iliescu stepped around the table to slug Jeremy in the jaw.

The Kosovar yanked Jeremy's hair, twisting his head. "Would you like *this* to happen to Ghensie?"

"She's a much softer specimen," Iliescu added, rubbing his fist, which might not have been used to striking blows. In truth, Jeremy had suffered much worse in his life, but he couldn't bear the thought of anything like it happening to Ghensie. "How do I know she's even alive?" he asked.

With a nonchalant wave, the Kosovar indicated the short hall. "Because she's under guard back there."

Chapter 37

*G*hensie, here on the premises! Jeremy's heart soared, though not for long.

"Interesting thing about torture," the Kosovar went on in his rational tone, "I find it most effective when a loved one is watching. Sort of kills two birds with one stone, if you get my meaning."

The grisly observation turned Jeremy's insides to ice. The thought of these bastards touching Ghensie in any way brought the taste of bile to his mouth and turned his anger into a fierce, focused flame.

He had only to hand over the coin. Or did he? Might he and Ghensie then disappear like Luan? Could the Kosovar and Iliescu afford to let them go? He thought of Iliescu, in particular, who would have to continue his Paris operation, conscious of Jeremy hovering out there in potential threat.

He felt the prickle of cold sweat. How much time had passed since he'd arrived? Thirty minutes? Maybe not even, but he had to get to the window. Sound the alarm—

Before he could even consider vaulting over tables, Iliescu pulled a semi-automatic from inside his jacket and waved it towards the hall. "Time to join your girl."

The gun gave Jeremy pause, but not for long. He had to see Ghensie before making any decision. As the barman and the Kosovar marched him down the hall, Iliescu's weapon pressed against his back, a further thought steeled him: who was in charge? Either Iliescu or the Kosovar was bound to assert dominance, though

Iliescu currently held a gun. Quick-tempered as Iliescu was, Jeremy would have preferred the Kosovar wield it.

It took about four paces to reach the storeroom. The barman opened the door to the very space in which Jeremy had manhandled the Moldovan, Rusu. Only it seemed Rusu's employment had not been terminated after all, for the redhead was standing at the end of the room aiming a pistol at Ghensie, who sat at the little table which once held a simple cup and saucer. Now it held Ghensie's arm, her hand supporting her forehead. She looked up, circles beneath her eyes like dark bruises. The sight of Jeremy turned her gaze feverish. She started to rise but Rusu waved his gun and snarled at her to stay put. He turned and stared hard at Jeremy, contempt disfiguring his face.

"So you've come for your Balkan bitch!"

"Shut up," hissed Iliescu.

The Moldovan blushed and muttered something to the effect of, "Sorry." If he was seeking a return to Iliescu's good graces, he had a ways to go. Jeremy took heart from the discord.

"Are you all right?" he asked Ghensie.

She threw Rusu a venomous look, then gazed back at Jeremy in a blend of fear and hope. She nodded once, but before she could speak, the Kosovar cut in. "Enough," he said, eyeing Jeremy. "You've seen her, she's unharmed, now tell us where the coin is."

"And then you'll let us go..."

"Sure." The Kosovar's eyes remained level, his tone reasonable.

Iliescu, in contrast, gave a deep, theatrically-gracious nod. If he had his way, Jeremy sensed, there would be no leaving here.

Jeremy licked his lips, thought to threaten them with the presence of the police outside, but feared provoking a hostage situation. *What fucking time is it?*

Rébert must know something's gone wrong. He resisted lowering his eyes to his watch, knew the gesture could give him away.

He drew a breath and announced, "If you let Ghensie go, I'll tell you where the coin is." A fleeting glance at Ghensie showed wide-eyed surprise. She said nothing, however.

"No," the Kosovar replied, an undercurrent of menace finally denting his tone." She's not leaving."

"You've got *me*," Jeremy insisted, "you don't need her."

"Don't *fuck* with us!" Iliescu's dark eyes were fiery and indignant. "I'm not sure which of you knows where the coin is, but if one of you doesn't tell us, I'll kill you both!" He strode over to Ghensie and hooked an arm around her neck. When she tried to resist, he pressed the muzzle of his pistol to her temple. Jeremy lunged forward but was restrained by the barman and Rusu's gun pointing at him.

He looked to the Kosovar, a useless appeal, for the *mec* was walking towards the shelves on the wall. He pulled a pair of pliers from a pile of tools and said mildly, "I find these effective, particularly on women."

"*All right.*" Slowly Jeremy lifted his hands in surrender. Knowing this might very well spell the end, he said, "The coin's in my pocket."

Another awe-struck stare from Ghensie. The Kosovar tucked the pliers into his jacket and held out his hand. "*Slowly,*" he ordered, as Jeremy fished out the coin and handed it over. The Kosovar adjusted his glasses, inspected both sides of the coin and its uneven edges. For the first time Jeremy perceived a twitch at the corner of his mouth that could have been a true smile.

"Let me see it!" said Iliescu.

The Kosovar glanced up at him, a glint of warning

in his eye. "In good time," he said coolly.

With Iliescu's pistol no longer denting her temple, Ghensie's posture had relaxed. She gazed from the Kosovar to Jeremy. *"But how?"* she uttered.

"Luan," Jeremy said, turning to glare at the Kosovar. "He hid it in Bekim's stuffed bear. I only figured it out last night."

"What?" Ghensie sprang to get up, only to receive a blow to her forehead from the barrel of Iliescu's gun. She slumped back down, her head dropping to the table.

Jeremy surged towards her, then was stopped cold by the thunderous clap of a gunshot. Iliescu had shot the ceiling above Ghensie and now aimed his gun and words at Jeremy. "Don't you move!" Then his ire swiveled to the Kosovar. "And *you*, show me the coin!"

"Yes," urged Jeremy. "Why *don't* you? Who knows if it's even authentic?"

"Shut up!" the Kosovar yelled, his sangfroid finally slipping. "Patience, Iliescu! There will be time after this mess is cleaned up."

"Are you sure about that?" Jeremy took a delicate step forward.

Up came Iliescu's pistol again.

"Don't!" the Kosovar warned him, glancing at the doorway to the hall. "No more shooting in here."

Iliescu scowled at him. "This is *my* turf! But if you're that jumpy about guns I'll deal with this piece of shit hands-on." He strode across the room to Jeremy, while Rusu resumed his guard of a still-unconscious Ghensie.

"What's your game!" Iliescu demanded. He grabbed Jeremy's shirt collar with one hand, cocked his other to bring his pistol down on Jeremy's head—and received Jeremy's knee to the groin instead, followed by a knee in the face as he bent, bone on bone emitting a dull *crack*. His gun fell to the floor. Rather than expose himself by reaching for it, Jeremy wrapped his arms around Iliescu, pinning him before the swooning *mec* could hit the ground. Clasped against Jeremy's chest, Iliescu presented a human shield to Rusu, who was lunging towards them with his gun. He halted, pointing his weapon at the blob of an embrace. For a moment it seemed like a standoff, though Jeremy's arms were loosening by the second around the dead weight. The barman, jolted from his surprise, punched Jeremy in the temple, and both Jeremy and Iliescu slid to the floor, Jeremy hanging onto Iliescu as they went down. Blurrily he eyed the pistol within his reach as he sat with Iliescu slumped against him. He shook his head, as from the bar proper came the sound of exploding glass and metal giving way. Everyone froze, including Ghensie who was finally on her feet. A clatter of rapid footfall followed, police shouting signals and thudding into the room from the miniscule bar.

"Put the gun down," Rébert yelled at Rusu, as another cop kicked Iliescu's weapon away from Jeremy.

"I'll shoot!" Rusu tightened his grip on his pistol, re-aiming at the Jeremy-Iliescu blob on the floor.

"And you'll die fast," Rébert shouted back at him.

Jeremy hugged Iliescu until at last Rusu dropped his weapon and a cop retrieved it. The Romanian was now rousing. He groaned, and Jeremy shoved him aside so he could get to his feet.

Rébert, taking in the scene, looked at Jeremy as if to ask *Why the hell didn't you come to the window?* Instead he declared, "You're under arrest!" Glancing at the rest of the crew, he echoed, "*All* of you are."

Chapter 38

Back-up cars were called in to accommodate six arrests, including Jeremy's own mock detention. "She's the victim," Jeremy emphasized to Rébert before Ghensie was taken away in one car while he waited to be whisked off in Rébert's own vehicle.

He hurriedly explained the saga of the stolen coins and told Rébert to get the prize coin from the Kosovar. "Before he can hide it."

Jeremy waited in the back of the police car until Rébert returned. Then they drove off, with Rébert in front next to his driver. "You couldn't have told me about this before?" Rébert said, holding the coin up for Jeremy to see, without turning to look at him.

You couldn't have broken into the joint before you heard the gunshot? Jeremy would have liked to counter. But as far as Ghensie's story went, he had little to offer except his ongoing defense of needing to protect her. Rébert turned and shot him a sharp frown. The bottom line was a question of trust, and Jeremy knew that confidence was lacking on both sides. *Otherwise, he would have his French passport by now.*

A passport was in fact mentioned. "By the way," Rébert said, "it's time to turn over that counterfeit job we bought from Iliescu."

Jeremy let pass a pregnant pause, picturing the *Martin Duroc* passport with his own discontented mug gazing from the middle page. Tucked away in his slashed bomber jacket, the forgery would never leave Paris, much less feel the hammer-stamp blow of a frowning customs official. "Right..." he finally muttered.

Most of the rest of the ride passed in silence, until the car came to a stop in front of Haley's building, as agreed.

"We'll spread the word that the American FBI is questioning you for now," said Rébert. "As for the boy, since you're the only one he knows, he's better off with you for the time being."

Jeremy nodded his appreciation. Under his continuing cover, he also understood he couldn't risk showing up at the police station to help Ghensie.

"I imagine she'll be freed soon, anyway," said Rébert, when Jeremy expressed as much. "You know, she'll have to become a witness against the Kosovar ring."

"*And* against Iliescu. She was kidnapped."

"Yes, she's been the victim of a crime." In the jaundiced light of a streetlamp, Rébert seemed to add a faint knowing smile. Jeremy took it for a truce.

It was early in the a.m. when Haley opened the door to him. He let out an exhausted sigh that seemed to last until he was well into the living room. According to Haley, Bekim hadn't stirred. Jeremy wanted to collapse into a leaden sleep himself, but he owed Haley the rest of the story, and as she brought out a bottle of Cointreau he sank heavily onto the sofa.

Haley listened to the night's tale with expressions of both marvel and relief. "So you'll be taking Bekim back home tomorrow," she said after a lengthy pause of reflection.

Jeremy nodded.

"And things'll go back to the way they were...I mean, however that's possible," she added, glancing away.

He could only give a weak smile and a weary shrug. Right now he couldn't even contemplate things *as they were*. Not after the last ten days...or week...or however long this ordeal with the Kosovar had lasted; and it wasn't finished. He thought of Bekim, hoped the boy could return to some semblance of tranquility. Then he recalled Louise's most recent revelation over the phone: *Ghensie was supposed to be a man*. Bekim's words, to be precise, and perhaps pure fantasy, though Jeremy would follow up all the same. *Later*.

Now he gave Haley another hug, releasing one more exhalation of relief. When they separated, Jeremy rubbed his eyes with the heel of his hand.

"You'd better get some sleep." Haley said, a look of distant affection in her eyes. "Plus we don't want Bekim waking up in a strange bed without you."

Jeremy nodded mechanically. As they rose, he felt an urge to apologize; thanking her again wasn't enough. And in that urge commingled a longing for things to return the way they were between *them*. He didn't trust himself to say it, for the only certainty that gripped him at the moment was exhaustion.

Later that morning, after promises of *Maman* coming home soon and other reassurances generated over breakfast, Jeremy took Bekim back to his flat. Haley had played her supportive role, no talk of anything else, although when they parted they once more exchanged a peck on the lips. This time a stare lingered between them. He didn't know what it meant, but he felt grateful.

Throughout the day, Jeremy debated whether to call Rébert. He considered it at the Square du Temple, where Bekim played on the slide and while they were shopping at the Monoprix. But he resisted—Rébert would make contact when there was something meaningful to report and he wouldn't appreciate any needling.

Jeremy did call Louise, recounting the prior night's events one more time.

"So it's all in the hands of the police," Madame summed up, "and Ghensie will be dealt with as the victim she is."

"The police acknowledged as much."

"Well thank goodness you finally called them, though I don't quite understand how you figured out where Ghensie was, other than having spotted the Kosovar near that café."

Jeremy's account had included that lie, not his first under the obligation to shield his RG work. All the same he hated misleading Louise, felt that after eight months of friendship he couldn't do so any longer.

He gave a long sigh, an apologetic note trailing along. "Well, there *is* more to it, and I'll be glad to tell you when we're face to face."

"Mm," she murmured, "Can't say I'm surprised. Come for dinner with Bekim, since you're off work again tonight. And if Ghensie's not free by tomorrow evening, Bekim can stay with me while you're at Le Prince."

That evening, as it turned out, Louise didn't seem the least astonished at Jeremy's freelance work for the RG. "I've always suspected something of the sort," she said after dinner, as they finished coffee at the kitchen table and Bekim watched television in the living room. "The way you passed yourself off as an insurance investigator last summer...and yet, for some odd reason I trusted you."

Jeremy returned a soft chuckle. "I'm glad you did. And I know I won't have to ask you to keep my little side job confidential."

Madame raised a mocking eyebrow, gave a playful

smile, and nodded.

Late the next morning, a call came from Rébert. They were releasing Ghensie Berisha pending investigation into her kidnapping and the theft of the coins. "She's agreed to cooperate on both fronts, and I have to say she seemed genuinely shocked about the location of that particular coin."

"That's all she's ever wanted," Jeremy emphasized. "The only thing that stopped her from coming forward earlier was fear of being implicated in the theft herself."

"Our Kosovar's already tried to do just that. We didn't find him convincing and now it seems he's willing to give up his partners in Brussels."

"Has he mentioned Ghensie's cousin? Last night he told me Luan was *out of commission*."

"We're just beginning to crack him. In the meantime, you can meet Ghensie when she's released. She says she owes you a great debt."

Chapter 39

Together, Jeremy and Bekim picked Ghensie up and brought her home. Hugs of relief were exchanged, though limited in emotion, for Bekim was ever curious. Ghensie dismissed the matter—*Maman* had business to take care of—and began busying herself in the flat. She rearranged Bekim's and her things in the bedroom, then attended to a couple of glasses in the sink as she roamed the flat in search for things to reorder. At first Bekim followed her, running his cars along whichever floor she trod, then eventually took Grizzly with him to the living room to draw. *Grizzly*: he would have to be examined by the police as evidence in the coin theft, and Jeremy had promised to deliver the bear to Rébert as soon as possible.

Jeremy stepped into the kitchen while Ghensie was bent over looking at the contents of the refrigerator. "Don't bother with that," he said. "I'll take care of my own messes."

She stared a bit longer into the cool depths, then sighed and shut the door. "We'll need to do some shopping," she said distractedly.

Jeremy was about to tell her that he and Bekim accomplished that task yesterday, but let it pass. Lightly he touched her arm and said, "I think we should sit down and relax a minute. You've just spent the night in custody."

As she faced him, worry filled her eyes. "I'm not sure the police believe me about the coin, even though they told me where you found it and what you said about Luan."

"I think they *do* believe you," Jeremy countered.

"Because you know them..."

"Because I know *one* of them."

"Ah," she said in a light laugh. "I've suspected you were involved with gangsters or police ever since you started that photo job...but these aren't regular cops, more like intelligence people..."

Jeremy nodded. "But I'm not an official employee, and my contact with them has nothing to do with you. I would never have told *any* kind of cop about you."

A trickle of tension drained from Ghensie as she allowed Jeremy to usher her to a chair at the kitchen table.

"Days ago," he said, settling across from her, "the Kosovar tailed me when I met with the Romanian Iliescu about those photos. Somehow he and Iliescu then met." Jeremy explained the deal in which Iliescu would have found a buyer for the coins. "Naturally I had no idea of anything until he lured me to the café. I was the one who called the police because they were supposed to arrest Iliescu for passport trafficking. I couldn't believe it when *you* turned up. I'd been looking for you everywhere."

"Well, I am *very* glad you came," said Ghensie, understanding beginning to show in her smile. There were things the police hadn't bothered to tell her while she was in custody. That the Kosovar was starting to reveal the plot, for instance, and that nothing was yet known about Luan.

"I still can't believe what he did," she said. "Hiding the coin in Bekim's bear, then tracking us all over Europe, accusing *me* of stealing it! And all to deflect suspicion from himself—he's not only a thief, he's a traitor to the family!"

Jeremy agreed. "I wonder how he planned to remove the coin and then sell it separately?"

"And how did he manage to sew it into the bear in the first place?" Ghensie added.

Jeremy shook his head. Only Luan himself would be able to answer. "Well, the police have it now. And we'll also have to bring the bear to them."

Ghensie grimaced. "That won't be as easy as digging out the coin."

Glancing towards the living room from where roars and crash-sounds now emanated, Jeremy nodded in agreement.

"So you figured it all out and your friend Haley helped you. I imagine I should thank her for taking Bekim in."

And for being willing to house you, too. But Jeremy hadn't mentioned that offer. "There's no need," he said. "I've already thanked her."

"She's the one who called that day while you were out..."

"Mm-hmm."

"She's a good friend..."

"True."

"Maybe more than that..."

Jeremy looked off in consideration.

"You don't have to answer." Ghensie gave a wistful sigh, or maybe it was philosophical. "We all have our private lives."

And our double loves.

And secrets: what of those?

Maman was supposed to be a man: Bekim's very words according to Louise Cholot. Probably part of the boy's rich, self-protective fantasy world, Jeremy repeated to himself. In any case it now sounded so absurd that he decided not to mention it. Of much more consequence were the upcoming meetings between Ghensie and Rébert. How long would they go on—weeks, months? Then what? Thoughts of the future heaped in Jeremy's mind. He thought of Haley. Now that they were back in touch, how would he handle these two relationships? He couldn't let go of Haley again.

His heavy gaze sank towards the table.

"Is there something else I need to know?"

Jeremy raised his eyes, watching Ghensie for a moment in quiet affection. "Just wondering about the bear..." he finally said, and told her that not only would Bekim have to give Grizzly up temporarily, he would probably be called to testify about Luan's deception.

That afternoon, Jeremy and Ghensie sat down on the sofa and called the boy over between them.

"Do you know what it means to *trick* someone?" Ghensie asked him.

A slight pause followed, then a hesitant nod from Bekim.

"It means to lie," Ghensie clarified. "To tell people things that aren't true in order to make them act a certain way." She waited for this to sink in. Bekim's eyes remained narrowed, so Ghensie repeated this in Albanian. "Do you understand?" she asked, returning to French.

This time the boy gave a firmer nod.

"Luan tricked you. Grizzly is *not* magic. He's a stuffed bear like any other you'd buy in the store."

Bekim snatched Grizzly off the coffee table and pressed him to his chest.

"He's a good bear," Jeremy took up. "He'll always be special, but do you remember what my friend Haley said?" He glanced at Ghensie, who knew the story. "She said real grizzly bears are big and ferocious, but they don't do magic."

"Luan told you a lie and he cut up your bear," Ghensie said. "He cut a hole under Grizzly's tongue and hid something valuable there. The police will have to examine him."

Bekim frowned, yanking open the bear's mouth. "What's in there?"

"Nothing, now," said Jeremy. "But my friend in the police will have to check him out."

Bekim was silent for a spell, gazing at Grizzly. Then he thrust the bear forward. "Grizzly's not afraid of the police."

"Good." Jeremy smiled in satisfaction. "And you can come with me to take him there."

The boy squeezed the bear again and grinned.

Ghensie did not smile, something not lost on Jeremy.

Later, when they were alone, she voiced objections to Bekim visiting Rébert's RG office.

"I only thought it would make giving up the bear easier," Jeremy said.

"I still don't like it. I've wanted to keep him as far away as possible from this coin business."

Jeremy sighed gently. "But he's going to have to repeat what Luan told him to the police and the judge involved.

"I know. And I also understand that you're trying to help, but I think you should go to the police on your own."

"You can't protect him from everything, you know."

Ghensie was quick to respond. "I don't need a lecture about this—I've been doing my best for five years. Do you think it's been easy?"

Jeremy regretted his useless cliché. Of course raising Bekim on the run hadn't been easy. All the same, he felt he had a modicum of common sense, though common sense likely played little part in

Ghensie's reading of the situation. She didn't trust the system. She was still locked in limbo, and she wanted to keep Bekim's awareness of that vulnerable, even perilous state as distant as possible. Jeremy thought he had lent some stability to her and the boy, and yet she had still ended up in mortal danger due to his dealings with Iliescu. So far she had refrained from mentioning it, but Jeremy judged it not far from her thoughts.

After a long pause, in which they both stood staring out the kitchen window, Ghensie reiterated her stance. "I'd like to keep Bekim as little involved as possible. We don't need to hurry things." Her face was drawn, still burdened with exhaustion. True relief was still beyond reach. "Please don't think I'm ungrateful. I don't know how we could have made it without you." She touched his arm and he pulled her to him. They stood in an embrace for several seconds, an ambiguous embrace, its warmth laced with the chill of uncertainty.

The next day Jeremy gathered up Grizzly to bring to Rébert, bracing himself for a possible meltdown on Bekim's part when learning he couldn't escort his tried-and-true friend.

Instead the boy asked, "When will Grizzly come home?"

Jeremy hesitated. He had no idea. He stared back at the boy with a feeble smile.

"Grizzly might need to help the police," Ghensie said quietly.

"He's the only one who knows what a bad man Luan's been," Jeremy added. "The police will want his cooperation for a while."

Bekim looked doubtful. Then a sly smile curled the corners of his mouth. "He's not magic, you know."

Jeremy grinned. "Right, you are!"

That night, when he returned from work, Ghensie was

ironing. She never did chores this late and Jeremy could tell she was still jittery. After hanging up his coat he settled on the sofa, watching her stack the last of the ironed items on the armchair.

"I guess I can put them away tomorrow," she said of the folded clothes that included one of Jeremy's own shirts. "I don't want to wake Bekim."

Jeremy agreed, though they both knew the kid slept like the dead. "Come and relax a bit."

He pulled her close on the sofa and wrapped an arm around her. "You know, I was really frantic while you were gone."

"I'm sorry," she said, blushing. "And I'm sorry I defied you by going to the hardware store."

Jeremy didn't like the word *defied*. Though he made no comment, he withdrew his arm and murmured, "It's in the past now."

"But I'm still going to have to find new work."

"You've got plenty on your plate for the time being, with the police and all."

"I wonder if I'll ever be free..."

It could have been a line in movie. Jeremy clasped her hand. "Of course you will."

"Free to..."

Her words trailed off. He wasn't sure what she wanted to say. Free to do what? He didn't exactly like the sound of it.

Chapter 40

The first week of March filled quickly with appointments involving statements to the police and judge. Ghensie and Jeremy accompanied Bekim to recount Luan's trickery with Grizzly. Ghensie, for her part, met with authorities to explain her entire journey, Luan and the Kosovars on her heels. In the search for Luan and the bald Kosovar, Interpol was called in and Jeremy gave his own testimony of being stalked in Paris and assaulted in Brussels. According to Rébert, the spectacled Kosovar insisted he'd left his two cohorts alive in Brussels, despite having threatened to make Ghensie "disappear like Luan," something the Kosovar dismissed as a means of coercing the coin from her.

Then there was the coin itself. Rébert could only shake his head in ongoing amazement as Jeremy and he sat in their habitual café across from the Parthenon-like Bourse. "I've never had a case end up so bizarre."

"I'd like to see that coin again," Jeremy said, savoring a memory akin to having tasted a lost bottle of wine belonging to Napoleon.

Both men sighed and took sips of their beer, Jeremy his Affligem, Rébert his Kanterbräu. For a moment they nursed the silence.

"And the rest of the coins?" asked Jeremy.

"Forty-eight of them—silver. Don't know what they look like, but Belgian police located them in a train-station locker in Brussels. Amazing how our Kosovar trusted the other two not to steal the whole lot while he was in Paris."

"*If* the other two are still around..."

Rébert gave a wry smile, then downed another draught of beer. "The coins will be sent back to Albania, of course."

Jeremy nodded. "And the Kosovar too, I imagine."

"Maybe—eventually, anyway, after the legal system finishes with him here and in Belgium, and wherever else he might have committed a crime."

Jeremy thought of Italy, the first stop in the trek to track Ghensie; when Luan and the Kosovars broke into Ruggero Vairo's house, threatening to hurt Ghensie and Bekim if he went to the police.

"You did well on the passport job," said Rébert. "There'll be a nice bonus coming your way."

"Mm," Jeremy responded, nodding. "And will I be congratulated or condemned over the coin business?"

"Maybe a little of both. I only wish you'd reported it right away."

From inside his jacket pocket Jeremy extracted the passport forged in the name of Martin Jacques Duroc and laid it on the table in front of Rébert. "I'm sure you weren't going to forget this..."

Rébert eyed it for an instant, then gave an amused grunt. "No," he said, picking it up, "not a chance." He flipped to the page with Jeremy's photo, studied the details for a moment, then shrugged as if unable to ascertain the quality of the forgery. He looked back at the photo's owner. "I haven't forgotten about your *real* passport business either."

"But it's a *long* process," Jeremy stated, mimicking his boss's refrain, then shaking his head in exasperation.

"It *is* a long process, and one that might have been shortened if you hadn't gotten involved in this coin business. Unfortunately it'll have to go down in the record."

"For the powers on high to mull over then use as an excuse to turn me down."

"I don't think so. You've done good work for us, and not without risk. You *will* get your reward."

At least this time Rébert didn't add the tedious mantra, *just be patient*. If he had, Jeremy might have slugged him.

Now Ghensie was under protective status in France. In addition to testifying against the Kosovar about the coins, she would have to denounce Iliescu and the Kosovar for kidnapping. Jeremy asked her how she had been led away by those who turned out to be Florin Rusu and another of Iliescu's goons.

"The redhead had a gun," she said simply. "And he said he had my 'half-breed son.' I figured he knew what he was talking about."

Rusu, the bigoted bastard. At their first meeting Jeremy had told him he wasn't worth a piece of lint off Ghensie's coat. Now Rusu would join the lint that accumulated on prison rags. Well, that had turned out for the best, though Jeremy didn't say this to Ghensie for whom a new set of trials was just beginning. Another transformation to go through in her odyssey from Tirana to Paris—from pharmacy graduate and translator at auctions in Albania to a ménage in Italy with Vairo, then on to Amsterdam and Brussels and hope of finally achieving a career dream; only to flee to Paris and start from scratch again. Gain, loss, adaptation, unsought evolution: the fate of the desperately motivated and perseverant migrant.

Transformations, he repeated to himself, and glanced at Bekim who was racing his cars down the hall floor towards the bedroom. *Maman was supposed to be a man.* What had the boy been dreaming? Granted,

Ghensie was big-boned, but under the sheets Jeremy had found nothing mannish about her.

He tried to return to the Italian-language novel that he had been reading for a month now. Yet he couldn't help looking over at Ghensie, who had set up the ironing board again to press one of Bekim's shirts that had fallen out of the laundry pile. He watched the rhythmic glide and halt of the iron, the steam that rose below Ghensie's calm expression. If three weeks of raging rollercoaster ride hadn't just passed, Jeremy might think he was back in the middle of February, with Ghensie freshly arrived from Brussels. He kept staring until Ghensie looked up. "What are you thinking about?"

Jeremy shook himself. "Nothing, really."

Ghensie put the final touches on the shirt's collar, then set the iron down. "Something's on your mind."

"*Whee!*" Bekim shrieked, as he sent his miniature Mustang careering into the living room.

"Stop yelling," Ghensie scolded. "Time for you to calm down and do something else."

The boy sent two more cars chasing into the kitchen and roared a final "*pow!*" Then he puffed out a sigh, retrieved his coloring book, and followed the cars into the kitchen.

For an instant Jeremy smiled, then a slight crease formed between his brows.

Ghensie folded the plaid shirt and crossed to the sofa to sit next to him. "Something's bothering you."

He gave a casual shrug. "Bekim's certainly wound up today..."

"I think he's just happy to be back here again. Hope it's not too much for you."

"No, no, glad he's back to normal." Bekim's humming wafted from the kitchen; Jeremy had Ghensie to himself for the moment. "He's got quite an imagination. Perfectly natural, of course..."

Ghensie gazed back expectantly.

"I mean all kids say...well...extraordinary things from time to time," Jeremy continued, feeling his way forward.

"And what has Bekim said that surprises you?"

"Well..." Jeremy cleared his throat, added a little laugh. "I'm sure you'll find this as absurd as I did, but he told Louise Cholot that his *maman* was supposed to be a man." He chuckled again, shaking his head in quizzical amusement. When Ghensie hesitated to answer, looking down at her hands instead, his smile started to fade.

She sighed and gave a helpless shrug. "Actually, it's not something he made up."

At first Jeremy thought he'd heard wrong. Turning to face her directly, he waited for her to go on.

"It's not what you probably think." She observed him with an uneasy smile. "I *was* born a woman."

This didn't do much to calm Jeremy's racing mind.

"You have to understand Albania," she went on softly. "Our culture."

Culture? Jeremy thought he understood Ghensie's culture—her Sufi Islam and so forth. He cocked his head in frustration.

"I'm an only child," she explained. "An only *female* child." She went silent, shifting her gaze to the ironing board across from the coffee table.

Jeremy's frown deepened as he waited for some kind of sense.

"In the case of no male heir," she finally went on, "a family can feel it has no honor. So a daughter can assume the role of a son."

"A son..." Jeremy uttered.

"A *son*," Ghensie confirmed, looking back at him candidly. "That's what happened in my case. I was supposed to become my family's male heir. It's a custom based in the mountain region north of Tirana, where my parents come from, a custom on its way to dying out, thank goodness."

Jeremy waited to hear more, but Ghensie had gone quiet again, her gaze retreating to her lap. "I don't understand," he said. "Do you *have* to become a son if there isn't one?"

"No," she said, her eyes rising slightly. But in 1985 our communist dictator Hoxha died and many people wanted to return to the old ways. My parents didn't have a son, so they encouraged me to become the male heir. I would have to dress like a man and take a vow of celibacy, which is part of the custom. Never to marry, never to have a sexual relationship with a man. *Sworn Virgins*, they're sometimes called," she added, flushing.

Jeremy shook his swimming head. "But you didn't want that..."

"No. Still, I did consider it. To help my parents, plus I had a great aunt who did this, and she gained much freedom, freedoms that not many Albanian women have—to come and go as she pleased, free to drink raki as much as she wanted, to shoot a gun, to have male friends...but if she had ever, *ever* entered into a romantic relationship with a man, society would have banished her. That was the worst part, plus that she had to dress in men's clothes and she couldn't have friendships with women. She must have regretted that. I know I would."

Ghensie paused, her head inclining again. "I don't even like to talk about it. It makes us Albanians seem alien. Anyway, I had time to postpone things while at university. And there I discovered Sufism, and love is the greatest component of that religion. Then I met the Serb who was Bekim's father. And when I got pregnant it caused so much grief to my parents, and shame throughout my family, that I couldn't bear to stay in Albania. So I left."

Left with the Italian, Ruggero Vairo. Had she been trying to prove she'd made the right decision not to be a *son*?

"I wanted *love*," she said, gazing across the room again," and I finally found it with Ruggero."

Jeremy continued to fixate her. So Vairo had been more than just a way to rebel against "sworn virginity."

"As far as Bekim goes," she continued, "he no doubt heard the gossip. So yes, at one point I was supposed to be a man."

Jeremy swallowed hard, his throat dry, his thoughts still spinning. How was he supposed to comprehend all this, let alone respond to it? This arcane Albanian culture. And Vairo, who seemed to be a pivotal part of the story and still might be. Back in Brussels she'd told Jeremy she still loved the man. If Ruggero Vairo had been her first true love, the hero who had rescued her from a loveless, desiccated fate, then what was Jeremy to her?

"You mentioned Vairo," he said," tensing his jaw. "Is he still on your mind?"

Ghensie's gaze drifted towards the window, towards a pale-blue sky whose sun was challenging the remnants of winter with its golden lengthening light. She seemed to be contemplating its promise, but Jeremy also sensed she was trying to gather words to convey a message he didn't want to hear.

And finally it came. Her eyes returned to him, trailing a gentle sadness. "He is," she said. "He's always been." Audibly Jeremy exhaled, trying to hide the stab of hurt he felt with a sober nod.

But he must have looked grim, for Ghensie tilted her head and said, "I'm sorry, Jeremy, but hasn't another woman been on your mind? Don't you think I can tell?"

Jeremy conceded a brief smile, one that didn't match the sting of resentment he felt. How could she tell that Haley meant more to him than met the eye, when he hadn't been able to guess the importance of Vairo? He had become complacent in their little household, taken Ghensie's exquisite attention to him for devotion. Whereas Ghensie had never been able to afford complacency, could never loosen her guard. Her life from Tirana to Paris was testament enough.

"I guess I shouldn't be surprised," he said, avoiding her penetrating gaze by leaning back and staring stonily at the ceiling.

Ghensie reached for his hand, then stopped when Jeremy withdrew both hands to behind his head. He let his head rest against them, trying to convey an air of indifference he hardly felt.

"Jeremy, I don't want to deceive you."

He flinched slightly, then looked at her in expectation of yet another revelation.

Which came immediately. "Ruggero has been more than in my thoughts—he's been sending me money."

"What?" Jeremy blurted, his back straightening, his hands dropping to his lap. This he had not anticipated, despite wondering how Ghensie managed to pay for groceries with her pitiful pocket-watch job. His thoughts flashed to the jar on the kitchen counter, filled with Jeremy's grocery contributions that never bottomed out.

"I couldn't let you support Bekim and me completely," she went on.

No, he supposed not, this latest discovery jolting him into looking at the situation realistically. "How long has he been sending you money?"

"Since I got here. Wired through the post office."

"And what does he think of you living with me?"

"He understands."

Jeremy had to stifle a smirk. *Then why isn't he here? Why isn't he here to protect you?* But he held that back as well. And though he wouldn't tell her, Jeremy couldn't help understanding the divided emotions.

"I said I didn't want to deceive you," Ghensie repeated shakily. "I love you for everything you've done for my son and me. I've loved being close to you…"

By the quiet tenderness in her voice Jeremy knew exactly what she meant. He was relieved that their intimacy hadn't also been a deception.

"But, you're *in* love with Vairo."

She drew a sharp breath and nodded.

"Then I guess he's won."

"Do you really feel you've lost, considering everything you have?"

There was more than a hint of misgiving in her tone. Again he had to consider his own attitude throughout the month of February. No doubt he had enjoyed a certain fulfilment in his makeshift family experience, yet he had always sensed it wasn't destined to last. He had experienced a "high" of sorts, never able, or perhaps *willing*, to answer the essential question: *Do you want to make this life permanent?* Spending time with Haley, following a two-month hiatus of dizzying change and much reflection, had him questioning all the more.

So, no, he hadn't truly lost, and he conceded as much to Ghensie. "I only hope Vairo appreciates what he's gained." *And can navigate the bizarreness of Albanian culture*, he added wryly to himself.

Stockinged footsteps padded into the room. "Are we going to see Ruggero again?" Bekim's eyes looked hopeful as the blue sky out the window. "Can I go to the mountains again, like Robertino?"

Jeremy sighed to himself. You never knew when the boy was eavesdropping. *Little Bekim in the Alps*: maybe the kid would get his wish.

Chapter 41

The second week of March brought another raft of appearances before authorities. The spectacled Kosovar faced prosecution in at least three countries. Iliescu and his band would be tried in Paris and, Jeremy hoped, deported. But that would take months, and in in the meantime he contented himself with picturing the Romanian behind French bars, his tics multiplying.

During week three came a bulletin from Brussels. Jeremy learned via Rébert that hikers had discovered a body dumped in the Ardennes, a gunshot wound to the back of the head. The corpse turned out to be Luan's. The bald Kosovar was still at large.

Jeremy and Ghensie mused over the news in a café where they met for coffee. *Meeting Ghensie for coffee*—Jeremy still found the idea akin to déjà vu, though Ghensie and Bekim had been living with Ruggero Vairo for over a week in a flat the Italian was renting in the Eleventh, near Père Lachaise. Strange and adrift was the way Jeremy now felt in the new and definite emptiness of his flat. He was eager to talk to Ghensie.

"I can't say I'm too surprised," she commented, after shedding her initial shock at Luan's demise. "I'm sorry for what he became, sorry for his parents, my aunt and uncle."

Jeremy nodded in rhetorical agreement. What else could be added?

"Will Vairo be staying in Paris during this whole drawn-out process?" he asked.

"He'll go back and forth to Italy," Ghensie answered, shifting in her chair.

She wasn't comfortable talking about Vairo, thought Jeremy with a touch of satisfaction. The wine grower and merchant had to be flush, and Jeremy couldn't suppress the idea that Ghensie preferred that kind of financial security to what he could offer with his precarious jobs. Still he took pride in being the man who stuck by Ghensie during the most dangerous period of her ordeal. "Is his French improving?" he asked, sticking to the subject of Vairo perhaps longer than necessary.

"A little." Ghensie shrugged, and Jeremy smiled to himself. He had met Vairo: the man wasn't very tall but appeared country-strong, intelligent looking, with an open and friendly demeanor.

Idly he suggested, "You might be eligible for residency in Italy after all this is over..."

"There's a good chance," Ghensie murmured into her cup of tea.

"Especially if he gets divorced and you marry him."

She shrugged again, perhaps trying to distance something she considered a painful subject for both of them.

But Jeremy wasn't in need of that kind of space. He needed to fill his own uncomfortable chasms. At least he was seeing Haley again.

"Then," he went on, "I imagine you'll return to working as Vairo's secretary."

"Secretary and translator," she reminded him, blushing slightly. Jeremy smiled. With her fluency in Italian and good prospects for residency in the country, she would undoubtedly take and pass the pharmacist test in no time.

He told her as much, and she nodded demurely.

"Of course you will," he said, "and rightly so!" Yes,

he thought with some melancholy, with luck her life would settle into some semblance of normality. And so would his. *Rentrer dans l'ordre*, as the French were fond of saying. Already he had noticed that even the roots of Ghensie's hair were turning dark again.

Then her gaze met his. "And would you come visit me eventually...in Italy?"

Jeremy's mind went suddenly blank.

"Come visit...with Haley, maybe..." she nudged.

That drew a wry smile from him. "Actually, I think she'd love a trip to Italy."

When he got home he called Haley, not to ask her about traveling to Italy, a distant prospect, but to tell her about Luan. By now he was in the habit of keeping both her and Louise Cholot abreast of events.

"So I guess the other Kosovar must've killed him," she concluded. "And who knows when they'll catch *him*?"

"If he's been following the news he'll be long gone."

"And he could end up getting eliminated in turn by whoever else was involved in the robbery of that ancient grave."

"A definite possibility!" He loved Haley's keen interest in things like this.

They agreed to get together the following evening when Jeremy was off work.

"I've got a new jazz album," she told him. "Duke Ellington's *In the Uncommon Market*. Recorded here in Europe in the sixties."

"Can't wait. Is it his really cool stuff?" Jeremy asked, knowing Haley understood what he meant.

"Yeah. Not every song fires you up, but most do. There's this one called 'Paris Blues,' with a tangoing type of violin—I can't explain, you've got to hear it for yourself."

"Tango and jazz..." Jeremy mused.

And on and on they went until they finally returned their receivers to their respective bases.

Jeremy retreated to the living room, sinking onto the sofa with a pensive sigh. The hollowness in his flat seemed to shrink a fraction. He stretched out, then turned sideways to pluck his Italian novel off the coffee table. With all the commotion over the last two weeks, he could now indulge in a bit of blatant idleness. He was wriggling back into a comfortable position when he felt something stab his lower back. He sat up again and felt around the cushions, pulling out a little car—the black Porsche Carrera that Bekim always gave him when they played.

He set his novel down and held the toy out, its chipped paint telling of a hundred racing crashes. Jeremy laughed softly. Did Bekim leave this car behind just for him? He gave the little Porsche a squeeze, then set it on the table.

Jeremy's boombox was whirling a cassette in the background—Serge Gainsbourg's *Du Jazz dans le ravin*, a duplicate Haley had made for him last year. If he liked her new album, she would undoubtedly make him a copy as well.

Le jazz: on rentre dans l'ordre. Order reestablished. He gave the little black car a push, sending it rolling against his book. *Well, sort of.*

Acknowledgements

Many thanks to my critique partners, with special thanks again to author and friend Paula Riley. Much appreciation once more to beta-readers Angela Sell, Cora Robey, and Barbara Stephano, for your excellent observations in my early drafts. And again, much gratitude to my friends in France and Belgium, Hervey L'Hostis and Steven Tijdgat, respectively. *Vivent les cultures française et belge!*